Acclaim for the Lambda Literary Award winner
Every Time I Think of You
(the companion novel to *Message of Love*)

"Provenzano artfully works in the theme of nature to suggest hope for Everett's physical recovery, as well as, in a difficult moment in Reid's and his relationship, the recovery of love... Their love is a force of nature."   – *Lambda Literary Review*

"There are so many levels of nuance to Provenzano's story. It's an exciting voyage of discovery. When the story takes its more serious turn, it becomes a tale of heartbreak, courage, and healing. It's a remarkable, uplifting story."   – *Windy City Times*

"The romance, simple and pure, yet heated and passionate, is strikingly genuine. Furthermore, they're both likable, so much so that the reader can't help but cheer for them. Even the most jaded among us will experience a renewed faith in love and romance after reading it."   – Edge on the Net

"*Every Time I Think of You* opens readers' eyes, minds and hearts to corners of the world they may never have realized existed. It's not easy to write a novel about sports, gay teenagers and sex in (and out of) wheelchairs. Jim Provenzano has done it, with grace and power."   – Dan Woog, The Outfield

"Provenzano's characters are rich and complex. His sense of pace and plotting are dead on, and his prose is straightforward and never showy. It's a well-told tale whose aim to inform as well as entertain certainly hits the mark."   – Out in Print

"A beautiful story of friendship, devotion and love, as well as a practical lesson on dealing with physically challenged individuals."   – *Echo Magazine*

"Displays writing and plotting well above the typical gay romance; recommended for all libraries that have significant LGBT collections."   – American Library Association

PINS
Monkey Suits
Cyclizen
Every Time I Think of You
PINS the stage adaptation

Message of Love

a novel

JIM PROVENZANO

Message of Love, a novel. copyright Jim Provenzano, 2014
ISBN-13: 978-0615669243
ISBN-10: 0615669247
BISAC: Fiction/Gay

Cover Art; Getty Images. Used with permission.

Cover Design: Kurt Thomas

"Accidents Never Happen" written by Jimmy Destri; published by Chrysalis Music Group

ACKNOWLEDGMENTS

Thanks to Gene Dermody, Carrie Euype, Paul Isaacs and Sean Drate, Michael Yamashita, T. Scott King and Scott Wazlowski for their support of this book's research project; to Dudley Saunders and Eric Himan for their music; to Joel Brown, Marc Brew, Robert Drake, Seth Eisen, Brad Lyman, Tom Mendicino and Nick Ifft, Kelly McQuain and John Cawley, Kile Ozier, Scott St. John and others who shared their memories and personal experiences; to the librarians and archivists at Temple University and the University of Pennsylvania, in particular Kim Bravo for her enthusiastic assistance, and to the Philadelphia Public Library Archives Department; but mostly to Stephen LeBlanc for amazing assistance.

for Raja Shortell

"Like the maji on the hill,
I can divinate your presence from afar.
And I'll follow you until
I can bring you to a perfect world."

– Blondie, "Accidents Never Happen"

Chapter 1
June, 1983

The smiling face of Everett Forrester looked down from a huge banner as guests assembled at the circular tables in the ballroom of Pittsburgh's William Penn Hotel. 'A Helping Hand,' read the text below it as Everett, posed in a blue button-down shirt, was seated in his wheelchair, with a hopeful look, about to shake hands with an unseen person.

Other versions of the ad campaign, featuring teenage girls and boys of different races, offset his banner, and were hung at different places around the ballroom. But the image of Everett bothered me, as if he was the one needing assistance. If anyone truly knew him, and all that he and I had endured together through the past five years, they would know that the opposite was true. Everett was more often the one providing help.

Across the ballroom, I snuck a brief glance at Everett's mother. In a stunning red gown, Diana Forrester's hair was bundled up in an elegant swirl. Her earrings dangled, glistening as if she'd positioned herself in a spotlight. In between cheerful hugs and measured shoulder pats offered to others, her brief glance across the room toward me was one of mild contempt.

Moving to a swanky apartment in Pittsburgh, and having a daughter with cultural connections, had given her a new social circle to join, and recruits. It hadn't taken her long to latch onto a local nonprofit and whip up a benefit dinner for handicapped kids in Pittsburgh. Everett simply had to attend, since he was one of the cause's poster boys.

A few feet away from me, the real Everett waved me over and casually introduced me to yet another wealthy patron.

"This is my boyfriend, Reid Conniff." His dark eyes sparkled, his bow tie tilting as he craned his neck up to them, smiling as he gauged their perplexed reactions.

The string quartet, positioned at one side of the ballroom, finished playing, signaling the guests to take their seats. Along with the mostly elderly donors, almost a dozen young recipients of the foundation's generosity had been strategically placed at several of the three dozen tables at the dinner. To accommodate them, one setting at each table lacked a chair, and wheelchair-using guests scooted in as others sat.

While of course I had wanted to sit next to Everett, the seating chart placed us at opposite ends of the table. I wouldn't have been surprised if I'd been relegated to the back of the room. But I understood the protocol. His mother helmed another nearby table, and Everett had been strategically placed between two of the more generous donors. His charm, I suspected his mother knew, might convince these patrons to give even more.

After a brief introduction, as Diana Forrester stepped up to the podium, a round of applause swept through the hall. I put on my glasses to see her more clearly.

Her speech was outwardly sincere, recited with a natural elegance and composure that showed her comfort in the spotlight. She spoke of the struggle of the foundation's clients and the opportunities given them, then segued to the story of her own son. Across the table, Everett's glance and knowing smirk said more than any speech. I was not surprised when the story about her dear son's struggle completely excluded me.

I didn't mind. It wouldn't matter how much she twisted the facts to suit her purposes. For the past four years of college Everett and I had lived on the other side of the state, separated by hundreds of miles and thousands and thousands of trees.

Although it was a well-timed holiday weekend after we'd graduated, for us to drive in Everett's new car across the state the night before, we still had to blow off a birthday party for a friend, rush through our move from Philadelphia, and postpone two rather somber visits to a few friends.

Since the entire event was planned around him, I had to go. It wasn't just out of obligation, of enduring what would be a celebration more of his mother's ego than the poor little kids for whom the gala was being held.

The sheer audacity of appearing again in a jacket and tie appealed to me as a sort of sartorial revenge toward his mother. Our relationship was much more acknowledged by her than at our first formal party escapade, back when we'd barely known each other.

While I'd grown accustomed to dressing up with Everett, I caught myself repeating a nervous habit, twisting the new piece of jewelry on a ring finger with my thumb.

Then I stopped, and relaxed. Because more, I felt a sense of fealty with Everett, which we had almost lost a few times; an argument, an affair or two, and the death of someone once intensely close to him.

That glint in his eyes toward me across the table wasn't just part of the applause, the show. In his eyes, those dazzling near-black eyes, more important to me than our love or lust or friendship, was a look of pure trust.

Chapter 2
February, 1980

Everett is standing wet and naked, his back to me, in a dark shower stall I don't recognize. Shampoo suds cascade down his back, over his rump and down between the dark fuzz of his legs like rain on a mossy tree trunk.

Tree stump? That's not right. Anyway, he turns, but I pull back around a tiled wall, knowing that if he sees me, he'll remember who he is, where we are, and he'll melt back into sitting, into that metal frame.

Then I'm following him, clothed, leading a cluster of people who are jogging in a train station, and up the escalator they go, and I've lost him.

But seated at the side of the cold steel ramp, the flat part before the escalator ascends, he's sitting, in shorts, and I worry that it would be cold if he could feel his legs, but then he smiles when I catch up to him and says, "Thanks, Bub," and I know it's a dream, because he never calls me that.

Once again, through the night I had curled myself up, turned away from him and hogged the blankets. I stirred, rolled over in our bed.

His tousled dark hair sprouted from the sheets across from me. I reached an arm over him to toss the blanket back over his feet and lower legs, even though he was wearing sweatpants and socks. The slim foam pad meant to lay between his knees had slipped down to his ankles.

In a sideways morning hug, he stirred, groaned an exaggerated stretch, and rolled over. Our groggy eyes met.

With his curly locks flattened askew, half of his face red and waffle-creased from the pillow, and a tiny eye booger dangling from a lash, the disheveled man of my dreams bid me our familiar greeting. "Giraffe."

"Monkey," I grunted in return.

He planted a kiss on my nose, then traveled lower.

"Are we going there?"

He mumbled consent from under the covers.

"Can I pee first?"

"No."

"Should I empty Mister Pee Buddy?"

But any concern for his catheter and bag were brushed aside. He had already slurped his way down between my legs. We were definitely going to be late for class.

Everett's occasional morning lust had begun to feel less like a simple urge, and more of an erotic gesture of ownership. Unconcerned, or perhaps enticed by the slight funk of my body in the morning, his kisses and licks continued along my chest, then lower. After an insistent tug of my shorts, and a little shift upward by me, I felt the warm wetness of his mouth around my erection.

Everett's slurping sounds under the blankets matched my quiet sighs. It had become a frequent ritual, dutiful almost. He wouldn't stop until I'd burst into his mouth with that overriding tingle, a consuming connection.

Rubbing his head, his shoulders, he responded with a hand crept up to fondle my nipple and the side of my nearly hairless chest. I knew better than to attempt rearranging our positions to a more democratic entanglement. He suckled on me, refusing too much variation on such mornings.

Satiated, I pulled the blanket and sheet down. My cock, glistening with his spit, still jutted up from my groin. Nestled next to it, Everett's flushed face looked up at me.

"Morning."

"Morning."

"What were you dreaming about? You were tossing like crazy for a while."

"Spaghetti," I half-lied. There was a moment in the dorm cafeteria, but he wasn't in that part of my dream.

"Must have been some speesy-spicy sauce," Everett joked. He toyed with my penis as it shrank. I quivered from his touches.

It was great to be his, to be all his. Wasn't this what we'd wanted?

And yet, it seemed as if this one-sided and brief sex were part of some checklist Everett added to his daily duties, as if to say, 'I have satiated you. I claim you once again.'

With an exaggerated groan, I rose from the bed and began another day. He followed with his own measured shifts; half-rising, elbows back, fully seated, grabbing his legs, shoving them over and off the side of the bed, tossing the foam pad aside, then shifting up and into his wheelchair.

Our dormitory room on the second floor of Johnson Hall, one of the few accessible rooms at Temple University, was filled with books, framed art prints, and even a fancy old Persian rug. Despite its slight impediment to his wheelchair, Everett had almost demanded we use it to cover the cold linoleum tile floor of the room, which, as he put it, was "too much like rehab."

When we'd moved in, I hadn't argued with him, comfortable to concede to his decisions. It did make the otherwise bland room in the high-rise dorm more homey.

I made what we called 'pre-breakfast,' usually a bowl of cereal or a few slices of bread slathered with peanut butter and washed down with milk or a protein shake. Neither of us could endure the lines at the cafeteria downstairs which connected to Hardwick Hall. Our growling stomachs couldn't wait. Making a quick breakfast became our preference to the cafeteria and its bacony odors, at least on our 'early' days when classes started at 8:30 in the morning.

He'd already rolled himself across the room and into the bathroom, where he took care of emptying his catheter, starting our usual shared morning shower. We loved being naked together, especially while wet.

Having laid out my morning's clothes, and stacked my books in preparation for the day's classes, I set our morning meal on the small counter above the mini-fridge, slipped off my sweatpants and T-shirt and joined him. With the tingling haze of my orgasm still making me a bit woozy, I nearly stumbled as I joined him, already seated in a plastic stool under the shower.

"Whaddaya got today?" he asked.

"Botany, Earth Science, then we both have English. You back tonight?"

"Not til after Poly Sci. See you at six-ish in the dining hall?"

"Hopefully."

"'Hopefully,'" he mimicked, as he grabbed me with a soapy hand. I stood, letting him lather my thighs and offer a few playful scrubs between my long legs. Even before his accident, I'd stood taller than him by a few inches.

"*Ecballium elaterium*," he said, as he toyed with my penis.

"Flying something?"

He replied with a sideways shrug.

We'd begun a game to help my near-failing attempt at Latin 101. Tested up to Latin 301, since he had taken it for years at Pinecrest Academy, Everett took a bemused pleasure in spontaneously tutoring me with floral names at seemingly random moments. He had only glanced at the plant name worksheet, while I pored over it for hours.

"Squirting," he hinted.

"Oh, the Squirting Cucumber. It's a flowering plant; little fuzzy fruit bulbs that squirt goo and seeds, like five, ten feet."

"Thus the name," Everett nodded. He gave my dick a few tugs until I brushed away his hand.

"This cucumber's pickled."

My hand traveled down along his arm to a shoulder, which I scrubbed and lightly massaged. He caught me admiring his changed body, his thinner legs, and the contrasting new muscled curves of his upper torso, gained from his months of workouts through his recovery.

Finished showering before him, I wrapped my waist in a towel, and stood at the sink near him. As he hummed another song I didn't recognize, I looked in the mirror as I shaved the two-day scruff from my cheeks, amused that my lanky frame, big ears and what he called 'doleful' eyes were what he considered handsome.

Dressed, I prepared a few midday snacks, a water bottle for him, and busied myself, refraining from doing things for him that he could do himself, which was pretty much everything.

This ordinary sexy morning, this somewhat monotonous intimacy, was all I had ever wanted.

The first few days we had shared the dorm room, I thought that the simple act of unrolling a pair of his socks and placing them on the bed would be helpful. He didn't, so I stopped being 'helpful' unless asked.

I didn't have to wait for Everett, but I wanted to leave our dorm and cross the campus with him. That was my form of claiming. Through the few more minutes it took Everett to get dressed, I reviewed my notes from the previous class lecture. It became a habit that actually helped improve my studies.

Accompanying Everett down the hall, I put on my glasses as we took the elevator down one floor and out onto the campus. We wove ourselves through the morning herds of students, backpacks slung over my shoulder, and the back of his chair.

We approached the Temple University bell tower, a vertical slab that resembled something out of a future-primitive science fiction movie. The campus was covered in a slushy blanket of snow that had been shoveled along the main walkways into bulky piles shoved to the side.

"See you in English?" Everett's breath escaped in a wisp in the cold air.

"You bet."

And then he wheeled away, and I couldn't help but watch him, his back slightly hunched over, his arms tugging the wheels with a quiet strength that, whenever he left me, sometimes tore me up inside.

Casual. Yes, that's how we may have seemed to the other students, many of whom still gave us curious stares. Who were those two, I almost sensed them wondering, that lanky jug-eared guy and his cute friend in a wheelchair? Were they friends? Roommates? Something else?

We were something else, all right.

Settling in at the usual third-row aisle in my day's first class, a sort of calm overtook me in the warmth of the lecture hall as I straddled my parka over the back of a chair. Everett was with me, in my mind, at all times. Alone, without him by my side, I could choose to chat with others, make new friends, just be myself.

But I knew I wasn't.

As I absent-mindedly took notes on the professor's lecture about gradient erosion, I was still thinking about my boyfriend, my Everett, the spoiled little rich kid who almost died, who almost pushed me out of his life, until I simply refused to let him go.

It was a Tuesday, one of my two favorite days of the week, the other being Thursday, when we both shared American Literature. Despite our completely different majors, a few general courses aligned us at first, and we made sure to get the same class.

After another brisk walk across the campus, I ambled down to the front of the lecture hall, where the gap in seating on the front right aisle was Everett's wheelchair parking spot. Expecting to casually plop down next to him as usual –his previous class was closer than mine– I was surprised to see someone already next to him, engaged in a friendly discussion. I slowed my pace as other students walked around me.

The larger lecture classes usually led to students taking the same seats. Everett parked himself in front, because the ramped access led to the front of the room, below the tiered rows.

Already midway through the semester, it seemed odd that some boy our age, with gelled spiky hair and a formal shirt and tie, had parked himself beside Everett.

I approached them cautiously, deciding not to play the turf game. Hadn't I just enjoyed my boyfriend for a pre-breakfast treat, or, more accurately, he me?

"Oh, hey, Reid. This is Gerard."

I offered a cautious nod, hoping that by standing near them, this Gerard would get the message and move elsewhere. I seemed to recall him at the beginning of the semester in the back of the lecture hall, slouching in the back row, a cigarette pretentiously parked above his earlobe. A few weeks later, I noticed him in a middle row. And now, there he was, in my seat.

"Gerard was telling me about this eighteen-and-over New Wave night at, where was that? We should go."

"Are there stairs?" I asked.

"It's in the basement," Gerard said.

"Well, too bad," I said, refusing to move, standing before them, hoping I could mentally push this poser out of my seat and out of our lives before it got complicated and this curious dandy had to be told off.

But Everett, knowing my protective intentions all too well, and that I had many times carried him up and down stairs with a quiet pride, dismissed my stern behavior and turned back to Gerard. They cheerfully chatted about the B-52s, until our professor entered the room, and the other students settled down.

I took a seat in the row behind Everett, yanked the folding retractable desktop from its slot. It flapped down a bit loudly. Everett turned back to me and shot a glare.

For the rest of the lecture, I stared at Gerard's shiny spiked hair every time he whispered some remark. I alternated by gazing at the back of Everett's head, making doodles on a page of my spiral-bound notebook in imitation of his dark curls. Then I focused on the back of his neck, the nape, where tiny wisps of hair trailed down to the pale skin that I'd so often licked and playfully bitten on nights when we'd made love, or tried to. A pink glow almost illuminating his earlobes made them seem like a pair of tiny trumpets. Had I nibbled on them enough times to claim them, to allow him this one slight? I noticed a small twitch in his right ear, as if he were biting down out of habit, or flinching at some quiet pain. Why had I never seen that tic?

The first time I had met Everett, more than a year before, he also had his back turned to me. Naked in the snow in a strip of woods that separated his former Greensburg home from the more middle-class neighborhood where I grew up, we had sparked a most unusual friendship on that cold winter day. I felt a warm flush recalling it, and our intrepid encounters in the ensuing days before we separated for months at a time. That short time before his accident, a spinal cord injury on a lacrosse playing field, kept me locked to him, beholden somehow.

And now, months after he had tried to spurn me, send me away, then reel me back with an emotional yoyo that aligned with his own physical recovery, we were together, despite his mother's protests and my parents' doubts. With our families on the other side of Pennsylvania, so far from Philadelphia, we had begun a life together.

The sudden rumbling of students and the flapping of folding desktops jolted me to the realization that I'd ignored the entire lecture. My notebook page was a dark swirl of ink, and all the while I'd been staring at his earlobes.

"You could have been a little nicer." Everett flicked a clump of snow that had rolled up from his wheels onto his gloved hand. We had planned to have lunch at the dining hall, but I feared he might find some excuse to dismiss me.

"He was in my seat," I replied. "You could have asked him to move."

"Are we connected at the hip or something?"

"No, I just–"

"We already discussed this, Reid. You're getting a little over-protective, and it's really not appreciated."

"I'm not being over-protective, I'm just–"

And then, out of nowhere, as was his habit, Everett broke into song, loud enough for a few passing students to smile. "In time the Rockies may crumble, Gibraltar may tumble. They're only made of clay."

"What, is that another of your Cole Porter songs?"

"Close; Gershwin. And if you'd let me finish, I'd tell you," another sung line; "Our love is here. To. Stay."

"Fine. A little off-key, but I'll take that."

He scooted ahead of me, apparently finished with the discussion.

The day had started out so well, what with my cock in my boyfriend's mouth and all.

Chapter 3
March 1980

"You coming?"

Marlene, who lived down the hall, had invited us to another of her video nights with a few of her friends. She made a big fuss about commandeering the rec room on our floor, plugging in her videotape machine to the communal TV. She would even bring popcorn, a sealed bag straddling her lap as she navigated her electric wheelchair and portly body around the room.

"What are you guys watching tonight?"

"*Whatever Happened to Baby Jane*," Everett said, grinning with anticipation.

"Again?"

Marlene, a quadriplegic art major, Devon, my friend from the previous semester, who lived in another dorm, but wheeled over for these nights, Everett, and Craig, a computer science major who was also an amputee (leg cancer, something I hadn't known even existed) had howled with laughter and recited a few of the supposedly famous lines. I thought it was depressing, those two fading stars screeching at each other in black and white, and Bette Davis torturing her sister.

Marlene's movies, rented at a store, or ones she owned, mostly featured characters in wheelchairs, like *The Men* (which was actually pretty good), and *Rear Window*. One of the strangest films was *The Rocky Horror Picture Show*, a very gay science fiction musical. Marlene had bragged that she'd spent a few dollars to get a bootleg video, saying the movie was "more fun live. There's a movie theatre downtown where people say lines and toss stuff."

I didn't understand, and the promise of attending such an event made me a bit uncomfortable. I also couldn't see the movies the way they did, as they critiqued or complimented what they saw as either stereotypical or accurate portrayals of disabled people.

Also, the previous gathering had been delayed by Gerard's extensive one-sided introductory conversation telling everyone about his French background; his father, of the Delannoy family, working class Canadians, and his allegedly royalty-descended great-great-someone coming from France.

Devon offered a bit of his family history, "descended from a proud Uruba tribe by way of the slave trade." His father had dug into their lineage back in the 1970s after the TV show *Roots* became popular.

"Well, I myself am descended from pure mid-Pennsylvanian white trash," Marlene announced to much laughter, except from Gerard.

When he and Everett broke into gossipy French, the party split up between the talkers and the watchers, until they settled down to watch the film. It just felt odd to find another group where I was left to feel a bit awkward without Everett's attention.

But then Devon rolled up to me, and we shared an update. He'd offered me a few pointers on relationship advice even before Everett had joined me in Philadelphia.

"How's things?"

"What things?"

"You know," he lowered his voice, nodded discreetly toward Everett. "You settlin' in with the boyfriend okay?"

"I guess so," I replied.

"Well, again, I don't know about the gay stuff, but like with the women I date, don't baby him. He wants a partner, not a nurse. You don't wanna emasculate him."

"What?"

"Gender Studies," Devon had offered a tap to his own forehead.

Despite such unusual advice and company, I was behind in my studies, and didn't want to watch another movie.

"So, you comin'?" Everett asked.

"I think I'll pass. I might go to the library."

"Suit yourself," Everett shrugged before heading out.

"Don't stay up too late. We have our park hike tomorrow."

"You bet, Ranger Reid," he saluted.

As the door closed behind him, I felt a familiar pang, a sort of drop in my heart that almost echoed through the room, which became suddenly quiet in his absence.

We knew college would be a more freeing environment, and in many ways it was. Walking –and rolling– across campus, greeting people and friends like Devon or Everett's new classmates, we could have passed for straight, even though we told otherwise to anyone we got to know.

The few wheelchair folks knew about us. Gossip got around faster. But I saw other people who couldn't see him as a complete being, and I might have appeared to be some sort of hapless human service dog.

Most of the other gay students that we'd met had been hit or miss as potential friends. One time, I'd caught up with the elevator while Everett was in class. The guy who held the door half-smiled, nodded a silent greeting, then asked, "So, that wheelchair guy. Are you his nurse?"

I'd wanted to reply, 'No, I'm his boyfriend!' but caution overtook me, so I let it pass, simply reducing my explanation of our relationship as mere roommates.

The oddest encounters were with people who either completely ignored Everett and only spoke to me, or they would lean down to him as if they were addressing a mentally challenged child. A few times, Everett just started babbling away in Latin, usually phrases involving their maternal parent and allegations of prostitution.

When we weren't in class or studying, we continued to explore and find accessible places; the pool, museums, or the closer campus theatre productions. "Hey, guaranteed front row seats!" Everett would joke.

The Temple University campus was busy that semester, with wide sidewalks and mostly flat terrain. Everett could be gone all day and I learned not to worry, even though he had taken a few spills on snowy days months earlier.

March was still cold and damp. Clumps of snow, dirty miniatures of the large piles from winter, clung to muddy grass along the campus walkways.

Since we'd been together, we had each made sacrifices. Everett joined me at Temple after my first semester, even though he could have gone to Carnegie-Mellon, but his standard line about Pittsburgh was, "too many hills." What we knew, and didn't state to others, was his preference to be away from his family; well, most of them.

Having enjoyed runs through Fairmount Park the previous fall, I was eager to share my new favorite place with Everett, perhaps too eager. The early spring weather was still a bit chilly, and not nearly as scenic with the colorful leaves not yet in bloom, but it would feel good to get out of our small dorm room.

When we had some time off from studying, on a few Sundays, as soon as winter had mostly passed, Everett liked to go driving in his van, finding back roads outside the city. On impulse, we'd visited Valley Forge, then King of Prussia's shopping mall. He said he liked the adventure, but I knew he enjoyed the sense of independence and freedom of simply driving.

His laughter, his almost buoyant humor, accented with a sardonic edge, gave each day a new small joy. Everett and I, together, then apart, had become constants; buds.

But even best buddies sometimes got on each other's nerves.

"Turn at Spring Garden Street."

"I know," Everett hissed as he checked the side rear-view mirror. He drove the van with ease.

"Sorry. Is something wrong?"

"No."

"Do you not want to go to the park?"

"No."

"Well then, let's go somewhere—"

"No, I do not *not* want to go."

"So you do."

"A double negative would imply that," he snipped.

I didn't reply. Something was bothering him that he wasn't ready to explain.

As we crossed the bridge over the Schuylkill River, the Museum of Art loomed ahead like a Greek temple. Everett drove around it, following the flow of traffic, until he spied a parking spot along Pennsylvania Avenue. But by the time he'd looped around a block, a car had already parked there. He found another one further up the street.

"There's handicap parking behind the museum."

"Fine."

And we looped back again. Finally parked, he fiddled with the various gears that made the van workable for him, and opened his door. "Could you just get my chair?"

"You don't want to use the lift?"

"The damn hoist is broken again. Just bring me the chair and let's not make a big production out of it."

Holding my comments, such as 'Why didn't you tell me?' 'We could have gone to an auto shop,' or 'We could just go home,' instead I just got him his chair, wheeled it to the door, where he hung from the side of the door frame and plopped himself down before I handed him his backpack, which he'd filled with snacks and a water bottle. He slipped it behind his chair.

"Can you get the door?" He handed me the keys, pushing himself away.

By the time I'd caught up with him as he rolled along the pathway, he seemed in a better mood. The sun had burst out from behind a cluster of clouds. Only a few people gave him the usual curious glances, which he ignored.

"So, show me your wonderful park."

The sudden burst of sunshine drew plenty of people, who dodged stepping in crusts of snow still on the ground and in gutters. We wore gloves and hats along with tracksuits that flopped at the laces of my hiking boots. I could have worn sneakers, but the treads were all smooth, and I figured there'd be mud and slippery trails where we might attempt a hike.

But despite the scenery, it was as if Everett wanted to zoom by it all. He seemed bored, or unsatisfied with the expanse of lawn along the river, the clusters of tourists, cyclists and joggers.

"Isn't there some more private path?"

"Further up," I said. "This is just the southern tip. It goes on for about eight miles."

"Let's go, then."

He yanked his wheels, churning them hastily, as if daring me to keep up. I tagged along as I broke into a brisk jog.

We passed the historic Boathouse Row and their racks of stored boats and oars. Further along, across grassy fields adjacent to the river, flocks of geese waddled along aimlessly. The pedestrian traffic gradually thinned out, but I kept a pace behind Everett, watching his back and arms flex, until he turned back, nodding his head for me to jog beside him.

"We're not doing the whole length, are we?"

"I dunno. Can you handle it?"

"Not really," I puffed between steps. I hadn't been training much, although my body was adjusting. Pacing myself along with him altered my stride, which felt like a harder workout than my usual running speed.

"You're welcome to catch a ride when you're pooped out," he joked.

After a while, I relaxed, found a steady pace, and just tried to enjoy the day.

By the time we diverted off to the more shaded Forbidden Drive, we slowed to a stroll. The path, although wide, was gravel, which forced Everett to push harder.

"Why's it called that?"

"I dunno," I sighed, panting a bit. "I guess it was forbidden, maybe for amorous Victorians."

"Do you wanna take a break?" he said, already veering toward a bench. This was his polite way of saying he was tired, too. An ingrained competitive instinct from his prior years of lacrosse were probably what could have pushed him further, but I was glad for the rest.

We shared swigs from the water bottle. Everett glanced around, pleased, it seemed. "You should get a job here."

"What, as a ranger?"

"You've done it before."

I considered it. My job the previous summer at Allegheny National Forest had been so different, distant. "I don't know if they're hiring. It's probably through the city."

"So? Find out."

"You want to stay in Philly for the summer?"

"Maybe not this summer, but you know."

"Where would we live?" By that, I meant, where could he live? Every apartment I'd seen had steps. I hadn't yet considered a life off-campus, and even the classrooms had proven a challenge for him.

"We'll find someplace."

"If you say so."

"I do say so. Now, how about that private tour?" He wriggled his eyebrows with a naughty inference.

It had been so easy those other times, when he could walk; our meeting in Greensburg, and in the woods near his school. But this was different. The only paths he would trek on wheels were so public.

"There's a bridge up ahead."

"Let's go."

The stone bridge's side walls, just above his vision, were too high for him to see above, so I hoisted him up so he could lean over it and see the river below it. A passing couple with a baby stroller gave us what at first seemed a curious stare, but the woman's smile seemed more appreciative. I smiled back.

Satisfied with his view of the river's muddy brown depths, Everett plopped himself back into his chair. The sprout of a tiny fern, one of many persistent plants that had grown from notches between the stone bricks, had fallen free and landed on his lap.

"And this would be?" Everett asked, ever the unofficial tutor, holding the leaf.

"Licorice fern, maybe."

"And the Latin?"

"I don't know; *polypodium…gly*-something."

"You're getting rusty."

I sighed. "Come on."

It could have been a perfect day, if I hadn't been so ambitious, if we hadn't been so determined to recreate that which could not be created; spontaneity.

A small tight hiking path led off near the bridge, a path I hadn't checked out beforehand. Everett suggested we simply park his chair off to the side and use our familiar piggyback method to find a private spot. He took his backpack from the chair and fitted it over his shoulders.

The path, on the opposite side of Wissahickon Creek, never became completely private, so I kept walking, despite the weight of him sagging on my back. He whisper-sang that old Beatles song, "Everybody's got somethin' to hide, 'cept for me and my monkey," then vocalized the twangy guitar into my ear, until all of a sudden the path became completely obstructed by a fallen tree.

"Damn."

"Yeah. Here, let me…" I stupidly thought I could just straddle it quickly, since it was only a few feet high, until he muttered, "Wait a minute," but it was too late.

I tripped and he fell off my back, hitting the tree trunk before tumbling down to the path. His head hit the ground with an awful thunk, his legs flopping about.

"Oh, my god! I'm so sorry! Oh, shit! Oh, fuck! Ev, are you okay?"

I rushed down to him, cradled him in my arms, reached down to straighten his legs. "I'm sorry!"

"It's not your fault."

"But I shouldn't have—"

"It's okay." He grunted, leaned forward and handed over my glasses, which had fallen as well.

"We need to. We need to– I have to–"

"Reid. Sit. Be still. I'm okay."

"You don't know that! This was so stupid. I'm so stupid!" Wrenched into a knot of guilt, I slapped my forehead. "We have to get you–"

"Reid! Calm down!"

I crouched down, touched him, hugged him, sniffed back what would have become a crying jag that was about more than just dropping him. He wrapped his arm over my shoulder.

The creek trickled, and a duo of gnats flew by. Everett waved them away.

"You sure?"

"Yes. I'm fine."

"But you can't–"

"Look." He pulled up his track pants to reveal his thin lower legs. "Nothing's bleeding. Nothing swollen. It'll be okay. Just sit."

I sighed, calmed down. "I'm sorry."

"Don't be."

"Let me take your backpack off."

We fumbled with it. I pulled out the water bottle, which fortunately hadn't leaked. He reached his hand up to my face.

"I'm sorry."

"Stop."

I settled down next to him. We leaned against the fallen tree trunk, breathed, held hands.

"Not as romantic as you'd hoped, huh?"

"What? I wasn't–" I sputtered.

"Come on. You wanted to find a private place to make out. It's okay. So did I."

I leaned over, kissed his cheek, wiped away a smudge of dirt.

"Look, I should be the one apologizing."

"For your cranky mood?" I asked.

"Yeah. I got this letter the other day, from Pinecrest Academy, all formal and full of pomposity. They want me to come back for some alumni honor bullshit event at this year's graduation ceremony." He rearranged his legs into a crossed position, pushed himself up to lean more comfortably against the tree trunk.

"And you don't want to go?"

"Hell, no."

"Are you embarrassed about…"

"About what? Being Mister Crip?"

"No, about being here, with me."

"No, sweetie. I want to tell the world. It's just that explaining Temple means explaining why I came here and they have expectations for alumni."

I understood, and wondered if he had made the right decision. While I was so happy to be with him, wake up with him, spend each day together, I sensed his disappointment. He had already placed higher in French and seemed bored by our shared American Lit course, having already read half the reading list when he was at Pinecrest. It was like my high school experience. I'd usually read several chapters ahead of most other schoolmates. My enthusiasm for learning was rare, even joked about, until I'd learned to hide my enthusiasm, except toward my teachers. What if his sacrifice had been a mistake?

"They just want to show me off," Everett shook his head. "It's just a big guilt trip for them, to make an example of me, what an 'inspiration' I am."

"You inspire me."

"But you don't need to present me with a plaque or a useless trophy."

"I could present something," I leered.

"Yeah, well, don't unzip unless you brought some bug spray." He swatted more gnats.

Chapter 4
April 1980

A chilly spring breeze seemed to blow up from the ground, whooshing iridescent leaf buds around my feet. I felt underdressed while rushing back from a late class.

Everett had a physical therapy appointment that afternoon at Magee Rehabilitation downtown. He insisted on getting there and back on his own, so I wanted to at least be back at our dorm before him. Sometimes he would be a bit exhausted from the stretches and rigors of the exercises they put him through. I think he liked the drive, and he said that he enjoyed hanging out with those he called "my fellow crips." He told me sometimes he headed out early, just to prove to himself that he could navigate the city streets.

Still, I wanted to make sure things would be ready for him back at our dorm, little things I wasn't even sure he noticed anymore; making sure he had something to drink and snack on, that the sheets were clean in case he was tired or amorous.

The cool wind should have served as a sort of warning, one of unexpected change. At the time, it just reminded me that it might be too soon to put away my winter coat.

So when he arrived, a bit disheveled, a slight scowl on his face, I thought it was mere exhaustion from a long day. I was wrong.

"*Sansevieria trifasciata.*"

I sighed, not really feeling up for our little Latin game at that moment.

"Um, snake plant; it's in the order Asparagacae, those spiky ones with the yellow strips."

"*Sansevieria trifasciata,*" he repeated, then translated, "Mother-in-Law's Tongue."

I nodded, distracted by getting my backpack unloaded. I didn't understand his reference.

"My mother called," Everett said.

"When?"

"Earlier today."

"How is she?"

"Fine, and plotting, and visiting."

"Us?"

"Yes. This weekend."

It was a Thursday. I scanned our room, wondering what dirty laundry or which of the somewhat gay posters we'd acquired might sour her opinion of our living quarters.

Sensing my unspoken 'Why?', Everett said, "Her excuse is a belated birthday lunch for me, a shopping binge and a visit with some old college lady pals, or so she said."

"But?"

"Of course she's checking up on us."

Although my own meager gift would pale in comparison, I knew Everett appreciated it, a cute Curious George children's book. It referred to our corny pet names for each other, he the monkey to my giraffe. Such intimacies –that we'd decided upon the names on our first night together– were kept hidden from others, friends and family alike.

Diana Forrester had pretty much let us be for a few months, so I shouldn't have been worried. She had enjoyed some time with her son, without my presence, over Spring Break, when Everett was in Pittsburgh staying with his father.

My train trips to spend the weekend with him had been carefully choreographed around her own requests to see him. His sister Holly had been more than accommodating, letting me stay with her when Everett visited his mother's fancy new apartment in Fox Chapel.

But her impending visit set me on edge. Although our initial clashes were nearly forgotten, I had a sense that she had merely been biding her time, and that time was up.

My efforts to scrupulously clean our dorm room were for naught. By Saturday, we were set to have dinner at her hotel, the Bellevue-Stratford. "Mother travels first class or not at all," Everett informed me.

I'd carefully ironed button-down shirts for Everett and myself, and had hung our jackets and pants at the ready that afternoon when she called.

"No, Mother, you don't need to send a car. We can drive," Everett argued over the phone, keeping his tone even while rolling his eyes at me.

"Yes, Seven o'clock. Yes, we'll be dressed appropriately." Across the room, I made a grand silent gesture of displaying our suits like a game show model.

"So, no grand tour of our r-r-rooms, Sir?" I joked, rolling my R's after he hung up.

"Apparently not. But a word of warning at dinner; don't order anything from the menu that you can't pronounce."

Out on the streets, having found a parking spot surprisingly near the hotel's entrance, I kept my sometimes worried nature on an even keel. Everett wheeled beside me, in a chipper mood. We approached a high unramped curb, but before I could even offer to help, he simply popped a wheelie and jumped over it. His jacket and tie, combined with his black fingerless gloves, gave him the look of some sort of classy action hero.

As we rounded a corner, a gust of wind, thick and humid, whirled around the nearby tall buildings and blasted us. I saw Everett recognize someone ahead of us on the sidewalk. He paused, reached into his inside breast pocket for his wallet, then extracted a ten-dollar bill, which he slipped inside his glove.

I saw what, or who, had inspired him. A lone Black man in a wheelchair, a bit disheveled, with a worn cardboard sign in his lap, was parked next to a newspaper rack on the sidewalk. Other people passing by gave him barely a glance, but Everett wheeled right toward him.

"College Boy!" the man called out, his face brightening at our approach. Everett leaned forward, shook hands with the man, palming the extracted cash like a discreet card trick.

"How's it goin', Ricky?" Everett smiled.

"Fancy duds," Ricky admired us. "Y'all goin' to the opera or somethin'?"

"Dinner with my mom. This is my best bud, Reid."

I shook Ricky's extended warm hand, felt deep calluses. He smiled.

"Any friend of College Boy's a friend a mine," Ricky said. "Where ya headed?"

"The Bellevue-Stratford, believe it or not."

"Ooh, fancy! But careful ya don't catch nothin'."

"Come on. That was years ago."

"Don't let me keep ya. Y'all have a good night."

"Thanks, my man. We'll bring you some leftovers."

Ricky mock-scowled. "Oh, that rich food's bad for my arteries! Y'all have a good time. Don' worry 'bout me."

"Alright, You keep dry, okay?"

"Oh, yeah."

As we headed away toward the hotel, I felt a surge of conflicting emotions; the thrill of the brisk evening, so wonderfully lit, with City Hall and its ornate elegance just up the street. My pride for Everett's innate good nature toward Ricky contrasted with the comparative luxury of our destination.

"What?"

"Nothing," I grinned. "I just… You're something else."

"He's an okay guy. I met him at Magee a few times. He actually has a place to live. He just likes to pester the tourists." He smiled up at me, nearly wheeling ahead of me towards the hotel. "Come on. I'm hungry!"

"What did he mean?"

"What?"

"When he said, 'Don't catch nothing.'"

"You remember Legionnaire's Disease?"

"Wait, when all those old veterans died?"

Everett gestured toward the imposing hotel's entrance.

"But—"

"We better find the side entrance." He looked up at me with an amused scowl. "Don't worry. They cleaned it up. It's not contagious...anymore."

Everett pushed himself in ahead of me with ease as a handsome bellman opened the door for us through the fortunately flat side door entryway. The grand lobby's floral displays jutted out from circular tables. Beguiled by the intricate patterns in the ceiling, I found myself gawking open-mouthed, nearly tripping on Everett's chair.

"This way, gentlemen," the bellman said, guiding us to a carpeted ramp around a corner by the reception desk.

Diana Forrester greeted us at the entrance of the hotel's restaurant like a diplomat welcoming foreign dignitaries, as if the entire hotel were her own palace.

She seemed taller than I'd remembered her. Her hair done up in a higher style, her red jacket and skirt angled with subtly wide shoulder pads, a thin strand of white pearls dangling from her neck just so. I couldn't keep a forced smile from my face as she bowed to hug her son, then approached me. She embraced me yet somehow managed to hug me while barely touching.

"Shall we go to our table?" she breezily said, leading us through the doorway.

As we followed, Everett offered a cheerful wink of reassurance. Yes, this would be fun. Yes, I should let go and enjoy this.

We settled at a table, prepared in advance, it seemed, with one chair removed to accommodate Everett. The white tablecloth and multiple glasses and utensils glowed under the warm lighting. Waiters busied themselves with a silent efficiency. Small bound menus were presented to us.

"Order whatever you like," Diana Forrester offered with a wry smile. "Champagne, perhaps?"

I looked to Everett for instruction. "Sure!" he beamed.

"Nothing but the best for my son and his good friend," Mrs. Forrester offered as she sipped what appeared to be a most perfect goblet of iced water.

I couldn't help but consider how she had qualified her description, 'good' friend as opposed to 'boy.' She prepared to woo us with luxury, mixed with a qualitative sliver of dismissal, that diminution of our bond.

Surveying the menu served as a distraction. Surprisingly, the prices weren't too exorbitant, until I realized I was reading the list of appetizers. We ordered, an effete waiter made a few suggestions, and left us as a silent busboy proffered warm bread blanketed by a napkin. A bottle of champagne appeared almost immediately after Everett's mother had ordered it.

"If you'll excuse me, I need to wash my hands. My wheels are a tad gritty." Everett removed his fingerless gloves before excusing himself.

With my 'good' friend absent, Diana Forrester's cheerful demeanor shifted to an almost businesslike pose as she toasted me with a fluted glass of bubbling wine.

"So, young Mister Conniff."

"Ma'am," I raised my glass and resisted the urge to reply, 'Old Missus Forrester.'

"I have a proposal for you."

"Oh?"

"I'm going to be quick before Everett returns. Now, don't be nervous. It's very simple. I acknowledge your… success and inspiration in aiding my son's recovery. All that…"

She made a gesture, as if to toss away that first tumultuous year of my relationship with her son, and her determination to destroy it, as mere bread crumbs. "… is behind us."

"Is there something…?" I'd gulped down a bit too much champagne.

"I imagine that Temple University is doing well by you?"

"Yes, Ma'am."

"I do, however, think Everett could do a bit better, in the long term."

"He's not going back to Pittsburgh, Ma'am."

"No, no, no. Settle. I'll be quick, before he gets back. Here's the thing. Despite his… undeniable… relations with you, our boy has a future, don't you think?"

"Of course."

"No, I mean, as a community leader, and a leader needs more… challenges."

"Challenges," I repeated.

"Academic advancement. I did a little tour; my driver did, actually. I didn't actually walk around, but I did give it a little survey. Temple is really more of a commuter college, isn't it? It's very … urban."

"I don't know what you mean." Actually, I did know what she meant, but didn't challenge her to admit it, or say, 'You mean there are too many Black people, right, Ma'am?'

"Here's the thing. Just blocks away, the University of Pennsylvania is much more… appropriate for someone of Everett's intellectual needs. What if I were to support his transfer? You could remain close to him, something I have no intention of preventing, and he gets an education more fitting his …"

"Pedigree?"

"Exactly!" she concurred, failing to notice, or ignoring, my sarcasm.

In a flash, I did agree with her. Perhaps it was the champagne, the expensive kind, which almost evaporated in my throat. But we found an accord. Everett had been noticeably antsy in his first semester. He was excelling in all his courses, and had barely studied.

But then, my stomach flip-flopped, perhaps from the champagne gulp. Where would he live?

"Of course, I would offer to finance your own transfer, but I imagine your parents might find that a bit unseemly."

"Um, they don't exactly have my major. I could switch to basic earth sciences, with a minor in–"

She silenced me by interrupting. "And while I'm sure the Penn administration will be most accommodating –I'm actually old college chums with one of the assistant dean's wives, and we had a lovely lunch this afternoon– there might be a housing change to accommodate his… situation."

"Disability."

"That's such a limiting term, don't you think?" She glanced beyond our table. "Oh, here he comes. So, in sum, I'll support you and you support Everett, and everyone's happy. Yes?"

At the moment Everett rolled himself up to the table, I had silently raised my glass.

"To what are we toasting?" Everett innocently asked as he settled himself.

"To your future," his mother replied, her catlike grin broadening.

"Our future," I added.

"All right then," Everett replied, a bit confused but smiling nevertheless.

Champagne swirled as our glasses clinked, and our entrees arrived with precision timing that made me realize the secret of such fancy restaurants; it wasn't what was served, but how and when.

It wasn't until dessert was finished that Diana Forrester unveiled her plan to her son. Through the entire dinner I waited for her to mention it, but the three of us chatted amiably. Everett wittily described one of our public transportation mishaps, in which he almost spilled sideways off a bus ramp.

"Why didn't you use your van that Mr. Muir got for you?"

"Parking downtown is almost impossible. It's only a few blocks from the train. We drove tonight, though."

"Very well. I'm just concerned for you."

She pushed aside her plate of what I heard called an orange liqueur tartlet, and rearranged herself, poised, ready to pounce.

It came to me then, with just a half-glance toward me, her silently saying, 'You agreed to support this.' It was then that I imagined an additional unspoken threat, 'Or else I take him away altogether.'

Coffee was poured beside her by white-gloved hands.

"My dear son," Diana Forrester announced after I nervously dropped a fork on my plate with a clatter. "I have a proposal for you."

Everett absorbed her words, fingers folded, elbows up, tilting his head a bit, and then I saw that ear twitch, him clenching his teeth.

He waited as she extolled the virtues of the university, our proximity, his advancement, until she did finally offer, "How does that sound?"

Everett blinked twice, turned to me abruptly. "Did she already pitch this to you?"

I nodded.

"And what do you think?"

I held myself contained, considered. "I want what's best for you, and this is." I nodded to punctuate my resolve, then winked at him. It said, 'No matter what, we're together.'

Everett inhaled slowly, dramatically, scanned the restaurant, as if looking for some other table where he really belonged.

"Let me think about it," which meant, 'Let me talk about this with Reid and not you.'

His mother burst out another litany. "You can shape your own major, Public Policy with, what did you say, a minor in Civil Rights or whatever. The student-teacher ratio's practically as good as Pinecrest. Which reminds me, did you reply to the dean's request to—"

"I'm not at Pinecrest anymore, Mother. I'm in this city, with Reid, and I'm happy. My advisor even told me I could start auditing classes in the Disability Studies grad program. Penn doesn't have that."

She countered again. "Do you know what the administrator who I talked with said? That a boy of your talents would be an asset to the university."

"For a mere, what, ten thousand a semester? Who do you owe a favor to at Penn?"

She signed the bill, which arrived via another silent waiter. "It's none of your business, and besides, it'll be they who will owe me." She smiled. "You wanted honest? There, your interfering mother's just doing her job."

As we returned back to the Temple campus, I followed him into the dorm. Everett had remained silent. It wasn't until we were alone that he yanked off his tie and tossed it across the room.

"I'm going to be like a mascot there," he said. "If they put me in one of the jock houses, it'll be like expanded frat parties and pseudo-intellectual twaddle nights. 'Let's be buddies with the crip for extra credit!'"

Everett had yet to fathom his mother's true motivations, but still ruminated on it with me as we undressed for bed. I wondered how many remaining days I would have with him in it.

"You really are okay with this?" Everett asked me.

"You're too smart for this school. It's only across town," I said as I nestled into bed with him. "Your mom said you just have to stay in the dorms for two semesters. It'll be romantic. We do long distance really good; really well."

I didn't clearly state that our daily proximity had sometimes made both of us a little cranky, whether either of us would admit it or not.

"It's twenty blocks," he said.

"I can just take the Broad Street train and transfer to the trolley. I'll be all over you. It's just for a while. *Pro tempore.*"

"Clever," he smirked. "I never thought you'd take sides with my mother."

"I'm not. I'm on your side. Temple's not… You need more challenges. Besides, won't some of your old classmates from Pinecrest be there?"

"Probably, the ones that are too stupid to get into Harvard or Yale." His sour look made me wonder if he'd want to see any of his former classmates. Was the memory of his accident still too strong?

"Besides, you're kind of sick of me, aincha?" I cuddled closer.

"Yeah, I am." He went along with the joke, scooted his legs into a crossed position, took me in, grinned slyly. "And as punishment for your treachery, you must dance for me."

"Again?"

He'd played this game with me before, demanding that I perform for him, let him watch, before we got to making out. He told me that seeing me move turned him on almost as much as touching.

Leaning over to the radio alarm clock, he fiddled with the dial. I jumped out of the bed, heard fragments of Pat Benatar, that Donna Summer-Barbra Striesand duet at its peak, news, static, then the middle of The Pretenders' "Brass in Pocket." But he pressed on.

"That was good," I said, swaying to the beat as I warmed up. Yes. We were going to have sex to celebrate his imminent departure.

"Wait," he said, and then the dirge-like synth of Gary Numan's "Cars" amused him enough to raise the volume.

Satisfied, he grinned, shoved a pillow behind his back and clapped his hands like a harem-keeper. "Now dance for me, you traitor!"

Chapter 5
May 1980

Everett hated buses.

More precisely, Everett hated the beeping sound the bus made, the only cross-town bus that had an accessible ramp, and the audible sighs passengers made when we got in or out, delaying their own journeys by a few minutes. He hated the disgruntled eye-roll of the drivers as they operated the grinding lift, and the constant threat of those who sometimes simply refused to do their job.

Still, we got around. Everett's van, bequeathed to us at a discount via the car salesman father of our Greensburg pal Kevin Miur, spent more time in his assigned parking spot on campus, except for out of town trips. Philadelphia's streets were sometime too busy, or quaintly cramped, too 'historic' and bricked to gut for a curb cut. With the van, we'd loop around our intended goal, a restaurant or movie theatre, several times before finding a parking spot.

More often, weather permitting, we walked and rolled. At busy sidewalks, I sometimes just let Everett clear a path, loping behind. It was more efficient.

That Saturday, we decided to take the afternoon off, and Everett offered to take me out to lunch for my birthday, even though he'd already given me a large book of nature photos by Ansel Adams.

We both skirted around the fact that only a few days after my birthday the previous year, his lacrosse accident had changed everything. "Forget it," he brushed it off. "Let's go play tourist." But I knew it weighed on him, and his mood was conflicted, a determination toward pleasantry.

Only minutes after hoisting ourselves onto the bus with all its lift-beeping and passenger eye rolls, a bedraggled man moved to face us on the opposite row of seats.

"Huh. Had a brother't lost both legs in Nam."

"I'm sorry for his loss," Everett muttered, before offering a false smile. The man continued talking, to the wary older woman next to him, or himself; we weren't sure.

Everett glanced at me, almost whispering. "You see? What I said?"

"About what?"

"People think I'm some sort of conversational entrée to their own tragedies. It's like the chair's magnetic!"

"Oh."

He seemed a bit snippy. Perhaps it was the man's nearly toothless grin.

We had decided to take in Independence Hall and the other historic attractions. The line to see the Liberty Bell was a bit long, the crowds were a bit tough to navigate, and I could sense that Everett was becoming irritated.

But what set him off was a little kid; actually the kid's mother.

No more than three or four years old, the child turned to stare open-mouthed at Everett, or more precisely, his chair. His mother kept trying to turn him around, glanced back at us, and scowled. But the kid persisted. When Everett's friendly wave made him smile, and his additional funny faces made him giggle, the child stepped toward him and reached out to touch a shiny wheel.

"Bike?"

"Sort of," Everett beamed.

But before he could get closer, the child's mother yanked him back and scolded him, which led to a responding howl that made more heads turn.

"I'm sorry," the mother said with a tone that implied blame on our part.

"It's okay," Everett replied. He then gave me a bewildered shrug.

The kid kept howling, until his mother scooped him up in her arms, muttered something to her husband, who left the line and they scuttled away.

"Well, damn."

"That was…" I didn't know what to say.

Everett shook his head, as other tourists offered wary glances. "Are you hungry? I'm hungry."

That was his cue to leave. He impatiently picked the first restaurant we found that didn't have too many steps. We ate quickly, and the service was abrupt. So we cut our trip short.

Once off the bus again, we headed back to our dorm.

"Sorry I ruined your birthday."

"Shut up. You did not."

He seemed relieved, though, to be back in the somewhat sheltered campus.

"I'm gonna miss this place," he said.

The paths were modern, open and accessible. So were the people. Somehow, the students around us seemed more disinterested in us, more easygoing.

We had made friends with nearly all the other disabled dorm residents. With five other wheelchair students, and a few women and a guy who used crutches, it was mostly a close-knit group. Their various categories of injury or disability made them sound like a fraternity of science fiction fans; C5 Tetra/quad, T-4 para, T-10 amp.

Penn's undergrad population of disabled students was four. He would be the fifth, and the only one living on campus.

Everett admitted that despite our impending separation, he was excited to transfer to Penn in the fall. His new advisor had practically gushed over his enrollment, he'd told me.

As the semester's end drew near, he spent more time hanging out with his Temple friends, Gerard in particular, who often brought over obscure European bands' albums for Everett to record to cassettes.

My remark one night that the music sounded "gay" induced a disdainful huff. Despite his over-styled manner, Gerard "did not identify with hierarchical gender constructs," whatever that meant.

Between the combination of whiny electronic sounds and Gerard's posed snobbery, that night I found an excuse to study elsewhere.

By the time I returned from the library, Gerard had gone, but Everett was still absorbed in taping selections from the pile of records by the stereo. He waved and smiled, his headphones on.

I'd settled at my desk with a textbook when he shut down the stereo and removed his headphones, apparently satisfied with his latest cassette mix.

Moving to the center of our room, he played with balancing his chair in a tilted still wheelie. I pretended not to notice.

Plopping his wheels back down, he said, "So! What are we going to do this summer?"

The 'we' part of his question heartened me. While Everett and I had become comfortable living together, despite the occasional turf war for shelf space, the summer was ours, with no restrictions from our families. I also thought I needed a break from it all. Everett living elsewhere would keep us from taking each other for granted. It would be okay.

Staying in Greensburg meant seeing Everett on weekends, I had hoped, and getting a job, not that my parents said I should. They supported nearly all my expenses, except for Everett's occasional splurge night out, or a small gift. My partial scholarship had been renewed for one more semester.

I knew I didn't want to return to Allegheny National Forest, where I'd spent the previous summer before college. While it had been a great experience, being so many miles away from Everett that first summer after his accident had made me ache for him. Feeling more strongly connected to him, that nothing like our abrupt break-up could possibly happen again, I also didn't feel the desire to escape the urban world and work in a forest. I no longer wanted an escape. Actually, what I needed more was money.

"Mom's taken up gardening again," I said. "She said they're hiring at Wolfe Nursery."

"Selling flowers to the housewives of Greensburg?"

I smirked. "More like hauling bags of fertilizer. I could come visit you on weekends."

"That'd be great," Everett replied. But I sensed some other plans in his tone, and he revealed them when he wheeled over to me and presented a brochure. "But I'm definitely sure I'll go stir-crazy at Dad's high-rise, and Mother no doubt wants to show me off to her new clique."

"What's Holly up to?" I asked, hoping his sister might provide an escape from their parents for my weekend trips to visit him. She was more than supportive, and had been helpful in getting us back together when Everett and I had sort of broken up several months before.

"The opera company's off for the season. Last I heard she's got offers from three different summer theatre companies; upstate New York, and two in Connecticut."

"Good for her."

"She'll be subletting her apartment," he said, reading my thoughts yet again. "So, no Squirrel Hill love shack for us."

"Oh." I had wanted to revisit her apartment, for sentimental reasons, since we had spent our first night together on her living room sofa-bed months before his accident. The stairs would be a problem, but that never stopped Everett, or me from hauling him up and down on my back.

"It's cool," he said. "At least Dad'll be cool, so long as we don't make too much noise in the spare bedroom."

Everett had mentioned his father getting more serious with his new girlfriend, but not so serious that she had moved in, since he had yet to reel her in with an engagement ring. She was also divorced, and had a young daughter, Everett had told me.

The mere thought of making out with Everett in a bedroom in that high-rise, with that view, by night or day, pleased me. His father's presence made me curious about his level of approval.

"So, what's this?" I asked as I reached for the brochure in his lap, which he teasingly yanked from my reach.

"This," he waved it like a sort of wand, "is my proposal…" –I liked the sound of that word– "…for us to spend a month together in the woods."

"You want to go camping? Great!"

"Hold on." He finally handed me the brochure: Cedar Springs Summer Camp.

"I got it from Gary, one of the rehab guys at Magee."

I read the address. "It's in Pine Grove? Where's that?"

"Actually up north near the park where you worked last summer."

"And it's wheelchair kids?"

"For a month, in July. Actually, it's not just wheelchair kids, but like, Down Syndrome kids, Muscular Dystrophy kids, and we could work all three months, but I kind of wanted to do a few other things this summer, too, with you."

"So, retarded kids?"

"The preferred term is 'developmentally disabled.'"

"I don't have any... I don't even have teaching experience."

"You taught kids last summer, didn't you?"

"I gave tours, told busloads of them about trees and bugs for a few hours a day."

"So, great. Put that on your application. You can do sports. They're really not that picky. Besides, I can tell them you helped me."

"You're not retar– developmental–"

"That's debatable. Look, they'll want me as a kind of role model. I can lead singing classes and, I don't know, French for deaf kids. It'll be fun, and a challenge, and the best, we can have a cabin of our own, knock on wood." He instead knocked on his head. "There's an actual town nearby if we need some civilization. There's a lake, and a pool, and, baby," he wheeled close to me, those dark little caterpillar eyebrows arching up in a flirtatious leer, "woods all around."

"Woods," I smiled.

"Yeah. The pay's not much, but we get housing and whatever their version of food is. Gary said it's great."

"Gary."

"The guy with one leg and the beard? He's on my basketball team."

"Right." I remembered him from the last scrimmage I'd attended, a big friendly Black Vietnam vet. With the rush of moving and transferring to Temple, Everett hadn't officially joined the team, having missed most of their winter season. But he'd attended a few practices. This was Everett's world, and I was going to be a part of it in a new way.

"Plus," he pointed, "This will totally satisfy Mother's request for a 'good deed' résumé-builder. But it wasn't her idea. I haven't even told her yet. I probably won't, until we're already there, just so she doesn't swoop in and take over."

"Hire a florist to cheer things up."

Everett smirked. I thought of us spending moonlit nights in sleeping bags under the stars.

Then I remembered the strange, almost forced-friendly demeanor of a group of people, all with large crosses around their necks, at the one summer camp my parents took me to, in Roaring Run Park. A weekend stay was planned, until the singing and blessings over potato salad at the picnic kiva seemed to irk my parents. We relocated to the Laurel Hill camp, further south, and had a wonderful time. They basically set me free to hike all day while they… reunited. On the way back, we drove Dad's old station wagon back into Amish country and picked strawberries.

"This isn't, like, a Christian camp, is it?" I asked.

"What? No. I don't think so."

"I don't want any…"

"Any what?"

"Are they gonna be… you know, have a problem, with us…"

"As long as we don't fuck in front of them, I'm sure we'll be fine. Hey, do you trust me, Giraffe?"

I looked at him, his warm brown eyes, that glint of anticipation.

"We can be together every night."

I did trust him, and I didn't. The spoiled rich kid I once knew had been transformed, hadn't he? He wanted to give back, and perhaps find a safe way for us to be together over the summer without all the distractions of college and our parents. Learning how to help him, to appreciate his challenges and little victories, could be extended to some eager kids, couldn't it?

"Sure. Let's do it."

"Great!" Everett leaned in, and so did I, for a kiss. It all seemed like a wonderful idea. But it was his idea, and he knew I couldn't turn it down. I had to relent. Besides, hauling bags of fertilizer for housewives would keep for a month.

As Everett wheeled back over to his desk for the application forms, which, it turned out, he'd already sent for, he casually added, "Oh, so, have you had your shots?"

"Shots?"

"You know, the usual; tetanus, measles."

"Shots?"

"It's kind of standard procedure."

"Shots."

"Just a quick poke."

"You're infuriating, you know that."

"I love you, too."

Chapter 6
June 1980

A crash of late morning light splayed over my bed through the window. We had the house to ourselves to make as much noise as we wanted. Instead, I merely gazed at my boyfriend's sleeping face. Resisting the urge to kiss him to waking, I instead crept out of bed.

With the house quiet, I was surprised to see my mother in a light jacket and matching skirt, keys in her hand. I had forgotten how professional she looked when dressed for work, her dusty-blonde hair neatly pinned back.

"Oh! There you are."

"Hi," I smiled, still a bit groggy.

"Forgot my purse, again," she smiled. "You boys sleep okay?"

I nodded, looked across the kitchen counter for a quick snack.

"There's plenty of food for breakfast. Do you boys drink coffee now?"

"Not really."

"Well, I'll be back this afternoon. I'll make one of my big fun dinners, how 'bout it?"

"Great."

She leaned in for a brief hug, her perfume surrounding me. "It's so nice to have you back for a few days."

"Yeah."

After she left, I looked around at the quiet rooms, longing for my parents' company, yet somewhat relieved by her departure. Our simple house had once made me feel ashamed compared to Everett's wealthy home. But now, it made me happy, content to return.

After eating half a banana and a gulping down some orange juice, I returned to my room. Everett still slept in my bed, and I eased myself back under the slim sheet. He stirred and grabbed my arm over him, as if wrapping me around him like a blanket.

After visiting Everett in Pittsburgh for a few days, we'd been apart for most of the week. His drive back to Greensburg was delayed and he'd arrived at my parents' house a bit later than expected.

My parents knew better than to call us to breakfast. Dad managed the account books at the Best Rite supermarket, and Mom was a paralegal at a small law firm downtown.

In between his or my visits between "the sbergs" Green- and Pitt-, we had still called each other almost every night. We muttered cryptic code words for entire adventures we had shared, like "*bidens aristosa*," named for the afternoon in a scrubby northern section of Fairmount Park where we'd enjoyed an open plain of hills to the east, and even a few horses in a distant field full of (in English) tickseed sunflowers.

We'd merely kissed that day, but it was splendid. I didn't want to offer a critique as to when he wanted to go further. He pretty much showed it.

Other times, in private, we would explore new positions, new ways of blending our love and lust with the new challenges brought on by what Everett called "my new body." I learned how to enjoy the experience without needing a finish, without trying to push him toward an orgasm, which in itself was, well, more complicated for him.

Retrograde ejaculation; just one of the many awkward biological terms that had become a part of our life, was reduced to a mere joke when he called it "Back-Ejac." I grew to understand his preference for spreading our sexual fun, not be so, as he put it, "goal-oriented," since him even getting an erection often didn't happen. I took my cues from him as he guided me toward other pleasures; caresses along his neck, his underarm, connected by deep long kisses.

Bare under the slat of sunlight, the sheets tossed aside, he awoke fully and tugged the sheet down, surveyed my body with a smile before reaching downward.

"Flip around," he instructed.

Everett had almost mastered a two-pronged approach of taking my erection in his mouth as deep as possible, accented by an increasingly insistent finger wriggle to greet my prostate, which invariably led me to an overwhelming orgasm.

With a slurp and a grin, he released my penis from his mouth. It plopped onto my thigh with a splat.

"How do you do that?"

"Practice."

I wiped his cheek and lips of a shine of milky saliva, brought it to my mouth and licked my fingers.

"You are getting the best lunch ever."

"Sounds good," he patted my belly.

Later, barely dressed in shorts, having eaten a pair of immense sandwiches, we lounged on the sofa that afternoon. He squealed with delight at my younger pictures in family photo albums.

"You were adorable."

All I saw was a gangly Dumbo with black-rimmed glasses. But his amusement spread to me.

"You know you're handsome, don't you?" he said.

"I never thought about it until you, we…"

"Oh, Giraffe," he sighed. "You should know by now that I have impeccable taste."

As he closed the album, I asked him if he had any family photos.

"I think my mother has most of those. I have my yearbooks. I'll bring them when we head back to Philly."

"That'd be nice."

"It's nothing like that staircase is; was."

His family photos, hung in ascending order up the mansion's two-tiered staircase, had beguiled me on my first visit. I wondered where they'd all gone, now that the Forrester's, truly split, had leased their semi-furnished home to a German businessman who had plans to open a new economy department store on the outside of town.

Unable to break with the source of their family traditions –Everett's grandfather had the house built to his exact specifications decades before– his father had managed to hold off on selling their house.

I had returned, at least near it, on my first spring break after the Forresters had all moved to various new homes. Sitting at the corner of the lawn, until a few cars drove by too slowly to ignore, the mansion seemed to loom. The Forresters' lives had moved to the city and glistening new buildings.

"Do you miss it?" I asked.

Everett shrugged. "Sort of. But the last few years, with just me and Mom and Helen, were kind of vacant." Helen, his mother's housekeeper, had found work with another family in Forrestville.

"I mean, she filled up her days with, I dunno, those women's groups, and the country club and all," he continued. "But really. All those rooms, all that maintenance."

"But do you wanna go see it?"

"Have you gone back?"

"Once."

While hoping to find the nerve to retrace each step in and around his former home, out of some kind of instinctual trail sniff, I'd merely stood at the curb for a few minutes.

"I do, and I don't," he said. "I mean, we were already falling apart. It's just a natural..."

"Shedding."

Everett huffed, pretending insult. "Well! If you want to get all botanical about it."

Feeling that I should keep him entertained during his visit, and having run out of things to distract him, I suggested we go for a visit to one of the nearby parks out of town. He rolled his eyes, taking it as a hint of some probable outdoor lechery.

"Aren't your parents coming home soon?" he asked.

"Well, yeah, but we don't have to–"

"I need to get cleaned up. We reek of sex and I need a shave."

He'd already begun hoisting himself off the sofa and into his chair, and rolled down towards the bathroom when I jokingly called out, "But I like you fuzzy!"

"Plenty of time for fuzzy at the camp next month!"

I understood, though. Despite any casual situation, Everett's life had been one of protocols and dress codes. As familiar as we had become, he still addressed my parents as Mr. or Mrs. Conniff, and gave them a respectful attitude.

"Can you get my shaving kit?" he called out from the bathroom.

Foraging through his backpack in my bedroom, I found the smaller pouch with a few toiletries. I noticed a few prescription bottles as well, something I'd never noticed during all those months at the Temple dorm. Why had he hidden them?

"Here you go." I handed him the pouch, hung out in the doorway as he ran some hot water over a disposable razor.

"Does your dad have—"

"Here." I opened the cabinet, found a canister of shaving cream.

"Thanks."

"So, what are those medications you take?"

He stopped. "Why?"

"Well, since we're going to be at the camp, I just thought I should—"

"You should what?"

"Ev, I just… In case something happens.'

"Nothing's going to happen. They're just antibiotics and an antidepressant, which I haven't been taking because it kills my sex drive, and I'm perfectly happy, and you should be too."

"Okay, I'm sorry. I just never saw them before."

"And now you have. Do you want to watch me shave now, too?"

"Um, yes?"

"Get in the shower," he commanded as he lathered his face. "You stink, and you might as well entertain me, too, nosy."

Chapter 7
July 1980

Everett surveyed our tiny cabin with a wary look. "Well, this is … rustic."

I walked past him, shrugged a duffel bag off my shoulder and to the wooden floor. "It's ours, alone. We're lucky."

Because most of the counselors were women, and two of the other men were married to others, we were able to finagle our own cabin. Being the only wheelchair-using counselor must have helped us get a little bit of special treatment. I still wasn't sure that Alice, our lead counselor and default boss, completely understood our relationship, or cared. To Everett, it seemed unimportant.

The cabin's windows were small, with dingy drapes that hid the sunlight. The room's paneled walls didn't seem mildewy, but the room felt stuffy.

"Let's get some air in here." I opened each of the windows.

"You want the top bunk?" Everett joked as he wheeled toward the two stacked beds. They were as small as twin beds, so it was going to be a tighter fit when we slept. After sharing our larger dorm bed for so many months, the idea of merely sleeping near or above Everett was unthinkable. Going to sleep and waking up by his side had become one of the joyous constants of our new life together. Even so, the bed looked small.

Our first day involved a lot of introductions with the other counselors in the main hall of the camp, poring over mimeographed sheets of instructions, schedules, safety guides and a list of the students' names and various disabilities.

Barbara, the other lead counselor, seemed to repeatedly eye me, and speak in a somewhat careful tone, as if I might not understand the seriousness of our duties. I got a feeling that she thought I was just along for the ride, that Everett, by being disabled, didn't need instruction. Not sure who had figured out our relationship, or if any such revelation would be appropriate, I just busied myself by taking notes.

We would be expected to be on call most of the next day when the parents and their kids arrived. We also received short-sleeved shirts with the camp name printed on them.

"Our first night together in the wild," Everett said as we finally settled into our bed. The single lamp gave the cabin a dim yet unintentionally romantic light.

"Hardly the wild," I said. "The town's two miles away."

"Ohh. Was that a coyote?" he joked.

He shifted closer, we smooched, and his hand reached down toward my thickening penis. We lay side by side, kissing, caught up in the new feeling of being together in a strange place. Surprisingly, Everett had removed his catheter and let me touch his dick, which was showing signs of excitement. He must have taken care of it in the tiny yet adapted bathroom.

Clumsily, at first, we negotiated the small bed's confines. I bumped my head on the bed above, then, in a moment of creative gymnastics, Everett reached up to grip the above bed's frame and hoisted himself up to sitting, then a higher pull-up position. His penis bobbed close to my face.

"Oh, yes!" He gasped in mocking tone. "We should get bunk beds at home!"

I continued licking and kissing his torso, which tasted of a day's sweat. Wrapping my arms around his waist, I guided him back to sitting, almost hovering over me. I wanted to just devote my attention to him for a change. His arms flexed, suspended, he snorted out breaths. I caressed his chest, cradled his limp legs into a position around me, and kissed his belly, then lower.

As the familiar erratic spasms made his body shake, my lips clasped around him, tugging, fondling. I took my time as he pulled himself up, then lowered down. I took a hungry pleasure in knowing I might soon bring him to an orgasm, a rare instance. Perhaps it was the new setting that aroused us so quickly.

He let one arm drop, grabbed my head to pull me away, but I insistently clamped my lips around him until I felt, then tasted, a fluid burst in my throat. I felt his weight drop onto my lap as he grabbed my shoulder. I caught him, held him.

Straddling him, I quivered as he dug down and toyed with my penis, which jutted up against his thigh. He squeezed it out of me, pressing my cock against his skin, until it burst with that satisfying abrupt tingle.

"Wow," I sighed as I licked a spurt from his shoulder.

"So, we really like the new digs," he grinned.

"Well, it's been a while."

I didn't want to harp on how our distance during the preceding weeks had limited our time together.

"Don't you jack off when I'm not around?"

I shook my head. "I like saving it up for you."

"Apparently!"

Relieved that I was able to do for him what he so easily did for me, I eased him down to laying, hoisted myself off of him, searched around in our pile of unsorted clothes for a beach towel, wiped us off, then retreated to the bathroom.

Even though it was warm in the room, and we only lay under a sheet, I pulled on a worn pair of favorite shorts. Everett tugged up a thin pair of track pants, and we nestled close before falling asleep.

Early the next morning, what sounded like a riot of birds woke me. I needed to pee, but having slept against the wall, I would have to gently crawl over Everett to leave the bed.

I pressed a hand on the mattress for support, and felt moisture. I pulled back the sheet and saw Everett's soaked track pants clinging to his legs. My movements roused him and he gave me a sweet look that switched to shock as he saw the stains.

"Fuck!" He pressed himself up to near-sitting.

"It's okay, just–"

"No, it's not okay!"

"Just calm down–"

"Get out of the bed."

"I was trying to."

"Dammit, Reid. Why didn't you remind me about my catheter? How are you supposed to take care of a camp full of kids when you can't even help me?"

"What? How is this my fault?" I hurtled myself over him, stood awkwardly by the bed. "Just take them off, and get out—"

We had forgotten to lay down a bed pad, and Everett had usually been fastidious with his catheter and tube. But the mattress was soaked.

Everett scooted himself to the lower part of the bed, started pulling down his pants, then fumbled and nearly fell over. "This is so fucking embarrassing."

"Wait," I said, impulsively rooting on the floor for the beach towel. I set it in front of me, stood on it and tried to relax as my erection subsided, and the tent in my shorts slowly became wet.

"What the hell are you doing?"

I sighed. Urine dribbled down my leg, until I clenched, stopping the flow. I'd made my point. "Now we're even. We're both embarrassed."

Everett's scowl brightened to a sardonic smirk. "I think you liked doing that, you perv."

I shrugged, bent over to mop up with the beach towel. "It did kinda tickle."

Crisis averted, as he cleaned up in the bathroom, I tugged the mattress to the floor, then switched it with the one above, reminding myself to visit the kitchen and find some Lysol for the mattress.

Whatever trepidation I had about being a camp counselor dissipated by the end of the first few days.

Whether they stuttered or spasmed or didn't move much at all, each of the kids had their spark, even the sullen ones who feared being left without their parents for a week or two. Some of the kids stayed for shorter lengths of time than others, depending on their parents' schedules and budgets.

Everett's immediate popularity with the kids didn't surprise me. They had someone like them to inspire them, particularly with his more physically adept maneuvers.

Certainly I was liked, or I hoped I was, but Everett and the kids seemed to share a common language and understanding. I found myself crouching a lot, since they were smaller.

But it only took one game of balloon toss, a bit safer than any heavy ball, to define it all for me. One of the girls just bluntly said, as we paired off into two groups, "I wanna be on Everett's team!" I let her roll away from me, blushing with an embarrassment that only his silent smile could soften.

My favorite had to be Kenny, who steered his motorized chair with his nub of an arm, and whose favorite phrase was, "This is amazing!" Since we both wore black-framed glasses, he took to me as a sort of role model, scooting himself wherever I went, until another counselor would corral him back.

After our group dinners, some nights Everett would lead the kids in sing-alongs. The kids weren't the only ones who smiled at the sound of his voice.

On quiet afternoons, the crafts cabin would be nearly still except for the scratching sounds of crayons on paper. Over the next few weeks, the blank walls of our cabin became decorated with pinned-up drawings by the kids. I had never thought of myself as a teacher or even artistic, but given the context of nature, something opened up in me as the kids opened up as well.

In the middle of one of the few rainy afternoons, the activities shifted as the other counselors helped me bring out paper, crayons and magic markers. I decided to offer a primer on different kinds of trees.

Kenny declared that he would make autumn leaves, because they were "amazing!" even though it was summer, which led to another kid asking why leaves turned color and if they died. I fumbled through a kid version of carotene, anthocyanin, and the photosynthetic pigment depletion, until Alice saved me with a simpler comparison to animals shedding fur.

As I was helping Jennifer, one of the cerebral palsy kids, pick out colors for her leaf drawing, she bluntly asked me, "Are you disabled, too?"

I looked at her curious wide eyes and smiled. "You know my buddy Everett?"

"Yeah. Ebredd sings priddy."

"Yes, he does. And my disability is, if I'm too far away from him, I can't breathe."

She gasped. "Really?"

"No, not really. It just feels like that sometimes."

"Are you brothers?"

"Something like that."

"You don't look like brothers."

I leaned close to her, "Can you keep a secret?" and whispered, "That's because we're in disguise. We're twin unicorns from a distant galaxy."

Her volley of giggles took on an almost goose-like honk. A few of the other kids just caught on, laughing for no reason, or at her laughter, until Alice suggested "we should all calm down," followed by a stern glare toward me.

"*Dodecatheon.*"

"Stars; shooting stars," I answered.

Everett and I lay on a blanket in a small clearing at the edge of the campground. It wasn't late, after nine. We had missed the nightly ghostlike firefly dance over the fields. But the kids were in bed, the other teachers and supervisors relaxing in their own cabins. We'd found a path that he could wheel over, settled down with a few beers I'd hidden in a cooler after a shopping trip in town. They were warm, but we didn't complain. The air was also warm, a thick verdant texture we could almost taste.

"The stars are pretty," Everett said.

"The stars are always pretty."

"Even the dead ones."

"That's a morbid perspective," I said.

I rolled over on my side, gazing at Everett's face in the night as he looked upward, then returned my gaze.

"It's a sad fact," he said, softly. "Those stars, sending out that light, millions of years after their passing. You know one of the boys isn't well. Kenny?"

"He's 'amazing'!"

Everett tried a grin, but failed. "He's got some congenital thing; his bones won't grow right. And his kidney's fucked up. People with disabilities, we ... sometimes we don't last as long, Reid."

"What do you mean?"

"It's… It happens. It's a health thing. We get sick. Our bodies don't process things right. Urinary tract infections, respiratory problems…"

"Stop it." I bolted up to sitting.

"I just want you to know, to face facts." I felt his hand on my lower back, touching me where his own injury had occurred.

"I want you to know what you're in for."

"I know. But you don't have be so…"

"What?"

"It's like… you're always trying to give me a way out. You're so sweet, and you challenge me, and you made all these changes to be with me, and you're patient with me about everything. But then you just point a little finger like, 'By the way, here's the emergency exit.'"

"Hey, you were the one who fell for my mom's plan before I even heard about it. That was not my–"

"I know, I know. It's all my fault you're transferring."

"I just want you to–"

"Don't."

We stopped, sat without moving. The sounds of the woods were much more reasonable.

"You've made my life so different," I said, after a while. "All these trees. A few years ago, I'd be just seeing them, not the people."

"The studious botanist."

"These kids. They just…" I fought back a surge of tears. "You know Madeline, the little blonde?"

"She's great. So sweet."

"I was sitting with her at lunch today. I think you were out on the playground somewhere. She just started humming this little song, so off-key, but so perfect. And it sounded so familiar. And then I realized it was that song you taught them last week, one of the tunes you sang to me from the radio in the van. I just…"

I shuddered. Everett hoisted himself up. "Hey, hey…" He rubbed my back, leaned in, grabbed his legs, shifting them a bit.

"I can't be without you, without this, seeing people, their sweetness. It makes me feel… my stomach and my heart just… It's like I see their innocence, and I worry and fear for them, and you, and at the same time I know you'll be okay, but it's like, I get all … squidly or something."

"Squidly. I like that; a quivering jellyfish of emotion."

I turned, wrapped myself around him, holding him tight. With my face crooked into his shoulder, I smelled the light salty odor of his sweat. His kisses started on my neck, and as I turned toward him, the night light gave his face an eerie glow, the quiet only disturbed by my snorting back a burst of emotion.

"Pick me up."

"Do you wanna leave?" I asked.

"No, pick me up to standing."

"What? How?"

"Just… like piggybacking, but in front."

I crouched, held him as he wrapped his arms tightly around my neck. Then I rose and felt his legs drop down against mine. I swayed, nearly faltering to avoid spilling the beer cans. I felt how heavy and light he was at the same time.

Facing me, he said, "Just dance with me."

He hummed a tune into my ear as I stepped cautiously, side to side, off the blanket and out into the open field. Then he softly sang, another one of his old-time tunes.

"You're all the places that leave me breathless, and no wonder, you're all the world to me."

He felt so strong, holding on to me. I pressed my face against him, wiping tears into his hair, then pulled back to see him grinning wide.

"See? One less thing I can't do, thanks to you."

"Sweet." I swayed with a bit more daring, swirling about.

"Would you do this with me at a wedding?" he asked.

"Whose wedding?"

"Let's say my dad remarries."

"If it's okay with you," I said.

"It's okay with me," he answered.

"Stick around, and I'll dance with you anywhere."

"It's a deal, Squidly."

Crickets, starlight, trees sleeping in the night; it was as if that thick summer night air held us up.

Chapter 8
August 1980

The van, parked in the driveway of my parents' house, was once again in need of repair. But Everett and I weren't concerned about it, and instead pondered Kevin Muir as he fiddled under the hood, his tight cut-off denim shorts pressing against his bent-over ass.

The van had conked out a few times, and Kevin provided a little in-home fix, shrugging off our muttered catcalls of "lemon" as I sat in a lawn chair with Everett beside me, basking in the sun like fans at a softball game. As Kevin bent over the engine, Everett changed the fruity chant to "melons."

I chortled. The afternoon sun made Kevin's thighs shine, and although Everett wore sunglasses, I knew that his eyes bore a lascivious glance, which I shared.

That was because we had both 'shared' Kevin, in a way. As a childhood neighbor over in Forrestville, he and Everett had 'messed around' a few times. And during his painful hospitalization after his accident, Everett had basically offered up Kevin as a form of amusement. That a few of our stoned evenings together had taken an occasional, if not one-sided, sexual turn left Kevin unfazed, even though he considered himself straight, with a series of girlfriends to prove it. I wondered how our lives might have changed if I'd known that my handsome high school track teammate was open to the occasional blow job.

"That should do it," Kevin wiped his grease-stained hands on a rag as he turned to us with a confused glance. "What?"

"Nothing," I shrugged.

"You two were checkin' out my butt."

"It was hard not to," Everett argued.

"Hey, I know we have, you know, history. But I don't go there."

"Of course not," Everett held his hands up.

"Yet," I added.

"Well, if you can keep from molesting me, you're welcome to swing by and party a bit before you head out. That is, if you're not the old married couple you act like."

Everett gasped. "We're not old!"

The van up and running, we drove over later that day. Although his younger brother was also home, Kevin seemed to have the rule of his family's house. Set down the street from the Forrester's larger now-leased mansion, the Muir's white neo-Colonial, with columns on the porch, remained one of the more prominent homes in the upper-crust neighborhood. The interior, however, displayed a modern style with abstract paintings and shag carpeting in some rooms.

A Rick Derringer album played in the den as Everett and I sat in haze of pot smoke, pondering the remains of a pizza box.

While it was nice to talk about "old times," even though it was only a year ago that we'd been in high school, it felt odd to return to the same room where I'd serviced Kevin.

Over the blare of the music, we let our host ramble on about his newfound interest in working at his father's car dealership, usually selling, but occasionally getting his hands dirty with repairs. He also bragged about his new girlfriend.

"I think she's the one," Kevin said, nodding to convince himself. "It's been, almost as long as you two've been together. Hey, you are somethin' else, by the way." He stood still, took us in with a glazed look of admiration. "You know, it's too bad you can't really get married. I could throw you a helluva bachelor party."

"With you as the entertainment?" Everett teased.

Kevin shrugged, briefly thrust his hips as if it were a possibility, then more casually swayed to the music. "I definitely owe you. There was this guy, single, lookin' over the compacts, but I kinda worked the charm a little," –another suggestive thrust– "Then I did whadyou call it, the gay radar."

"Gaydar," Everett corrected.

Kevin pointed a finger in agreement. "Anywhose, I laid on the charm, got him to get behind a new Corvette; jet black."

"Did you give him a test drive?" Everett leered.

Kevin hooted. "Damn near."

Somewhere in my stoned haze, my befuddlement at the course of the conversation made me wonder if we should leave or start taking off our clothes. Were we supposed to admire his known cockteasing talents, and thereby admire him more directly?

"Say, how's the job doing?" Kevin asked me as he offered another bong hit. I declined.

"Okay," I said, a bit hazy. "Planting season's mostly done. I helped a few folks put some small shrubs in; that and mulching, selling leaf blowers."

My part time job at the Wolfe Nursery was providing some extra money for me to save up for school. But as late in the summer as it was, I spent more time piling up bags of wood chips and shelving pottery.

"You still visit Ev on the weekends, right?"

"Oh, yeah," I smiled at Everett.

"Fun in the big city. Hey, I oughtta come with. You guys could show me around."

"Sure!" Everett said, a bit too enthusiastically.

I considered a drive to Pittsburgh in Kevin's Camaro, our odd relationship, and what might happen. Kevin's offer seemed innocent enough, but I didn't agree to any specific plans. Back in high school, being alone with Kevin led to our unbalanced sexual connection. With all this joking flirtation, I wasn't quite sure that link had been broken.

"We only have two more weeks until we drive back to Philly, and I'm tryin' to get as many hours as I can, so I'm not sure when …"

"Sure, whenever," Kevin said, a bit dismissively, as he sauntered across the room, ending his macho dance.

Once we were comfortable enough to feign sobriety, Everett drove the van back to my house where he and I managed to dodge any parental interrogations. It was still early evening, but we retreated to my room, having called out to Mom that we'd already eaten.

"He seems happy," Everett said as we undressed and got settled on my bed. I made sure my door was locked. The pot had made me a little amorous; that and Kevin's company.

As if reading my mind, which became a more frequent occurrence with Everett, he broke our first embrace with a question.

"Would you have, if Kevin had wanted to?"

"What?"

"You know; a return engagement."

"With him? That was just... I was miserable then. I thought you were gone for good."

"No, I mean, if I were with you, and him."

"What?" I pretended to be shocked, but actually the idea had occurred to me, if Kevin's brother hadn't been there. "I don't...think so. Besides, he's not... I mean, big dick and all, he's not very good at it."

"But if he was."

"Are you–?"

"Forget it. Just horny stoned thoughts. Come 'ere. I prefer your big dick anyway."

Although he seemed to have dismissed it, as we fumbled about on my bed, quietly, with music playing more to cover our sounds than inspire us, I began to wonder if I wanted such a situation.

Did I need sex with an able-bodied guy? I'd grown used to the difference, helping Everett move his legs as we adjusted our bodies, focusing on his chest, on kissing and caressing the more toned muscles in his shoulders and back, and letting him explore my body with increasing ease.

Once again Everett kept the sex fairly one-sided, him eventually pleasing me, and unable or uninterested in getting an erection or reaching an orgasm, or even a 'back-ejac,' as he enthusiastically persisted in giving his attentions to me.

He must have thought he wanted to share an opportunity, something that could possibly strengthen our connection. But it instead left me with a lingering doubt.

59

Halting his insistent clutch to my lips, I rearranged myself and did the same to him, for a long time, stroking him to a rigidity that surprised him. I shifted upward to face him, plant our lips together as I humped him, groin to leg, thrusting between his legs, occasionally poking behind and into him, until I finally got a few spasming bucks of relief out of him and myself. But I kept kissing him, licking and caressing under his arm, longing to cover every inch of his skin with my own, until he shivered and begged me to stop.

After cleaning ourselves up and cuddling close for the night, I slept well, having convinced myself, having proven that I was enough for him, that we were enough for each other.

Chapter 9
September 1980

"Did you know…?"

"Not another 'Did You Know.'"

As Everett sat at his desk, I lay on the carpeted floor, stretching, since I'd decided to jog across town after taking the Broad Street line from Temple to Center City. Despite the jostling of the books in my backpack, I enjoyed the brisk fall weather. I would take the usual bus and train back, but wanted to enjoy an excuse for a workout, and Everett told me he liked me a bit sweaty.

Ware College House embodied all the gothic style and historic charm expected of the University of Pennsylvania, at least on the outside. The halls and rooms had been renovated and divided up into small white-walled near-cubicles, one of few with a private bathroom and other adjustments for 'the handicapped,' a phrase Everett disliked.

His room's front window next to a desk let in afternoon light. A second window, set back under an angled ceiling arch, faced the historic quad with other ornate brick dormitories squared off to resemble what I joked as the set for some PBS mini-series. Despite its inconvenience, Everett had asked to have the bed scooted to be underneath the window.

The small Persian rug Everett brought had proven to be a great addition to his almost overstuffed décor. Despite the cautious drive, with wobbling boxes spilling in the back of the van, it had been worth it. A few days before classes began, we'd managed to cram a lot of items from his family's storage garage in Greensburg into the van, then up and into his new dorm room. A few other guys helped out. Despite our new separation, I had to admit that Everett's mother had been right about his transfer to Penn.

"Yes, another 'Did You Know,'" Everett stated over the quiet classical piano music playing on his radio.

The phrase had become our sort of running joke, a lead-in when a long passage of reading and note-taking had to be broken with an outpouring of the cluster of information we'd just absorbed. My own homework, a chapter on common parasites among deciduous trees, had yet to reveal anything worth sharing.

"Until recently," he read, "the seventies, actually, some states had what were called 'ugly laws.'"

"Ugly laws?"

"Pennsylvania had them from the 1890s. Chicago passed one in 1911. Get this: 'No person who is diseased, maimed, mutilated or in any way deformed so as to be an unsightly or disgusting object or improper person shall be allowed in or on the public ways or other public places in this city.'"

"Fut the wuck?"

"The fine was 'not less than one dollar and nor more than fifty dollars for each offense.' Can you imagine?"

"Wow."

"Just think; if I'd been born fifty years ago, and been paralyzed, I could be fined for simply going outside."

"That's sick."

He tapped his textbook. "Even a few years ago, if my parents weren't wealthy, I'd be locked up in an institution."

"Damn."

"Historically speaking, I'm now a double minority," he said with a slightly confused tone of astonishment.

"Well, I would think," I strained a bit as I stood, stretching my legs before approaching him at his desk with a hovering hug, "that even some old-timey version of you, as cute as you are, should be fined for not displaying yourself."

He took the bait, returned my hug, turned away from his desk and offered a smooch, actually our first that night. It didn't promise anything, but I was hopeful. I rubbed his chest, brought my hand up to guide his face back to me for a more forward kiss.

"Am I staying over tonight?" I asked.

"Do you want to?"

"Of course I want to. I just need to know if you want me to, before they roll up the sidewalks."

While I made light of it, I didn't want to take a late train back to Temple. The student newspaper had reported a few muggings at different stations.

His tiny dorm room had become homey, due to the older buildings' more historic design. My own new single dorm in the bland modern high-rise at Temple felt bare, and not just because it lacked his presence. There hadn't been much room for my own stuff after we'd packed the van with boxes of his books, pillows and that cumbersome rug, so my room remained sparsely decorated. My poster of the Amazon rainforest adorned one wall. On a shelf sat the forlorn small stuffed giraffe Everett had given me the previous Christmas. I had also had a few of the drawings from summer camp framed, including one of Kenny's 'amazing!' trees.

My nights alone were warmed by calls to or from him, and I did find a few things to fill up my room, but mostly it felt cold and functional.

So Everett's room at Penn became our default scene for weekend trysts, only occasionally added by a midweek phone call that sometimes became an impromptu invitation. I quickly learned the quickest train and bus routes, and admitted that I liked his campus more. The autumn leaves and old buildings were quite pretty.

That night hadn't been a romantic invitation, but a mere, "Come on over," command. While gauging his interest, I thanked the lulling tones of the music and the warmth of his room.

"Did you remember to bring a change of clothes?"

"Uh…"

"Because I'm tired of you stealing my clean socks. You got big feet; they stretch mine out!"

"I'll bring a whole bundle next time. Now, may I romantically pick your 'ugly' self up and bring you to the bed?"

"I appreciate the offer," he shifted away from me and toward his chair. "But I'm going to 'the library' for a bit first. See you in the bed."

The 'library' being his tiny yet accessible bathroom, with an added reading stack for his somewhat time-consuming toilet details, I undressed and settled into his bed.

Back when we shared the room at Temple, when I'd asked him why he spent so long in the bathroom, Everett had mentioned the more unpleasant details of his various techniques for basically forcing himself to poop.

At his request, I sometimes left the small confines of our dorm room so I wouldn't overhear the various sounds of his sometimes-needed douche, the repeated toilet flushing and running sink water. It was one thing he really disliked, but just stoically dealt with, accompanied by a slight obsession with cleanliness. It also became something else I realized I took for granted, that basic human bodily function. He'd offered a concise description as being "like scooping out frozen ice cream with a plastic spoon, behind your back."

The radio music continued, and he hummed along from behind the closed door, then emerged, declaring himself "Fresh as a daisy!"

After hoisting himself over to the bed, he stopped. "Oh, the light."

"Can we... just leave the music and the lights on? I want to see you."

"Aw. Ain't you roman-ical." We embraced and his hand trailed quickly to my groin. "Jeez! You are in a good mood."

"I haven't wanked all week."

He switched back to a cartoon voice. "You really know how to impress a guy."

I chuckled as I shifted closer. Under the covers, I tried to adjust his legs with my own, but fumbled. He sighed, shifted up and shucked off his shirt, then scooted his butt sideways to tug his sweatpants down.

Rubbing his chest with my palm, I marveled at the definition of his muscles, the rounded curves of his shoulders. I kissed and licked around his neck, and around the small necklace he wore, a gift from me. I then trailed lower as he lay back. Although he couldn't feel it, he liked to watch as I caressed his legs, tugged his penis to a slight hardening, then grazed over the darker fuzz of his legs.

When we had first begun sleeping together, after his accident, he at first shied away from my touches to his lower body. But I had begun to be more persistent, and he allowed me to caress all of him. I delicately lifted his leg, held it, then nestled my face between his legs as he rubbed the top of my head.

His hand guided me back up after a while, and he rolled himself over. I grazed a few fingers over the scar on his lower back as he leaned over to grab the little bag where he kept a few small bottles of lubricant.

"Can we…?" I almost stuttered.

"What?"

"I just want to…" Although I kept a hand between his legs, I brought his face to mine. "I just want to kiss you, see your face."

"Okay." He seemed resigned, perhaps disappointed. I hadn't clearly explained my discomfort with fucking, how my concern over hurting his desensitized areas prevented what had a few times become a series of too lustful thrusts.

We settled side by side, then I rolled atop him, happy to have a night with him.

"Missed you."

"Since Tuesday?"

I nibbled his ear, nuzzled his neck, then probed my tongue deep into his mouth as our hums of pleasure mingled. My humping on his lower belly led to him reaching down to clutch my erection, until his push at my hips signaled his desire to take me in his mouth.

When I winced at his forceful tugging, he asked, "What's wrong?"

"Your hands; they're getting callused."

"Sorry. Pushing my wheels bare-handed. I promise I'll wear gloves more often."

"Okay," I stroked myself for a while.

"Don't spill all over me," he instructed, and I followed, quivering at the sight of his handsome face and lips distended by my thrusts as I straddled him. I scooted the pillow closer behind his head, pushed further in, and he grunted consent, his hunger and insistence making me once again nearly lose control.

My reach back behind for his penis was allowed, but eventually his hand took my wrist and led it back to his chest. I knew to twist a nipple, tickle his armpit, anywhere he could feel it. His hands then clutched my butt, explored between my legs, then inside me, and I spilled into his mouth as he offered a volley of pleased grunts.

He made a familiar joke of slurping his lips after I withdrew and collapsed by his side. Determined to offer the same, I leaned down, licked and tugged on his penis, which he allowed for a while, until it seemed he wouldn't, or couldn't, find his way to an erection. His leg twitched a bit, a minor spasm, which sometimes happened. He sat up, rubbed his leg until I took over, and the jiggling motions subsided and he guided me back to lying beside him.

"It's okay. Just—"

"But I want you to—"

"Next time."

He cradled an arm over me, made an amused forced burp, and muttered, "I noticed you followed my dietary suggestion."

"Pineapple juice. Two quarts this week."

"Dee-licious and nutritious!" he almost sang.

"There wasn't any on campus. I had to go to three grocery stores before I found some."

I pulled the covers up, nestled close to him, until he reminded me to turn out the light and turn off his stereo, which I did, then resettled back into his bed. "I wanna do whatever you want."

"We do," he assured me. "It's okay. It's more than okay."

I offered a sheepish smile and a goodnight kiss.

In the dark, always one to have the last word, he muttered, "Besides, you could stick that big thing in my ear and I'd be happy."

As considerate as Everett was at night, by morning, he could be brusque to the point of rudeness. He basically shoved me out of bed before his alarm clock went off. Those years at Pinecrest must have instilled a need for order.

At the same time, I was reassured by his previous comment on his private school years; "I haven't had a room to myself since I was a kid. I mean, I love you and all, but this is great."

And it was great, for one person, with the low ceiling and small space, great for one person who never stood up. His small shower stall, adjusted for accessibility, had only room for the plastic and aluminum seat, so I had to bathe either seated or while standing at an odd angle.

By the time I re-entered, clad only in a wet towel, he'd already made his bed, laid out his clothes, the pants rolled up for easy entry.

"Friday," he stated as I dressed, acknowledging that we would spend that night together. But also, I sensed an air of dismissal. Only two days away, and yet I knew his intent. I had to let go of him until then, allow him get on with his busy life without me.

Dressed, my backpack slung over my shoulders, I stopped him from wriggling out of his sweatpants before his shower, then leaned in for a smooch. "See ya, Monkey."

He smiled, waited until I was nearly out the door before shouting out, "More pineapple juice!"

Chapter 10
October 1980

"You guys look fabulous!" Gerard cooed as we crossed through the Penn campus in our costumes.

I, however, felt nervous enough just being near Gerard, whose thrift-store tuxedo and make-up got more than a few stares all the way through the Temple campus, and particularly on the trolley to Penn.

Everett didn't want to park the van in the dodgy neighborhood where we were headed. A side window had been smashed on a previous movie night and we still hadn't had it replaced with more than a slat of cardboard and some duct tape.

So we waited at the bus stop, he and I looking normal to anyone else, at least compared to Gerard. My tan windbreaker, with a patch on the shoulder, my old dark-rimmed glasses and greased-back hair might not have raised an eye; the high-waters and white socks, however, were a bit off.

Gerard looked quite comfortable in his tuxedo and pale makeup accented with thick black eyeliner. "We're fine," he reassured me. "It's Halloween season."

I had yet to see anyone else dressed up as anything unusual, but I did get over my nervousness.

Everett's suit and fake beard might have set off some of the stares at the bus stop. But as we ascended the ramp, as the beeper beeped, Everett didn't seem to mind the sound. Under his plaid blanket, and under his sweatpants, he wore black mesh stockings, a pair of high heels in his backpack.

My frustration had started with our argument over how to get there. Everett wanted to take a crosstown bus, the only one with a lift. Gerard seemed a bit disappointed that we wouldn't be using the van, and offered to splurge on a cab, but we let it slide.

It wasn't about the fishnets. Everett wanted to test the public transport system. He was working on a paper for his Public Policy and Accessibility paper, which he'd been poring over for months, as his final paper for the class.

Daring us to take a late bus in costumes that appeared to be normal, at least he and I as Brad Majors and Doctor Scott, was his new idea of "an adventure." After a bit of pleading, despite Gerard's tickled joy at the prospect, Everett consented to wearing track pants over his hosiery.

His dare, and my caution, turned superfluous when we saw that half of the other people on the bus were dressed as other black-clad costumed characters just like Gerard. "Is this cool, or what?" he beamed.

Everett agreed. "I think we've found our people."

Outside the Theatre for Living Arts, a slightly run-down art house cinema on South Street, more dressed-up fans crowded the entrance to the midnight screening of *The Rocky Horror Picture Show*. Assuming the role of tour guide, Gerard insisted on buying our tickets.

We won the Halloween costume contest's second and third place. Since we were the only ones dressed as Brad Majors and Doctor Scott, we got to sit in the front row.

"We don't have a Brad. You've simply got to help us!" squealed a tiny woman dressed as Janet.

Some people were missing from their little acting-it-out cast. Marlene was dressed as Magenta, but preferred to watch from her spot across the aisle. "Get up there," she encouraged from her electric wheelchair.

An awkward recruit, I stole glances up at the screen to figure out what to do. 'Janet' led me around the aisles through the "There's a light…" "Over at the Frankenstein place…" song. Along the way, about twenty people squirted us with water pistols.

As "The Time Warp" started, everybody in the theatre danced in place, even Everett, whose chair version made me smile. I started to dance a little, but Janet tugged my jacket sleeve.

"We don't do that," she said, nodding up at the screen.

After the song, my pants got yanked down. To be honest, I was asked first by the other Magenta. But when it happened onscreen, Everett and Gerard could not stop laughing and cheering for me. I just stood there, my stuff making a visible tent as I was shoved around by a girl playing a guy and a guy playing a…whatever.

The … person playing Frank N. Furter pulled open a red velvet curtain below the nearby EXIT sign, then danced around me like a temptress. To halt a nervous burst of laughter, I just smiled at Everett, which left the contents of my shorts a little too inspired. I bashfully dressed and returned to my seat.

"You quit?" Everett asked.

"Brad's no fun," I scowled.

"He loosens up later."

"Well, if he made out with Rocky instead, I'd be interested." I nodded toward the husky blond sitting across the aisle from us. A black bathrobe covered what would be revealed as his mummified bandages and subsequent strip-down to a gold bikini.

Everett leaned forward, then offered a sardonic sigh. "Oh, Brad."

By the time Everett/Dr. Scott entered, we had tried to echo the catchphrases, always a bit too late. But of course Gerard knew them all, and Everett knew all the lyrics for his song, singing along while spinning around on back-wheelies. People went wild. But he, too, was not up to acting out every line.

"Monkey," I said to Everett as he returned to my side amid shouts and tossed pieces of toast. "You just got yourself a constituency."

"Tenk ewe, Brad. Tenks for supporting my pre-campaign. Von schtep at a time."

"Which will all be eliminated and turned into ramps."

"Precisely. My evil plan foe rampire vuld domination vill be a suck-sess!"

Had we, like Riff-Raff and Magenta, a mansion-spaceship with which to magically transport ourselves back to Everett's dorm room, the night would have ended well enough.

But Gerard's insistent invitation to join a gaggle of hardcore *Rocky Horror* fans, all still in full costume, to invade a nearby all-night diner, insured that the festivities were far from over. And sadly, the adorable Rocky left with his girlfriend.

As we bid Marlene and her assistant-friend goodnight, I almost longed to hitch a ride, leaving Everett to sort out the inevitable stair and seating situation. But I remained by his side, until Gerard quickly squeezed himself between our seats, leaving me huddled in the corner of a cramped booth.

Declining the coffee everyone else seemed to crave, "It's two in the morning," I muttered, I instead ordered food. And while no one repeated the callback line tossed to Brad Majors, after the cheerful congratulations on my participation, I could almost feel my awkward disconnect with the more festive characters.

Gerard held court, spouting on about yet another club night, a new band, and a new vintage clothing store, while his friends replied in perky affected tones, as if always quoting some clever line or lyric whose significance eluded me.

The other Magenta sat across from me. "You guys simply must come back."

Not if returning meant acting out a hump session with a drag queen alien, I thought. "Well, I don't know if we can–"

"It's so perfect, Everett doing Doctor Everett Scott." She glanced at him, charmed, of course.

"Yeah, kind of a funny coincidence."

"And him being…"

"A paraplegic."

"Sorry." She hunched her shoulders, wincing. Her heavy mascara almost completely blacked out her eyes.

"No need. He's cool about it." I glanced across the booth at Everett as he laughed at another of Gerard's jokes.

"So, you guys are…?" She wagged her finger in a motion that implied a connection.

"Yeah."

"That must be…different," she said softly.

"Well, we kinda dated before his accident, before college."

"You went to high school together?"

"No, actually–"

Distracted by Gerard's question about some bit of movie trivia, Magenta's attention returned to the louder group chat. I ate.

It was fun, for the first hour. But the others were not interested in geologic surveys or environmental issues, so I didn't have much to say. Perhaps I should have brought up asexual plant reproduction. Instead, I listened, half-smiling and nodding. Everett ignored my repeated silent glances, so I dug into my omelet and hash browns, which were actually pretty tasty.

Long after my empty plate sat un-bussed before me, and the others continued to nurse their coffees amid relentless chatter, Everett finally noticed my silent smiling stare.

"We should get going, but this has been great," he finally said.

Outside, a fuss ensued over who among the two people with cars would have the honor of driving Everett home, until one of the Transylvanians said, "I can fit him and one more."

"Oh!" Gerard practically leapt forward.

"But I'm going with Everett," I said.

"Oh, why?" Gerard asked.

"Because. I'm his boyfriend."

"Well, I just thought you were going back to Temple."

"No. Thank you."

Visibly miffed, and his other potential ride already off in the other direction, he bid us an abrupt goodnight and left to chase them down.

As our Transylvanian led us to her car, Everett muttered, "You didn't have to be so–"

"Apparently, I did; otherwise I'd be walking home."

"I hope you had fun, at least."

"Yes, but it's four in the morning."

Squeezed into the back seat with his wheelchair beside me, as we rode toward Penn, I ignored Everett's pleasantries up front with our Transylvanian, wondering how many more times I would have to declare my connection to Everett, and how to do it without being, well, an asshole.

Chapter 11
November 1980

"Reagan isn't going to change anything for the good," declared Jacob. "It's a lot of corny rhetoric."

"Corny rhetoric that sells," Everett said as he flipped through a stack of note cards strewn around him on the carpeted floor of his dorm room.

"Oh, right, like 'It's morning in America?' That's a breakfast sausage commercial, not a campaign slogan."

"Well, it worked."

Seated at his desk across his room, I looked down with an affectionate smile as my boyfriend and our new friend continued their seemingly endless conversational debate.

Comfortable in his new digs, Everett enjoyed relaxing in various positions on the carpeted floor. With a pillow under his chest, up on his elbows, he scooted himself, his legs dragged along a bit. One of his socks was coming off, but I wasn't going to interrupt him.

Near him, our friend Jacob Isaac leaned seated against a wall and adjusted an overstuffed pillow on Everett's bed. It was essentially one of our 'date nights' when I slept over, but it could wait. The fact that Jacob was on his bed might have unnerved me if he wasn't such a nice guy; that and the fact that there wasn't another chair.

"Carter's being blamed for the oil crisis, even if he didn't cause it," Everett countered.

"But his policies were sound," Jacob said, "and the Arab embargo—"

Everett cut him off. "The public is resistant to energy-saving measures, no matter how many statistics tell us that turning off a light bulb is going to do anything."

"Citation, please," Jacob scolded.

Although Everett encouraged me to accept invitations from friends to events that aren't accessible to him, more often

I declined. I never wanted to have any intentional reason to not be with him. But any invitation to meet up was welcome, even being the odd man out in their study session.

His first semester focused on Classics, then Public Policy classes took over. After auditing a few classes, he decided that he had no patience for Pre-Law.

While I enjoyed watching him at a few preliminary student debates, I at first shied away from accompanying him to out of town tournaments.

Everett caustically joked that he loved to watch his opponents squirm while "fighting with a cripple." Besides, I'd endured enough of his superior argumentative skills the previous semester over amusingly petty topics like the arrangement of shirts in our dresser drawers.

The truth was, Everett's real major was becoming a hybrid of arguing for disability rights and perfecting his innate charm.

People seemed to adhere to him, flirt with him, as if defying the prejudice of not considering him approachable would gain them some sort of status. I didn't know what to make of it, usually ignored it or endured it when it was done in front of me without being acknowledged. Declaring us boyfriends seemed arrogant, defensive, in front of his new friends.

Jacob Isaac, however, was different.

The first time we met him, we were naked. Actually, we'd been swimming at the Penn pool. After letting himself be photographed for the *Daily Pennsylvanian* newspaper in the pool's fancy handicap hoist, Everett got an unlimited guest pass when I accompanied him. Apparently the device had come at great cost, and Penn's public relations department wanted to show off their 'commitment to accessibility.'

Nevertheless, he refused to use the hoist afterward, preferring to wrangle himself out of his chair, to the pool's edge and into the water on his own, diving in if the lifeguard wasn't looking.

It was then that Everett told me of his glimmer of understanding about his mother's pact with the school. We'd claimed a corner of the wider lane, circling each other. "Your boyfriend is a poster boy," he'd said simply.

We'd been casually paddling back and forth, swimming around in lazy circles along with a bit of mild horseplay that no one else realized was our own form of foreplay. The combination of being wet and nearly naked together usually led us to return to his dorm for a different sort of exercise.

One swimmer adjusting his goggles between laps, then gave us more than the usual curious stare. It seemed one of recognition.

We had been joking about the continuance of horseplay of a different sort at our lockers when Everett made a playful grab for my crotch. A giggle, a cautious glance between us, and there stood the curious swimmer, toweling off, his light brown curls damp and glistening.

I stole a brief glance at his wiry muscled body, his smaller lean frame and the fascinating fan pattern of his chest hair, along with the perky, almost friendly way his penis bobbed as he rubbed his back with his towel.

"I'm right behind you," he said apologetically. Everett made a move to back his chair away, but it bumped into the wooden bench that ran between the rows of lockers.

"It's okay," Jacob had said, as he hopped up around us and opened his nearby locker.

As we dressed, he introduced himself, quickly revealing his knowledge of who Everett was.

"You won state in forensics last year. Pinecrest, right?"

"That I did," Everett smiled as he dug in his locker for his clothes. Jacob introduced himself to Everett, reminding him of some prep school debate where Everett had trounced Jacob's team at some other private school in Western Pennsylvania.

I dressed quickly, so I could make myself available for any assistance. But when I leaned in to help him, Everett returned my gesture with a scowl. In public, he preferred to perform such basic tasks on his own. I'd forgotten again.

"Thinkin' about joining the debate team?" Jacob asked as he shucked on a pair of boxer shorts.

"I don't know. I've got a big course load," Everett said.

"We could really use you."

Jacob offered his phone number, scribbled on a notepad which Everett always kept handy in his backpack. As an afterthought, before leaving, he also introduced himself to me.

"You interested?" I asked after we'd left the locker room.

"I'm not sure. I'd have to look up what the topic is this year." College debate teams followed a national schedule, choosing pro and con sides according to some obscure regulations whose rules eluded me, despite Everett's explanation.

"He's pretty cute," Everett said.

"You think?"

"I saw you checkin' him out."

"Well, he was kind of showing off."

"You think we were being hit on?" he feigned shock.

"I think you were being hit on."

It turned out we were both wrong. Jacob, while okay with us being gay, and a couple, had not been hitting on us, despite being naked when we'd met.

Now, more than a month later, their informal debate continued in Everett's room. I glanced up from my chapter section on monocotyledon and dicotyledon plants. Leaf veins, flower petals and other parts had subtle differences. I noted an amusing 'Did You Know,' that banana trees were actually large grass plants and not trees at all.

Jacob shifted forward to grab a cookie from a bag on the floor. He joked about having narrowly escaped one of many group activities in his dorm, Stouffer Hall.

Jacob's rapid speech, his talkative nature about everything from his Jewish family heritage to local cuisine, combined with what he called, "our mutual cultural history of oppression," made him one of our few shared friends at Penn. He never asked questions about Everett's disability, but listened if the topic was brought up. His studies in social justice paralleled both our interests.

So when he and Everett spent an evening in his dorm room at least once a week discussing politics, even while veering off course from their topic and what Everett called his Notes and Quotes card box, I enjoyed listening in while doing my own work.

"What do you think, Reid?" Jacob crumpled the bag of cookies, tossed it into the trash can, and licked off a coating of crumbs from his fingers.

"Me?" I'd been poring over a half-assed chart on plant cell walls, coloring in a mimeographed drawing to differentiate the cellulose from the hemicellulose.

"You're obviously into the environment," said Jacob. "What's your solution to the energy crisis?"

I glanced at Everett for assistance, but he merely offered a coy grin, his chin resting on his palm.

"Uh, well, solar and wind power, for starters."

"Okay, but what about fuel?" Jacob asked. "Diesel, petroleum?"

"Well, we need to cut off dependence on foreign oil, of course."

"Catch phrase," Everett muttered.

"Hey, I'm just answering his question," I shot back.

"And I'm critiquing the argument structure, not the emotion of the presenter," Everett tossed off his reply.

"Okay, purely for the sake of argument," I aimed that last word at Everett before going on full attack. "We cut off OPEC, halt all logging, subsidize hemp for fiber and paper production, offer tax incentives for all new housing that includes solar and wind upgrades, and, and fine polluting industries into extinction, before we're extinct."

Everett sighed as he rolled himself over onto his side, then yanked one leg up a bit, pulling it into a forced stretch. "And there you have it. The liberal approach taken to its extreme is isolationist, anti-business and totalitarian in its basic ideology."

I shook my head as if stunned. "Well, he asked for my opinion," I muttered before returning to my stupid little cell cartoon.

"You're lucky you're just his boyfriend and not his debate opponent," Jacob joked as he stood. "We'll have to solve the entire world's problems some other night." He gathered his notes and books.

Everett rolled over. "Hey, we were thinking about going to movie night at the quad tomorrow night; *Escape From New York*. Wanna come with?"

"Actually, I have a date. Marcy; freshman and very blonde."

"Girlfriend material?"

Jacob stuffed his papers in his backpack. "More like a hot shiksa who's slumming before getting her emarress degree."

"Her what?" I asked.

"M. R. S. Missus. You know, girls who aren't really getting a degree, just husband-hunting, and I don't think I qualify, or want to."

Everett chuckled. "That's something we don't have to worry about."

"No, what with you two already being practically married," Jacob joked. He offered a low-five as Everett shifted to sitting on the floor, folding his legs in front of himself. "Don't get up on my account."

Everett laughed. Jacob offered a quick hug as I led him to the door. "Stick to your guns, Reid. We'll save the world from these dirty imperialists one day."

I watched him trot down the hallway before closing the door, almost afraid to be alone with Everett. Jacob seemed to provide a buffer between us, and now he was gone for the night.

After closing the door, I returned to his desk. "You didn't have to skewer me in front of him," I muttered.

"Reid."

I didn't respond.

"Giraffe."

"Yes?"

"Debate is the attempt at objective argument. It's not about personal feelings."

"Fine." I closed my books as if I might leave. He knew I wouldn't.

"Come 'ere."

I hesitated, then relented, walking across his small room, his little universe, then settled down on the floor next to him. He wrapped an arm around me, offered a light kiss to my forehead.

"Nobody else knows how much you love the planet, and trees in particular." He grinned, knowing that remark spoke volumes, not just about my hopes, but our own intimate past.

"I know," I whispered. "It's just ... you get so ...cold when you argue."

"It's not cold. It's practical."

"So, you're like your parents. You're a Republican."

"No. I'm not defining myself by them."

"But you're conservative."

"Not in the way you think."

Everett held me closer, but then gestured with his arm, waving above us. "The argument is outside us. That's how it works. The emotion," he pressed his hand to my chest, "stays inside. It's fragile."

I kissed him. He tasted of the cookies we'd been eating. I shifted my mouth across his jaw. His beard stubble sent a surge of desire through me. We adjusted the pillow, but I could sense his discomfort as I moved to lay atop him.

"You wanna move up to the bed?"

"No, let's do it here," he grinned. "Just get a few more pillows."

I stood, tossed a few from the bed toward him, which he caught. "And a towel." I walked to the bathroom.

"And some lube!" he called out.

"Anything else? Dessert? Coffee?"

"Your butt."

"Coming right up," I replied, as I stripped off my clothes, and helped him yank down his sweatpants.

As we jostled and repositioned ourselves, kissing and licking, we gradually ended up in one of Everett's other preferred positions; me straddling his chest, teasing him by flapping my erection toward his mouth, his eager tongue darting toward it, then me finally succumbing to his grunting moans of pleasure as I plunged in and out. It seemed strange, feeling a surge of lust at the sight of my own body distorting his cheeks, that perfect face.

His reach upward toward my own face confused me.

"Your ears turn so red when you get excited."

He held them like handles, pulled me downward for a kiss, until I leaned back up. Behind and under me, he stealthily lubed up a few fingers and gently, then insistently, probed up inside me.

"Ow, jeez."

"Hello."

As he found that tingle-inducing spot, as I gave myself to him, letting him have his way again, I became overwhelmed, not by the familiarity, and not by his expertise.

What brought me to an almost tearful explosion was the shock that, after all this time, I still barely knew who he was.

Chapter 12
December, 1980

Mountains parted for us, rivers conjoined with us, tiny towns approached and were forgotten through our drive across Pennsylvania, with Everett at the helm. With only one break, despite my repeated offers to take the wheel for part of the way, for most of the trip we were silent or sang along to Beatles songs on the radio.

Our anticipation of holiday joy had been overshadowed by John Lennon's death. Back on campus, the night of his murder, candle-holding students had appeared from all over, a spontaneous memorial on both campuses, I learned when Everett called me in tears. I had rushed across town to be with him, and through my journey, it was as if the entire city were lulled to a somber tone. It was such a strange day, how quiet everything was, until strains of "Imagine" and other songs echoed from windows. It wasn't the first time we had shed tears together, but it was altogether different.

When we finally pulled up to my parents' house, both of them met us in the driveway, insisting that Everett take a break. Although he had less than an hour to get to Pittsburgh, after a pleasant meal of catching up, he asked to take a nap, and I let him alone for an hour before sneaking quietly into my room, just to watch him sleep in my bed.

His pants slung over an arm of his wheelchair, his shoes lay on the floor. The curls of his hair poked out of the blanket, his back to me. I resisted the urge to join him, and instead considered all we had been through together, our first abrupt encounters, and an additional one in my own room.

What problems would he face in Pittsburgh? Between his generous yet somewhat indifferent father, the protective pressures and silent disappointments from his mother, would his sister Holly's defiant support get him through the next few weeks?

As if sensing my presence, he rolled over, tugged an arm under the covers to flop his legs over, offered a groggy smile, and opened the blanket as an invitation.

"Just a little cuddling," he warned with a smirk. "I gotta get back on the road."

"Well, I'm not quite sure of the protocol. 'Merry Christmas from the parents of your son's...boyfriend.'"

"You're not writing that, are you?"

"Well, we're not exactly friends, or in-laws."

"Anne?" Dad called out from the garage. He was packing his car for our annual visit to Mom's brother's family; the holiday trek to Scranton. We'd begun to limit our visits to a single day, and thankfully booked a pair of hotel rooms. I had even offered to help pay for them, since the previous year I'd been relegated to a sleeping bag on the floor of my younger cousins' bedroom.

Although ready to go, Mom was still sitting on the couch with a small stack of cards, envelopes and stamps, poring over a few of what she called her "late entries," the Christmas cards she felt she had to send because we had received cards from them, but forgotten to send one back.

"It's still good through New Year's Eve. That's how it works," she half-joked. "Here, you sign them, too."

Before he'd left, Everett had given my mother the separate addresses of his divorced parents and his sister. He'd also reminded me of his invitation to join him and Holly in Pittsburgh for an overnight New Year's Eve visit.

"Just one more," Mom said as she handed me a third card, addressed to some family whose name was new to me. "One of your father's coworkers."

I scribbled my first name as Dad tromped into the kitchen. "Anne. I'm ready for the cake, then we should go."

Mom pointed to a large Tupperware container on the counter, then licked the envelopes and sealed them. I grabbed my parka and followed Dad through the kitchen door to the garage.

We sat in the car as he clicked the door opener attached to the visor. From the back seat, I saw his shoulders slump, then he caught my glance through the rear-view mirror.

"Another family gathering," I half-groaned in an attempt at a sympathetic comment.

"It's just for one day," he replied. "Let's just pretend to enjoy it. That's what the holidays are about."

"Woah."

"Sorry, son. It's just…"

"Dad. It's cool. I don't like them either, except Gramma and Grampa, of course."

Mom remained in the house, and we waited.

"Why don't we ever visit your mom in Tucson?"

Dad sighed. "You know why. Your mom doesn't like flying, and after my father died, my mom went a bit wild with her jewelry-making and took up with a man whom I consider to be a racist idiot."

"Okay then."

Her holiday cards and infrequent phone calls were a bit eccentric, but I resented his deciding for us which part of our family was worth visiting.

After Mom finally got in the car, we endured a long drive, and a day of dinner with my uncle and aunt, their brood of kids, and our doddering elders.

That Everett and I didn't celebrate Christmas together until days afterward frustrated me. Our initial encounters over that first holiday together had served as an incomparable gift. Mere packages wrapped in paper paled by comparison.

Still, I had carefully placed my few gifts for Everett and Holly in shopping bags inside my duffel bag, so as not to harm the wrapping paper, along with innocuous cards for his parents.

The train into Pittsburgh was a bit crowded with people traveling to and from family visits. I spent most of the ride adding up the days I would be away from him, and how much closer we had become with just a little distance between us.

Our time together was special, and sometimes, with a phone call, the distance was eased.

Although Everett's dad's apartment would offer a great view of the city's skyline, and the possible view of the fireworks (only partially blocked by a few skyscrapers), his mention of Holly's party invite had intrigued me.

"It'll be full of theatrical types," Everett had teased. We would finally be able to celebrate as ourselves, sharing a kiss and a champagne toast among friendly company.

While my own parents settled for awkward hugs and plain conversation through the many holiday visits and greetings and cheerfulness, Everett's parents lobbied for his affection in different ways, and from opposite sides of Pittsburgh.

He split up his time by spending a few days each with either parent, bracketed by visits with his sister.

Although Holly had promised a party, Everett suggested the possibility of a night alone, especially when I arrived, and his father told us that he would be going out to "a business party; just us old people," he smiled before retreating to his own bedroom.

As I unpacked, Everett mentioned that I had received an invitation from his mother to stay with him in her new apartment, but "with the barest shred of sincerity," he said. I begged off, repeatedly, as he teased me about the possibility of staining her fancy sheets.

"Besides, the whole place," he shook his head when he told me. "Lots of the old furniture. It's amazing how much stuff she's got crammed in there. Maybe she's going to sell it off. I don't even know how she makes a living. She won't discuss it."

As I'd remembered, Mr. Forrester's apartment had hardwood floors, and Everett said that the spare room off to the side was okay. I hadn't seen either bedroom when I'd visited his father the year before. It appeared a bit sparse, and the wooden floors made sounds echo a bit.

"It's kind of drab," he admitted. "But wait'll you see this." He wheeled off and I followed him into the bathroom.

"Thank you, Jeeee-sus!" I bellowed a bit loudly in what was an enormous open shower with no tub, a few aluminum safety bars, a plastic chair, and a small plastic table.

"Dad got it remodeled."

"It's like a porn set."

"How would you know?" he shot a glance.

"I seen plenty," I lied.

"Well, shall we test your proposal?"

"Now?"

"No, like, before bed. Let's exercise, go for a run or something later. That'll be a good excuse."

"To be sweaty."

Sweat we did, despite the cold weather. With the triangular Point Park set at the apex of the three rivers, and only a few blocks away, he pushed as I jogged. The skyline, river and connecting bridges glistening in the sunlight.

More energized than exhausted upon returning to his father's apartment, we explored the expansive shower. I removed my glasses and peeled off clothes as the hot water sprayed. Everett offered a clumsy strip tease.

Our antics became a giggling splashy romp. The sheer size of the shower almost demanded multiple positions. He sprayed water with the detachable nozzle, aiming at my bent-over butt. I lathered his chest, rinsed him off, slurping up and spitting water as it cascaded along his chest. I slipped a few times while trying to straddle one leg on a safety bar. The loud thumps made us giggle.

The pounding at the door, and its half-opening, stopped us.

"You okay in there?"

"Yes, Dad. We're fine, we're just…"

"Okay."

He whispered it; "…playing."

More stifled laughter covered whatever his father tossed off as he closed the door behind him.

The next morning, I woke before Everett with a groggy hunger, and snuck into the echoey marble-countered kitchen, where I encountered his father making coffee, in a robe and not much else, and felt a surge of desire. His legs and chest resembled Everett's from before his accident. His stature was a sort of cocky side stance, and his eyes were framed in the face of Everett's future handsome self. I fought off a pang of loss, tried to shut away the thought of trying to recall the last time I'd seen Everett stand so casually.

"Sleep okay?"

"Uh, yes sir."

He smirked, offered me a cup, which I nodded for, despite having rarely drunk coffee.

"I take it you like the renovations."

"Yes, sir."

"Coupla years, we'll start moving from leasing to selling; from luxury apartments to condominiums."

"Really?"

"I'm still holding a single for Ev. It'd be nice to have him, and you, nearby." His smile was playful, but his intent was clear. "Look, I'm really glad you enjoy it here. But you boys are gonna have to keep it down, or else do that when I'm not in."

"Yes, sir. Definitely. Understood." I sipped the cup, retreated abruptly, saying I preferred to dress before breakfast, and joined Everett for an entirely non-sexual shower.

New Year's Eve afternoon, Everett's father again offered to take us to his hotel gala, but Everett begged off on my behalf. "We have plans," he assured his dad, who seemed mildly relieved.

"So, what time's the party?" I said as we lounged in the living room, flipping channels on the enormous TV.

"Oh, it'll keep. You hungry?"

"A bit."

"I got us reservations at a fancy-ass restaurant."

"Who's paying for it?"

"My mom; a sort of extra Christmas present."

"I'm not too comfortable knowing your mother's paying for it."

"Don't worry," Everett brushed it off. "She has family money. It's not all my dad. Besides, once I turn twenty-four, my trust fund's released and then we're on our own."

He took the remote, switched channels.

"Your trust fund?"

"Dad's been investing it; stocks, mostly. He invested low during this wonderful recession your hero Jimmy Carter created. And now, thanks to some evil conglomerates, plus some smart real estate deals, we'll be set after graduation, or grad school."

"How set?"

"A hundred thousand or so."

"Dollars?"

"There's some gold, but I'm not supposed to touch that."

"So that makes me a gold-digger?"

Everett hit the mute button, scrunched his face in mock concern. "I think prior knowledge of said gold would be a prerequisite."

"Okay, then."

"So, let's get dressed." He shut off the TV.

"For what?"

"Dinner at eight. And speaking of gold, wait 'til you see the menu!"

"You spoil me."

"I can't spoil you since you're worth it."

Chapter 13
January 1981

"A holocaust; a damn horticultural holocaust," I sighed.

Dad didn't want to miss the truck as it approached down the street, the loud grinding noise having roused us to drag the dried-up Christmas tree to the curb.

There would be later days for the tree pick-ups, but Mom had already stripped the tree of the ornaments by the time I trained back from Pittsburgh after New Year's Day. In Greensburg, the clouds had shifted to a drab grey, uncertain whether to rain or snow.

Everett had a few more family days before we would drive back to Philadelphia and was due to pick me up later that day.

"We really should get a fake tree."

"Don't you like tradition?" Dad asked as he tried to wipe off a bit of sap from his hand.

"The sacrifice of a few million spruces is not one of my favorite rituals," I replied with a dry edge. The truck slowly approached, and with it the chomping noise of the mulcher attached to it.

"You know they're farmed," he said. "It's not like forests are being stripped for the holidays."

"I know, but it's the concept. Douglas Fir, Blue Spruce; proud trees bred to be tiny, like pug dogs. They're a mutation."

"How is that different than farming? Where would we get all those vegetables growers put in cans for me to sell so I can pay your tuition?"

"It's a vicious cycle," I shook my head, pretending to be some wise philosopher. And yet, we stood curbside, fascinated by the approaching roar. I couldn't help but feel a strange combination of satisfaction and horror as the gloved worker nodded to us, took our tree, and shoved it into the machine, which chewed it into bits.

As the truck passed, Dad offered a supportive shoulder pat, continuing our half-serious debate as we returned to the house.

"Wolfe Nursery sells live trees," I offered. "We could get one next year and plant it after the holidays."

"In the middle of winter? You want to dig a hole in frozen ground?"

"We could dig it in the fall, or we could buy a fake one. It'd be campy."

"Campy?" Dad asked with a confused glare.

"Yeah, Mom would love that."

I caught myself, and wondered if I'd let slip a too-gay comment.

The New Year's Eve party had been as festive as Holly had promised, with several older gay men who shared flirtatious and funny comments through the night. I had forgotten to reign in my newly acquired expression.

Dad shrugged in surrender. "It's your call. I'm staying neutral on the subject."

"Think of the money you'd save!"

Our trail of needles in the living room to the porch door was already being vacuumed to a mere memory by Mom, whose enjoyment of the holidays seemed matched by her efficient removal of its evidence.

Dad grabbed a scrub brush and washed his hands over the kitchen sink, then, once Mom shut off the vacuum, said, "Our son the environmentalist suggested we go artificial next year."

"What, the tree?" Mom asked.

"Or a live one," I added. "We could plant it. I can do it."

"Oh, and leave me to clean up a bag of dirt?"

"We can put it in a bucket," I suggested.

"So we have to buy a bucket, too?" With her hands on her hips in mocking astonishment, I couldn't help but grin at her.

"Well, the Christmas decorations are all fifty percent off right now."

I clapped my hands in partial victory.

But as I put on my coat and gloves to go shopping, the phone rang. Feeling giddy, I raced to it ahead of Mom.

"Hello?"

"ETA's about an hour, sport," Everett said with an abrupt clip.

"Okay. I gotta–"

"Be ready to roll, okay?"

"Oh. Okay."

I hung up the phone, discarded my coat.

"I thought you were going out. I need some things, too."

"But Everett's coming."

"When?"

"In, like, an hour."

"Well, hurry up then."

"But what if he–"

"We'll keep him company. Don't worry. We'll get him inside."

"But–"

"We won't eat him. Go."

Was I really afraid to leave him alone with my parents? They got along, certainly better than I did with his.

Distracted in thought, I drove across town to the Greengate Mall, where, in the variety store, after impulsively grabbing the first half-off artificial tree I saw on a shelf at the store, I didn't even notice who was standing in line behind me.

"Conniff?"

I turned, surprised that I couldn't recall the name of a former classmate from high school.

"Hey, how's it going?"

"Greg."

"Right. Greg Harris. How ya doing?"

"A little late for a tree, innit?" He gestured toward the box under my arm.

"Oh, you know, after-Christmas sales. My mom wanted me to–"

"Yeah, sure."

I looked at him, a twelve-pack of beer under his arm, a John Deere cap on his head. I barely knew him, and could only recall some tossed-off insult from him back in grade school. Greg was by no means a friend, not even an acquaintance.

"You hangin' around for the holidays?"

"Actually, I'm leaving, today."

"I was jus' gonna say. Havin' a little post-post-holiday party."

"Sorry. I'm–" Some people ahead of us checked out, moved on. I stepped away.

"Whatever. Hey, you were friends with that rich kid, the one't got crippled, right?"

"What?" I dropped the tree box on the conveyer belt. It slid past me. I heard a few beeps from the register.

"Yeah, the Forrester guy. I heard about you."

Confused, unsure where this was going, I asked, "From who?"

"Yeah, Graff tole me."

Wendell Graff. Then I remembered. Greg was friends with the only person I had ever punched, only after being punched, all because back in high school some country club waiter had told anyone who would listen that he saw me and Everett making out on the golf course at a party.

"Yeah, whatever." I turned away.

"Well, 'scuse me for breathin'."

The cashier almost sang, "That'll be thirty-seven thirty-nine."

I pulled two twenties out of my wallet.

"Do you need a bag?"

"No." I tried to rush off, the boxed tree under my arm.

Greg hooted with a tone I pretty clearly understood. "Hey, I'll tell Graff I saw ya!"

I walked off, then turned back. "You can tell Wendy to go to hell."

A hundred other retorts swam through my mind as I raced through the parking lot, half expecting Greg to follow me for another confrontation. Waiting at a stoplight, I switched off the radio, looked around, and felt a grey drabness take over the streets of Greensburg. All my life I'd lived here, but it no longer felt like home.

By the time I got to the house, as I'd worried, Everett's van was parked in the driveway. Once inside, I didn't even bother to take off my coat.

"Hey."

"Well, there he is," Mom said, a bit too loudly.

"I still gotta finish packing."

"Hurry up," Everett said impatiently. "I don't want to move back in after it's dark."

In my room, I shoved clothes into a duffle bag, then tossed a stack of books into a cardboard box.

"I made sandwiches for your trip," Mom called out.

"Thank you!"

Everett had almost snuck up behind me, and parked himself at the door.

"Fut the whuck, dude?"

"I'm sorry," I sputtered. "I… gimme a few minutes."

"Something wrong?"

"I'll explain later. Let's just get the hell out of here."

As he drove east on I-76, Everett listened patiently to my frustrated complaints, how high school haunted me with each return visit, how gossip spread. He'd barely said a word until we approached Bedford. Waiting until I finished and started fiddling with the radio, he instead turned it down, gave me a look, and said, "Just remember; some day, that's not going to be your home anymore."

"Yeah, but–"

"Just, just find us a nice song to sing to," he nodded toward the radio dial, hands on the wheel, eyes on the road, moving us forward.

Chapter 14
February 1981

I'm running to the Walnut Street Bridge, but it's tangled up in a sort of M.C. Escher knot with the Market Street Bridge and about a dozen connecting steep staircases, none of which appear to lead across the immense gulley of the Schuylkill River, and it doesn't help that even though I know it's a dream a failing Psych 101 student could analyze, I can't escape it, but wait· there's a button that could unravel the gnarled tangle of steps, if I could only reach it, but my fingers are too frozen to touch it, since I've forgotten my gloves and can't feel my hands, and watch in amazed horror as the chasm between the riverbanks gets wider and wider.

Despite our demanding course loads, we did find time to enjoy some on-campus events. On nights when Everett didn't have basketball practice or a game, we took in movies, a wrestling tournament, and even a gymnastics meet. Fortunately, Temple had a bigger program and Penn didn't have facilities, so the gymnastics tournament was held at my school.

Bleachers were an understandable barrier, and Everett often forgot to bring a seat pad to prevent pressure sores, so we more often asked to be allowed to sit at floor level on the sidelines, with me finding a folding chair to sit next to him.

People sometimes thought our courtside position was due to some connection to the competing teams. That led to the benefit of introductions to athletes, like Kyle, he of the puppy dog eyes and grapefruit shoulders.

"You used to be a gymnast?" was his friendly presumptive greeting to Everett. Kyle was a red-shirted junior on Penn's team, he told us after shaking hands. His palm was deeply callused, and thick as leather.

Everett's chair led to an unsolicited comparison, Kyle also told us, as we chatted between ring and pommel events, that he had been one of two male cheerleaders at his high school in

Shreveport, where one of the girls fell in a botched hoisting move and broke her neck. "She's a quad, quader–"

"Quadraplegic," Everett finished.

"Can't even move her arms. You're not–"

Everett explained his different condition, and even opened up about his lacrosse accident, sparing Kyle one of his fictional tall tales. Perhaps it was the jock kinship. Perhaps it was the fact that he was so damn cute.

Kyle and Everett exchanged phone numbers, hoping to meet at the gym for shared workouts.

"Yeah, right; workouts," I smirked.

Everett had gone to the gym on his own more often since his transfer to Penn. I tried to contain myself, but I knew what kind of other extra-curricular activities that environment could inspire.

But usually, for such events, it was Everett luring me to his campus, so I had to navigate the public transportation system, and suffer his impatience if I was late, again (his Christmas gift of an electronic wristwatch said as much), as I was one frigid night in February.

7:10. I'd only laid down for a few minutes' nap, after four classes and a rushed workout at the gym, all the while hoping Everett might notice I'd been working on my shoulders. Calling Everett's room at Penn got no answer.

7:20. Showered, with clothes thrown on, my down parka made the same odd sounds as the nylon fabric brushed against itself while I fumbled with the almost-broken zipper. I would have forgotten my gloves and ski cap if I hadn't learned to just stuff them in the parka's pockets. Almost reaching for my backpack, I remembered it was night, a cold night, and not class time, and I wouldn't need it. I almost slammed the dorm door shut without my keys.

7:36. The train was late, and packed with sniffling passengers in heavy coats. I felt hot and cold, steaming on the inside from running, face thawing from the hurried race to a stagnant underground stalled train car.

8:04. After a few minutes waiting for a resident to enter the dorm, I snuck in behind him before the door closed. He gave me a suspicious sidelong glance, but I didn't explain. Hurriedly trotting up the stairs to a door, I knocked repeatedly.

"You looking for Forrester?"

A tall Nordic-looking student with a casual air balanced a stack of books and a six-pack of sodas as he stopped to offer his assistance.

"Yes."

"He left a while ago."

"Thanks."

"Sure." He turned away.

"Hey, do you know how to get to the Iron Gate Theatre?"

He gave me directions to Houston Hall, even took me to a hall window and pointed across the quadrangle. I thanked him and tore off down the hall and to the stairs.

8:13. The usher refused to let me in until a burst of laughter seemed to be enough to cover the sound of the theatre door, and my entry.

The house was full, but I knew exactly where to look. The theatre more resembled a small cathedral with arches and stained glass windows. As my eyes adjusted to the bright stage lights and darkened rows of seats, I spotted the familiar shiny bars folded next to a front row aisle seat. Shifting my stance behind the back row, I recognized Everett's dark curls, the back of his neck, and his alert posture.

In a moment I thought he may have felt my presence, instead, during one moment where one of the actors recited a rhymed jest that made the audience erupt in laughter, instead of looking back to me, Everett turned to whisper some smiling comment to a guy seated next to him.

At intermission, I made my way down the aisle as others jostled past me toward the exit.

"I thought you forgot." His tone was dismissive. He turned away, refusing my attempt at an apologetic hug. I cut short my travel ordeal, and the truth that I had slept late, when Everett's new companion appeared, offering a box of Sno-Caps.

"Connor, this is Reid."

We shook hands. Connor seemed friendly enough, if not a bit confused. Taller than me, and handsome, he gave off an air of confidence.

"What did I miss?" I said, trying to break the ice as some other patrons excused themselves to get past us.

"Are you familiar with this Shakespeare play?" Connor asked with an air that I took as haughty.

"No."

"You didn't have Danforth's class yet?"

"Reid doesn't go to Penn," Everett explained. "He goes to Temple."

Connor offered a glance that packed a sliver of unspoken thoughts, I didn't know what; dismissal?

As Connor offered a Clif-Notes version of the first two acts, I stood, pretending to care. I hadn't even wanted to see the play, but one of Everett's classmates was in it, and when he asked me to go with him, I agreed. I always agreed, even if I was busy, or exhausted from my own studies, my own attempt at a life that existed in this annoyingly inconvenient distance from him, and the fatigue of having endured the previous night in his bed as he had yet another fitful night of sleep after our brief round of half-sex.

None of this was spoken, but it hung over us like a storm cloud waiting to burst. My contorted logic reasoned that it was his fault I was late. As the houselights began to dim, realizing that neither Everett nor Connor had made any gesture to move or let me sit with them, I simply said, "Well, I'll see you after the show." Then I retreated up the aisle to the back of the theatre.

The audience laughed as the actors, in elegant witty verses, wooed each other as men, and women disguised as men, pretended to be people they weren't.

The wonders of something called 'venture capitalism' were explained to us by Connor as we trekked through the bitterly cold night to O'Hara's, a café and bar that was popular with

Penn students. Connor had invited us, and before I could interrupt with an excuse, Everett eagerly accepted on my behalf without even asking.

Connor had apologized for forgetting the six stairs down to get inside, but Everett, as usual, was resolute, and I shook off Connor's attempt to assist as I carefully guided his chair down bump by bump.

"I thought this was our date," I muttered as Connor stood at the bar ordering drinks. The jukebox seemed stuck on a Hall and Oates tribute. We sat at a table where I'd removed a chair for Everett.

"It was, until you didn't show up," Everett snipped.

"I went to your dorm."

"I told you to meet me at my room, and then you were late. It takes me… The building isn't easy to get into. I gave you the address."

"I forgot to bring it."

"Well, there you go."

"And Clark Kent just came along and saved the day?"

Everett sighed. "I was on my way out and he offered to help, and he was going anyway."

"How convenient."

"Are you going to be jealous of every guy at Penn who wants to be my friend?"

"Yes, if you're gonna dump me at the first sighting of–"

"Now you're being silly."

"Wasn't I the one who came over last night when you called?"

We had agreed upon planning nights when I slept over, which were different than nights when we went to some play or lecture or movie that might or might not become a night spent together. Intuiting the difference became my burden, it seemed.

"Yes, and thank you for that. We had a good time, which we're not having now, since you're determined to blame me for you being late."

"Did you even tell him?" I asked.

"Tell him what?"

I rolled my eyes to the ceiling, looked away, anywhere but at him.

"Reid, don't do that. It's really not becoming."

"Becoming what?"

"Not everyone needs to know."

Know what, I simmered. That I loved him, that we were boyfriends? That before college, we had endured a long-distance passion of near-felonious proportions? That only my steadfast refusal to let him destroy our fumbling relationship before and after his accident had brought us back together?

"Here we are, gentlemen," Connor announced as he placed three mugs of beer on the table with a wet splat.

Once seated, Connor hoisted his glass, offering a toast. Everett and I reluctantly joined in.

Not noticing our cold demeanor, Connor postulated on his expected brilliant future in business, thanks to the glory of Reaganomics. He and Everett continued discussing topics that had nothing to do with me, until Connor noticed that I hadn't said a word. He abruptly stopped, then awkwardly attempted a segue.

"So, Reeve. How do you know Everett?"

"It's Reid," I glared at him, gulped down half of the beer, then set it down a bit too loudly. Despite the chill from our walk, I was burning up inside.

"I'm sorry."

"Don't be."

"So how are you guys friends?"

"You'll have to ask Everett," I said as I reached for my parka. "Because apparently, I have no idea." I stood.

"Reid," Everett frowned.

"Excuse me, gentlemen, but I have an early class and a few trains to miss."

"Reid. Don't." Everett sighed.

"But tomorrow's Saturday." Connor seemed confused.

I grinned at him before storming off, "No rest for the lower classes!"

By the time I arrived back at my dorm, having missed the trolley by seconds, chilled from the twenty-minute wait, then the Broad Street train, which was on time, my phone was ringing. I unplugged it, for four days.

His letter arrived on Wednesday. Unlike the silly one-word postcards we'd sent through the fall, this one was typed, no doubt on his electric typewriter, a leftover from an office upgrade after Everett's father's real estate firm had expanded.

The almost stuffy diplomatic tone made me smile.

'You are invited to a mutual apology session and private dinner, Saturday, February 14th, at Seven P.M.' He'd added the address of a restaurant in Center City.

Saturday. I looked at my datebook. Valentine's Day. Relieved that our fight had happened the weekend before, I took this as a blessing. Everett's more mature nature refused to let my impetuous immaturity interfere.

After jotting down the address of the restaurant, I flipped back a few pages to the days where I had scribbled a capital E with a circle, each noting our nights together, our "dates," and the curving doodles and smiling faces for our weekends together before we'd returned to Philadelphia. Then I dug into my desk drawer and found my 1980 book. Flipping backwards week by week, the notations and little E's accumulated until I'd lost count through each month.

How could I have been so stupid, so selfish, to think him uncaring? Yes, he was rude to me that night, or so I thought. He would explain it all away, reason with me, argue his way to victory.

Determined to arrive on time, early even, I trekked to the train, my jacket and tie peeking out from my parka, my nose dripping from the chill. I didn't have a proper overcoat, but knew he'd appreciate my dressing up.

Once downtown, I walked briskly to the Reading Terminal Market. If the floral market there didn't have what I wanted, I could try a florist in Rittenhouse Square who said over the phone that they did. Both of them would close by six o'clock, so I would have an hour to spare in the cold.

Deciding to just go to the restaurant and wait, I asked for a table in the back, had the waiter remove a chair, and asked for a vase for the flowers. He smiled, as if sensing my obvious eagerness.

I'd been gazing at the front of the restaurant when he arrived. I let the maitre'd help Everett up the one small step in the entryway, then beamed as he wheeled toward me. As I had anticipated, he also wore a jacket and tie. The maitre'd took his coat and offered us menus.

A plastic-wrapped bundle of flowers in his lap, Everett handed them to me, then I leaned in for a brief hug.

"You got flowers, too." Everett eyed the vase as he scooted to the table.

"Marigolds."

"And I got roses; so cliché."

"No, they're nice."

"So, the Latin?" he gestured to my flowers.

"*Calendula officinalis.*"

"Very good."

"It's supposed to have medicinal qualities, too. People used to grind them up and hope for prophetic dreams."

"That's spooky. Maybe I should—" He made a playful gesture of nibbling on a petal.

"Careful. It's also a diuretic."

"Good to know." He pulled his hand back, wiping it on a napkin with an exaggerated flair.

After the waiter took our drink orders (champagne seemed out of our league, so we had sodas), we shared smiles and a bit of silence held as we looked into each other's eyes. I felt a bit of the nervousness of a first date, not that I'd ever really had one with anyone other than him.

"So."

"Yes?"

"A bit of Paris Peace Talks, and then we can just enjoy ourselves. How does that sound?"

"That sounds good," I said, as I folded my fingers together, sat forward, and waited.

"The reason I asked Connor along to the play; first he's a housemate, and you know the guys like to help, even when I don't need it. It's different at Penn. People just...get in and make friends."

"We made friends at Temple."

"Yes, but, it's... Also, his dad's in politics, and yes, he's a snooty old-money arrogant preppie. But my world, I'm sorry, it's different. Unlike you, I can't trust in the beautiful serenity of nature for my future."

"Okay."

"And I can't just rely on my parents' connections after college."

"Okay."

"Some people don't need to know about us. Some people don't deserve to know."

"But hiding–"

"I'm not hiding, Reid. We're not hiding. I'm not afraid of people knowing. Connor's not dumb. He figured it out. A lot of people know. And the important people; we tell them. We have plenty of friends who know."

"Okay, but maybe they're not going to be my friends."

"And that's fine. I'm sure some of your classmates at Temple are ... not going to be my friends."

"You like Devon."

"Of course!"

"And you like Eric, don't you?" My former roommate from my first semester had kept in touch, but had only hung out with us a few times.

"Eric's great. But are you sure he's not gay?"

"No. He's just really cool about it."

I actually hadn't seen Eric in weeks. Although he'd been understanding when I'd come out to him, and told him about Everett, the two had only spent a few hours together one night when Eric came over to visit. As before, he'd unspooled a volley of curious questions about Everett's life from a technical angle.

Still, our lives didn't intersect much, and like other classmates and guys on my new dorm floor, I hadn't opened up much to friendships. Every spare moment was spent with Everett. That left me with no one to talk to about Everett when such little tiffs sprang up.

Our salads arrived, and the waiter made a show of grinding a large wooden pepper mill. After he left, Everett still hadn't lifted his fork. Quite hungry myself, I was chomping of some lettuce when I had to stop. Everett had a sad, ruminative look.

"I'm sorry. Was there something else?" I swallowed.

"Just… the other reason I asked Connor to go with me was… It was cold, and dark, and with the damn plowed snow up to my nose in the gutter… I couldn't even get across the street. And you weren't there. I know I'm all about being independent and everything, but sometimes, going out alone, I just get scared and frustrated."

"I'm sorry."

"It's not your fault. Let's just… We need more space."

I fought a surge of panic, that neediness, of wanting him, of wanting to be wanted. Was he enjoying living alone more than he let on?

"Wait. You say you need to be away from me, but then you need me."

"No, Reid. We need more space together, bigger than a dorm room. I want us to find a place to be together."

"Oh!"

"It won't cost much more. I saw a few apartment listings, and next semester we don't have to be in the dorms. My mom can still get whatever payoff she probably got out of all this, and–"

"Are you sure you want to leave Ware? You seem really comfortable there."

"Well, architecturally speaking," he took on a faux-snooty tone, "It is the style to which I am accustomed."

"But you want to do this?"

"Sure."

"So, we can be together again?"

"Yes, off-campus, somewhere nearby."

As I jumped up from the table, my salad fork flipped off the plate and I nearly knocked over the vase. Reaching around to hug Everett, I kissed his cheek a few times, until his hand touched my face.

"I take it you like the idea."

I retreated back to my seat, and noticed a few couples in the restaurant were giving us an assortment of glances, both admiring and curious.

As the giddy anticipation settled, we ate our dinner, smiling, speaking little, except for small intimate jokes. Yes, it could work. It had to work, playing it cool. I would learn over the next months that it did work, for a while.

Chapter 15
March 1981

"Treat your babies with care," our professor cautioned with a half-serious air as my classmates and I took our share of small trays with seedlings just barely growing in their tiny square plastic containers.

Months of Botany studies had finally developed into actual growing. Our assignment was to nurture the sycamore saplings and eventually plant them as part of the university's landscaping program. I had held the little tray of plants carefully as I returned to my room.

When Everett called to tell me he'd be a bit late with "some dorm thing" until about eight o'clock, I told him I'd meet him later. Then, on impulse, I decided to bring him a few of the saplings. He didn't have any plants in his room, and I thought it would be a nice gesture.

Since it was a Friday, I wasn't planning on studying in his room, so I filled the bottom of my backpack with a few clothes; a pair of socks, a T-shirt and underwear. I nestled the small pots inside my backpack, and carefully hung it over my shoulder.

It happened so fast, I hardly had time to react. The Broad Street train car wasn't crowded, yet I stood, and placed my backpack on a seat near a train door. I didn't want to risk jostling the plants.

At one stop, almost the moment the doors started to close, somebody shoved me. I fell to the floor of the car, and from my lower, almost sideways view, I saw a small kid rushing out of the door and across the platform with my backpack.

"And nobody did anything to help!" I said, frustrated after retelling the story to Everett.

"I'm sorry." He consoled me with a hug.

"And then," I fumed. "Some woman just said, 'You gotta watch yo bag onna train.' Like it was my fault."

"Damn."

"At least there wasn't anything important in it." I'd always kept my wallet and keys in my pockets.

"That sucks."

"I know."

"No, I mean your imitation of a Black lady sucks."

"Ev! Be serious. What if he had a knife or a gun?"

"Sorry. I was trying to make a joke. You have to be careful. From now on, you should just come by earlier, and stay over."

"That would be nice."

"Yes."

"So much for the survival of my sycamores in an urban environment."

"That kid's gonna be disappointed when he opens the bag."

"What the hell would he do with the plants?"

"Probably try to smoke them."

I shook my head. "It's just so…creepy." I felt nervous with the prospect of taking the train again without a returning fear.

"Do you still want to go out?"

"Sure," I said. "Let's just go get drunk."

"My teammates don't really do that. I think there's a change of plans."

Everett's debate team had won regionals, and were headed off to finals in a few weeks, which would be held at Rutgers. The celebration had migrated to a larger party down the block, where to them, access to a keg and sorority girls was the lure.

Perhaps I'd hedged a little too long when Everett asked me to accompany him. As what, debate team cheerleader?

But he didn't have to ask twice for me to go with him to the party. Two of his classmates, members of Lesbians and Gays at Penn, had been harassed by a cluster of other male students when they were putting up meeting flyers. As he was told, they were called names, threatened, and chased across Locust Walk in the center of the campus.

Other students were threatened, too. Residents of Dubois House, where many of the Black students lived, had received anonymous phone calls and threats of violence. Suddenly, like the crime-ridden city, his elite school didn't feel safe either.

But parties were parties. I'd been used to Everett deciding on a seat, always a sofa, so I could sit near him. But I didn't get why until I'd sat down at the sofa's mid-section to devour a bowl of chips, having missed dinner to meet up with Everett.

It was in his territory, over the bridge, in one of Penn's multipart mansion rentals on the main drag, just south of the campus. One of his debate team pals knew they had a ramp in the back, not for wheelchairs, but for the sheer volume of beer kegs they rented.

Once again we'd parked in a main room. I did have to politely ask a couple to move, but they kind of jumped up anyway when Everett wheeled up by them.

Everett scowled, resigned himself, lifted his brow in a hint, and hopped off to the sofa. I followed, folding his chair and leaning it against a nearby wall.

I stood over him, as a waiter, mimed a beer-hoist. He nodded.

Upon my return, we sat. Beer sloshed a bit. He urged me closer against him.

I sensed a decidedly 'not at all gay' environment from the party. Every guy was talking to a girl or two, and the noisy talk resonated on two levels, a sort of growling assertively male rumble, sprinkled with frequent forced female cackles.

"Who are these people?" I wondered.

"Looks like… two sororities, a crew team, a bunch of Rosemont girls, and a herd of Whartons."

"Where are your teammates?"

"Probably playing Trivial Pursuit in a bedroom."

He sipped, we smiled. I hoped someone would bring us pizza. Out of his chair, just sitting, no one noticed him at first. Until some guy, apparently girl-less, struck up a conversation with Everett and I. What I more remembered was what the conversation wasn't about; Everett.

When he sat in his wheelchair, and was the only one, especially in such a group, he basically took audiences, paired or single. Without his chair, he didn't have to, what he called, "do the script," his terse summation of the how he got injured, the yeahs, the whens, the what ifs, and try to steer the guy, all such people, the Brads, the Connors, to just talk about other stuff.

"But why aren't you comfortable with–"

"I am comfortable. I'm just bored with that. Is there food here?"

"You read my mind."

As I returned with a paper plate full of anything edible on the already scrounged dining room table, Everett already had two admirers, both blonde young women, I stood back, nibbled on pretzels, until he saw me across the room leaning in a doorway. With his plaintive eyebrow raise, a helpless tiny shrug, I realized I had to save him.

The girls actually turned out to be a lot of fun, and amid this babbling four-way chatter session, I decided to just move toward a segue, jostling myself back beside Everett, dislodging the more buxom of the pair, who, it seemed having just learned of Everett's disability, had begun to nudge herself just a bit too close to him.

They didn't get the message, until my arm slung across Everett's shoulder, and I rubbed his neck.

A gasp. "Oh, mah gawd. Are you guys…?"

"Yeah."

Another gasp. "Figures. The two cutest guys in the room."

The party was so noisy, I wasn't sure whether we were offered drinks, or that they were leaving. One of the girls walked off, apparently put off by us being gay, but the other hung back.

"So, how did you guys meet?"

Then came what had become a familiar mutual smirk. Everett would choose one of many euphemisms, obscure yet declarative, which referenced that wintry day in a forest where we nearly froze our butts off in a first-time smooch and yank session.

"Arbor Day Club!"

The intent sailed over her fluffed hair and into the kitchen, where someone else laughed at something else.

"That's nice," she smiled, then didn't. "Look, I don't remember whether it was in *Cosmo* or some sister told me. You both seem set for the night, but we're kind of on the prowl, if you will."

"Okay," Everett withheld a full-on smirk.

"So, I read that women who are with guys attract other guys' animal competitive instinct, and I think half the crew team is here."

"So, we're bait," Everett nodded.

"Now you got it." She winked, then stood. "Beer or the hard stuff?"

Drink orders taken, I tickled Everett.

"Wow. I ought to sell autographs."

"Why?"

"They knew who I am."

"Ev, you're, like, famous. You've been in the student paper, how many times?"

"Yeah, but see, they're just nice to us because we're a cute innocuous pair of homos. That's why."

"That's why what?"

"That's why I want to sit by you, without the chair. It's easier for them to just be at ease, themselves, not all ...sympathetic, apologetic; mentioning some crip relative–"

"Right."

"And thank you for moving in." He leaned against me. "So can we have fun now, my little crime victim?"

"Yes. Fun. Now."

"Okay, cool. So just...scoot over."

"Okay."

And then I gave him a smile and an affectionate head rub, and perhaps a few heads turned, but we didn't bother to look back, until the ladies returned with beers.

We watched from our vantage point, as, true to her promise, a series of paired male suitors presented themselves, until, through some secret code between them that Everett pointed out to me in the whisper of a golf tournament announcer, the ladies chose bachelors Number Two and Three, and retrieved them through what Lindsay, her name, I finally discovered, called, "a retrieval." Their suitors hadn't been dismissed, just put on hold. We saw them hook the boys in at the end of another room.

"Marvelous," Everett clapped his hands like a mad professor. "The mating ritual of their species is so complex."

"I couldn't disagree more."

"Then you agree."

"How?"

"That's a double negative."

Both of us a little buzzed, that night Everett offered a woozy confession as we prepared for bed. A light rain had started as we were headed back to his dorm. As we undressed, I hung our wet clothes on a chair and a coat rack he'd attached to the back of his door.

"So, I'm going to be getting kinda naked with some other students."

"Naked?"

"I've been asked to participate in a series of physiotherapy students' practicums."

"Say that again?"

"Prac-ti-cum."

"More poking and prodding?"

"Sort of. They're going to chart my workouts and do some kinds of tests. And," he peeled off his undershirt, tossing it to me, "I'll get massages."

"With some hottie doctoral student?"

"No. It's with a bunch of different students. It might be a little weird. There's one cute Japanese guy, though."

"Should I be jealous?"

"Aren't you always?"

I offered him a sour face. "Can I offer you my services now?"

"Sure. Get the unscented stuff. That last bottle was like strawberry creamcakes."

As the rain outside continued, after getting the lotion and a towel, he stripped and lay down on the bed.

I rubbed his skin, his calf hairs swirling out as I circled what remained of his leg muscles. He blushed, perhaps just from the blood circulation, or from seeing his legs admired as well. It seemed to make him feel good. As my hands traveled up his back and to his shoulders, he started singing softly, another of his old time songs, so I must have been doing something right.

And later, atop him, the lotion making a few funny sounds as our skin pressed together, I felt that scar rubbing against my hips as I slid, occasionally poked, or dabbed, inside him, just to say hello.

But I couldn't do what I'd done with him before his accident. With Everett, I had to be careful. Besides, just nibbling his ear, with his arm reaching back to clutch some part of me, and the rain tapping on the window, despite all our odd adjustments, it felt right.

Chapter 16
April 1981

Thick spring air nearly hit me in the face as I almost tingled with anticipation while waiting for the bus. I didn't want to run through the city blocks to get to the south entrance to Fairmount Park. I never liked dodging pedestrians and traffic.

But when I stepped off the bus with a gaggle of tourists before the entrance to the Art Museum, the almost endless hill of steps up to the monumental building daunted me. Could it have stated any clearer its foreboding inaccessibility? Surely there was a ramped entrance somewhere, "In the rear," as Everett so often joked.

We'd made plans for a quiet dinner together following his afternoon with a few students in his study group. They were somewhere on the Penn campus, debating world affairs.

Ever since our pact on Valentine's Day, conceding to his schedule yet again, knowing the occasional night would be ours together, I felt freed, released to spend an afternoon alone.

Nevertheless, his needs clouded any sense of solitude, and before I began my run in earnest, I found the handicap entrance to the museum, made a mental note, stretched my legs at the base of a huge circular group of bronze sculptures of a moose, buffalo, and what I guessed was some historic Native American, the city's tribute to the people and animals whose fate its growth helped extinguish.

The path around the museum led into the park, and I began a steady jog, sometimes passing smaller or slower runners, men and women. Dodging parents with baby strollers and waddling walkers, I adjusted my old black-framed 'Brad Majors' glasses, the small fanny pack that held merely my house keys, wallet, a small water bottle and a few snacks.

I popped a piece of chewing gum to moisten my mouth, remembered to keep my lips closed for as long as possible, to avoid dry-mouth, and after a while, found a steady pace as the Schuylkill River passed to my left.

I should have been at ease, but with every pace, I thought, 'This is flat. Ev can do it,' like some sort of rhythmic chant. I knew the terrain, had studied a map, and visited before, but not dressed for a run. Striding with comfort and ease, seeming carefree to onlookers, I found myself checking the pathway for bumps and cracks. I didn't want anything to happen to him again.

Scuttling flocks of geese ambled along the expanding grassy lawns to my left, as opposite the roadway, oaks and elms in full spring bloom swayed in the light breeze.

I passed the boathouses while dodging slow-walking or photo-taking tourists. At a point further north where the path divided, I took an inland course, passed distant open baseball fields, more historic buildings with obscure pasts that failed to concern me that day.

As two kilometers became three, then five, I measured the distance by my fatigue and signposts, in the hope of estimating how long a trek Everett could endure, were he to one day visit the park with me again.

I'd mentioned it a few times, invited him, promising to keep a steady pace with him. He'd joked about rolling past me, saying it in that joshing tone that I felt betrayed his own doubts.

My pace slowed a bit as I veered off to Forbidden Drive, the popular wide path with a series of benches set along the tree-lined western side. To the right, the creek curved alongside. A few bicyclists zoomed past me. I trotted around to avoid some adorable little dogs on leashes.

But all the time, I remembered how the gravel path had slowed Everett down. He'd so often found some other reason to stop, or brush off an invitation, denying fatigue. I didn't want to push him, but at the same time, I hoped my repeated invitations would encourage him.

Had I learned the difference between suggesting and pestering? He could react so differently, depending on his mood. Was this year spent being a bit farther away from each other better? His interests were so heady, while mine were so simple and earthly. He wanted to change the world, and I just wanted to make trees grow.

By the time I reached the sort of bottleneck of a white criss-crossed bridge that served a sudden influx of cars, and an open area that led to residential homes, I checked the map on a bulletin board. Yes, I could continue north, push myself, but what was the point? I'd already covered more of the park than Everett could manage at one time. Couldn't I just enjoy this for myself?

No, actually. Collapsing to a grassy area I panted, sipped water, wolfed down the dry trail mix and chased it with more water, and rested for the run back.

'He can do this,' I told myself. 'Just don't push him. Let him want to do it.'

"You have a nice day?"

"Yep," said. "Ran up along the river in the park."

"Cool."

Everett was understandably distracted. His radio, set to a news station, reported updates on the assassination attempt on President Reagan, which had happened more than a week before. Some crazy guy had shot him in Washington, D.C.

"They said his press secretary's still in the hospital, probably paralyzed for life."

"Damn."

I'd pretty much inhaled my food as Everett recounted his afternoon. We were seated on the floor of his dorm room with a few boxes of Chinese take-out food set before us. While he deftly managed a pair of chopsticks, I settled for a plastic spork.

"We didn't get much done in study group. Everybody started arguing about gun control, and then politics, and mental health, and Reagan, and then violence in movies, and some of the guys know guys at Yale, and how the crazy shooter was stalking Jody Foster there."

"It's all so weird."

"Some strange days."

I nodded agreement, unsure what to say, except to eat, then try to change the topic.

"You should come with me again."

"Where?"

"To the park."

"Oh, right."

"I promise not to drop you."

"Okay," he smirked.

"Okay, stop asking you, or okay, you'll go with me?"

"Okay, I will go with you if you stop bugging me about it. I see you like the Szechuan chicken."

"Mmm."

"You want some of mine?" His shrimp something looked tempting. I forked a mouthful.

"So, when we move in together," he said.

"Again."

"Again, but off-campus."

"I thought that was the plan."

"Yes, well, remember, we have no idea yet where we can live." We knew which neighborhoods were cheap, but they were also not the nicest, either.

"Mmfm." Mouth full, I shirked off my concern that Everett was about to address something else, something that might separate us further.

"Can you cook?" he asked.

I swallowed. "Of course I can cook."

"Have you?"

"I've helped my mom a lot. It's easy. It's just chemistry, backwards."

"Ex-squeeze me?"

"Whatever takes the longest goes in first. That's usually the meat. Then the starch, then the vegetables. And don't forget the bread, which always gets forgotten. Mom always made a big joke about that. What, you don't like cooking?"

"I love cooking; at least, I did in the old days, with Helen." He gestured toward his legs. "But if we can't find a place with a stove I can reach, that's going to have to be your domain."

"As beta male."

"You would look cute in an apron."

I set down my spork and flipped my wrist about in a sort of impersonation of Gerard. "Don't impose your antiquated gender constructs on me, young man."

"Don't overdo it, Blanche."

We took our time finishing off the food, then shared fortune cookies.

"This is perfect," Everett said. "'A fresh start will put you on your way.'"

I read mine. "Not sure about this one; 'Every flower blooms in its own ... sweat time.'"

"Sweat time?"

We giggled. It would have been another wonderful romantic evening, if the exhausting run that day, and the overload of calories and delicious food hadn't made me sluggish by the time we cleaned up and settled into his bed. Despite his affectionate kisses and hugs, I dozed off in his arms.

About an hour later, a series of banging and knocking noises out in the hallway woke us.

Thinking it was some sort of fire alarm or emergency, I bolted up and opened the door just as, about to knock on Everett's door, a tall, muscled and quite handsome guy, holding a stack of yellow papers, stood, surprised to see me standing dumbfounded in my undershorts, which was odd, since he was wearing a short skirt and had what appeared to be balloons under a tight pink sweater.

"You're not Everett," he said.

"You're not a girl," I replied.

"Here," he handed me a flyer, then dismissed my protective stance in the doorway. He poked his head inside, grinning at Everett, who sat up in his bed. "Forrester! Mask and Wig tomorrow night! Ya gotta come!"

"Okay!" Everett replied, grinning.

The girl-man waved his cluster of flyers, then pranced off down the hallway to join his friends, who were stuffing more flyers under doorways, showing off more than a bit of thigh as they bent over.

Closing the door with relief, I joined Everett back in bed and handed him the invite, which promoted *Between the Covers*, a variety show at a Penn campus theatre.

"Is this another wonderful part of Ivy League life I'm missing out on?"

Everett shrugged. "Just another strange tradition." He tossed the paper aside. "It's actually supposed to be a hoot."

"So, you're going?"

"Well, yeah. We're going. They are my house mates."

That was just another of the eccentric things that made Penn so different than Temple, calling dorms houses; that, and muscled jocks prancing about in the hallways with inflatable breasts.

Another Saturday that I would have preferred to spend alone with him would become a public affair. Actually, I was curious to see the show.

"Is it accessible?"

"They don't have a space for my chair. We'll just fold it up like usual and I can sit in a regular seat."

"Front row, hopefully," I half-joked as I wrapped us under the sheets. "If he's any indication, those gals are gonna be kinda sexy."

And they were, in a strange way. The next morning, after we'd parted, I headed back to my relatively non-festive dorm, wary on the train as I held my new backpack close, despite the fact that my textbooks and spare clothes weren't that valuable. I did some studying and laundry, and returned to Everett's 'house' in plenty of time for us to find the theatre.

As we'd predicted, there weren't any spaces for him to arrange his chair, so after he hoisted himself into an aisle seat, I folded his wheelchair and set it aside against a wall.

As we perused the program, Everett pointed out the names of housemates whom he knew, including Harris, who had abruptly greeted us at his door the night before.

Everett had become friends with several of the guys. With only a few weeks of living apart left, I let it go. There would always be others who wanted to be close to him, brag that they were his friends.

And as we saw some of those friends strut about onstage in various inane yet hilarious sketches, the giddy appreciation from the audience built in anticipation toward the finale, when the jocks would appear in makeshift drag.

Throughout the show, Everett had kept his hand either on my thigh or in my hand. I'd casually hung my arm over his shoulder, resting it on the back of his seat for a while. At one point, I'd casually grazed the back of his neck, and felt him shiver from my touch. But then he shrugged it off, what I took as a silent rejection of that small gesture of affection.

"What's wrong?" I whispered.

"I'll tell you later."

His response was to creep his hand closer to my inner thigh. It was a semi-public yet secretive form of affection, a silent understanding we had, with no Connors or other guys in between us. We couldn't as easily engage in the reckless public sex of our furtive pre-college days. But just the slightest bit of public display, I knew, meant more to us. So I was concerned that he had brushed off my hand.

After congratulating his friends on their performance, he thankfully declined an invitation to the cast party on my behalf.

His joked suggestion in his room that I don a T-shirt as a skirt made me bold. Stripping down to nothing else, once again I danced for him, this time to some old soul cassette mix he'd made. He clapped his hands, pretended to toss me tips. I shimmied and swayed, until the feeling of being a young man pretending to be a woman felt a little strange.

"You're much sexier than any of those guys," he beamed.

"But I don't have any knockers," I joked, squeezing my lean pectorals together.

"Well, you're my knockout."

As I dropped the shirt/skirt and got into bed with him, I hesitated to ask, but did anyway.

"So, what was it you were going to tell me?"

"You didn't hear about it?"

"About what?"

"Did Reagan die?"

"No."

Everett huffed out a breath, as if preparing, and scooted himself under the cover, reached down to adjust his legs. "The reason I got a little... cautious with you in the theatre... It was in the *DP*. I don't know who it was, but... some gay student got attacked."

"What?"

"In his dorm."

"What?"

"It wasn't here. It was in another house, one of the highrises. And after you got sort of mugged, it just... scared me."

"What happened?"

"I saved the paper. It's over there in my stack. Don't, don't read it now." He stopped me from leaving the bed, held his arm along my back, pulled me closer.

"I was gonna tell you, but I didn't want you to worry."

"Of course I worry."

"I'll be fine. Nobody's going to hurt me. I just... It might be a good idea if we kept it cool for a while."

As if the threat were closing in around us, I could only sit and stare about his room. Was he safe at all?

Everett diverted my concern by saying, "It is kind of ironic. My presumably straight schoolmates can perform a sloppy kickline in tight skirts and wobbling fake boobs, using a theatrical guise to express some sort of sex-reversal ritual. But if we merely touch in public, we could cause more outrage by just being ourselves."

"Your scholarly analysis doesn't make me feel better."

"Sorry," he said.

"Maybe you should come visit me more often."

"Sure, if I can find a place to park the van."

"You still have the parking decal from Temple."

"Yeah, I guess I could fake it. The handicap card's good anywhere."

"Come 'ere," I said, drawing him close. We kissed, and touched, and explored and licked and caressed, but it became a cautious, quiet form of lovemaking.

Afterward, I held him close, not falling asleep until much later in the night. Every sound in the hallway yanked me from sleep, as if a potential threat lurked just outside the door.

Chapter 17
May 1981

As Penn's lacrosse team prepared to compete against Princeton, the bleachers were about half full. Penn's mascot, a guy dressed as a Quaker, had yet to rouse the crowd to respond to more than a few half-hearted pre-game cheers. We parked ourselves on the grounds in front of the bleachers.

"You sure you want to be here?"

"Why not? It's a game."

"It's more than that," I said.

"Yes, 'facing my demons,' just like my physical therapist said." Everett made a comically fearful face that made me grin.

As if to lighten his mood, he offered another 'Did You Know.' "The traditional football huddle…"

"Yes?"

"Not used in this sport, but nevertheless, was invented at Gallaudet University for the Deaf."

"Huh."

"So the opposing team couldn't see their play calls being signed."

"Really?"

"Yes, really; in 1892."

"Wow."

"By a professor Hubbard."

"So then, why isn't a huddle called a hubble?"

Everett offered a confused look. "Let me get back to you on that."

As the team's warm-ups ended, I saw one of the players staring at us, then walking toward us. A husky guy with short blond hair and a questioning look approached us, his helmet and stick in his hands.

"Forrester?"

"Nickerson!"

"Hey, man!" He dropped his equipment, leaned down and surrounded Everett in a bear hug. "I thought that was you."

"What gave it away?"

"Oh." Nickerson frowned, then offered an embarrassed smile. "I get it."

"So, a Princeton man."

"Yup. And you're here at Penn?"

"That I am."

Nickerson looked at me.

"Oh, sorry. This is my best bud, Reid."

"Drew."

We shook hands.

"Nicks here's one of my old classmates from Pinecrest," Everett said.

"Oh," I nodded. "Were you in the same grade?"

"Naw," Drew glanced behind him to see if the game had started. "He was a year ahead. I was JV. So, wow. I remember when your…" He gestured vaguely toward Everett's chair.

"You were there?" I said, a bit too urgently.

"Well, yeah. We had a game before his, then he fell and everything stopped and it wasn't until that helicopter swooped in, man, that was pretty amazing, sorry, but…"

Drew continued his account, but my ears were ringing, and a tautness in my stomach overtook me. I almost got up from my seat and turned away, until I felt Everett's hand grab my elbow.

"Sorry," I muttered.

"It's okay," he whispered.

"You get the cards we sent?" Drew asked.

"Yes, I did. Thank you."

Drew appeared oblivious to what I read as Everett's contained frustration.

"So, how are you?" Drew asked.

"Other than being a paraplegic, pretty good. You?"

"Huh. Sorry."

"Why? You didn't do it."

Stunned, Drew's mouth hung open.

I glared at Everett.

"Sorry. I can be a little caustic. Right, Reid?"

"Oh, yes. Very," I added.

Everett patted my shoulder, then sort of kept his hand on me, lingering, as if undecided about whether to caress or choke my neck, which made Drew seem even more uncomfortable.

An awkward silence was broken by Everett's segue, "So, now I play basketball."

"Really?"

"Yeah, it's just for fun."

"Don't listen to him. He's wicked on the court," I added, feeling reconnected to the conversation, calmed. Drew smiled.

They shared some more disarming chat about their classmates and teachers at Pinecrest, until one of Drew's teammates called out his name from the field.

"Gotta go. So, who ya gonna cheer for, me or your team?"

"I have to say, my allegiance is now torn."

"Ha. You gonna hang after the game?"

"Actually," Everett turned to me. "Reid's got a …thing in a bit."

"Um, okay then. Great to see ya." Drew leaned forward again, offered a briefer half-hug, parting nods and trotted off to the field.

"Well, that went well."

I shrugged, determined to not pass judgment. "Was he one of your 'demons?'"

"No, he's harmless."

"Right."

"And not on the 'need to know' list."

"Not a problem," I assured him. "But I think he got it."

"I'm not so sure. He wasn't the brightest bulb in school."

"So, how'd he get into Princeton?"

"The same way he got into Pinecrest. His dad's a defense contractor; richer than mine."

"Oh."

As the game started, Everett shared several disdainful critiques of the Princeton team's skills. He held a stoic attitude, and offered critiques on moves, explaining various strategies. When we weren't talking, I stole a few glances sideways and saw his jaw clench several times, and that familiar slight wobble of his ear.

Just before the game's end, Penn was ahead 13-10.

"Come on." He started wheeling off ahead of me. "Let's beat the crowd. We have to go apartment-hunting."

"Did you ask again with the guys at Magee?"

"Yes," Everett said with a sharp tone as we trundled along Spruce Street a few blocks west of the Penn campus.

Our search for housing off campus had not been going well. He said he'd seen a listing in the *Daily Pennsylvanian* that sounded right; modern apartments (meaning no Edwardian grand staircase entrances) and an elevator, for $450 a month.

Gerard heard about our plans, thanks to Everett, and offered to move in with us and apartment-hunt, but I squashed that as soon as he called me with suggestions for row house rentals in Center City. I had to remind Gerard that no amount of fabulous decorating ideas would improve a series of steps. Also, as much as I'd finally warmed up to him, the idea of Gerard living with us was unthinkable. We had to find a place of our own. So we looked, and had narrowed down our search because our options were limited.

Hidden away between older houses, a few with Greek letters on awnings and doorways, the Sprucewood Apartments seemed out of place. Set back with a first-floor parking lot, except for the street view, the grey-bricked box-shaped building's windows faced the lot, and probably saw no direct sunlight. That was proven when the reluctant manager let us see one of the vacant rooms where the windows faced a wall.

The bathtub had an aluminum bar. The kitchen had a lowered work table with a cutting board on it. The living room and bedroom were grey boxes with some recently removed ghost-like carpet stains around where a sofa had been.

"There's free cable." The indifferent manager added, as if tossing a carnation on a block of cement. Even Everett couldn't hide his hesitation, but added, "It's functional."

What was also functional was one tenant's loud stereo thumping through the wall. We asked for a day to decide.

But by the time we rounded back onto Spruce Street, for some reason, Everett turned off to South 42nd Street with a smaller row of houses, a few elegant ones. I pulled back behind a row of shoulder-high hedges, which had just blossomed with spring flowers. In front of them, black wrought iron gates repeated a crest of what seemed a plant, no, an oak tree. At the top of each crest, a tiny cluster of acorns hung.

Everett had been pushing ahead of me, but the sidewalk's bricks rolled under the roots of a curbside tree, or the remnants of one. A stump had become a chopped out bench.

Finally, Everett stopped, since I wasn't following him. Instead, I leaned over to stick my nose in a cluster of tiny white hedge flowers.

"Pretty," Everett said, having jumble-rolled himself back over the bricks.

"Lilac."

I had to stay calm. We had no choice but that boxy apartment around the corner. It might work with a little lighting, some carpets, a request for Gerard's help, to please Everett, but also out of necessity. I didn't want to just put up posters, but that's about all we had.

"Look, sweetie, Monkey, honey, etcetera," I said, resisting the urge to pluck a cluster of the hedge flowers. "I don't know where else we can go, other than that one on Eighth Street."

We'd checked out a large modern apartment building, but it looked and felt more like a hospital, since it had been a veteran's rehab building built in the 1970s.

"The other one's got a doorman, and high ceilings, but it's really for seniors, mostly," he said. "And that's so out of the way for me, especially winters; unless I drive."

"That reminds me; the carburetor."

"What?"

"Something's wrong with the van."

"Again?"

The ignition worked fine, but some other clanking noise irked me. We'd kept it parked too often, simply walking and rolling instead, and fast-paced sometimes, too. It became our default aerobics; hunting for a home, zooming across the Walnut Street Bridge as spring rains poured down around us, the blast of wind from the river basin side-slapping us.

"I don't know," I said. "Let's just …"

"Excuse me," One of the hedge flowers spoke.

Then a head popped up from behind the hedge, an elderly woman with a ragged sailor cap, green gloves and a pair of clippers in one hand.

"I'm so sorry, but I was actually kneeling and clipping some stems when you young fellows passed by and I thought you'd just keep going, so I didn't get up, but then one of you, oh, your friend; did he leave?"

She had been looking right at me, completely missing Everett below the hedge. He could have raised his hand. He instead convulsed in silent laughter at my side.

"Did you say you needed a place to stay?" she asked.

"Excuse me?"

"He'll be out in September, or else June, if he gets that doctoral fellowship trip to Honduras for the summer; my current tenant, that is. Normally I only rent to graduate students; keeps the place a bit more quiet than the undergraduates. No offense, but at least they're not like the fraternity boys down the street."

"Are they noisy?"

"Oh no, only for the occasional pagan holiday disguised as an academic ritual. But anyway, are there two of you?"

"Yes, Ma'am." Everett raised his hand.

Her pop-eyed look of astonishment, followed by a thrust upward on her toes, was finally met by Everett's dazzling smile.

"Oh!" She darted up, then down, with a wobbly flair, disappeared, then the black gate swung open and she rushed forward to shake Everett's hand.

"Well, this is our lucky day," she smiled. I remained befuddled.

"I do hope this rooming problem is about you," she said. "I mean, there's only one room, but I suppose it could fit another bed. You're Penn boys?"

"Ma'am, actually—"

Everett shot a panicked silent 'Shut up a minute!' glare my way, then doled out a series of compliments and handshakes after the woman introduced herself as Suzanne Kukka.

"It's an old Finnish name, my husband's. I'm Irish-Albanian. But he was a Kukka. It's Finnish for flower; appropriate, since that's been my hobby for years and years."

Everett beamed, glanced around, said softly, "Flowers."

I returned his grin, nervous. The woman hadn't quite figured out what to do with her clippers, and apologized for the bricks. She seemed a bit flustered, but a certain spark in her eyes made me smile in return.

"We'll get that fixed right up. I know a fellow. It's about time. Oh, but do come in. You'll understand my excitement when you see."

And see we did.

Past the gate, whose handle was only waist high, and wide enough for Everett's chair, the sidewalk led down at a wonderfully discreet angle, all the way to the right of a side porch that led inside to the kitchen. The yard's garden included a variety of shrubs, small clusters of flowers and, in the back, a maple and pine tree, with a smaller redbud in a far corner by a fence.

"No steps," Everett said to me as we approached the side porch.

"You noticed," Mrs. Kukka turned back, smiling. "My mother used a chair for her later years," she said as she led us inside.

We both stopped first to admire the enormous kitchen and a sidebar counter, a lowered separate stove, and a large refrigerator. Beyond it, a warm yet somewhat darkened dining room was lined with shelves filled with books, but lacked a central table.

"Ninety-five she was, before she left us. Of course, she didn't get around as much as I would have liked, but there's plenty of room to move around. You look like the athletic types. What were your names again?"

We re-introduced ourselves as Mrs. Kukka showed off cabinet doors, which slid sideways, not out. "Otherwise gets in the way of the feet, I imagine you've found," she glanced down at Everett, who nodded.

"Darling, we've found our dream house," Everett whispered as our host chattered on about some university trustee. "Let's not fuck it up."

"Did I say anything?" I shrugged.

Mrs. Kukka led us through the living room, which managed to be cozily cluttered with what appeared to be African and other ethnic antiques, and more built-in bookcases in a dark wood that matched the trim and mantle. Below the front bay window was a large sofa.

Everett rolled ahead, spun around back to the hallway, then instinctively sought out a door. He pushed it open.

I froze, but Mrs. Kukka called out as she followed, "Yes, that would be the bedroom. The bathroom's on the left across the hall, and a washer and dryer in the storage room by the back door, which has steps, so..."

We trailed behind Everett, who had already wheeled around to the other side of the low, surprisingly simple bed and spartan furnishings. The current resident's belongings included stacks of papers, a stereo, and what I first thought was a chair, but it was a waist-high suit holder.

Through the window, a florid back yard beckoned. Beyond that, the back of the drab apartment building we'd just visited was thankfully blocked by an ivy-covered fence.

Mrs. Kukka stood in the doorway. "I'm upstairs. I'll be out of your way, and I mostly stay in the front rooms. I have a little kitchenette, but I'll use the big kitchen down here sometimes."

"That's cool," I said.

"I have a gal who comes by to clean once a week, but she'll stay out of this room, if you prefer. Oh, and my daughter might come for a visit every now and then. She likes to check up on me; thinks I shouldn't be alone. But I'm not in agreement. I host little dinner parties and gathering in the front rooms. You're not obligated to attend, but certainly welcome; mostly retired faculty and their widows like me who still like to prattle about primitive cultures."

She seemed to have finally run out of patter. I didn't bother to add anything, but nodded mutely.

Everett smiled, said something in Latin, "*Domum dulce domum.*"

"Which translates to?"

"Home, sweet home," Mrs. Kukka said. "I think we're going to get on just fine."

"Thank you, Mrs. Kukka, But, you see…" Everett glanced at me, his eyebrows raising, as if to say, Here it comes, "This isn't just for me. Reid and I are together."

She stopped, blinked. "Oh. You mean *together* together."

"Yes, Ma'am."

She pondered for a brief moment, as if distracted by something else. "Well, I guess that, unlike a few previous gentlemen, there won't be any problems with ladies coming by."

By the time Mrs. Kukka had trod upstairs and back down after having dug up a copy of a lease, which noted that payment was due upon signing, a demand she shrugged off, Everett and I had already imagined moving in.

"I can park in the driveway," he marveled as we departed. "It's ramped. This kitchen kicks ass, and there's no dead grandma feel in the bedroom."

"Well, no. She said she'd been renting it since–"

"Yeah, plus, maybe she'll cook for us."

"She'll probably kick us out if we make too much noise," I muttered. He knew I meant sex noise.

"Maybe she's a little hard of hearing."

"We can hope."

Chapter 18
June 1981

Since I'd started college, I hadn't helped Dad work on any house projects. When I was younger, he had taught me some of the basics about plumbing, electrical wiring, and other small projects that didn't require professional help.

So when I casually mentioned over dinner that I would once again invite Everett to stay over for a few nights between our trips to and from Philadelphia and the summer camp, and that a small removable ramp might be a good idea, he immediately said, "Sure. How about we make one for the kitchen door in the garage? Then we can just store it there."

His enthusiasm heartened me, signaling in his quiet way that he understood Everett and I had remained more than close, that we were together, and that that wasn't going to change.

When I found him that Saturday morning kneeling by the kitchen door taking measurements, he offered a chipper, "Get dressed. We're off to the hardware store."

Picking out two-by-fours and a sheet of board, we kept the conversation in the abstract; my plans to make more ramps for parks as a sidebar to some as-yet undefined career, his mention of a disabled employee at one of the stores where his company distributed food. We were talking around Everett.

Mom welcomed us back as we unloaded the lumber, then took a bag of peat moss she'd asked for. She continued working on her vegetable garden in the back yard, where I was looking forward to assisting her.

As the band saw rang loudly in the garage, Dad and I donned goggles and sanded the parts, and re-cut them to fit. Once he finished cutting the wood, I saw this as the time to ask him things I had never considered aloud.

"So, you and Mom."

"Yes?"

"You both really get along."

"We do. I'm lucky."

"How does that work?"

Sensing that a 'discussion' had commenced, Dad put down the saw, shifted to picking out screws, then chose a compatible drill bit for the battery-powered screwdriver. "We talk about things. We have had arguments. Just, you usually aren't around."

"About what?"

"Well, getting a bigger house, having more kids."

"Which you didn't do."

"Well, I like this neighborhood, so I won that one, and your mother pretty much has to bear the burden for the other …discussion, so I left that up to her."

"So, you don't…?"

"We do. I got a vasectomy, which took about ten minutes, and it didn't hurt, and we figured if we wanted more kids, we'd adopt. But we were so happy with you, we left it at that."

"Come on."

"No, really. You were just a wonderful kid. You still are."

"Thanks."

"Is this about Everett?"

"Yeah."

"Are you having problems?"

"Not exactly. I just… We're going to be living together. And it's different than the dorms. How do you get around, you know, the daily stuff, the 'Put the dishes away like this,' or being around other people he doesn't like, or that I don't like but he does, or doing things–"

The specifics of our unusual sex life, the feeling that we might just become mere friends if the passion drained away; these worries I couldn't explain to him.

"Don't sweat the small stuff," Dad said, a bit too glibly.

"Okay." I had expected a few platitudes.

"No, really. Half of getting along is just letting go of things that don't matter. You got along in the dorms last year, didn't you?"

"Pretty much. It was a little cramped. I just basically let him have his way. We have this joke about who's the alpha male. But we're moving into an apartment, or part of a house. It's really... I just want to... make it perfect for him."

"What about you?"

"Me?"

"Yeah, you. Look, I know you have to make accommodations for him. That's what we're doing here." He tapped the board in front of him. "But I don't know if your... relationship is any different than anyone else's. I see you...you're really devoted to him, and that's fine. But, you have to make yourself happy, too."

"But I'm happy if he's happy."

"But if you're not, he won't be. Sometimes, you have to think of yourself, too."

"Well, see, he wants me to work at the summer camp again, but the nursery's just more money. I love those kids, but I don't know if they'll take me back again in August, and he pays for stuff, but I just want to make my own way, you know?"

"Exactly my point."

As he returned his attention to a plank, I assumed the conversation was over, but he said, "Also, I like to surprise her, remind her that I don't take her for granted."

"Ah ha."

"You know, our twentieth wedding anniversary's coming up next year."

"You going to get her something nice?"

Dad nodded.

"So?"

Dad offered a sky grin. "Keep a secret?"

I mimed zipping my lips shut.

"Five days in Hawaii."

Mocking a gasp, he shushed my little hummed hula wave with a finger to his lips, which failed to stop me, so he revved up the saw, which worked.

But after a few deft board cuts, he pulled up his goggles once again, and said, "Anyway, you should know about making things grow."

"I Iuh?"

"You don't just plop a plant into the ground. You care for it, nurture it, right?"

I nodded. "You're pretty smart for an old guy."

Chapter 19
July 1981

Returning to the camp at Pine Grove gave me a sense of anticipation and belonging, combined with the mild apprehension about returning to the 'rustic' cabin with Everett.

Some of the kids hadn't returned, because their parents couldn't afford it, or because of health problems. And we learned about the new campers' needs.

I was relieved that "Amazing!" Kenny had returned, his affection for me as sweet as ever.

During our recreation and therapy in the small pool, Kenny was at first nervous about the water. I held him carefully as he paddled about in his unique way, his inflated life vest glistening under the sun.

It was only after the second week's work, with a few other staffers relaxing over some snacks and a discreetly shared bottle of red wine, that any sort of problem came up.

Two of the kids' birthdays were celebrated within a few days of each other, and Everett had pushed the boundaries of standard activities. He'd bought a few boxes of sparklers at a store in town, leftovers from July Fourth. Just after sundown, we taped the sparklers to the kids' wheels, and they giggled and hooted as the swirling sparks lit up around them.

Karen, a rather enthusiastic new staffer, had expressed concern about "bedtime irregularities," preferring more traditional entertainments.

She had brought a box of children's books, and read to the kids on a few afternoons. They seemed rapt by Karen's enthusiastic oration of a few fairy tales. But something about them bothered me; Everett, too.

With the kids all in bed, we were free to discuss adult topics as we enjoyed the warm night air on a back porch for a well-deserved break. But our talk still came back to the kids.

"They really liked your story time," Alice, the senior staffer said.

"Thanks," Karen smiled.

"Are there kids' books with disabled characters?" Everett asked.

"What do you mean?" Karen asked.

"You know, stories about kids in wheelchairs, blind kids."

"I haven't found any," she said.

"We should write some," he suggested. "Let the kids write stories."

"Well, moot of them don't have motor skills for that."

"I meant, they could tell the stories and we could write them. And then they could illustrate them," Everett added.

"What's wrong with the fairy tales? They're classics."

As Everett started in, I felt a burst of pride, and held back a smug grin, knowing he'd just been given the easiest bait for a debate.

"Sure, they're classics," he said. An expert tactic; agree with your opponent before unleashing the attack. "But don't you sense, underneath it, a rather consistent form of sexism in the role of women in those stories?"

"Because they want to find a prince?" Karen sounded confused.

"Because they need a prince to save them," Everett countered. "Snow White's basically a quad in a coma until some prince kisses her. And think about the representation of disability, or deformity, if you will; dwarves, witches who use canes, people with physical abnormalities are always depicted as evil."

"But that's what they wrote," Karen countered. "You're saying we should ban them?"

"Not ban them; rethink them. Why do we have to tell them the old way? I mean, these stories were written when kids like the ones here were locked up."

"Tossed into ovens by witches," I joked.

"Who are always depicted as disabled or disfigured seniors," Everett piled on the last smackdown.

"So you agree with him?" Karen asked me.

"I…"

She pushed out an exasperated sigh. "Of course he agrees with him. You're both…"

"Both what?"

"Well, you're …friends."

Everett stated a bit too loudly, "We're more than friends. Come on, Karen. And you think we don't argue?"

I stifled a burst of laughter, then added, "Also, sorry, I don't mean to pile on, but what about the depiction of forests?"

"Forests? You think, along with being sexist, fairy tales are, what, anti-tree?"

"Well, think about it," I said. "It's always some mysterious woods; Goldilocks, Little Red Riding Hood."

Alice inserted a comment. "Actually, she did okay in the woods. Grandma's house was the danger zone."

"But still," I continued. "They all make the woods out to be some dark evil place, when the truth is, like you said, the creepiest dangers are their own families."

Karen huffed. "That's an entirely different argument."

I sipped my wine, tried to sound as eloquent as Everett. "I'm trying to get these kids used to nature, to let them be a part of it, to appreciate it, and then they get a bedtime story guaranteed to give them nightmares, thanks to the Brothers Grimm."

"Well, maybe you should take over story time. I was just trying to entertain them." Karen crossed her arms.

"We're sorry," Everett said. "Please don't take offense. It's just, we could evolve our teaching and entertainment to reflect their lives in an uplifting way."

Alice stood, waving her empty glass. "Okay, speaking as someone named after a preteen drug addict who consorted with tea-gulping rats and bunnies, I declare the sermon over. Who wants more wine?"

In spite of Alice's intervention, I sensed a distance from Karen after that night. It kind of soured the remaining weeks, and a sort of turf war for the kids' attentions began, culminating in a seemingly innocuous drawing.

The idea of a book made by the kids got going once we let Karen have control over its production. That maneuver on Everett's part was calculated and on-target.

Since the kids' imaginations spiraled off into a series of stories, it worked out better to separate the contributions into chapters.

Karen got an estimate from a local copy store in town for spiral bound color booklets. It wouldn't be cheap, but since the copy shop owner had a soft spot for the camp, he offered a discount.

The first day, we got the kids to make drawings of any creature they wanted, which resulted in a lot of cats and bunnies. Karen's creative idea, days later, was for the kids to draw their favorite monsters, which unleashed some surprising results. Dragons, balloon-like Great Pumpkins and a giant snake were among the contributions. But Kenny's drawing caught my attention.

"What's that?"

"Doctor Monster," he whispered with a wary tone, as if the mere mention might conjure the big-headed green-faced man-ogre in a lab coat with knives for arms.

"Pretty gruesome."

"He likes to operate a lot."

"Ouch."

"I'm spozed to get another one, but I don' wanna."

"I'm sorry."

"You been to hozpitals?" Kenny looked at me with a wide-eyed concern.

"Yep, when I got my tonsils out. I was about your age."

"Did it hurt?"

"No, but I don't remember much. I got ice cream."

He looked away, returning to his drawing. "Ebrett said he had two op-rations."

"Yep, and I visited him a bunch of times."

"Did you feel bad?"

"I cried buckets," I nodded.

His little arm reached for me, and I held his hand, what there was of it.

"Are you guys friends?"

"The best."

"Best friends?"

"Best best friends."

"Then don't let him go back."

"I promise."

Karen hovered nearby, offering a wary glance. "Let's finish up before lunch!" she announced.

After the monster drawings were collected, she instructed everyone to pick someone from the camp and make drawings of themselves or each other. I felt a bit too much 'childhood therapy' in her tone, but it seemed like a good idea.

Our staff cook asked for some help hauling boxes of food, so I ducked out and assisted him on the loading dock for a while. When I returned, Everett was beside Kenny, beaming in appreciation.

"Check out our junior Matisse," Everett pointed.

"Who's that?" I asked Kenny.

"It's you and Ebrett!" he grinned.

In the drawing, a big-eared bespectacled version of me with really long legs stood next to a curly-haired Everett in his chair. We were holding hands.

"Aw, that is so sweet!" I leaned in and hugged Kenny.

"You can have it," he said, almost casually.

"Don't you want it for the book?"

"Okay."

But then Karen's clapping hands signaled a summing up, and as she scooped up the various drawings, we had to get the kids ready for lunch.

"Were the two of you acting … inappropriately in front of the kids?"

The way Alice said it, sitting behind the cluttered desk in her office, as if she were already exhausted by the absurdity of the situation, should have calmed us. But Everett was understandably upset, and I was disgusted.

Karen sat on the edge of a chair, lips pressed together, eyes on fire. She had seemingly forced Alice into this meeting just after lunch, and this little scandal she'd cooked up couldn't wait.

"No. We were not," Everett simmered.

"I think we need to think of the parents, and what they would think. Surely I don't have any problem with you two being–"

"Really, Karen?" I let Everett take the reigns of our defense.

"No, I don't! It's just that, how did Kenny come up with such an image?"

"We hold the kids' hands when they're scared of getting in the pool. I hug. Is that a crime?"

"Well, no, but you two–"

"We two," he almost snarled, "have respect for the camp, and don't do anything in public that would be 'inappropriate.'"

"Well, it's not going in the book. I have to limit the pages anyway–"

"Fine, Karen," Everett snapped. "Maybe we can ask Kenny to redo one with us, far apart."

"This is absurd," I muttered.

"Well, I'm sorry if you think I'm over-reacting," Karen snipped.

"Perhaps you should take the drawing and keep it for yourselves," Alice suggested.

"Gladly," Everett reached for it. "I know a nice frame shop back home. It'll look great over our bed."

The books made great gifts for each of the families, and the kids liked them, too. But as our time there drew to a close, Everett and I knew we had finished our service, and with Karen having dug in and pretty much spoiled any sense of innocence, we were done, just like in the book, excised and edited out of the picture.

"You think he ever saw us?" Everett wondered as we packed up in the cabin for the last time. He placed Kenny's drawing of us carefully between two pieces of cardboard.

"How could he?" I replied. "The windows are too far up for him to have spied on us."

"Maybe he just knew."

"Pre-teen gaydar?" I suggested.

"Well, you know, he is amazing."

On our last day, as we bid farewell to our co-workers, except Karen, who was conveniently elsewhere, I wondered how many other people could sense our connection, and what they really thought of it.

Chapter 20
August 1981

Everett had asked, then begged, then almost demanded that I accompany him and his father on a road trip to upstate New York to visit Holly and see a closing weekend performance of a summer theatre musical and the elaborate costumes she had designed. It seemed absurd to him that I couldn't just drop everything, since they would pass by Greensburg anyway.

"So, you really can't go with us?" his voice on the phone still sounded bewildered.

"I told you," I said. "I have to work."

"Fine. See you in a week or so."

I knew the trip would have provided some nice time with his family, or part of it. Everett's mother had taken off for the month to Martha's Vineyard with her sister's family, I'd been told.

Everett's dad was more relaxed about spending time with us, I felt a pang of loss to miss the opportunity to see Holly as well.

But economic realities interfered. My scholarship at Temple had not been renewed, due to university budget cutbacks. Sometimes, Everett and his family's affluence made him seem indifferent to my own situation. I wanted to save up my limited funds. With an additional tuition hike at Temple, plus other potential expenses and the rent on our new apartment, I simply had to work.

The rest of my summer would be spent discussing peat moss with housewives, or so I thought.

"Excuse me, young man. I'm told you're the gardening expert."

I turned from shelving a rack of withering baby Petunias on the sale table to see a portly older man in a colorful madras shirt, khaki shorts and sandals offering an expectant glance.

"Well, I wouldn't call myself an expert, but… What can I help you with?"

"You see," he glanced at the plastic nametag pinned to my shirt. "Reid. I bought a few little cherry trees to perk up my back yard, and–"

"What kind?"

"Excuse me?" He took on a haughty tone.

"I mean, are they Cornelian, Bing, Yoshino…?"

"Goodness, you are quite the expert!" He folded his arms.

The Latin terms for the various cherries jumbled around in my head along with an obvious realization; the man was gay.

"They need well-drained soil," I added. "You don't want to over-water them."

"Well, one of them, I'm not sure, but I think it might be…" he sort of whispered it, "dying."

"Oh, well, if you want a refund, you need to go to–"

"No, no, that's alright." His hands fluttered. "I just wondered what I may have done wrong."

"Well, it could be root shock."

"Really?"

"When did you plant them?"

"April."

"That should be okay. Sometimes, too much fertilizer can hurt them, if it has too much high-nitrogen. You might add some B-1."

"The vitamin?"

"Liquid form; Aisle Three." I pointed.

"Oh, alrighty then. I was wondering if you could come and look at them to sort of check them out."

Oh, yes; definitely gay. "Um, Ernie's the delivery and home guy. I could ask him to–"

"No, no, that's fine. But I could use some help getting my purchases into my car, at least."

He turned aside to reveal a cart full of items; mulch bags, a few decorative planters, and other supplies. It seemed odd for him to continue his gardening so late in the season. With another gesture, almost an intentional eye flutter, it dawned on me. I was being cruised. It felt kind of nice.

"Did you want to get anything else before you go to checkout?"

"Well, I suppose I could do with those vitamins you mentioned."

"Great. Follow me."

After I led him through checkout, I pushed his shopping cart as he led me to a rather fancy Cadillac. The trunk easily fit all the supplies.

"So, thank you, Reid." He offered his hand.

We shook. "Thank you…"

"Richard, but you can call me Rich."

"Rich."

He withdrew his car keys, and fiddled with them for a moment. "I hope you don't mind my harmless flirtation."

I must have blushed. Perhaps it was just a flush from the effort of hoisting the bags into his car.

"No, no, but… did you..?"

"Oh, sweetie, if you'd visit my home, you'd know I live in Forrestville, with my mother. She's a pip. And we know the Forresters."

"Oh." And then I got it. "Oh!"

"We do miss them. That German clan is a bit noisy. We're just across the road."

"I see."

"Don't worry. Your secret's safe with me." He patted my shoulder.

"Actually, it's not a secret."

"Well, then. Give Everett my best. You know, I never saw him after it all, you know…"

I nodded. "He's fine. We're…we're fine."

"Good. It's a small town, you know."

I nodded. "Something I find out more every time I come back."

"Well, don't make my mistake." He leaned in, as if offering a secret. "Get the hell out while you can."

As he drove away out of the parking lot, another hand flutter emerged from his rolled-down window, and I felt a combination of feelings; proud that I had been able to help him, worried that I had somehow betrayed myself by acting or looking gay, even though he knew who I was. But he had a point. It was a small town, and getting smaller.

"Oh. My. God. Richie Gunders?"

Everett was more than amused by my encounter with his neighbor. He had called me to apologize for being snippy a few days before, and to regale me with his description of "the only motel in town. It makes our summer camp cabin seem like the Ritz."

"So you do know him."

"Of course. He was always barging in pretending to share recipes with Helen. But I knew he just wanted to ogle me whenever I was home."

"Sounds a bit odd."

"He is."

"How's your dad?" I asked, changing the subject.

"Fine. He and Holly are having drinks at the only bar in town, settling old scores, I guess. I'm just here in my bed, thinking about you."

"That's sweet. So, are you gonna swing by my house before we head back to Philly?"

"After we get back. What's up?"

"Mom and Dad have invited you for Labor Day; backyard barbeque, the works. Your dad and Holly can come, too."

"Dad's probably otherwise engaged with some real estate swindle back in Piss-bar, but Holly might."

"Cool."

A silence followed, where I listened to his breathing, longed for him.

"Do you ever…?"

"What?"

I paused. "Nothing."

"Come on. Wait; do you have your hand in your pants?"

"No! I'm in the kitchen."

"So. I recall our first New Year's there."

A popped cork, kisses. I felt a surge in my heart.

"Ev, do you ever… think about us, a long time from now?"

"What's the matter? Are you afraid of becoming a lonely spinster living with his mother and hitting on stock boys?"

"I'm not a stock boy! I'm a 'gardening expert.'"

Everett's laugh was so loud I had to pull the phone from my ear.

But then his tone went soft, as if it were one of our quiet nights in bed. "Reid, Giraffe, my hunky spunky man child. I don't think about the future…"

"You don't?"

"If you'd let me finish; I don't think about a future without you."

"You always know the right thing to say."

His voice called out, away from the phone, "Hey, Dad!" then closer, "Gotta go. See you… in the future?"

"Okay."

Two days, later, half a dozen postcards from upstate New York's "Scenic Catskills!" arrived, each one from him, with a comical series of tiny drawings. My favorite was a depiction of what I assumed was an aged version of he and I in a pair of wheeled and non-wheeled rocking chairs.

Chapter 21
September 1981

"Ugh; Jerry's pity-fest."

My father nearly dropped a tray of uncooked burgers on his way out to the back yard. Everett's comment had obviously confused him.

"Don't care for it?" Dad asked, trying to keep things light. "Gimme a minute. I'll turn it off."

"That's okay."

"No, it's fine. Reid, can you get the buns?"

He set the tray of meat down on the brick edge of our fireplace, shut off the television, then fiddled with the stereo, settling on one of his old jazz albums. It was hardly Labor Day-appropriate, but the melody calmed us.

"Much better," Everett said as he gave me a concerned glance, then smirked, "Nice buns."

We joined my mother and Holly, who were sitting at a table and chair of patio furniture on our back yard, sipping colorful drinks with a good portion of rum probably mixed in. They too raised an eyebrow as Dad and Everett continued their discussion. Everett bumped down the one step off the porch, settling his chair on the lawn.

"What is it about that telethon that upsets you, son?"

"Dad," I said, feeling defensive.

"No, it's okay," Everett said, waving me to silence. "It's just... it creates an industry of pity, not empowerment."

"I see."

The burgers sizzled as Dad slapped them onto the grill. I stood, unsure where to place the tray of buns. The nearby table was full of speared vegetables mom had arranged, each of them proudly plucked from her nearby back yard garden.

"Are you going to offer a lecture again, brother dear?" Holly said. She wasn't exactly soused, but working on it. While I was glad that she had made the time to visit with my parents for the holiday, I didn't appreciate the sibling friction she and Everett seemed to share.

Having finished her job as the costume designer for a summer theatre company in upstate New York, over appetizers and a first round of drinks —we 'men' had stuck with beers— Holly had regaled us with the gossip of the various philandering theatre professionals' not-so professional behavior.

"I'm not lecturing," Everett said, although he did seem prepared to wait for our attention. "Sister, dear," he added with a light tone of sarcasm. He turned to my dad, who listened, standing sideways at the grill so his back wasn't turned, "I just think it's a kind of pageant of condescension that doesn't really help disabled people."

"But they raise millions of dollars," Mom said.

"Sure, but for what? Administrative costs for nonprofits that spend most of their budget on advertising and more fundraising. How much of it goes to research? A cure? Or even job placement, skills training? They just parade these kids out for a has-been comic to make you cry. It's a self-perpetuating industry."

"They are kind of pathetic," Holly muttered. "No offense," she hoisted her glass toward Everett.

Everett offered a bemused scowl at his sister, who pretended to ignore him as she sat under the shade of the lawn furniture umbrella. These were the kind of almost cruel comments Holly seemed allowed to make, knowing Everett understood and even appreciated her caustic wit. I never joked about such things with him, except when we fumbled in bed, where things often became a bit comic.

"You're an accountant, right, Mister Conniff?"

Even though Dad had repeatedly asked Everett to call him Hal (not Harold, his dorky full name), he never did. It was one of his many respectful gestures toward adults that I admired and tried to emulate. Even dressed in a casual shirt and khaki shorts, he carried himself with that private school formality. It was one of those rare days where, in the company of family, he didn't appear self-conscious about his legs. They'd thinned considerably, but his dark fuzzy hair maintained the nearly simian masculine physique underneath his clothes.

Dad flipped a few burgers. "Well, yes, but to compare, every can of peas we distribute doesn't actually cost more than a few pennies. We sell it, and the grocer sells it, and people make money. That's how it works."

"But donations shouldn't work that way," Holly added. "Ev's right. Shouldn't it be the state or the government's responsibility?"

Everett sighed. "But that's the argument that we're a burden, millions of people paid off to get out of the way, not contribute to society. The kids at the camp where Reid and I work; if they don't get a chance, that just leaves them at the mercy of charities. How can they make lives for themselves?"

"Do you get," my mother asked, "I'm sorry if it's not, if it's a private matter, but don't you get Social Security? Disability?"

Everett shook his head. "My parents make too much money. When I'm independent, then maybe, but I'm too rich. But for others, that's just an incentive to not work. If I wasn't 'a Forrester,' I'd want to get a job, but if I do, then I don't qualify. The entire system's set up for a victim status."

Dad had added the buns to the grill. The smoke churned up, wafting too close to me. I stepped away, feeling the impulse to add something to the conversation, but I wasn't sure how I felt. I knew Everett was excited about returning to school, getting back in the world of being busy, part of something. He sounded as hungry for yet another debate as he was for the food.

Although we'd spent most of August apart, except for one weekend visit, I knew he was anxious, about more than school.

While it was great to hear him inadvertently stating a kind of purpose, a focus he might want to take with a career after school, it seemed he had yet to figure out where or how to accomplish that. Would my being with him become a mere afterthought?

His van, parked in the driveway, and nearly packed with both of our belongings for fall semester, fortunately didn't include any furniture. My parents were enthused about our return, although assured that we didn't need them to travel with us.

They were understandably curious about our new apartment, and Mrs. Kukka, our eccentric-sounding landlady. I was just looking forward to spending a cozy night with him in my old bed, then heading off the next morning to Philadelphia to restart our life together.

"Well, I can't imagine you taking charity," Mom said. Her gesture back toward the woods behind us, beyond the open field, implied a reference to Everett's former home and his wealthy Forrestville history.

"Well, no, of course," Everett answered. "I'm not like the veterans, you know."

"Like the guys on your basketball team?" I said.

"Yeah. I mean, they have great support at rehab, but economically, they're struggling, and their families sometimes have other problems. But I have an advantage as well, kind of a former outsider's perspective. I never…"

He paused for a moment. Dad continued tending the barbeque, as my mother, Holly and I waited as Everett struggled to explain himself. Holly sat forward, as if ready to offer him something, a hug, perhaps.

"Did you see *Coming Home*? The movie?"

"Yes, of course," Mom said. "Remember, Hal, we all could barely speak after it, it was so upsetting."

"Ann?" Dad interrupted. "Could you help me here?"

Although she rose to assist him, stacking the burgers in between toasted buns as if it were nothing, I knew his reason. He wanted to change the topic.

Those few years ago, me a hapless high school junior, before any of this had happened to Everett, or we'd met, as the credits had rolled for the film, I remembered glancing over to see tears glistening from my father's eyes. It was probably one of the only times I'd ever seen him crying. Later that night, my mother had quietly visited me in my bedroom and explained that two of Dad's high school friends had gone off to Vietnam and hadn't returned alive.

I looked at my father's tall frame, his back to me as he fussed over the grill, and wondered how many dark mysteries he would always keep to himself.

"Well, the guys at Magee, the older ones, said that was exactly what it was like, only worse," Everett continued. "Things only got better a few years ago."

"It was very tragic," my mom added. "But here!" she perked up, bringing a plate of food to the table. "Who's hungry? Don't worry, we can still talk seriously," she assured Everett.

"That's okay," he sighed. "I'll stop. I can be a total downer sometimes."

"You?" Holly joked. "Never!"

The four of us sat at the table, sharing bowls and plates full of potato salad, seared peppers shucked from spears, corn on the cob, and burgers done to fatherly perfection. We passed condiments, ate silently for a while as the music from the living room echoed softly. Everett squirted a bit too much ketchup, the flatulent sound inducing a few giggles.

"You know what was really tragic about that movie," Holly said. She sipped her drink, pausing as we waited. "Jane Fonda's hair!"

After dinner, as dusk swept over the expansive field beyond our yard, and Mom took away the dishes, Dad closed up the barbeque and retreated inside, as if sensing that Everett and I wanted to be alone for a bit.

Holly stood close, grinning and almost whispered, "Your parents are so sweet." She offered to drive Everett and me to take a nostalgic glance at her family's former house, but we declined. So instead, she bid us adieu. "I think I'll walk off my cocktail buzz before heading back home. See ya in a bit."

We watched her walk across the field, where she almost became lost amid the darkening light and a few errant fireflies.

A breeze passed by us, still thick with summer's weight, the kind that, when I was a child, had filled me with a longing and a nervous anticipation for the coming school year.

Somewhere in the middle of her trek, Holly breezily waved back toward us, taking almost the same path Everett and I had made years before, when we hardly knew each other, but were connected by a sudden passion.

"Funny," Everett said as he waved back to her, then took my hand.

He didn't need to explain.

That night, a moth fluttered outside the screen in my window. I had kept my small desk lamp on since Everett was still adjusting himself into my bed. A warm breeze wafted over us from the window as I stripped down to my underwear and stood over the bed. Although he had slept over several times, I still marveled at his presence, so relaxed.

"You're very lucky," he said as I lay down beside him.

"To have you? I know."

"No, I mean your family."

"Oh. Yeah."

"They're just so comfortable with us."

"They are." I leaned in and kissed him, realizing that despite their understanding, I still felt a bit awkward being affectionate with Everett in their presence. Kissing and touching him held so much meaning for me, but still felt more comfortable in private.

And yet, he had a point. How many other couples like us got to do this? I didn't know. The few gay people we had met in Philadelphia were all single.

Everett had described the few gay and lesbian students he'd met at a Penn meeting after the attack on a student. He said they were frustrated and concerned, but none of them were in relationships.

Everett's roving hand pulled me back from my distracted thoughts. Everything might change once we began living together again.

But I had to put such thoughts aside. As we quietly giggled and rustled about, while knowing any sounds wouldn't bother my parents in the next room, our attempts to soften our caresses made them more intense. Pressing close to him, I felt a new desire, slower but more secure, a new anticipation for our life ahead, while that moth kept fluttering against the screen.

Chapter 22
October 1981

Our new 'home sweet home' proved to be as comfortable as we'd hoped. With the Penn campus only a few blocks away, Everett managed to get to classes with relative ease.

The tedium of my trolley and train commute to and from the Temple campus was countered by Everett's affectionate daily farewells; a kiss in the privacy of our new home, with a more platonic light hug on the street when our morning departures matched.

We shared enthusiastic greetings when I returned to find him toying with Mrs. Kukka's expansive array of kitchen equipment as he prepared a simple yet deftly served dinner. Other late afternoons I'd find him in the cozy living room, studying or napping on the sofa, his chair nearby. With an almost tranquil smile, he'd remind me that it was my turn to cook with, "What are you making for dinner, darling?"

We became domestic.

As Everett and I figured out a routine in those first joyful weeks, we got to know Mrs. Kukka as a kind if not eccentric woman. She had been more than reasonable to hold the room for us over the summer and not charge rent, despite inviting us to leave some of our stuff there.

I had only been upstairs once, when she asked me to move some boxes. The middle room had a small kitchen, and I could see her bedroom in the front. But the door to the room above our bedroom was closed. She mostly kept to herself, with occasional visits to the kitchen.

But the small house was old, and creaked a little. Fortunately, Mrs. Kukka's bedroom was in the front of the upstairs, yet her padded feet above us squeaked a few floorboards. On weekends, her early morning routine nearly prevented the need for Everett's alarm clock.

Early one brisk October Saturday morning, the sounds of her preparing something in the kitchen woke me.

Everett was not holding me when I awoke, nor I him. The sheets, a tangled mess, contorted between us, left our legs exposed. I sat up, my stomach growling already, my bladder pressing for relief against my stomach.

"Good morning!" our landlady called out from the kitchen as she spotted me cross the hallway to the bathroom.

Holding in my need to pee, I shyly approached her as she fussed with a gurgling coffee machine.

"Oh. Thank you. I was just on my way to—"

"Yes, yes, don't let me interrupt. I'm on my way out."

She seemed a bit distracted. I headed back down the hall.

"Oh!"

"Yes?" I turned.

"There was some article in *The Times*, I can't recall. Something about, well, of concern for your community. I'll have to look it up."

"Okay. Thanks."

She returned upstairs as I ducked into the bathroom. My hunger outweighed my need for a shower, and Everett joined me in the kitchen.

"What was she going on about?" he rolled in, also still in his sweatpants and a T-shirt.

"Who knows?"

Everett dismissed it. "Probably some gay-friendly resort in Borneo."

"There was something in the newspaper. She has a lot of stuff up there."

As we settled at the table to eat, we heard Mrs. Kukka coming down the stairs again. Wearing a coat, but looking a bit distracted, she hovered near the table.

"Couldn't find it. Perhaps Rosita moved it."

She inquired about our studies, and after reminding us of her upcoming pre-Thanksgiving party, to which we were invited, she left us with a cheery farewell.

As we cleaned up in the kitchen, Everett asked, as if merely curious, "Have you met the maid yet?"

"No, have you?"

"Once, for a minute. Remember when I got caught in the rain?"

"Yeah."

"And you were at classes all day."

I nodded as I rinsed dishes.

"I got out of the bathroom and she was mopping the hallway, muttering, 'De wheels, de wheels,' then pointed to my treadmills."

"Oh." I pondered a response. "Was that... did you feel offended?"

"No, I thanked her," he said. "She was just showing me what she does for a living." He shut a cabinet door with a slap of finality.

Everett's affection for Helen, his family housekeeper back in Greensburg, didn't match up with his dismissive attitude toward Rosita, our new mystery maid. And as quickly as he abandoned the subject, he changed it again.

"So, I'm off to Magee. Wanna come with me?"

"For your rehab?"

"Actually, I only stop by for that every once in a while. I need to do some recruiting."

"For what?"

"You'll see."

Since it was only a few blocks from City Hall, I had met up with Everett several times after his physical therapy sessions at Magee Rehabilitation Center, and a few times after his occasional gathering with his basketball teammates. But I'd never been inside for long.

The stout brick building, set on a side street not far from the highway, had an adjoining parking garage, which Everett eased into.

"Can you get the flyers?" he said as he transferred from the driver's seat to his chair.

Everett greeted the woman at the reception desk before heading for the elevator.

"Thanks for coming," he said, smiling, almost eager.

With a sort of pride, Everett toured me around each floor of the building. The first was quiet, more like a hospital. On the second floor, he led me into a large room with about a dozen people sitting or lying on a series of large square padded tables. Each patient had a therapist who helped them with exercises. Some tossed balls a few feet, others had their legs stretched, while a few more struggled across a few parallel bars with braces.

Almost overwhelmed, I calmed as Everett greeted several people, waited for others to finish their tasks, then followed him as he chatted up several people. With each interaction, he handed them one of the flyers.

After finishing with tacking a few flyers on bulletin boards on each floor, he handed me the last of them.

"And one for you."

As part of the United Nation's International Year of Disabled Persons, Alpha Chi Rho, one of the Penn fraternities, had joined up with the United Way to organize an event in two weeks at Fairmount Park called Runfest, which would include a wheelchair race.

Scheduled for an early morning, I at first shied away from considering it, since I hadn't run seriously in months. But as usual, Everett had already gotten application forms. Despite his usual cynical dismissal of such "touchy-feely" events, he had engaged me with a dare, claiming he could beat me in the race.

"Fine. Let's do it," I said as I followed him down another hallway and into the elevator.

"Maybe we can meet some cute jocks," he smiled.

"Like the ones you flirt with at the gym?"

"I don't flirt. I'm just friendly."

"You're a regular belle of the balls."

I noticed the elevator was going up. "You pressed the wrong button."

"No, I didn't. Come on. You gotta see the roof."

"The roof? It's freezing outside."

"It is not."

The air was brisk, but he was right, it wasn't too cold. The view of the downtown buildings, City Hall and nearby parks did offer a terrific view.

"They used to play basketball up here, believe it or not. Now," he scooted around a corner, and I followed. "They mostly work out here."

Set before us was a series of recreated curbs and sidewalks. "Folks have to learn how to navigate," he huffed as he hopped his wheels up and down the ramps and curves. Finally finished, he wheeled over to the edge of the roof.

"Come 'ere." He waved me over until I was beside him. "Closer."

I understood, leaned down for a kiss, bashful for a moment. Our breath escaped in misty trails.

"It's okay. There's nobody else up here."

I felt his comfort there, his sense of being, and understood how it energized him. We kissed some more, and he toyed with my ears. "Cold."

"Good cold."

I could have stayed with him there until the shivers overtook us, but he had other plans.

After we left, Everett pulled out of the parking garage, steered carefully onto the street, and said with a casual air, "Do you know anyone who smokes pot?"

"Why?" I asked.

"Um, to get high?"

At first I thought he was joking, but Everett explained.

"It might help us with the back end merchandise." Another euphemism for 'the butt sex.'

"I don't need to do that."

"But I want you to. You get ... amorous."

He was right. I did get more excited under the spell of a pot high, but I sometimes lost myself and forgot to be careful with him.

"Well, it works on you, at least."

He did have a point. But I dismissed it, at first. "You should have gotten some from Kevin when we were in Greensburg. We can't smoke it in the house anyway. Mrs. Kukka would smell it."

"I know. Just. Okay, whatever."

A few minutes passed, each of us looking at the traffic and passing buildings as we drove through downtown and back to the house.

Then, not at all unrelated, but chirped by Everett in a bald-faced attempt to make it seem so, "How's your friend Devon?"

"Wait. You think Devon knows how to get pot because he's Black?"

"No. Your implied racism contravenes economic probability."

"What?"

"He lives in West Philly. Statistically, it figures. Plus he's my friend, too." Everett braked at a light, the van lurched to a halt.

"I haven't seem him in months."

"Neither have I. He doesn't go to Magee anymore. He doesn't play basketball. That's my crip crew. I don't– Just…"

"Fine. Whatever. I'll call Devon." He drove, humming some tune I couldn't recognize.

We shared code words in front of guys we considered befriending, or whose company we preferred to leave, like when some drunk guy would half-sob out a sympathy pity-patter Everett couldn't stand. And, there were a few out-and-out jerks. It was college.

There were also guys who withheld their pervy intentions, so we cautiously befriended a few. We hadn't sorted that out yet.

But the real stares were in the gym. I spotted Everett, helped him hold steady as he grunted, pushed and pulled on bars and weights. Other athletes looked on, admiringly or just curious.

Some of those fit guys got to see us naked together, me in the next shower stall, or sometimes with Everett, between transfers to and from his chair. Guys sometimes stared at us from a distant stall.

Training gave me an excuse to touch him. We enjoyed being seen. Despite the exhibitionistic tickle we both shared, being naked together offered a feeling of liberation, Everett refusing to hide, and me with him. And that had an allure, sometimes made clear by the pointed interest aimed at us by certain guys.

One of those guys befriended us as we left the gym. His point of entry was being in Everett's Poly Sci class.

With a few casual introductions that dodged his having cruised us in the gym, Rodger "with a D," told us he lived off campus and he and his several housemates were hosting a party that Friday night. What kind of party it would be left me confused.

"A lot of creative types'll be there," Everett repeated one of our inside jokes. "It'll be fun."

Everett seemed to be waiting for my response.

"What?" Everett blurted as I stood, waiting for him to continue rolling until after he'd stuffed a piece of paper with Rodger's phone number and address into his backpack.

"Oh, nothing. It's just fascinating to watch as some 'creative type' hits on you right in front of me."

"It's just a party. I should invite Gerard."

"Sure," I shrugged it off as we continued on our way.

"Besides," Everett added. "What makes you think he was just hitting on me?"

Blondie's "Accidents Never Happen" blared from the house as we approached the daunting porch steps. Neighbors in the nearby row houses in the run-down off-campus area didn't seem to mind the noise.

Since the house was only six blocks away on Pine Street, and our intended goal was to get drunk, stoned, or both, we decided not to drive the van.

As we reached the steps of the row house, he said, "Are we ready?"

"I suppose," I sighed as I backed up toward his chair. Everett wrapped his arms around my neck. I pulled him up behind me, spied a ratty lawn chair on the porch, placed him delicately onto it, then trotted down the stairs to retrieve his chair.

Two other guys entering the house offered curious stares, then a too-late, "Need any help?" to which I replied, "I got it. Thanks."

After we entered, to a few more glances, Gerard gave us a friendly wave, amid a cluster of green and red-dyed hairstyles on girls who smoked cigarettes. The guys varied, from overdressed imps to generic frat types ("The theatre techies," Gerard later explained to us. "They're all hot; and straight.")

Even though the music continued blaring, the cigarette and marijuana smoke filling the air, conversations halted for the briefest moment, until Everett rolled ahead of me into the main living room, where he found some space beside a sofa after I slowly pushed back an end table.

There seemed to be an air of contrived bohemia among the party guests. I noticed a few other daring fashion attempts, and a few of the more high-pitched laughs and hoots were coming from men as well as women.

We sat, established our space. I'd learned not to rush to get drinks, knowing I'd be left hovering nearby as a cluster of curious new fans would have already gathered around my boyfriend.

And, as anticipated, our host Rodger happened by and offered to get us drinks.

Everett's attention was drawn to a coffee table in front of the sofa, where a small pile of sifted marijuana, papers and a small bong sat atop the cover of a Soft Cell album.

Some chubby guy finished with his sincere yet unoriginal compliments about Everett being "cool" for "getting out" despite his "handicap," words that made Everett veil his mild annoyance with a smile.

Not bothering to wait for an invitation, I retrieved the bong, stuffed it, lit it, and handed it to him as Rodger returned with two plastic cups of beer.

"Digging in already, huh?"

"It seemed the polite thing," I smirked as the smoke escaped my mouth. Everett toked, handed me the bong, then puckered his lips, signaling me to lean in for a shotgun kiss.

My lips were dry, so I took a gulp of beer, quietly happy inside to feel comfortable enough, or carefree enough, to kiss him. We toasted. The high settled around us like a blanket.

Everett generally let others circulate around him. People were kind, offering yet another beer, a slice of pizza, a napkin. He took it in with thanks. I endured the same questions, or the conversations that skirted around their most basic avoided inquiries, some of which had been clarified by our kiss.

"Let me know if, you know if you need to cut in the bathroom line," I offered.

"I'll be fine."

"Just one more beer."

"Yes, sir!"

Our figures of speech for bodily functions had become rather expansive. Everett, a few times, despite knowing beer would do it, had offered various whimsical code words for our need to excuse ourselves at gatherings, or his sudden rush to the bathroom. "Time to see man about a horse," became "the dogs have left the kennel," and the more succinct, "Shit happened."

As the evening grew on, someone put on the television and we watched a series of music videos on the new station, MTV. Gerard plopped himself down beside me on the sofa. His eyes were as pink as his skinny tie.

"Oh, here's a new show I'm coordinating next Saturday." He handed me a red flyer with black text and graphics, zigzagged magazine clippings photocopied alongside the barely legible words for a show at some nightclub on South Street.

"Thanks," I said, putting the flyer on the coffee table. "But we're both gonna be up at the crack of dawn for this race event."

"Oh, Everett's going to cheer you on?"

"No. We're both competing. There's a wheelchair race, too."

"Oh. Quelle butch. Anyway, you guys having fun?"

Everett saluted. I nodded. We began to loosen up, and offered a plastic cup salute.

"Oh, I love this song!" Gerard hooted as the B52s' "Private Idaho" induced someone to raise the volume.

We nodded along as the roomful of heads bobbed, and Gerard began rattling off the upcoming concerts he'd be going to, to which we could be invited, it seemed, if I played nice.

"Everything's happening now. It's so," he gestured toward the TV screen, some muted new music video. "Fast."

"Really?"

"Yeah, I mean, sure; Reagan's in. But people are fighting back, making change…"

There had been several anti-Reagan rallies on both the Temple and Penn campuses, but I didn't see what good they would do. I offered a dismissive comment. "With flyers for art rock fashion shows?"

Gerard offered a withering glare. "You know, I know you don't like me. I just don't know why."

"Wait. What?"

I didn't add how surprised I was that he hadn't tried to squeeze himself next to Everett on the sofa. I simply never got up.

I faced him, spoke softly. "Look. I like that you're our friend. Just know that I think you're fabulous and we really like being out and everything, you know … out. But Ev and I are together, like, really close, and you have no idea what it took to keep that, for both of us."

"I'm sorry. I–"

"It's okay. Just…" I simmered. "Just be our friend."

"Okay."

"Okay?"

"Okay."

"Now tell me more about this rock fashion show or whatever it is."

But as Gerard unspooled a series of talented acts, amid some pedantic assessment of "cultural zeitgeist," as he called it, I was really half-listening to Everett talk up to a guy standing beside him. He was telling yet another artful fib, and had cued me in when he'd crept his hand across the sofa like a spider to tickle my exposed lower back.

I tilted my head as Everett wove another increasingly fanciful tale to explain his injury; a train derailment, wild game hunting, and a new one, "Blimp wreck. Oh, the humanity!" Watching their befuddled reactions was his form of sport.

I turned to him, grinned sarcastically, "I love that story."

I excused myself to find the bathroom, after Gerard spun off to some late-arriving friends. A random girl who parked beside me inspired a seesaw-like reaction. "Save my seat, please?" She nodded consent.

As I considered my ability to relieve myself in such a tiny bathroom, with a line of people waiting, Rodger sidled up to me in the hallway line.

"You guys having fun?"

"As well as can be expected."

"What's wrong?"

"Nothing, it's just…" I really had to use the toilet, and didn't care to explain.

"Hey, there's another bathroom upstairs," he said, tugging at my sleeve. I followed Rodger, and turned back to see Everett chatting with the girl who'd scooted in my place on the sofa. He saw me, offered an apologetic shrug. I nodded my head, then rounded the stairs to follow our host.

After using the bathroom, I found Rodger waiting for me in the hall. He led me to another room; his, I guessed.

He didn't waste more than a minute after the door was closed before his mouth attached itself to mine.

It did feel good to kiss a guy while standing, almost dancing around the room, he trying to lead me toward his bed, me diverting his moves. He didn't understand, wouldn't understand, how different it felt, why I consented, allowed this, knew this was inevitable.

Finally pulling apart, he surveyed me, pawing under my shirt. "You guys were so hot in the gym."

"Thanks."

"You a couple?"

"Yeah."

"We should get together."

"What? You want me to haul him up here so you can–"

"That'd be hot."

"Maybe some other time."

He pressed himself close again, reaching, grabbing. I wanted to kneel, feel the banal thrill of clamping my arms around a guy's legs, full muscled legs, risk being thrown off-balance. I didn't.

"I should–" I pulled away.

"Lemme know if–"

"Yeah, that's probably not gonna happen."

As I trotted downstairs, I adjusted my pants and the contrary opinion of my erection.

Everett's new friend was still doing most of the talking when I returned to his side with a fresh beer. He took it, leaned up and, with a single brief kiss, pretty much gave her the cue to exit.

"How we doin'?" I asked.

"Uh, the music's good. The beer sucks. What was that?" Everett nodded toward the stairs.

"Our host wanted to show me his etchings."

"And?"

"You're right again. He's definitely…interested."

"Oh, well, shut my mouth."

"Let's go out on the porch. The smoke's getting to me."

"Hmm." Everett adjusted himself into his chair.

The air was brisk, but our jackets sufficed. We sipped our beers. I sat on the rickety lawn chair beside him.

"You know, we need to set some parameters."

"For what?" I asked.

"If you want to... explore some purely recreational options."

"Like what? Bowling?"

"Sex. Other sex."

"I don't want to have this conversation right now." It would have been perfect timing, what with me washing down Rodger's tongue action with the beer. "I'm not– He's not– I was joking, and he's really drunk."

"Well, I'm not."

"Drunk or joking?"

I simmered, felt more exposed for having tasted the possibility. I just wanted to protect Everett from any difficult reactions from a guy like Rodger.

"Fine. You wanna go back in, grab a guy for the night? I'll see you at home. You know the apartment we moved into? Together?"

"It's not like we're married. We can't even get married."

"Yeah, but we should trust each other."

"That's exactly my point! You're my everything! *Mon raison d'etre*! Anything else would just be like ...dessert!"

A few other people had come out on the porch, and gave us a concerned glance.

"You're shouting."

Everett leaned in, softened his voice. "It's just... Things are getting a bit predictable."

"What do you want to do? It's not like we can just sneak into a museum or the woods like... before."

"Wow."

"Sorry."

"No, you're right. You've been so great. It's just... it's just sex, Reid. It's not love."

"Which is my point."

"Okay, but I just think it's gotten a little..."

"Predictable. Got it."

He shrugged.

"Well, maybe next time, you can give me some pointers instead of just chowing down on my dick and shoving me off you when I want to get you off, too."

"Fine. Let's go. Me and Mister Pee Buddy should get home."

As I helped Everett out of his chair and into the lawn chair, the others on the porch intervened, offering assistance. I directed him to take Everett's chair down the steps, placed him back onto it, and we rolled off down the street. All the while, I secretly wished I could abandon him for the night, walk off in a huff.

That was when we saw her, on some dark side street. Still a bit inebriated, I at first mistook her for some sort of shaggy dog foraging on hind legs in a garbage can. But when she turned to face us, a ragged homeless woman in dirty clothes, we both were stunned by a ravaged, crazed stare in her eyes.

She took one look at Everett, shivered or convulsed, and uttered some unintelligible shriek of fear.

"Cripple! Cripple, cripple, goddamit!"

"Fuck!" Everett shouted back. "Fuck you, bitch!"

I didn't know what to do; protect him, shove his chair away from her, or scream back with him. I chose the latter.

But before we could shout back again, she'd already waddled away in a babbling trail of profanity.

"Damn. What a buzzkill," Everett offered in an attempt to gloss over our confusion.

"That was … odd."

"These are the people in your neighborhood!" he sang, as he adjusted to yet another bump in the cracked sidewalk.

After the night of the party, we swore off anything unhealthy for the next week.

My nearly abandoned competitive spirit saw a small surge as I eyed the competition, dozens of people warming up in Fairmount Park for the Runfest.

Even though the race was for charity, and all in good fun, my high school memories of cross-country races flooded back. Runners of all kinds stretched, flexed their legs and sipped last gulps of water as more than a hundred runners clustered before the starting line. Behind us the Museum of Art and its imposing staircase loomed.

The early morning chill had many others rubbing their hands and trying to keep warm. With my sweatpants still on, I cautiously wove my way through a crowd of wheelchair racers, who would start later. Everett was in the middle, chatting with a few others.

"Hey, you ready?" I asked him.

"Ready as I'll ever be. You running in those?" Everett wore a smart dark blue tracksuit and a pair of fingerless gloves.

"I was hoping you could stuff them under your chair."

"And roll with the added weight?" he scoffed. "Fine. Take 'em off."

Feeling a little self-conscious as the only standing person in the cluster, I yanked my sweats down, and Everett folded them, then shoved them under his seat pad.

"See you at the finish?" I said.

"Yeah, I'll be waiting for you!"

That got a laugh from a few others.

The idea of running a full marathon daunted me, so I had signed up for the ten-kilometer race. I'd put on a few pounds, and worried that despite our hasty few weeks of practice and gym workouts, I might tank.

But once the starting gun shot off, and the herd of runners took off around me, I eventually found a good pace while dodging others.

At first, the pounding hurt; it always did in the beginning. But once I got my breathing under control, and was able to glance up at the colorful autumn leaves, the race was half over before I noticed how many people had passed me. I cheated a glance back. Far beyond the others in my category, I saw a cluster of chairs approaching in the distance.

Part of me wanted to fall back, just run alongside Everett, competition be damned. But I turned back, got a good kick, dodged a runner who had stumbled, and kept going.

By the time the first of the wheelchair racers approached the finish line, I had recovered from the dry heaves, managed to stand, gulp some water, and wait for Everett to approach. Viewers cheered and clapped, and I checked the times.

The mean, determined look on his face stunned me. I had seen it on him during a few tense moments at his basketball games. But something about that last long haul just got to me, and I found myself screaming for him as he narrowly edged out another racer.

I brought him a bottle of water as he veered off to the side so others could speed by. The cold sweat and pounding of his chest almost frightened me as we hugged.

"You did good, Monkey."

"Hell yeah, I did," he panted.

We stayed for the kids' race, and the numerous awards. Everett had placed among the top ten, and held up his little ribbon for a few photographers.

"Here," he scooted his butt, extracted my sweatpants, which were wrinkled and damp. But I didn't care. The sheer elation overtook our exhaustion. As we cooled down, hands were shaken, palms were high-fived.

"That was great," he said after we tumbled back into the van and headed home. Everett had shared phone numbers with several of the other racers, and I knew that although it was great for us to be together competing, he had found a kinship beyond his basketball teammates, an expanded idea of a community.

Chapter 23
November, 1981

'Ninety percent of 9,700 bird species mate for life. In mammals, only three percent of nearly 4,000 species are reported to remain monogamous through their mating. Among that list are bald eagles, beavers, ba n owls, red-ta led h wks k'

The electric typewriter ribbon had nearly run out. My paper on native species for Principles of Zoology 101 had become a bit sidetracked as well, so I was relieved when Everett popped a question during the pause in my typing. Of course, I was already thinking about him, and us, in comparison.

Only weeks before, on a race to crank out several midterms, he'd run through three ribbons on the typewriter, until some wing of the library offered what he derisively called "Computing for Crips," a city-funded course. That way, he got to print it out in sputtering reams of hole-punched paper, just not at home.

I was distracted by the music Everett had decided to play during our study session. A perky, almost magical sound distracted me as well as the imminent death of the typewriter ribbon.

"Who is this we're listening to?" I asked, a bit loudly, since I was in the dining room where a small desk had become our typing space.

Everett sat on the floor, a few throw pillows under his folded legs. He had just had a new wheelchair delivered, and decided to adjust a few parts. The wheels, body, and various tools lay on the floor before him. The front room had almost become our second home. With the trees across the street bleeding down to ochres and russets, the day's sun filled the room.

"Benjamin Britten; composer and notable deceased homosexual!"

I rose, walked to him. "Note-able. A pun?"

"Oh, I get it," he deadpanned.

"Pretty snazzy ride ya got there." I parked myself on the floor by his new chair and toyed with a wrench.

He tossed a rag at me. "Make yourself useful." He pointed to the other wheel. I reached for it, handed it to him and watched, fascinated as he fit the pieces together, snapped and twisted a few parts, then reached under the seat to pull the brakes. As he hoisted himself up and onto the seat, he hopped around a bit, adjusted a cushion, then released the brakes, and broke into a spinning wheelie.

"Damn!"

I remembered the first time I saw Everett's first chair, looming in a corner at his makeshift downstairs bedroom back in Greensburg. At the time, it had represented a gloomy moment of finality. He had since gotten a newer model, similar to his new one. But his active life had worn that one down in little more than a year, and the Runfest, he told me, had pushed his old chair's limits.

Without the old-fashioned armrests and push handles, the angled wheels and new frame gleamed in the afternoon sunlight.

"It's so much lighter, and the camber's better."

"You should get some decals."

"Oh, like a flaming skull? It's not exactly a Harley."

"Maybe a flaming nerd."

"Pretty sweet." He rolled over to the dining room into the kitchen, then scooted down the hallway and back to me. "So, a shopping trip is in order this weekend?"

"I could just go to the student center for the cartridges."

"No, no. Let's make a day of it," he announced. "Haircuts and shopping. New chair, new hair."

"Haircuts? When did that come into it?"

Everett wheeled over to a small stack of newspapers on the floor by the sofa. He had been reading a local weekly newspaper, the *Philadelphia Gay News*. I had seen it, and read a few copies, but Everett was more interested in it since attending a few meetings of the gay and lesbian student group at Penn. In addition to his studies, he read through local newspapers, keeping up on current events, suggesting a movie or play to attend.

"Did you know there's a gay bookstore?" he said turning a page of the newspaper to show me an ad.

"I did know that."

"How could a pair of brainiac homos like us not have visited it before?"

I shrugged. Being boyfriends with Everett, and having a few gay friends, felt like more than enough. Shopping for stuff to be more gay hadn't occurred to me.

But I had asked him what he wanted for Christmas, and he knew. My previous year's gift of a small necklace, similar to ones he'd begun wearing, was met with mild appreciation. He wore it often enough, but with my comparatively small funds, I thought just openly asking him what he wanted would be better.

"Yeah, we should get some snazzy new haircuts. There's a salon Gerard goes to. It's right near the gay bookstore."

Gerard had bragged about his plans to move off-campus at the end of the semester, after befriending a pair of older gay men who shared a swanky apartment near Rittenhouse Square. Even when he wasn't around, he called every weekend to lure us, or more precisely, called Everett with me as an afterthought, with invitations to an eighteen-and-over dance night, a coffee house, a music concert or a poetry reading. After a few times, I just let Everett go without me, claiming I had to study.

"We can get New Wave haircuts. We're looking a little seventies."

I actually liked Everett's hair longer, especially on weekends when he skipped shaving. The beard he'd grown at summer camp made him look more masculine and sexy. I also liked the feel of his face, but knew he preferred a clean-cut look when he had debates or yet another photo shoot for the university's public relations department.

My own longer hair was a bit dated, but being self-conscious about my jug ears, I preferred my hair long. Still, he asked for it, so I relented. "Okay, let's be trendy; change our... plumage."

He made appointments for us on Saturday. He drove the van a few blocks to the student center, where I got a few ribbons and more paper while he waited at the curb, then drove the dozen blocks to Center City, the quaint part of town with a lot of historic brick townhouses. Every home, adorned with small shrubs or potted plants, seemed to hold a bit of Americana, shaded by elms along the sidewalks. I could almost imagine horses and carriages maneuvering the narrow streets.

But most of the shops' front doors included a few steps, making casual shopping a challenge. Everett seemed to ignore the barriers, and instead narrowed our selections.

The receptionist and hairstylists saw Everett, and at first seemed a bit put off by his chair. But when he hoisted himself from his own into the salon chair, and I scooted his wheelchair off to the side wall, the lengthy bib wrapped around his neck and Everett and the stylist chattered away about plans for his new 'do.

Shortly afterward, as I leafed through a copy of *Rolling Stone* from a stack of magazines, a voice called out my name, and a woman welcomed me to her barber chair.

"So, what look are we going for? Something new? It looks like your friend's getting a makeover."

"Yeah, he wants to look like a rock star, I guess."

"And what rock star do you want to look like?"

"Just a minute." I got up, retrieved the *Rolling Stone*, flipped to a page, and found an article on a new British band called Madness, whose lead singer looked rather handsome.

I pointed. "That'll do."

"You got a flat top?"

"So?" I said, as I helped Everett down the two steps of the salon and onto the sidewalk.

"No, it looks great. It's just a little old-fashioned."

"You said 'rock star.'"

"So, am I 'rock star?' Whaddaya think?" Everett coyly turned his head in a few directions.

Sheared at the sides, with a wavy sort of pompadour on top, he looked…over-coiffed.

"Kinda Duran Duran, right?"

I wanted to say, the missing member of that band; their poodle. But then I remembered my mother's words of relationship advice: 'You don't have to be honest about everything.'

"You look very stylish."

"You don't like it."

"I do like it," I said. I just knew I wasn't going to make out with him until I'd hosed off all that hair gel.

The door to Giovanni's Room had two cement steps, so I opened the door, then backed Everett's chair up and into the bookstore. A friendly bald older man with an earring asked if we needed any help.

"We're fine," I said, as Everett turned and took the place in.

"I can get you something from upstairs," he offered.

"Thanks," Everett smiled. "We'll just look around first."

It looked like a home converted into a store, like many in the historic neighborhood. A few of the aisles were a little tight, so I brought him a few books he couldn't reach. The array of titles overwhelmed me at first, books with shirtless men on the covers, lesbian health books, and further off, an entire shelf of porn magazines.

"Check this out." Everett handed me a large paperback with large curling letters on the cover.

"*The Joy of Gay Sex*?" I whispered.

"I figure we could get a few pointers."

"'An intimate guide for gay men to the pleasure of a gay lifestyle.' Does it include decorating tips?" I joked as I flipped through it, opening it to a page with a drawing of two guys going at it in an entirely unfamiliar position. The chapter heading read 'Fisting.'

"Woah." I handed the book back to him.

"Prude." He perused it as if it were a textbook.

"Do you have any complaints?" I muttered.

"No, it's just, you know, we do have… challenges."

"Yeah, but—"

"It's what I want for my birthday."

"Your birthday's in February."

"Okay then; an early Christmas present."

"Fine."

"Besides, I have a feeling you're going to enjoy this as much as I will."

The eager clerk appeared before us. "You sure you gentlemen don't need any help?"

"He needs a little Gay 101," Everett said as he handed the clerk the sex book. "And I need an owner's manual."

He also ended up buying himself a small stack of books, magazines and a videotape that he said was "a surprise."

When Carl, a Masters student in medicine, had approached Everett and asked him to participate in a study using massage, hydrotherapy and a different series of exercises, he had given Everett a small chart of a human body's nervous system to use when he made notes of any changes in sensation.

While he'd said he felt healthier, and energized, I wondered how he would feel when the semester ended, and the Masters student, Carl, whom I'd never met, and pretty much didn't want to, went on his studious way elsewhere. Who was he to get Everett's hopes up when he'd already adapted, really begun to challenge himself, and others, by accepting who, or how, he was?

Yet Everett had become focused, with some sardonic jokes, on the possibility of regaining sensation in his lower body. He repeatedly pointed at the chart when the subject arose, with a hokey Ironside-like impersonation.

"Sir, may I provide the evidence."

Over our desk hung the body chart of spinal nerve connections, how one vertebra's nerves connect with different areas of the body. Everett had it enlarged at the copy shop. His amusement was about less than research, but more probably because the lower checklist included the odd phrase, which he announced in Lawyer-ese, "Anal Stimulation? Yes or No?"

Basically, I think he wanted to try fucking some sensation back into his tush. I blamed the porn. All those positions just made him competitive.

Everett had installed a videotape machine sent by his father. It was one of many appliances and comforts that would randomly show up via UPS, signed by Mrs. Kukka, packed and waiting by our bedroom door; pillow cases, books, socks, pre-framed family portraits, and forwarded stacks of letters and cards from his former classmates. Everett dutifully placed them on a side desk in the alcove in our room.

After our shopping trip to the bookstore, I had to turn away from the smiling family portrait.

We were in the middle of our third rather intense attempt to enjoy more than about twenty minutes of *Fox Studio presents School Daze* when we halted abruptly at the sound of our landlady descending the stairs.

Everett discovered that he got excited from watching porn. We had to keep the volume down, because the apartment walls were a bit thin, and Mrs. Kukka, despite her easy nature, probably wouldn't appreciate the sounds of butt-slapping sex on tape. The sex sounds were dubbed from what seemed a silent film, and the music was awful, anyway. It was kind of creepy in silence, until I put some other music on and dimmed the light on the TV, which gave the room a harsh glare without another light on.

After watching the brightly lit butts getting plowed by glistening huge appendages, almost to the end, we were a bit wiped out, changed in a way.

Several positions had pretty clearly displayed themselves as being a lot of fun, but while watching the muscular oiled-up men, mostly we just lay there, a bit stunned. Maneuvering ourselves into those positions later was a little different. The gay sex book felt tame by comparison. The feelings from sex with Everett started in my head, fluttered through my chest, then stirred my body further down. Watching the videotape seemed to induce a strangely stiff erection with no connection to the rest of me.

"Spread your legs a little more."

"Like this?"

"Ow. Wait. Not on my arm."

"Sorry."

"Okay." His hand pushed my thigh. I adjusted a pillow under him, arched my back and, despite my misgivings, as he lay below me, I aimed my ass at my boyfriend's face.

"Oh. Oh, there it is."

"What?"

"Your butt, that's what!"

With an abrupt slap to my hindquarters, I quivered, then relaxed as I heard a familiar squirt of lubricant somewhere behind me. Perhaps it was his own lack of feeling in his rump, or a nostalgic craving for that New Year's Eve urgency when we had barely known each other, combined with the comparatively gymnastic porn video we'd watched.

Whatever the inspiration, Everett was determined to fully enjoy my ass. He couldn't exactly fuck me, but knew how to give me more than a bit of pleasure while having a sort of positional advantage under me.

While his own penis, inches from my face, had only sort of roused itself, I became quite erect as Everett began to toy with my butt. I had followed his instruction with a disposable douche kit, something he himself occasionally used for merely medicinal purposes. This time, it was all for him.

"Oh!" I squirmed again as one of his lubed fingers poked inside me. I felt his tongue grazing along my buttock on one side, then a playful bite. His other hand continued stroking my erection downward onto his chest.

"Enjoying the view?" I joked.

"Enormously," Everett mumbled before grabbing my hips and shoving me closer to his face.

And then I felt it, his tongue, exploring, darting, lapping, slathering around my butt. It was wonderful, giving myself to him, submitting. I dug my face between his legs, hoping for some reaction from his penis, which seemed to involuntarily respond to my touch. But it was really about his having his way with me. Our awkward position became more comfortable as I relaxed into this groin-to-groin juxtaposition.

And then, all too soon, as it happened whenever I truly let go and forgot all the difficult mechanics, and let Everett dig and probe and have his way, I spurted atop him, or at him. I wasn't sure where he was aiming my cock, until I felt his lips surround it, savoring it, humming with pleasure.

Settling atop him, I felt his hands rub my buttocks, caressing me with a sort of satisfaction, even though I knew he hadn't, and probably wouldn't, get anywhere near an orgasm.

After a few moments, I got up and wiped down with a towel. A sliver of guilt, that it has just been about me, about his desire to please me, brought me to curl up by his side and offer him a thankful kiss.

"You taste like butt."

"I refuse to hear a word of complaint," Everett shook a finger at me.

"I wasn't complaining."

"Good."

"I just wonder… Why do you like …doing that?"

"It's your body. You're just so vulnerable, spread like that, trusting me. You've got this little swirl of hairs. Also, you know, since I can't feel anything down there, it's fun to let you feel it."

"Okay."

"Satisfied?"

I nodded, because I was. But I didn't think he was, and I didn't know if he was content, or if he ever really would be.

Chapter 24
December 1981

"Are we supposed to give the cleaning lady a tip?"

Everett looked up from his book, a confused look on his face as we sat across from each other at our bedroom desk.

"We don't pay her," Everett said.

"So…"

"Have you even seen her?"

"No. That's why I'm asking."

Once a week, usually on Wednesdays, the kitchen and living room were cleaned, which I didn't exactly notice, except to find a few items moved around. Mrs. Kukka had mentioned the mysterious maid, and we opted out of having our room cleaned. But every now and then, a few stray cereal boxes would be neatly arranged or put away on a counter, and each of us, for a while, had thought the other had done the cleaning.

"I'll stick a twenty in a Christmas card," he said, dismissing it, and me.

"But what's her name again?"

"Rosita," he blurted without looking up.

I had thought about asking Mrs. Kukka about her maid when a few newspapers I'd wanted to save went missing. The *Daily Pennsylvanian* had published an article about Everett's debate team having won another tournament, but I couldn't find the paper.

I'd even gone to Penn's journalism department to get another copy. Proud to have retrieved it, Everett shrugged it off with a smile, and dropped the article into a box in the closet. We had finals for the end of the semester coming up, and he was more intent on studying than I was.

My copy of his little bit of print fame was above the wall near my side of the desk. It helped when we studied, because too often I would simply gaze at him as he did pushups atop his chair's seat. He pored over a textbook, reciting Latin in a soft voice.

"What?" he barked, forcing me to blush and turn away.

So I gazed at the picture of him instead, as a gift to myself between pages of note-taking on "Comparing the Values of Urban Forests in New Community Development." We had to do studies of trees in heavily populated areas, compared to parks and forests. For a few field trips, we went to the Ambler campus, forty-five minutes north by bus. Even after the blooms withered in the gardens, the mini-forests and a beautiful greenhouse were almost enchanting under an early winter snow.

I'd asked Everett if he'd like to go with me, but he kept postponing it. He was busy, and we liked studying. But that became difficult while knowing that I could just lean over at any moment, merely lick him once, and he'd shiver, and then we would kiss, and our academic routine would be tossed off with one touch.

The newest article included a photo of the entire debate team, all six of them, among them Everett, our friend Jacob, two Asian guys and two young women who, Everett had said, were "really smart, but they could do with a little makeover."

What struck me about the photo was that while the photographer had arranged Everett in the front row, no mention was made of his being in a wheelchair. I took that as a good sign, one of simple acceptance.

And yet, it reminded of the first time I had seen Everett's smiling face in newsprint. Back when I was in high school, the Greensburg local daily's usually innocuous news features had splayed the story about his lacrosse accident across the front page. Seeing the new version of him in the pages of his school newspaper brought out my pride, yet a bit of remembered fear.

Everett had simply glanced at it, and tossed it on his desk. "I was in the Pinecrest newsletter all the time," he shrugged. "It's no big deal."

My high school cross country efforts had also been documented, usually as just with an also-ran mention, twice in group photos, and saved in a scrapbook my mother kept back in Greensburg. True, in a way, it wasn't a big deal.

Apparently, it was a big deal enough for word to get around. Shortly after the article was published, we got a few odd phone calls.

The first few were hang-up calls. The second, a girl's voice, giggly, asked for Everett. When I said he wasn't in, but offered to take a message, the voice replied, "He's cute. Does he have a girlfriend?"

Apparently this member of his fan club hadn't also noticed his quote as a member of Lesbians and Gays at Penn about the group's plans to sue the university for discriminatory practices by letting the Army recruit on campus. Everett was quoted critiquing no less than Penn's President Hackney, and while a bit proud of it, he had also tossed that clipping into the same box.

I resisted the urge to bluntly state, "No, he has a boyfriend, and I'm it." But after a few giggles in the background, she had hung up.

Everett's indifferent response to my mention of these calls was simply, "I'll buy an answering machine." He didn't.

But the oddest of calls happened a few weeks later. Already defensive every time the phone rang, I offered a cautious, "Hello?"

"Yo, Mutt!"

"Excuse me?"

"This Forrester?"

"No. Who is this?"

"Who're you?"

"His roommate."

"Oh. Forrester in?"

"You mean Everett?"

"Yeah."

"No."

"When's he due back?"

Across town at basketball practice with his Magee teammates, I expected Everett to return within the hour. But I wasn't about to offer that information to someone who called my boyfriend 'Mutt.'

"He'll be back later," I said.

"Cool. I'll call back. Happy holidays."

"Okay. Happy–"

The line went dead. I stared at the phone, and considered unplugging it.

About an hour later, Everett did return, elated if not a bit exhausted.

"You didn't take the van?"

"One of the guys picked me up and drove me home." He casually tossed off his sweatshirt, took his backpack from his chair, and offered in a naughty tone, "Shower time?"

Although I didn't need one, I rarely missed an opportunity to bathe with Everett, particularly with such an obvious invite for a little wet affection. He didn't need my assistance, but I was happy to offer it, in exchange for some steamy shenanigans.

Not wanting to spoil the fun, I resisted the urge to ask about that mysterious caller until we'd enjoyed some soapy yet inconclusive fondling.

Dried off, our hair damp, we settled in, me at my desk, Everett sprawled on the bed, after having tuned in a classical radio station playing some Bach piano solos. Prepared for a contemplative evening, I was surprised when a while later, like some coy harem sheik, Everett coaxed me with, "Meester Kawn-neef?"

"Yes?"

His curled finger was all it took. It had been weeks since he'd deliberately invited me so bluntly. We held each other, kissed and began toyfully displacing clothing, when he leaned over and produced a tube of rubber.

"What is that?"

"Page 72; Cock Rings."

"Will it work?"

"I auditioned it while you were out on Thursday."

"Really?"

"Yes. You should get some lube, though. It ripped my ball hairs; not that I felt it."

Although not as spontaneous as we'd liked, I brought a few other items, a towel as well, and damned if the thing didn't work. Happy to see his cock stiffen, Everett eased me from our clamped sixty-nine to admire himself. I stroked him slowly.

"Pretty neat!" I knelt down to slide my tongue up and down his dick.

"I can't keep this up, though."

"Oh?" I leaned in, kissed him again, arched a leg over his waist and began humping his bobbing erection. I tried to keep my sexy kisses going along his neck as I shoved a few dabs of lubricant up my butt, then repositioned myself until I felt him slide up inside me. Tingles of pleasure shot up through me as I plunged onto his hips.

"What are we doing?" Everett asked.

"I think you're fucking me."

Everett tucked his chin up to enjoy the view, then sprawled back, gasping in relief, then back up on his elbows, grinned at me. "Page 34. So you've realized you're a bottom."

"That's not in the book!"

He reached up, pulling me closer to him, as I tried to maintain my awkward crouched position.

"Stop laughing," I smirked. "You're spoiling the mood."

"Just tryin' to get my rocks off before our holiday parting."

His hand behind my neck, he pulled my face back down toward his, and in between more kissing and giggles, we did, in our way.

A sweater.

It was a nice sweater. Although I already had a green one, at least it didn't have snowmen or reindeer on it.

The sweater wasn't the problem, nor was my gaggle of cousins, the eldest male demanding to show off his newly received arsenal of plastic weapons. I had years before been elevated to the adult table, so no cranberries would be flung my way at dinner.

My docile grandparents' compliments about the food, amply prepared by my equally ample aunt, were not a problem, although holding my tongue as she extolled the virtues of the First Lady, and her inspired new red dress and its accompanying shoulder pads, along with her interesting hairdo, might have been a problem, especially when she compared my mother to herself as "still skinny after all these years." That was Mom's battle.

No, the problem began with a seemingly innocuous question. Like the acoustics in the many rooms of their garishly large home that managed to be cluttered and empty at the same time, my uncle's question echoed for a moment before I replied.

"So, Reid. How's your, uh, roommate?"

It wasn't the leering grin my uncle added to his question. It was his inference of other knowledge that I knew neither of my parents would dare to divulge, not due to any embarrassment. No, it was the predicament of responding to, as Everett had said, "people who don't matter."

And yet, there it hung, the implication, the loaded question, the silent glance from each parent as a sort of warning.

"He's fine," I answered as deadpan as possible. "He's in Pittsburgh. I'm going there for New Year's."

"That's great. They do fireworks over the river, don't they?"

"Yes. His dad's apartment has a great view."

"He got a big place?"

"Not too big. But he bought the building with his real estate company, and he got one of the upper apartments for himself." I held back a bragging tone, even though bragging was an integral part of nearly all my uncle's talk; his bigger house, his bigger job, his bigger family.

"How many bedrooms it got?"

"Pete, how about we–" Dad attempted interference.

"Two," I blurted.

"So you–"

"Yeah, Uncle Pete, I sleep with him. And I sleep with him in Philly, too. You happy?"

The kids giggled. Mom tossed her napkin onto the table. "And you wonder why we only visit once a year."

"I was just asking about–"

"What's this?" Grandma chimed in.

Aunt Nancy practically shouted, "I'll put on the coffee!"

The cacophony of chairs scooting on hardwood floors, three arguments at once fell behind me as I left for the foyer closet, and my coat. Dad rushed up beside me.

"I'm going for a walk."

"Don't be long," he scolded.

"No, it shouldn't be long–"

"Good."

"–for me to walk back to the hotel."

"Reid."

"Dad." I saluted him, and then I walked off dinner, all the way back, after getting lost and having to find a gas station with a phone book to call the motel for directions.

The nearly silent drive home back with my parents the next morning halted around Stroudsburg with a heart to heart in the car, where Mom offered pointers on "understanding and tact."

Considering the small size of our home, it was surprising how quickly we each found separate spaces to relax after the trip. Dad busied himself with some project in the garage, Mom had lots of leftovers to sort through, and I parked myself on the couch, put on one of Dad's old jazz albums, and contemplated our new tree.

The metallic silver branches reflected more light than the prior real cut trees from prior years. The colors almost glared in the room, and several of the ornaments seemed to be lost in the metallic fringe.

"I don't know what to make of that," Dad said, standing with his head cocked to one side. "So, when are you off to Pittsburgh?" he asked.

"Day after tomorrow. Ev's got split parent visits, then they're going to some other relatives in Bradford Woods. I'm waiting for the all-clear."

Dad nodded, as if understanding, when I sensed that he didn't. So I blurted out, "If we were a straight couple, like engaged or something, not even that, I'd be invited to all that."

"Do you want to be invited to all that?"

"That's not the point, Dad."

"I know. I'm sorry. You know Everett's welcome here anytime."

"I know. You guys are so different. I am so lucky."

"We love having you home. We miss you."

"Thanks. I just…"

He looked at me, waiting for more. I wanted to beg him for an answer; how can I make a life with Everett if we're so disconnected, if half of the people in our lives are just waiting for him to outgrow me, to move on to whatever they think he should be, and the other half, my half, either refused to acknowledge us, or considered it worth innuendo-laden prying?

Instead, I declared, "That tree is hideous. It's like a robot tree."

"You bought it!" Mom chimed in from the kitchen.

Was it my duty to remain, to return, to fulfill their lives? And if so, for how much longer? I loved them for their casual wit, their amused nature toward this whole family concept, which was occasionally foiled by bursts of sincerity and honesty that could make me blush.

My anticipation to be away from all that, and on to Pittsburgh, was all that mattered. The now annual visits for a few days before and after New Year's had become a new tradition, as did disassembling our new wobbly silver tree.

New Year's Eve almost turned sour. I almost left him, all because he was honest with me.

We had settled in to the guest bedroom in his father's apartment, then, the night before the holiday, had dinner in the living room while watching a basketball game on the huge television. I maintained a moderate interest as Everett and his father cheered for the 76ers with enthusiasm.

After their predictable trouncing victory, his father bid us goodnight, and Everett handed over the remote.

"I vote that we just go to bed," I suggested.

"Seconded."

"Or the shower."

"Amended, but we better keep it down."

The next night, Holly showed up an hour early with a limo and two of her friends, ready for the party at the opera house. Holly had "borrowed" a pair of vintage tuxedos from the opera company's costume shop.

While we dressed, they got an early start at her father's bar. Then we poured ourselves into the limo, enjoying ourselves at the party for less than two hours, until Everett impulsively turned Cinderella, insisting that we make a mad dash back to the apartment, courtesy of the limo driver. Once back at his dad's, some nighttime antics took place timed with the fireworks.

Celebrating with a crowd of people had been fun, but we had managed to celebrate in private; well, semi-private. It felt like an audience, with his room lights off, the night skyline behind us, the curtains pulled wide. I strode across the room naked, and retrieved a bottle.

Everett had pilfered one of his father's 'spare' champagnes. Mr. Forrester and his girlfriend were, according to Ev, "having a ball in the ballroom, and again several flights up at the William Penn."

With their comparatively romantic setting paired with our own –the champagne, the view, and the connected, almost choreographed situation of it all– I appreciated how his family knew we were together, and gave us our space.

As he finished up in the bathroom, I stood at the large window, surveying the fascinating lights of the night skyline and the bridge lights beyond it. Had it really been two years since that first drive to Pittsburgh, where we had approached the city for the first time together, singing and smiling with anticipation?

"Hey. You're naked."

"Hey. You noticed."

I settled into the bed as he shifted from his chair, tugged his legs up and then under the covers. Despite its blandness, its sparse décor, the room had taken on a familiarity. I felt safe, comfortable with him.

"Where's the bubbly?"

"Oh." I got up, walked to the shelf by the door.

"You sure nobody can see us?" I asked as I hovered near the window.

"Only if we–" The light flashed on. I hurriedly turned around, grinning at him, then jumped upon the bed, where we fought over the light switch in and out of darkness.

Once our battle concluded, over another shared bottle swig, I asked him, "So, are you gonna live here?"

"I don't know. It's like they're each auditioning for me."

Mr. Forrester had repeated his offer of getting Everett a studio apartment in his building.

"I got an offer from Holly, too, in her new apartment, and from my mother," Everett. I had yet to visit his mother's home during these visits.

"What are you gonna do, flip a coin?"

Cozying up in bed, the curtains still open to enjoy the view, the champagne slightly slurring my words, I understood what he had said about the distance between his parents. For all its panoramas, the guest room felt cold, unfilled, still lacking any real character of Everett.

I asked him if he had thought of bringing more of his old things, trophies or old toys, to keep at his father's apartment.

But he shook his head. "This is 'new dad.' This is like, you know, homey like a hotel room; dormant. I don't think I can live with any of them, re-nest, you know?"

"Hmmm." I found his dilemma puzzling. I took my parents' welcome back for granted. Whenever, if I'd wanted to work at the nursery fulltime, I assumed they would be fine with it, for a few years, perhaps.

But they knew I had ambitions to leave Greensburg. I'd pretty much established that at my fifth birthday party, a story my mother told more than I remember. Inspired by some illustrated children's book, I had declared that I would one day 'live on a big mountain top in a forest by the sea.'

The parks and nature and wildlife and moss, those were all part of my future, even if my studies were mostly limited to books and igneous rocks. The idea of home was still my parents', but what Everett was already facing, in addition to the family guilt-trip triage, was the unmet goal of true independence.

"Besides," Everett mused. "Why redo the room for me? He's probably sizing it up for a nursery if he knocks up the girlfriend."

He sounded so sad to me. I offered a hug, hoping it would lead to more, despite the late hour, and our being slightly drunk.

"So, New Year's resolution; I want to tell you something, but I don't want you to be upset."

I sat up in bed, wondering what new surprise he had in store.

"Remember Kyle the gymnast?" he asked.

"Puppy dog eyes? Grapefruit-sized shoulders?"

"That would be him."

"Yes."

"Well, we'd been working out together. He's got all these amazing upper body routines, and he's so hyper."

"Yeah? Whatever happened to him?"

"This was, March?"

"And?"

"He came over to my dorm, just insisted on visiting."

"Insisted."

"Well, we kind of… He kind of privately showed me some of his moves, naked."

"Naked."

"He's very flexible."

"One would assume," I nodded, lips pressed together.

"It was just the one time. I promise it'll never happen again."

"What won't happen again?"

"We kind of had sex."

"Kind of." And then, an emptiness swept over me where anger or jealousy was supposed to flood in.

"He was showing off, and just curious about me, I guess." He explained the brevity of the act, and Kyle's comparative gymnastic upside-down talents.

"It was just a little, you know." He began mimicking the motion of an upside down blow-job, as if to joke about its inconsequence, while admiring its ingenuity.

"No, I don't know."

"It was fun. I don't feel guilty. But I am being honest."

"Why are you telling me this?"

"Because it happened, and I'm sorry I didn't tell you."

"Why be sorry? It sounds like you had fun."

Was I supposed to be angry, leave, shout at him? It all seemed rather inconvenient, it being late at night, and me unable to imagine leaving, what with being drunk and naked.

"You could, you know, have a little dalliance and it would be okay," he offered.

"A 'dalliance?' What the fuck is a dalliance?"

"I told you before. I want you to have a full experience. I don't want to hold you back."

"From what? You think sucking some other guy's dick is just extra credit?"

"It doesn't mean anything. He's... You should try it; have an adventure."

"An adventure. Is that what it is to you?"

"Yeah. It's like that Amish holiday. Rumspringa."

"I should go back to Holly's. I'm not feeling very Amish."

"No, Reid. Please. It didn't mean anything. It was just fun."

"Fun."

"Yes."

"All this 'fun' must be what's giving you some memory lapse. I fought for you, to keep you in my life."

"Thank you for reminding me, again."

"And it's also kind of an anniversary, which is like the worst time you could have admitted this." But what made me feel worse was how his admission cracked open my own door to infidelity.

"Yes. We stuck on New Year's Eve that first time," Everett said, then joked, "It was very sticky."

"You're impossible."

"I know. Let's be together. I promise. No more fooling around."

"Maybe I want to have a little, what did you call it? A dalliance?"

"What, as revenge?"

"To even the score."

The fact that he had managed to have an encounter with some elfin jock seemed unimportant, at least to him, and I was supposed to agree, because we were continually negotiating our place together in each other's lives.

Perhaps this was the moment where someone else might have stormed off and gone home. But where could I go in the middle of the night? And where was home; my parents house, where my old toys lived? The odd little room we rented in Philadelphia? And where was his home, where would I run from? Did he even know?

"Well, we might as well enjoy the view," I said as I rose from the bed.

"What are you doing?"

"You'll see."

And then, with half of the skyline before us, I repeatedly, somewhat drunkenly attempted, and finally succeeded in managing a naked handstand.

Chapter 25
January 1982

Driving back to Philadelphia, we agreed to stop just after Harrisburg, for lunch and a bit of "freaking out the locals," as Everett called it.

Interstate 76 Turnpike led us through drab industrial towns, but more green hills and mountains of pine and spruce forests. Despite the cold, I almost wanted to stick my head out of the window like a tongue-wagging dog.

"What say we have a little adventure?" Everett teased.

"What kind of adventure? I don't see any hitchhiking gymnasts."

"Keep calm; nothing too outrageous. Get out the map."

I obeyed, but didn't know what I was looking for.

"How do we get to Lancaster?"

I checked. "Route 283, then we can stay south on 30. You want what, to seduce an Amish boy?"

"Maybe. Look just past Lancaster."

I scanned the map, then found what I knew was his goal. "Intercourse?"

He grinned. "We have to go once. Do you have the camera Holly gave you?"

"Yep." Holly had given me one of her older 35-millimeter cameras as a Christmas present. Although she apologized for offering what she called a hand-me-down, I was thrilled. It was better than the cheap Instamatic I'd been using, and Everett and I had been taking more pictures together.

I folded the map to isolate our route, and shook my head. "You planned this."

"Well? Come on, it'll be fun. We can take pictures in front of a road sign."

He was trying to cheer me up, remind me that we were still a couple, that I was more important than anyone else, and still able to have fun.

Due to the season, and the record freezing temperatures, we found few tourist attractions open, but we did stop at a convenience store disguised as an old-fashioned Dutch-style home. One lone black Amish carriage was tied up in a nearby parking spot, but we didn't see their owners, and knew better than to try to take a picture. Besides, the horse looks absolutely miserable.

We finally approached some other amused tourists bundled in parkas who had the same idea, and grinned like silly kids as we traded places under the faux-antique 'Welcome to Intercourse' sign.

A few restaurants were open, if not busy, and after a bit of fuss up the one step of a folksy-themed restaurant, with a flustered hostess who acted as if she'd never seen a wheelchair, we got a table.

"What happened to you, honey?" our stout waitress asked.

Everett whipped off his scarf and gloves. "I got hungry and dragged my boyfriend to this dive."

"No, I meant… I'm sorry. Would you like something warm to drink?"

"Yes. And we're ready to order."

As the waitress excused herself, Everett shook his head as is if to brush off the awkward exchange.

"I don't know how you deal with that." I had mostly stood silent as Everett dealt with such people. It was his decision how to react, depending on his mood.

"Well, I can always tell the blimp story!"

"You need a new tall tale."

He shifted in his chair, yanked off his parka and stuffed it on the booth seat beside him, looked around, out a window. "Hey, what say we get a room at one of those hideously quaint inns?"

"Ev, Philly's an hour away."

"But we're in Intercourse!"

"I'm sure they're all tired of the jokes."

"I'm not."

"You really want to?"

"No, I was just kidding."

I fiddled with a ketchup bottle, considered squirting him with it.

"Spoilsport."

"If you want quaint, we could go shopping at Ye Oldee Giftee Shopee."

"Arth thou craving a trinket, young Mathter Conniff?"

I smirked. "We only got Mrs. Kukka a Christmas card. Maybe she likes candles."

"Or a pewter olden denture cup."

Once again, we got stares for laughing a bit too loudly.

Our giggles continued unabated after lunch as we pulled into a gift shop parking lot, even though it was just across the street.

Having to distance myself from him when his muttered 'olden' comments kept me withholding snorts of laughter, I settled on a shelf of candles and porcelain figurines. I calmed down, a grin still stuck on my face as the thick scent of perfumed gifts became a bit overwhelming. I was surprised to see Everett near a small model bed, having what seemed to be a serious conversation with a saleswoman.

"That's a bit lavish for a landlady, don't you think?"

"Which one do you like?" He reached for one of the quilts the saleslady had produced.

"I don't know her taste."

"They're not for her, silly." He gestured for me to come closer, and said softly, "It's for our bed. Us together. None of that other stuff matters," he waved his hand, as if to brush off the likes of Kyle, he of the puppy dog eyes and grapefruit shoulders. Then his voice regained an open tone. "How about this one?"

I gazed confusedly at a pattern of dainty triangular fabric pieces, unable to think. "Uh, the one with the green patches."

"We'll take that one," Everett declared.

"A lovely choice," the saleslady smiled. "Anything else?"

"Um, this." I held out the candle I'd chosen.

"I'll just ring you up." As she walked away, I muttered to Everett, "Isn't that a bit lavish?"

"Sweetie, this is for us. That room is friggin' cold. Besides, if we're not going to have intercourse here, we might as well do it under something from Intercourse!"

"You're a nut."

He swatted my butt. "That's why ya love me."

Shoveling a few inches of snow from the front yard's sidewalk all the way to the hedge gate, I then had to attack the street sidewalk with the edge of the shovel, like an ice pick, because the bumpy bricks refused any even form of scooping.

Mrs. Kukka had promised to have the bricks repaired months before we had moved in, but it was just one of many things she'd been forgetting to do, like deposit our rent checks.

She did, however, remember to thank me for my work the night she was having some senior faculty over for dinner and "a slideshow from my late husband's trip to Paraguay," an event which Everett and I had to decline an invitation. The sporting life awaited.

Basketball, which usually disinterested me, became fascinating when Everett played. Despite needing to study, on some nights I accompanied Everett, with at least one textbook on my lap, and watched him practice at Magee, and at his games at Drexel University, a few blocks west of Penn. They used it a few times through the winter.

With Everett's basketball team, there became something for me to do; retrieve equipment, even take tickets on a few occasions. I had an additional excuse to be with Everett in his own special environment. Even if I didn't go with him, I knew he'd be protected.

Drexel was more like Temple, with newer bland cement buildings, a campus square, and, since we were at the gym, jocks, of which there were many. Some of them happened upon the wheelchair basketball practices, offered curious stares, compliments.

One of those jocks became friendly during the few minutes between his volleyball practice and the basketball team's court time.

By friendly, I learned what was more of a direct cruise, as Everett conjectured when I told him about talking with Chuck, a blond-furred hunk who coached women's volleyball. We'd both shared appreciative glances mixed with new friendly waves each week in the gym.

What I didn't tell Everett was that I once encountered Chuck in the showers, as I sidled up to the nearby urinals. My prolonged glance led to him not turning away, but almost presenting himself. Fearing some sort of trap, what with the reports of antigay behavior on several campuses, I'd rushed back out of embarrassment.

I didn't tell Everett that the next week, as his team warmed up, I returned, timing my entrance. He wanted me to have an adventure on my own, didn't he?

Chuck seemed to have been lingering. Since he was the only guy from the women's volleyball practice, he was alone, drying off with a towel.

He waited about a minute, a long heart-thudding minute of me refusing to not look, before he offered a quiet yet full-court press.

"You, uh… work with the wheelchair guys?" he said, a towel his swirling prop that displayed, then hid, his torso, legs, and swaying penis. His chest was enormous, still damp, broad with a sort of pelt of blond hair.

I'd stopped peeing, but held my dick, pretending not to finish.

"Yeah."

"Cool."

"You play volleyball?"

"I coach the intramural team."

"That's cool."

"It's not NCAA, but you know, it's competitive."

"That's cool."

"You play?"

"No. I run." I had to face him. He wouldn't move. I zipped up, stepped closer. "My …roommate does wheelchair basketball, obviously."

"Cool."

I wasn't cool enough at the time to reveal anymore. It had become a cautious game. Who seemed like they wouldn't understand the 'boyfriend' word?

Chuck the volleyball coach seemed like he would know. But he wanted something else, and as he teased me with a revealing towel dance, his penis was proving it.

A whistle tweeted out on the gym floor.

"Gotta go."

The next week, the women's volleyball team was nowhere to be seen. Out of town game? I wasn't sure. I helped the guys get set up, then sat a few rows up in the bleachers.

Everett's team dominated their competition for the first half. The sparse crowd remained enthusiastic, and although he was focused on court, he did glance over to me a few times with a nod when I cheered a few of his bold basket shots.

The whistle tweets, the scattered shouts, the occasional clash of metal on metal, echoed through the gym as the players faced off. Even from a distance, I could see Everett's ferocity, the clipped shouts of formation reminders, and an occasional almost scornful look as he or another teammate fumbled the ball.

The players took a break at halftime. Everybody had their towels and water, so I snuck off to the locker room, scanned the showers, saw no one, then bent over to tie my boot lace.

I wasn't alone more than a few minutes when Chuck appeared by my side, hands in his jacket's pockets, a ski cap covering his golden locks, and a demeanor that made him almost unrecognizable.

"Oh, man, Wow. You what? Wait, did you have practice?"

"Naw. But I knew you did. Or, your team."

I glanced at the hips that swayed at my eye level, then stood up to meet his gaze. He was very tall.

"You're friends with that wheelchair guy, right?"

"Yes. I think I mentioned that before."

"Sorry, I'm just…"

"Curious?"

"No, I'm…"

"You're…?"

"You're like roommates?" He seemed genuinely nervous.

"No. We're a lot more than roommates."

"Oh, great." He sort of melted a little. We shook hands. That simple contact seemed to have set off some electrical charge in him.

He led me to a bench, where we sat, and he unleashed a whispered cascade of confessions, frustrations, cloistered fraternity rituals that verged on sex but never followed through, plus a few random encounters in parking lots. Parking lots? Which ones?

"Wow, dude." I had no idea what to say.

"But you're, like, boyfriends."

"Yeah."

"Do you mess around?"

"No, we're happy." I smiled, lying a bit too assuredly.

It was then that his eyes flared with a lurid edge. "Whaddaya do?"

Initially put off by his imposition, his attempt at charm was amateurish compared to Everett. But he was handsome, a lot of handsome. The prior week in the locker room promised even bigger handsome.

Still, I didn't tell him, or anyone, that between the pull-up bars, our now well-read sex manual, and a growing collection of pillows, we pretty much had a three-ring circus.

"What we 'do' is kind of personal."

"I'm sorry. I didn't mean to—"

"Yes, you did. You're flirting with me, or us. That's cool. It's kinda nice; flattering. You're…" I hissed out a breath, muttered, "You're fucking gorgeous."

"Oh. Thanks."

"Yeah. But we don't …"

"Well, if you change your mind, I mean, if that's okay, maybe, just you, at first. I don't know if I could…"

A few weeks before, Everett and I had gone to one of those art film nights at the Temple student center. The John Waters line Everett repeated often that night afterward had been, "Dismissed! May we suggest Mister Ray's Wig World?"

I longed to shout it in the locker room's silence. Nevertheless, I took his number. He seemed put off when I asked for his last name.

"I got propositioned, again," I said when we'd returned to the house.

"By whom?"

"Coach volleyball hunk."

"The blond?"

I nodded.

After sharing the details of my flirtatious talk with Chuck, omitting most of the whispered spillage, Everett smiled. He leaned back from the desk, the green lampshade tilted back to silhouette his curling locks like a noir halo.

"My good man." Twiddling his fingers faux-maniacally a la Dr. Scott, he smirked. "You haff done vell."

You see, it was part of his plan. It was his fault.

"He wants just me, first."

"Only?"

"No, I mean, he might want you, but I don't know yet. He's a little fucked up about the gay thing."

His evil genius face soured. "So. Zis is a solo mission."

I was kind of put off by the way he joked about it. In fact, I was really put off.

But I tried to find a way to be nonchalant about this potential extra-curricular possibility.

As we made out, I told Everett about a few gym shower experiences I'd had back at Temple before he had come to room with me. Guys kept looking at me, I got excited, then they did, but each time had led to nothing more than a few minutes of furtive soapy dick-stroking from a distance.

Each of them gave me a taste of that exhibitionistic thrill Everett taught me before his accident. Retelling the experiences was fun.

But each one left me feeling uncomfortable. Twice I saw guys approach along a campus sidewalk, and the look they shot me months later, seeing me alone or paired with Everett, caught their gaze; a curious glance of recognition, then a darted turn away.

Having been given permission by Everett made it more familiar. But it had turned out awkward. Coach Volleyball, aka Chuck, was the first guy I talked with while having an intention of this deliberate attempt at outside sex.

We went out for beers, and got to talking. Actually, he did most of the talking. Only after he took me to his apartment had he made me feel small and pliable in his arms. Tall and nearly coated in a fascinating flaxen fuzz, his body could not have been more different from Everett's.

Chuck didn't understand why I wanted to do it standing. It was the one thing I couldn't do with Everett. Eventually, he guided me to lean against a wall, and thrust himself deep into my butt, lifted me atop him with a Herculean flair, until we fell back to the bed. I rode him, my own cock bapping to and fro on his chest.

On the verge of coming, I thrust my hips toward his face, tugging on my cock. His hand swatted my dick's aim away from his face.

"Don't," he grunted. His thrusts up into me became more insistent, but I felt an imbalance, almost a moment of shame. I pulled myself away from him to lie beside him, where each of us finished off on our own, barely touching.

After a bit too fastidiously wiping himself of any spurts, he sighed with an almost smug satisfaction.

"I'll bet that was fun."

"Um, yeah."

"No, I mean, different; what with your boyfriend, you know, being–"

"Actually, we're pretty good. This was just–"

"Well, whatever. I just thought. You were kinda really into it, like you hadn't had any normal sex in a while."

"Um, that's not how I'd put it."

He continued wiping himself.

I asked, "Do you...? You're not into, you know, the cum–"

"Oh, well, you know, all these strange diseases going around. You never know."

"You think I could have–"

"Well, no. But, I mean, who knows, right?"

While I understood his caution, it seemed an inconsistent opinion, particularly after he'd rammed himself into my butt.

Then Chuck mentioned some conservative group that was planning a Student Republicans party in advance of the mid-term elections. Our subsequent brief political argument pretty much spoiled the mood.

After excusing myself, I returned home to Everett, and coaxed him into watching me scrub myself in the shower.

"Well?"

I joked that I felt that dirty, and the Republican thing was more of a ruse. But it was the possibility of romantic anything elsewhere that turned me off. I was glad Chuck was a jerk to me when he'd abruptly asked me to leave.

"So, we're even," I said with a hoped-for finality as I settled into bed with him.

"If you say so."

"If we're not, I don't want to know about it."

I asked Everett to never tell me if or with whom he might ever 'expand our relationship' on his own. And I knew there were plenty of opportunities for him, too.

Sex was still a bit complicated, but the touching, caressing and intimacy wasn't. We'd been forced to find so many other ways to express our love, frankly, after all that playing around with Chuck, who basically ignored me after that, I didn't care what other people did.

Chapter 26
February, 1982

Perhaps it was the twenty-one inches of snow that made him long for warmer climates. With a few days of classes cancelled, and the city basically shut down from the storm, Everett's mobility was hampered even afterward by the un-navigable mounds of plowed snow blocking a lot of sidewalks. Shoveling sidewalk corners around our block became futile after snow plow trucks shoved the muddy snow back. We spent more than a few afternoons nearly housebound, reading, watching movies and keeping warm under the covers.

We did risk one playful afternoon in the yard where we made a snowman that fell over twice. Everett's attempt to roll a ball into a base left him with more snow on him than the snowman.

"So, where do you wanna go for Spring Break?"

Our outdoor clothes hung to dry in the hallway. I'd made hot cocoa as he soaked in a tub of hot water, then joined him. I spun my eyes around as if checking an invisible U.S. map on the bathroom wall, limited it to a drivable distance, even though I knew Everett would insist on flying somewhere.

The previous summer, he had flown to Chicago with his family since his accident; some cousin's wedding to which I was thankfully not invited. I had wanted to go with him, but didn't consider asking either his or my parents for money for a ticket.

Of his trip, though, Everett had said of the airline staff, "They treated me like royalty."

So I figured he wanted to fly somewhere, this time with me. I'd wanted to offer a week in the Adirondacks in a cabin, but I could sense another dare.

"How are we paying for this?"

"I told you. Mother gave me a credit card 'for emergencies.' This is an emergency." He splashed a bit of water.

"So we're telling our parents?"

"I think we better. But maybe, like, the day before we go. Then they can't protest."

"How much do you have?"

"About two grand. I think I've got us covered. But I'll do it on the card."

"Thanks, Monkey. But I have about six hundred from work, so I can carry some of my own weight."

So I thought about it, trying to guess his first pick, or the most preposterous ones. His legs bobbed in the water, and I maneuvered them to rest on my hips.

"Miami?"

"Too tacky."

"We could drive to Cape May."

"Too cold. Wait until summer."

"Maui? Mali? Manila?"

"Domestic only. Do you even have a passport? Have you ever even seen one?"

"No. But Maui is actually domestic."

"So, change letters. No M's."

Going out into the world, like a sort of oddly teamed Ironside and Kato, would become another dare, the kind that brought us together in the first place.

I relented. It would be his decision anyway. "Where would you like to go with me, oh, adorable one?"

He smiled, splashed water again. "Someplace warm and wet."

Our playful splashing came to a halt when we heard Mrs. Kukka descending the stairs above us. Everett held a finger to his lips, as if our silence could deceive her into thinking we weren't in the bathroom. But then a light knock on the door broke that hope.

"Boys?"

"Yes, Ma'am," Everett replied.

"I'm going out, but I saved some newspaper clippings for you both; some important articles I think you ought to read."

"Thank you," he called out, as we held back giggles.

"I'll leave them in the front room."

"Thank you!" we both repeated, then almost held ourselves in the tub water until we heard her shuffle around, then close the front door.

"What was that all about?"

"Probably some wheelchair pity feature or something about nature for you."

"I low nice." I flicked a small splash of water at him.

"She is." He splashed back.

By the time we had dried off and dressed, the pile of clippings was forgotten.

Since leaving the campus, Everett had struggled a bit with the few extra blocks, mostly in bad weather, but he refused a shuttle bus because it was too short a trip and usually arrived late. The van more frequently stalled in the cold weather.

But he still kept up with goings on, telling me about an anti-apartheid protest he'd approached, then joined in, and made a few activist friends. He'd even attended a small rally by the gay student group about the Army recruitment on campus.

In bed, textbooks in our laps, I was ready for either cuddling, studying, or a little of both. The warmth of our bed's blankets, topped by our new 'Intercourse' quilt, induced a drowsy comfort in me. I leaned over, lifted his shirt to rub his stomach, hoping it might distract him enough to put aside his book.

But he wasn't in the mood for that.

I peered over at his book and saw a picture of Franklin Delano Roosevelt. "Kind of a role model for you."

"You'd think so. We're supposed to do a paper on world leaders, but he wasn't all he was made out to be."

"I sense another 'Did You Know' coming on."

Everett flipped pages, then pulled a few photocopied pages from some other book. "He hid his polio from the public.

There are hardly any pictures of him in a wheelchair. And on top of his administration turning away Jews escaping Nazi Germany, an entire ship full of them… wait." The photocopied pages fluttered. "You know the WPA?"

"Yeah, the Works Project thing; the murals and dams and stuff."

"Well, his administration created jobs for millions of people, but they deliberately excluded the handicapped." He pointed at the pages. "I had to dig for hours to find this. It's not in any regular history books. There were fully trained people, some who'd had polio, like him, and his…underlings wouldn't even give them jobs until they protested, for weeks."

"Wow. But did they?"

"Get jobs? Eventually. But this is just another example… This is my history now. I never would have noticed this before, or cared."

"Well, things have changed. Now you're… enlightened. Is that the word?"

He wondered aloud, "What if we did a protest for accessibility on campus?"

"Don't they have ramps all over? Wasn't that the purpose of them showing you off?"

"There's still half a dozen old buildings they won't adjust. The few automatic doors at Houston and other halls are always locked. I had to get one of my classes moved because it's in a building with no elevator."

"Jeez." I adjusted myself in bed. It was not going to become a romantic evening until I managed to calm him down.

"And there are even buildings downtown. The problem is, you only demand it from public spaces. Stores, businesses; they stall and it's just not an easy target. Starting on campus would be something, right?"

"Sure. I'm with you."

I could almost hear him silently planning, yet returned to a Botany chapter on broad leaves and opposite compound leaves.

Our studious silence continued, until I heard the phone's other line ring upstairs, then Mrs. Kukka talking to someone. The sound reminded me. "So, I got another odd phone call."

"From who?"

"I don't know. He asked for 'Mutt.'"

Everett froze. He seemed to appear outwardly relaxed, but I noticed his hand was gripping his textbook a bit too tightly.

"Huh. Did he say who it was?"

"No. He said he'd call back later; wouldn't give me a number."

"I'm getting an answering machine."

"You know, it's getting a little weird, these calls—"

"I said I'll get an answering machine!"

It was my turn to freeze. "Okay, Jeez."

Everett slammed his book closed, and tossed it on the floor.

"Why don't you just let it ring sometime? It's not like—"

"What is wrong?"

"I'm tired." He rolled over, snapped off his bedside light, and yanked the quilt over his shoulder.

"Okay, then."

I pretended to study for a while, angling my own bedside lamp away from Everett, until, after a while, he half turned, saying, "He's just another guy from Pinecrest; probably wants to say how sorry he is; the usual crip-iddy doo-dah bullshit."

"Oh, okay."

"Did you see the mail my mom forwards me?"

"I may be nosy about your phone calls, but I do not go through your mail," I asserted.

"I still get sympathy cards from classmates. It's been almost three years."

It seemed like a nice gesture, but I understood his anger, somewhat.

"I'm sorry I got mad at you."

"Thanks," I replied.

"Gimme a kiss."

"You bet." I leaned down and we shared an off-angled smooch. "Can't go to bed angry," I added.

"Who said that?"

"My mom, I think."

"You talk to your mom about me?"

"Sometimes, when I don't have a clue how to deal with you."

"You're sweet." Everett offered a smile, then nestled close to me. "I love you, no matter what I say."

Despite wondering what the next 'what' might be, my Botany textbook became suddenly irrelevant.

And yet, as I turned off the light and lay in bed next to him, I pondered what sort of friend, or former friend, would call my boyfriend a mutt, when it was pretty obvious he was a purebred.

Two days later, I returned to our room to see a small box on the floor next to the garbage can. On the desk, next to the phone, and connected by a wire, was what appeared to be a small cassette player and a smaller instruction manual.

The little red light wasn't blinking, so I figured there weren't any messages. I clicked the 'Message' button anyway, and heard the outgoing recording, Everett's voice, in a clipped tone, stating simply, "Leave a message." No names, no funny sayings.

About a week later, Everett and I were casually studying, more listening to Elvis Costello croon that "Accidents will happen, we're all a hit and run..." when the phone rang.

I glanced at him, shrugged. He wasn't getting up from the floor, where he was doing a few stretches.

Then, after the beep, the answering machine projected a voice, that same somewhat abrupt rude voice.

"Forrester! Everett Mutt Forrester. It's Swagger. Gimme a call." The voice left a number with a 212 area code.

Everett seemed to stare at the phone as if it were possessed.

I waited for the click and ending beep of the machine.

"Do you want to call him back?"

"No. Not now."

"Okay."

I would have let it go, but a long while later, after I'd fixed a snack in the kitchen, offered him some, gotten no reply, eaten it, then trod to the bathroom to brush my teeth, I stole another glance at him across the bedroom. He was still staring at the same piece of wall.

I waited, then sighed, got up, turned off the stereo. The Elvis Costello album had finished.

"What?" he turned.

"Do you wanna talk about this?"

Everett offered a scolding glance. "You're saying that like, 'I want you to talk about this.'"

"We can keep ignoring your… fans, or ex-friends or whatever they are. It's up to you."

I pretended to return to my textbook.

Everett sighed. I resisted the urge to watch as he crawled on the floor, then hoisted himself up to his chair. He rolled around a bit, doing that scary off-kilter stunt, rolling on his back wheels, for a while. Then he finally said something that threw me for a loop.

"Remember that Polaroid I sent you?"

That time, I froze.

How could I forget it? Only a few months into our friendship, which was barely held together by flirtatious notes and gifts mailed to each other while he was at Pinecrest, Everett had sent a casual note, explaining the photo as 'an early birthday present.' In it, he posed wearing only a pair of undershorts as he flexed his little arm muscles, standing proud and apparently a bit aroused. It had remained an unspoken mystery, one of so many that had gradually unspooled as we had grown more comfortable living together. I was so envious of whoever got to take that picture that I never brought it up.

So I felt a bit of impending satisfaction, like a detective unlocking a secret, as I retreated to our clothes closet, dug around on the floor, extracted a cardboard box, and another smaller box inside it, and, after rifling through a stack of his letters to me, I found it.

"You mean this Polaroid?"

"Yeah."

"The one I smuggled to Allegheny National Forest and drooled over every night? One of the few pieces of you that got me through that summer before you tried to dump me?"

"Yes, Reid. I remember it."

"So, was this ... Is this from this Swagger guy?"

"Sweigard."

"That's a funny name."

"It's his last name. Private school guys... We usually just use last names... Wesley Sweigard."

"He took it."

Everett nodded.

"Are there more?"

He shrugged. "If he still has them."

"Were you wearing less in those?"

"Yes."

"Do you have any other pictures of him?"

"I threw them out."

'Too bad,' I thought. 'We could burn them.'

Everett pushed over to the bookshelf, selected one of three Pinecrest yearbooks he'd brought with him when we moved in. At first I thought it odd for him to do, but we had spent a wonderful night months before, Everett telling me stories about various classmates as he pointed out photos. But he'd never mentioned this Sweigard guy.

"Why didn't you tell me before?"

"I am now. Just... stay with me, okay. Don't get all..."

"Squidly?"

After flipping through page after page, he found what he'd been looking for. I leaned over as he pointed to a portrait of our mysterious caller. I saw a handsome, somewhat arrogant and assured smile, wizened eyes, a square jaw, and a closely cropped haircut. He was stunning.

Below each name were tiny lists of activities. Among Sweigard's were lacrosse and other sports.

But then I noticed the year. "1976?"

"He was a senior."

"And you were…?"

"I was fourteen."

"But the photo…"

"It was before I met you. Honest. We…"

"Wow. Wait, you don't have to–"

"He was my first."

I stared at the face in the yearbook, pondering it all, until Everett delicately took the book, placed it on his desk.

"What about Kevin?" I asked about his childhood neighbor, and a track teammate of mine in Greensburg, who, at an odd moment after Everett's accident, had become my brief sex buddy.

"That was just … We never really had actual sex until later."

"Oh… kay."

"It wasn't… I was. I wanted to, you know? But he was…"

I instinctively reached for him, hugged him, not knowing details, not wanting to know, but at the same time, desperately wanting to let him tell me.

"Wesley was different. It started with just some flirting," Everett said, sighing, as if he were finally unloading a heavy burden. "I never told anyone. This…"

"Take your time."

"It… there was this arts seminar at Pinecrest, guys from several different classes. The professor was talking about early Modern Art, and he showed us a slide that made everyone laugh. It was a signed urinal, this supposed great work of absurdist or, no, Dada art, by the painter, what's his name. He did "Nude Descending a Staircase.""

I had no idea what he was talking about.

"Duchamp. Marcel Duchamp."

"Okay."

"Anyway, he made up this signature, 'R. Mutt' on a urinal, and everybody in the lecture laughed. And then, after the lecture, it was like he followed me. I'd seen him, of course. Sweigard's huge; big muscles, dark red hair. And he just came up beside me in the boy's room after it, and was like showing off, I mean, really showing off, you know, like turning toward me when he pissed, and he caught me looking."

Everett noticed as I adjusted my sweatpants.

"Is this making you horny?"

"Well," I shrugged.

"Okay, fine. Anyway, it was hot. But, he just kind of forced himself on me."

"Like I did when we met?"

"No! Hell, no! You… You were so sweet, and well, kinda dopey-sweet. I'm sorry, Reid, but you're so different." He reached toward me, patting me and tugging an ear as a sort of consolation prize.

"I'll take that as a compliment."

"Do that. So, anyway, I'm sharing here, so try to keep your hand outta your pants."

"Sorry."

"He just… After a few times, he became really manipulative and mean, and kind of forced me to… One time, he kind of raped me."

"What?"

"Then he got all apologetic and I threatened to tell on him and it was just fucked up, all this mind-fucking bullshit…" He covered his face with a hand, as if trying to wipe the memory away. "And then he graduated and just abandoned me, and that's about the time I stole my mother's Mercedes, and that's why I'm such a slutty freak."

"You're not a freak. Fuck, Ev! I mean, we should call the police or something–"

"No! No. I will… This is just a phone call. And that's all. I don't hate him. I don't want…"

I dropped my head to his chest, just held him. I didn't know what to do or say. He rubbed my head.

"But, if he hadn't turned me into a freaky little horndog, you and I might never have met, so I hate him but I don't hate him."

"Damn."

"Yeah, so hearing from him now is kinda weird."

"I bet."

"Yeah."

I tilted my head up. "So, do you want me to erase the message?" I knew damn well that I wanted to.

Everett put a hand over his mouth, as if deciding, or as if he were a magician about to guess a card. "No. I'll... later. He probably just wants to–"

"'Sorry you're all crippled, yada yada.'"

"Right. Mother probably gave him the number."

We sat there for a while. I thought to get up and play some more music, but it was late. I had no idea what to say. On the wall behind us, Kenny's innocent drawing of Everett and I holding hands hung in a simple frame. I longed for such simplicity.

Everett fidgeted with his legs, shifted closer to me. "No matter what he wants, if he wants to see me, even for a visit, just promise you'll be with me."

"Sure." I looked into his eyes, those dazzling dark brown eyes, so close that I once again saw those tiny slivers of green and gold.

"No, I mean, don't leave me alone with him. I'd probably jump for his throat."

I whispered, "Of course."

We held each other tight, then softened our embrace, then kissed. And although I knew he was with me, so close, licking and grabbing with a ferocity we hadn't shared in weeks, I felt a strange fear, as if we were fighting him off, this Sweigard. His unseen presence entwined itself between us, like the toxic vines I'd read about that grow in the Amazon; *Rafflesia arnoldii* and *Thonningia sanguinea*. They wrap themselves around older trees like a parasite. The common name is Woe Vine.

Chapter 27
March 1982

Spring Break.

The paramedic.

Nick the paramedic.

Nick, the suntanned Italian feathery-chest-haired paramedic, didn't so much hit on us as not leave our company for hours after introducing himself to us.

Everett made sly glances at the bulging green Speedo of Nick the paramedic, from Islip, who stood, his crotch hovering near Everett's face as we sipped drinks poolside under the glare of a Fort Lauderdale sun.

Before meeting Nick, on our first day in Florida, we endured a bumpy cab ride from the airport where the driver seemed disturbed by the hassle of Everett's chair barely fitting into his trunk, or our destination, The Marlin Beach Hotel, being a gay resort. It was probably both.

"Well, here we are," Everett said as he eyed the nautical décor and stuffed marlins hung on the lobby wall.

As we entered the hotel, we endured a few raised eyebrows from other guests, all men, most wearing little more than swimsuits and flipflops. The desk clerk with a blond mustache offered a flirtatious smile.

"Welcome, boys!"

As Everett dealt with the reservations, I looked around. Through a glass window, I saw the pool, the source of some disco music being played.

"If there's anything you need, just let us know," the desk clerk smiled. "The tunnel's right by the dance floor, but it's got stairs, so you might want to take the street. Tea dance is just getting started, so I hope you're ready to have fun."

After squeezing ourselves into the tiny elevator, we finally found our room on the third floor. While I plopped our luggage onto the bed, Everett wheeled past me to pull open the drapes. Beyond the street below us, we marveled at the beautiful expanse of blue-green calm Florida water, and a wide strip of sand already filled with people.

"Wow," Everett said.

"Wow, indeed," I replied.

"This makes up for the tacky décor."

"So, what first?"

"The beach!"

We changed, stocked up on towels and lotion, hats and sunglasses, and crossed the busy street to the beach.

After rolling as far as we could, he parked at a cement wall. Carrying Everett through the sand, I set him down, then placed a towel down, and left him with the small duffel bag. I retrieved his chair, lay a towel over it so it wouldn't get too hot, and despite a generous slathering of lotion, we both tried to act natural until the various glances passed.

All around us, men lounged on towels, or further back, under cabanas.

"I never felt so pale."

"That'll change."

"I never saw so many mustaches."

"Are they all gay?" I asked as I looked around. Nearly all the men were tanned, fit in various sizes and shapes, and some even held hands as they walked along the shore.

"Pretty much," Everett agreed. "How about we get wet?"

Since there were no waves, the warm blue water was easy enough for Everett to swim in, except for getting to and from the surf edge, where I carried him piggyback into the water. He wore a pair of old sneakers to prevent his feet from getting scraped by any underwater rocks. Once into deeper waters, we splashed about with some abandon, but I always stayed close, just in case.

"Now this," he said as he shook water from his face, "is what I call heaven!"

I spat a volley of salt water, grinning in agreement.

We splashed about, dove around and on top of each other, frolicking like dolphins, until Everett, panting a bit, grabbed hold of me. "How 'bout we head in?"

"Okay. Hop on."

I guided us toward the shore, ignored the curious looks from others, then plopped down at the surf's edge. We sat, letting the waves wash up around us.

Once we'd settled back on our towels, we rubbed lotion on each other, and tried to relax. I still felt self-conscious in nothing but a swimsuit, until Everett's hands on me felt warm as he massaged my shoulders.

"You boys better take it easy on your first day," a man nearby called out.

"Is it that obvious?" Everett grinned.

The man's friend leaned forward, surveying us with a grin. "You don't want to spend all week like a pair of lobsters."

We shared a little more friendly chat, then relaxed and lay together for a while. I held Everett's hand, content to feel comfortable surrounded by so many other gay men.

Exhausted after returning to our room, we spent the afternoon napping. Despite our oceanfront view, I could still hear the faint thump of music by the inside pool.

After showering off the fatigue and lotion, we enjoyed a hassle-free dinner at the restaurant, and spent our first night cuddling under some scratchy sheets and the relentless hum of the air conditioner.

"We need to mingle," Everett declared as he led me to the resort's pool the next day.

"You don't want to just go back to the ocean?"

"It'll keep."

I followed him out to the pool, but felt daunted by the cluster of mostly older gay men, whose looks made me feel like we were freshly sunburned prey.

Everett's chair glistened a bit too brightly for a few among the gaggle of men in sunglasses, tanned attitude and hair gel. They parted for us, or in most cases, avoided us and made what appeared to be more than a few catty whispered comments. At one point, I thought I heard one of the lines from *Whatever Happened to Baby Jane?* muttered by one man, and laughed at by his friends.

But not Nick the paramedic. Emerging from the pool like a hirsute Neptune, he walked right up, got us drinks, and reluctantly told a rescue tale or three.

"You boys doin' okay?" he asked as he noticed my somewhat uncomfortable fidgeting in a beach chair.

"You're one of the first guys who's said hello that doesn't work here," I said.

"Well, you are the youngest, and the cutest," Nick smiled.

"Sir," Everett raised his cup, by then a bit sloshed after two drinks. "Flattery will get you everywhere."

"It's also, maybe some of the other guests think you're…" he nodded toward Everett's wheelchair.

"What?" he asked.

"They probably think you're sick."

Confused, I asked, "Is that what you think?"

"Oh, no!" He gushed, apologetic. "I know injuries, and you're what?" He gave Everett an appraising look. "T-4 para?"

"L-4," Everett corrected.

"Yeah, see? These queens," Nick waved his hand dismissively. "Some a them're runnin' around like headless chickens."

Our conversation continued in a somewhat morbid, almost cloistered manner, as Nick and Everett debated ideas, tossed facts, rumors and news they'd heard about GRID, gay cancer, or whatever they were calling it.

Finally, I thought, someone who can talk with Everett on his level. Despite the disturbing nature of it, Nick had moved closer to us, seated himself, and I felt a sort of comfort with him.

Our discussion eventually steered away from diseases to other topics, mostly the two of us, which seemed to interest him more. Nick kept buying us drinks. By the fourth round, he brought us sodas. "Otherwise, I might take advantage of you boys."

Everett grinned. "Or we might take advantage of you."

I resisted the urge to toss my soda on Everett, partially because I agreed with him. Nick was nice, and smart, but he was also incredibly handsome. One slim over-tanned guy even sauntered by with a catty, "Someone caught a whopper."

The sun had long before set behind the hotel, and most of the other guests had left the pool for other areas of pleasure, or what I learned was called a 'disco nap.'

Nick's offer of dinner later on clinched it.

"Shall we?" Everett asked that night as we donned decidedly un-trendy Hawaiian shirts and baggy shorts.

"We shall," I smiled, opening the hotel room door.

"No, I mean, shall we with Nick?"

Wasn't this the reason we traveled so far, to have 'an adventure?'

"Hey, we're on vacation. I'm game if you are, champ."

The food was lavish, the servings enormous, the waiter flirtatious, and all, at Nick's insistence, on him. He later guided us to the lower level Poop Deck, a subterranean bar with big wooden seahorses on the walls near the semi-circular bar, and window views inside the pool.

What charmed us both was Nick's ability to share his amazing accomplishments of saving lives, but without sounding boastful. He also kept asking us questions, and his curiosity and admiration seemed genuine.

What possibly kept Everett relaxed was that Nick never doled out the standard sympathy catch phrases about his disability. It just was.

As he offered to take an evening tour of the boardwalk across the street along the beach, I did, however, take a moment aside with Nick to ask, "So, you're not, like, into guys just because they're disabled?"

"What? Oh, no. Look, I'm sorry if I come on too strong."

"No, that's cool. We're just–"

"But, hey, look. I have seen a lot of stuff at work; some bad stuff. You know, bodily speaking. You're both hot to me."

"Uh, okay. That's cool." And then I touched his large muscled shoulder, dared to touch him on my own. Everett had slowed his pace, wheeled around, and saw me. He offered a sly grin.

There was a self-serve brunch in the dining room at the hotel each morning, with scooped melons in bowls, bagels, French toast and several kinds of juice. Savoring Nick the paramedic with Everett was like that; a buffet.

Sex with Nick was amazing. Everett kissed me while Nick sucked my cock, then simply leaned back to watch as I straddled Nick's hips, my back to him, my gaze intent on Everett's astounded smile, his dick jutted up from his groin as he stroked it indolently.

What made us realize that we were still a couple, in the midst of all the positions, all the licking and grabbing, were the sly grins Everett and I shared, alternating slathering laps and kisses upon Nick's wide furry ass spread before us. We were sharing him, having an adventure.

At one point in our lustful tumble, Nick coaxed me into thrusting into him, and Everett began his poking and playful swats at my rear end. Connected to them both, I found myself in a panting moment of lust, and almost knocked Everett out of the way before collapsing atop Nick's back. Other positions were tried, and enjoyed, but that moment, releasing myself into a pliable man who felt every thrust, surprised me with how much I needed it, wanted it.

The three of us slept in a tangle of limbs until late the next morning, ordered breakfast in, and tried a few more variations in the bathroom, but our laughter and exhaustion from the previous night made it more playful than plow-ful.

Nick rented a car, and we spent the next two days enjoying his guided tour of the Everglades, or at least the areas where the parkway cut through them.

"No, take your shirts off, both of you!" Everett insisted as he aimed the camera. Nick and I complied, arms around each others' shoulder, and smiled.

Standing in front of a rather un-photogenic expanse of swamp by the side of the road, it didn't matter. We were having fun.

We kept hoping to spot an alligator, but saw mostly herons and other innocuous wildlife. While driving, Everett sat in front as I lounged in the back seat, enjoying their conversation and the radio music. While I was fascinated to be in a part of the country that resembled a prehistoric marshland, Everett made his restlessness clear.

We spent another night together. Our passion was a bit more measured, and Everett ended up more watching Nick and I hump, rather than joining in, but I thought Everett was enjoying it. It was cool, or so I thought.

At one point, while driving inland the next day, Nick offered to take us all the way to Key Largo for a day trip.

"How far is it?"

"About ninety miles."

Everett turned to me in the back seat, and for a moment, saw me staring almost lovingly at Nick, until I turned to him, as if caught. His face, already tanned from our days in the sun, seemed more serious.

He then countered, somewhat abruptly, "I think Reid and I need to just spend some time together."

"Oh, sure. No problem," Nick said casually.

But after that, a silence followed, until Nick turned on the radio.

That was the last day we spent with Nick, who was leaving in two days.

Whether it was a royal palm or a silver palm I wasn't sure, but I wanted to know, and getting samples of the leaves was easy enough. Everett sneered at my bagged collection as we packed at his insistence, even though it would be almost an hour before our taxi ride to the airport.

"Really, you're bringing palm tree samples."

"Extra credit on southern foliage," I defended.

"I mean, you could actually buy a few souvenirs. If you're low, I could spot you."

"I don't need another T-shirt."

We were both a little exhausted, and not just from the sun.

Our hurried packing and the bumpy cab ride to the airport were mostly spent in silence.

It wasn't until we had settled into our seats on the plane that his resentment began to creep out.

"Go ahead; order a drink. They're not going to check your ID."

"No, thank you." I shook my head at the stewardess after Everett ordered a cocktail. On our flight to Fort Lauderdale, Everett had instructed me on the basics of air flight with a bemused yet condescending tone. The fact that I'd never been on a plane amused him.

But on our return trip, everything seemed to annoy him, particularly the flight staff's insistence that he check his own wheelchair and board with one of their antiquated models.

But the drink comment was a dig at my inability to count. I'd overspent during our first few days, and had to ask Everett to pay for our last few days' meals and drinks.

His snippy attitude sparked when we'd met Nick again, and he was understandably friendly. But when he hinted about a return engagement while patting my shoulder, my enthusiasm put Everett off. He declined abruptly, leaving me to apologize to Nick and bid him a confused farewell.

"You might as well have jumped into his lap," he'd griped.

As Everett downed his drink, the plane veered higher into the clouds. We didn't talk through the safety instructions or the beginning of the in-flight movie. It wasn't until his earphone got tangled up in my armrest that he audibly stewed.

"What?" I stared at him.

"Nothing."

"It's not nothing. I'm sorry about the money, but you said you were going to—"

"It isn't about the money," he snipped in a sort of growling whisper.

"Then what is it?"

He stared up at the small screen, then down, then at me. "You really enjoyed yourself."

"Yes, for the most part, until you–"

"With Nick."

"Didn't you? Remember, you were the one who–"

"Fucking him. You never did it like that with me."

"You… you're different. I thought we… You need a little more…preparation."

"Even before; those first few times, before the accident. You were never like that… I mean, wow, Reid. You were just slamming into him. You nearly knocked me off the bed."

"I'm sorry. He was just so…"

"What? We used to fuck."

"I didn't even know how back then, Ev. You might remember, I barely knew how to kiss you."

"But why…? Why can't you be like that with me?"

I blushed, looked to see if the people seated across from us were listening; headphones on all of them. I turned back to him, still keeping my voice low.

"I'm afraid of hurting you. You can't… You can't feel it. It's…"

I couldn't tell him what he already knew. For so long, what I thought had been his persistent preference, doing things to me, was fine; enough, it seemed. But when he was completely naked with me, I felt different, cautious, caring and loving. We had to be careful with positions, and his butt, once curved and inviting, was half gone.

And the scar; that inverted, elongated T along his spine, took me back to his accident; holding his hand in a hospital room, his drowsy drugged smile, and later, his angry dismissal, which had kept us apart for months.

"Fine. I get it." He shoved his headphones back on and pretended to watch the movie.

I should have ordered that drink.

"Where are you going?"

"For a drive; maybe back to scenic Amish country."

I sat stunned, watching him pluck summer shirts out of, then winter clothes into his backpack as his chair bumped into the opened drawer, then fumble as he attached it to the back of his chair.

Exhausted from our trip, confused by his continued resentment, I hardly protested. "You can't just–"

"Just what? Go somewhere without your approval? Maybe I need a vacation after our vacation."

And then he took off. I heard the van outside rumbling to a start, and he was gone.

The next few hours passed in a strange hollow silence. I didn't eat, read or put on any music. Sitting on the bed, waiting, brushing my fingers over that damn green quilt, seemed enough, for a while.

Then I grew restless, and wandered about the house. While the wood cabinets and furniture in the living room portrayed a feeling of comfort, I felt alien, reminded that we were merely temporary visitors in Mrs. Kukka's home.

While not exactly hungry, I glanced inside the refrigerator, as if waiting for some delicious meal to surprise me; a bag of carrots, a jar of mayonnaise, a nearly empty carton of milk. I thought to make a list of groceries, then wondered if I had enough money, or if I should even leave. What if Everett came back?

Then I noticed the month's rent check still attached to the fridge door by a magnet. Mrs. Kukka had once again forgotten to deposit it. Thinking that placing it someplace where she would see it as a good idea, I took it and crept up the stairs. I'd only briefly visited the upstairs a few times, and had merely stood in the hallway to ask her a question or have a brief chat about raked leaves and garbage cans.

Creaking floorboards heightened the feeling of emptiness. But when I walked cautiously into the main room, I saw more small stacks of books, magazines and newspapers. Shelves full of trinkets from her and her deceased husband's world travels intrigued me. I lightly touched a small African sculpture.

The closed office door to the room above our bedroom tempted me. Mrs. Kukka had never said we couldn't go in there, and Everett had dismissed my offer to carry him upstairs for a peek when she had once invited us upstairs.

It wasn't locked, which calmed me. Inside the small room, at the center, a large cluttered desk sat amid more bookshelves. At each side were waist-high stacked cardboard boxes. I lifted the lid of one of them; files and papers, thick clusters of them, filled each box. The remnants of her husband's teaching career, I wondered why she had kept them, then realized, why wouldn't she? Was this what it would be like, to spend a life with a partner, then, after he died, salvage the scraps?

Retreating downstairs, it seemed better to just remind her of the rent check later. I returned to our room and, in darkness, fell into a dense slow sleep.

"H'lo..?"
I dropped the phone.
"Hello?"
"Reid."
"Ev?"
"You need to come get me."
His voice cracked, almost pleading.
"Ev? Where are you?"
"The van broke down."
"Where are you?" I pressed.
"On the expressway near..." His voice called out. I heard another man's voice say it, then Everett repeat, "Exton. I'm at a gas station with an auto shop."
"What happened?"
"I told you! The van broke down and somebody stopped and drove ahead to get a tow truck and..." Near tears over a spill he took getting out of the van, and some nasty exchange with the tow truck driver, he said he had money, but it would be hours before the van could be fixed.

"Okay, just… Give me the number and the address. I'll figure something out. I'll call you back."

Mrs. Kukka had long since come home. I didn't want to wake her, since she didn't even have a car. Could I rent a car at night? Did I have enough money? I didn't have a credit card. Who among our friends even had a car?

And then I remembered. The only person we knew who wasn't hundreds of miles away, and who had a car, was the last person I wanted involved in anything this personal, anything that proved we'd had a fight and this had been the result.

"Hello?"

"Gerard?"

He had tried to convince me to just take his little VW Bug, even though I had no idea how to work a manual gearshift. When I explained to Gerard that the van would hopefully be repaired by the time we got to the garage, and that it would better that I just drive the van back separately, he sighed, coughed, yet agreed.

"I really want to thank you for doing this."

"Please, forget it. Just take over the wheel if I pass out." Gerard was just getting over the flu, and when his sputtering Volkswagon pulled up in front of our house, I was already outside, impatiently sitting on the tree stump at the curb.

"Just let me drive back with Everett," he said as we drove in the darkness against the string of headlights in the opposite lane.

"Why?"

"Don't worry. I'm not planning any 'I told you so' speeches. I just need someone with me so I stay awake."

"Okay."

I could drive back alone. I pored over the scribbled directions, frustrated that our road maps were all in the glove compartment of the van. But Gerard seemed to know where we were going, even in the dark.

He didn't ask, but after a long silence, I just spilled it out.

"We had a little… Stuff happened in Florida. It was totally

unexpected, and it got all intense, and I think Ev just got upset, like, after it, and he just took off."

Gerard nodded his head, then offered, "You'll work it out."

"I hope so."

"You'd better."

The nervous hug I offered Everett led to some whispered apologies, which were interrupted by the mechanic telling us he had the parts he'd need, so it would be a few hours, but not overnight. He recommended a Denny's across the intersection.

Keeping a wary eye on Everett, I searched for that panicked tone from his voice on the phone, but he laughed it off in Gerard's presence.

"The stupid tow truck guy could not comprehend that 'a crippled guy' like me could drive a van," Everett said. "He kept trying to blame the adjustment gears, but the garage mechanic told him that wasn't the problem." He shook his head, still astounded by such ignorance. I knew he'd been hurt by the man's comments, but brushed it off in front of Gerard.

Once we'd gotten our food, we all cheered up. Gerard started off telling some French joke, until Everett replied, but then waved off Gerard's reply.

"I'm switching to Spanish."

"*Pourquoi, mon coeur?*"

"Well," he perked up, or impersonated perking up quite well. "Since it'll be a while before I'm a dashing worldly diplomat, I figured I'll probably start off in social services, and maybe… an urban version of the camps where we worked?"

"That is a swingin' idea, Monkey," I joked.

Gerard faux-sulked. "Well, I guess I must *oublier sons lessiones*." He shifted to a play-by-play account of his near front row view of a recent Todd Rundgren concert.

From behind his milkshake and cheeseburger, I caught a sheepish grin and Everett's glance at me, a moment when his cheerful mask slipped, and his eyes softened under a bashful eyebrow furl.

'Thank you,' he silently said.

We finally got home around two in the morning. Gerard's VW pulled in a few minutes before I did in the van.

"So," I said after we'd bid Gerard an exhausted and thankful goodnight, and we settled under our heavy quilt. "What was all that?"

"What was what?"

"Come on. Why you took off. Were you upset? It was Nick, right?"

"It wasn't just him." Everett fussed with the quilt, gazed down, almost ashamed. "It was… I thought we could just have fun."

"Well, it was fun."

"No, I mean, fun without … without caring. And I felt like you were getting too close."

"Yeah, it was pretty intense."

"And I just got afraid."

"Well, don't be. Nick's back on Lone Guyland," I joked. "And I'm here. And you're here."

I wrapped him in my arms, dotted his face with smooches, and we held each other, and finally settled to a quiet exhausted sleep. It became unspoken, our fight, and by proxy, the entire incident. We told no one else about it, and Gerard promised to keep it *entre nous*.

Chapter 28
April 1982

Although he said it would be part of some special project for one of his classes, I knew the reason why Everett had invited so many of his and my friends to participate in an accessibility protest. He had experienced discrimination firsthand, and it hurt.

Mrs. Kukka delighted in welcoming our guests into her home. Devon, Marlene, and three of Everett's basketball teammates were those who used wheelchairs, and Mrs. Kukka supervised as I moved some furniture out of the way, then prepared a tray of sandwiches and sodas.

"We should sneak a ramp up Independence Hall," suggested Gary, who had been part of a few demonstrations years earlier. Arranged in a loose circle, we listened to his experiences, and others made suggestions. Although the Penn campus was a worthy target, the fact that Everett, Jacob and his new girlfriend were the only students there, and Everett the only disabled student, made it a moot point.

"What if we get arrested?" asked Marlene in a somewhat fretful tone.

"Then we should get lawyers," Everett countered. "Let's think local. Campus cops are slower. They wouldn't attack us, would they?"

"Isn't the mall part of the Parks Department?" Jacob stood, leaning against a wall, his girlfriend nearby.

"What, no police?" asked Devon.

"No, just park rangers and tour guides."

"Park rangers?" Gary said in a mocking tone.

Somebody snorted. A few others laughed. I turned beet red, but said nothing. The debate took place around me.

Everett looked up and saw my silent glare. Mrs. Kukka's living room amazingly fit everyone. It was as if the room felt larger. But the laughter echoed.

I gestured to him with a shrug. "I'm gonna step outside."

But no. He had to do it, play peacemaker. He had to defend me while getting us wrapped up in his most heroic dare yet.

"Let me tell them."

"No.

"Please."

"Whatever." I stood back.

"Excuse me. Everyone? I think you've met Reid. He's... he's my boyfriend, and he's worked as a park ranger, and they are the most wonderful people." He sniffed. "And they will give us trouble if we don't think this through. So don't laugh, okay?"

"Sorry 'bout that," Gary said.

I nodded.

There was a pause after Everett's thanks. I was certainly touched, but his emotion felt a bit polished. This trait would become clearer as I attended the public functions where he, his mother, his professors, everyone at Penn, it seemed, who connected him to an opportunity, provided a situation where he needed to perform.

Yet here he was, ringleader-apparent for a half dozen people, mostly in chairs, ready to bite a slothful bureaucracy on the ass with an accessibility protest.

The agenda seemed to have been forgotten, some other announcements were made, but in a pause, Jacob said to me, loud enough for others to hear, "So, Reid. You still have a uniform?"

That time, I was the one laughing.

The decided target became an administration branch of City Hall. I held off my concerns until everyone had left.

"Ev. I could lose my summer job, get banned or something."

"Look; technically you were an employee, so you're not impersonating an officer, or ranger. You were on the payroll."

"Which makes it worse."

"No, which makes it a misdemeanor and not a felony, probably."

"Look, I just can't. I'm sorry."

"That's okay. We'll do something downtown. City Hall's fine. I'll just never get a job there. So we're in the same boat."

"I dunno," I pondered. "Didn't other politicians who got elected, like, protest the Vietnam War?"

"Maybe."

"But what if you get arrested? Don't you need bail money?"

"I don't know. I should probably get some cash. Mother's little helper."

"Your what?"

"The credit card?"

"Right." I put away the cleaned cups and dishes and let him head off to our room.

"But if you did do it," Everett said, about twenty minutes later, in bed. He sat up, cleared his throat, thought a moment, and said, "*Eperiri in uniformis et nutrientibus tue erecta gallus.*"

"I heard 'erect' something."

He sighed, then offered a flirtatious grin. "If you try it on, you get a prize."

The morning of the protest was sunny and brisk, calm and quiet, since it was a Saturday. Everett spent a few hours making calls to the various participants with reminders and an eager enthusiasm that encouraged me. And yet, by the time we headed out for our drive downtown, inside, my stomach growled from nervousness and hunger. With all the preparations, I'd forgotten to eat anything since breakfast.

We found a parking spot a few blocks from City Hall, then headed toward the nearby corner where we'd agreed to meet the others.

"Remind me again why we're doing this on a Saturday?" I asked I walked beside Everett.

"Slow news day," he said as he tugged on his wheels. "That means more coverage. Jacob's been working with one of the Penn student journalism majors on a big feature."

"But nobody's here," I said as I gestured to the sparsely populated street.

"That's not the point," Everett countered. "We get our visuals, make our statements, and that becomes the story. See? Some of the guys are already here."

He pointed toward the corner where a few of our conspirators were gathered.

"Hi, yes. I'm Park Ranger Connitt. I have the wheelchair tour group we'd scheduled."

"You say you scheduled it?"

The City Hall guard looked put off, until he saw half of the people in wheelchairs already outside on the sidewalk.

"I don't know where the ramp is." He clicked a walkie-talkie, "Hey, do we got a ramp?"

I raised a hand. "Actually, we have our own."

A wooden plank was being unfolded on the steps below him. The steps had been measured by one of Gerard's hunky straight tech carpenter pals three days before in the scene shop, where I'd assisted in seeing my crude design made real.

"Oh." The guard seemed surprised. "Wow. Come on in. Check in at reception."

Everett wheeled up next me, recited, "*Udaces fortuna iuvat or fortes fortuna iuvat.*"

"Not now!" I muttered.

Despite me, he said as he rolled by, "Fortune favors the brave."

Once up the first set of stairs, the group of volunteer protestors lined up along the base of a large set of stairs inside the building. They stayed put and waited as a photographer took pictures. The hallway echoed as a group of tourists offered curious looks.

After a few minutes, with people coming up and down the stairs trying to shove their way around the wheelchairs, the head of security, or at least the largest one to loom over me, demanded one thing or another, and then said simply, "Sir, have you asked your tour to step asi- roll aside?"

"Three times, sir."

He simmered, looked at them, then at me.

"Who's in charge here?"

"Not me, sir."

He stepped away briskly, stood before the row of people, seven, including Marlene, Devon and others from Temple, and the guys from Everett's basketball team, who'd parked their chairs in front of the City Hall stairs. They didn't shout, they didn't pull out signs or banners. They just parked.

"Ladies and gentlemen, if you are intending to stay here, you are risking arrest."

"Our legal counsel's the guy with the beard," I nodded once to Jacob, the savvy member of the group who'd called a few newspapers and a TV station. "If it's not on the news, it didn't happen," he'd said. Determined to wait for more of them to show, other than the eager student photographer from Penn, Jacob stalled as he talked with the guard.

They conferred. Everett offered a steely determined grin.

I had to lean against a cool marble column. After facing off against the campus security men, I'd lost about half a pound of water weight in sweat.

Finally, a TV camera crew and a photographer from one of the daily papers joined the Penn student journalist, got interviews, and after less than an hour, the point had been made.

"That's it?" I asked as the others began to disperse.

"That's it," Everett beamed.

"I'm glad nobody got arrested," I added, calmed and a bit underwhelmed.

"Please," Everett scoffed. "No cop or security guard wants a picture of himself dragging some cripple into a paddy wagon."

My twenty-first birthday party, combined with the post-protest celebration two days later, brought together the most unusual collection of people. Gerard's artsy pals mixed with Everett's older teammates from the basketball team, his debate teammates, and my own classmates Devon, Eric, who chatted with a few of Mrs. Kukka's colleagues. I felt a bit overwhelmed to see these people from such different points in our lives mingling, laughing, discussing everything from politics to gardening.

The wheelchair traffic once again made for a slight challenge, solved by moving some furniture. I'd set up some folding tables Mrs. Kukka had borrowed from a church down the street, arranged them in the driveway, and for a while the party spread from the yard to the rooms of the house, until the cake and food were served. Most people wheeled or walked inside as dusk fell.

Even though we had said 'No gifts,' a colorful stack of wrapped boxes and cards in envelopes had accumulated in the dining room side table.

Everett beamed with pride over his additional bit of fame, perhaps because it was all a successful group effort. Copies of the local and student newspapers articles were stacked on the table beside the gifts, and everyone marveled over them.

"Just make sure you all show up for the city council meeting next week," Everett scolded as he handed out copies of the clippings.

The protest had gained the attention of at least one local politician. While we knew that strength in numbers might persuade the city to step up some aspect of accessibility improvements, it might also fall on patronizing ears. Nevertheless, Everett had been chosen to be the lead speaker at the upcoming hearing.

By the time the cake presentation and "Happy Birthday" singing took place, Everett turned up the cassette mix he'd prepared —nothing too raucous, a medley of new pop songs and old standards from his collection.

At one point, Devon wheeled up beside me in the driveway, a bit cheerful from a few beers.

"I'm headin' out before I get too drunk," he grinned. "I just wanted to congratulate you." We shook hands.

"It's just a birthday. Oh, you mean the protest? That wasn't my—"

"No, I mean you and Ev." He nodded toward Everett, who was on the other side of the yard, laughing at someone's joke. "Remember when I met you, back when you were a freshman? You were all sad-eyed and tellin' me how much you wanted to be with him."

"Wow," I must have blushed. "That seems like so long ago."

"Well, you did it."

I reached down to hug him, until a car horn tooted out on the street.

"That's my ride. You keep on keepin' on, Reid."

"Okay."

"An' if he gets on you, tell Ev I said you're a good man."

As the afternoon shifted to dusk, some of the other guests bid us goodnight and left in small groups.

I stepped outside to drop a bag of garbage into one of the cans beside the driveway. In the darkness, a tiny coal of orange lit up, swirled.

"Just me; a fag for a fag." Gerard stepped into the porch light.

"Just make sure the butt's out and put it in the garbage," I said. "Our beloved landlady's picky about her garden."

Gerard held up his nearly empty plastic cup, dropped his cigarette in with a wet hiss.

"Congratulations on your fabulous media event. Sorry I couldn't make it."

"Well, it was kind of focused. I was just the decoy."

"Still, it's good. Much more focused than Gay Jeans Day."

I chuckled. While pretty much the gayest friend we had, even Gerard dismissed such attempts at visibility.

"I should get back inside."

"Wait. Come sit." He parked himself on the porch, patted the plank beside him. "The party's great. It'll keep. Relax."

I wiped my hands, reluctantly sat. "Certainly an interesting mix."

"Our friends are a reflection of who we are."

"I guess so. And thanks for the present." Gerard had gotten me a snazzy vintage dress shirt. He had thoughtfully spared me a gift in any wild colors; just a deep green that I actually liked.

"Feel any different, being twenty-one; legal?"

"Nope. Just happy,"

"You should let me take you boys out to a few bars."

"Oh, I don't know how long this'll go on. Besides, I don't know if Ev'll want to. He gets a little tired sometimes, doesn't show it. But I can tell."

"Maybe some other night."

"Let me ask him, after we take a, what's it called? A disco nap."

Gerard sighed, stretched his legs. "You know, I really admire you. I always have."

"Really? For what?"

"You're …what's the word? Stalwart."

"What do you mean?"

"Strong; steadfast. You're so protective of him. I knew when we met, you were always going to be there for him. It was so funny you being jealous of me. I would never–"

"I'm sorry. I was so stupid. But I don't see that as being strong."

"Maybe not, but you are, and you know, it's not about him or you. It's what's between you, the connection. People can see it, even when you're trying to act casual. They don't want you, or him. Well, some do. But I think it's more… they want that energy, that ungraspable …something between you two."

"Is that love?"

Gerard smiled as he patted my shoulder. "Maybe someday you'll find out."

Chapter 29
May 1982

"Those daffodils are a bit brash, don't you think?"

Mrs. Kukka knelt before the flowerbed, giving the brightly colored blooms a doubtful glance. I'd helped her plant the bulbs back in the fall, but she wanted to trim the grass around them. The canvas pad below her knees was similar to one my mother used in her own garden, but our landlady's was more worn from years of use.

Crouching beside her, I compared the new plants jutting up next to the settled blossoms of more subtly tinted plants; the ferns, lavender and wild thyme. She'd even let a cluster of wild daisies spread beyond the outskirts of the lawn, and a few varieties of common moss had formed a fuzzy coating over a few decoratively placed rocks.

We had pruned the side yard's clusters of jasmine and a lovely blue ceanothus bush, the clippings of which she saved for later. "Perhaps some bouquets for a few of my friends, oh, and in the living room," she said.

But the daffodils did sort of stick out. "They're definitely perky," I surmised, not wanting to be critical.

"I suppose we should give them a chance."

A month before, when she had casually mentioned that she needed a few gardening supplies, I offered to drive the van with her to a shop outside of the city. Everett perked up at the mention of shopping, and the three of us had made a day of it.

"You know, Eugene's ashes were buried right under that redbud." She nodded to her left toward the small tree at the edge of the front yard's garden.

I didn't remind her that she had already told me that, but simply admired its still-flowering magenta buds. In my mind, I was playing the Latin-naming game, but without Everett nearby to coach me, the terms eluded me.

"I'm so glad I found those clippings," she said.

"Which ones?" The week before I'd helped her carry a few boxes downstairs in the hallway. I'd peeked inside one, found a series of magazines and newspaper clippings sorted in manila folders. The next day, they were gone.

"The ones about that disease. You boys need to be informed. Part of my husband's work, the basic sanitary structures prevented so many cholera and malaria outbreaks in some of those countries he visited. You know, an anthropologist isn't supposed to interfere with a culture, but sometimes he would just rail over the ineptitude of those governments, as if they were deliberately allowing those poor people to die."

She wiped her hands of dirt, then fumbled to rise, until I helped her up.

"A little gardening tip for you; ashes don't make the best fertilizer, no matter what anyone says."

"I'll keep that in mind."

"Now, how about you get the hose and we give it all a sprinkle."

As I walked around the side of the house, I admired the simplicity of Mrs. Kukka's plants. At first it had seemed somewhat haphazard, the arrangement of various clusters of flowering plants and shrubs. The trees offered a bit of shade without darkening the window views, and it all seemed to have a sort of balance.

As I handed her the hose, uncoiling it to stretch to the front yard, she continued one of her stories about her husband.

"He was always off on some adventure," she said as she used a finger to tighten the water's spray. "We often set in new plants, but never anything too exotic."

"Did you travel with him a lot?"

"Oh, sometimes. Most often I had my own work at Penn." She turned to me, almost soaking my leg before giggling lightly and turning the hose downward. "It must be so wonderful to have the world ahead of you, you boys."

I smiled. "Yes, ma'am. I just hope we can figure out what we want to do after school. Ev wants to go to grad school, but

I just like getting my hands dirty. All this studying's getting to be a bit much."

"You know, it takes finding a balance." And then she offered another bit of advice. "You have to figure out where you can both be happy. Are you excited about working in the park?"

"I guess so."

I had told her about my job interview at Fairmount Park, how I'd barely gotten hired. Despite being qualified, there simply weren't that many openings, and my work would probably be relegated to groundskeeping, at first.

"You know, if the nature study out in the woods doesn't work out, you could always give landscaping a try; it'd keep you in the city, if that's what you boys decide on."

"Well, thanks. That's…I'll consider that."

Her suggestion did sort of make sense. Instead of trying to take on an entire forest, shifting to a smaller goal, the beautiful microcosm of nature before us, contained in one home, began to resemble a possibility.

Later that afternoon, Everett returned from his second to last final exam. "Cause enough for celebration," he declared.

We sat on the porch, sipping lemonade that Everett had spiked with a little bit of vodka he'd pilfered from a gathering of Mrs Kukka's colleagues. We'd offered Everett's video player, and a former professor showed converted films of his documentation of tribal dances from Ghana.

"Anyway. What's the job? So, you'll be doing what, weed-whacking?"

"Pretty much," I said.

"Forgive me for saying it, but it sounds beneath you."

"It's more money than I could ever make at another state park, and I don't want to be gone all summer again."

"But you won't come to the kid's summer camp."

"Aw, Ev. I loved it, but it's just not gonna work out. I'm sorry."

Everett sighed. "Well, the kids'll miss you. Kenny'll miss you."

"Please don't guilt-trip me."

"I'm... Reid. I'm just trying to make plans. I can probably get something like that in the city, some summer school program. I'll check with the Magee folks."

"Are you sure?"

"No, I'm not sure. I'm just making it up as I go."

We settled, sipped out drinks.

"The garden looks great."

"Thanks. She's been growing it for years, told me about some earlier versions."

The last of dusk's sunlight glinted off the tops of nearby trees, giving them a golden shimmer, then fell away. A warm breeze passed, whirling across the porch.

"So," I said, after a moment.

"So, if we don't go back to work with the kids, do you wanna go camping this summer?"

"Sure, if I can take a few days off. Where?"

"Jacob and his lady pal mentioned Susquehannock."

"Did they? That's a mouthful."

The sprawling trio of forests, including Elk, Sproul, with two smaller parks to the west, were high up on my to-do list. I'd never camped there. It seemed perfect. Going with a straight couple who knew who we were, and were cool about; it seemed great.

"So, I could get the camping stuff when we go back home, unless we go someplace west, closer."

"Why don't you help us figure that out, Ranger Reid?"

I would have preferred to go alone with Everett, but if there were an emergency or anything, we'd have backup. Our previous few overnight treks were more limited, keeping near flat park areas. We took trails, but wide ones. I refused to carry him on any smaller trails. I told myself that he understood. He acted like he did. I was just happy that he wanted to make plans where we could be together.

"Are they gonna drive?" I asked. "We should take the van."

"Well, yeah. I kind of already offered it."

"Oh. You already–"

"Well, yeah, but I told them I'd ask you first."

"Well, it's your van."

"Yeah, but it's your camping equipment."

"Can you make sure it won't break down again?"

"I guess I'd better," he said.

"They have their own stuff, too?"

"Yeah, Jacob said he does."

"They better. I'm not sharing a tent with anyone but you."

"I'm sorry, I just–"

"No, it's cool. It's cool. When do you want to go?"

"Memorial Day Weekend?"

I couldn't help but roll my eyes. It would be the most crowded weekend of the season. Amateur week. Beer cans. Human raccoons.

"Uh, how about a week later?" I suggested.

"Uh, why?"

"It'll be a lot less crowded."

"You're the expert."

"I mean, if it's not–"

"No worries. I'll tell them I can't, use some medical excuse, a rehab appointment or something. Always works."

I grinned. "Yeah, but ask them. It'll be fun."

"Cool."

I got up, leaned over and hugged him, and thought to call it a night, but Everett was doing a little happy dance in his chair, pumping his arms up and down.

"Plus, the idea of Jacob humping his date in the next tent sounds pretty sexy."

"A fourway via proximity?" I joked. "I mean. Yeah, sure…you slut."

"Whore."

"Hey, I never charged admission."

He chuckled, inched his chair closer to mine. While I longed to keep this sweet moment, savor it, I had to ask him.

"Hey, since we're discussing sex…"

Everett offered one of his Groucho eyebrow-raised double-takes.

"Not like that. Did you read those news clippings Mrs. Kukka saved for us?"

The small stack had grown, and I'd noticed that Everett had moved them to his accordion file with his debate topic clippings. The label read simply "?"

"Yeah. It's pretty creepy," he turned away, swirled with the ice in his glass.

"So, what do you think?"

He glanced at me, offered merely a raised eyebrow. "As I said; creepy."

"But is it just about gay sex?"

"One article talks about blood. Another goes on about these multiple infections, mostly pneumonia, and some weird bird flu."

"But do you think it's just some combination of STDs that could–"

"I said I don't know, Reid. You're the nature expert. I haven't even taken a Biology class since I was at Pinecrest. Maybe it's like those tree diseases you studied, how it just spreads through squirrel shit."

"That's not–"

"I said I don't know."

"Okay. Sheesh."

"One thing's for sure. We might want to curtail our 'dalliances,'" he said with a declarative tone.

"Okay then."

"Let's just–"

"Talk about something else?"

"Yes."

Ice clinked as he took a last sip of his drink, even though his glass was empty.

"Do want some more?"

"No, thanks."

"Well, I do."

He pushed off behind me. I didn't look back. The sun had set, but a few blooms in the garden seemed to glow in the fading light.

After a few rounds of phone tag, the summer's weekend plans bounced back and forth with various interferences; Jacob's girlfriend's internship at a medical laboratory, Jacob's brother's wedding, Everett's Pittsburgh visits, and my work schedule.

We finally decided on the weekend after the July Fourth holiday. It seemed a long way off, but worth it. I made notes to myself to get a few new camping gear items.

I was casually checking the messages on the answering machine, expecting yet another change of plans via Jacob's almost flirtatious tone, when I heard one from that Sweigard guy.

"Everett. Look, I really would like to see you. I know... I know it's been a long time, but please. Call me."

I almost erased it; almost.

It wasn't until he got home from an afternoon of his final exam at Penn that I silently pointed to the answering machine, then left our bedroom.

Pretending that I wasn't listening as Everett replayed the message, I made us lunch, telling myself that the sound of that stranger's voice didn't disturb me.

When I returned with the tray of sandwiches, he hadn't moved.

"I'm doing this." He stared at the phone.

"You want me to leave?"

"No." He sighed with a resolve, then an almost pained determination, and dialed.

After a series of awkward greetings, one-way pauses, forced laughter and a few minutes of watching Everett nervously fold his legs, peel off a sock, pick at a toenail, I felt like a voyeur.

"I'll have to ask my boyfriend."

A pause.

"Yes, I have a boyfriend."

a

Pause.

"Two years."

I held up three fingers.

"Three years."

A longer pause.

"No, he's coming, too. Hey, what about…? When is Gay Pride?"

Another pause.

"You don't …? Well, we'd like to … Maybe." He looked up to me. I nodded. "The last Sunday? Okay, for the weekend."

After a few repeated goodbyes, he hung up the phone and seemed relieved.

"You want to go to New York City?"

"Uh, I guess."

"He said we could stay with him."

"Are you okay with that?" I asked.

"I'm okay if you're okay."

"Um… I'm not okay."

"Let's reserve a hotel room, then," he said as he dug in his drawer for his wallet. "Mother's little helper's due for some action."

b

Chapter 30
June 1982

As Jessica, my supervisor, had warned me, the bulk of my initial work at Fairmount Park was spent cleaning up after partying crowds who took over picnic areas and left garbage cans overflowing. When I wasn't working with my new coworkers cleaning up, we tooled around in pairs on the little electric carts or in pick-up trucks to check on fallen trees, clear brush and make lists of damaged benches for the construction crew.

As I grew more familiar with the immensity of the many divisions of the park, and its wooded and open areas, all the way up to the grounds near the cemetery, it all took on a daunting immensity. As soon as we alerted the construction crew of a precarious broken railing overlooking the river, another task took over, like disposing of a few discovered dead animals; a dog, a goose or two.

Still, I found moments during my lunch breaks to just sit alone and enjoy some cool shade under an oak, or to watch a casual softball game at one of the playing fields. At times, in between a few pesky flies, a butterfly would land near or on me, and the quiet pleasure of being outside all day returned.

After two weeks of what became a sort of exhausting boot camp, I stopped by the cramped offices of the Parks Department after a Thursday shift. Jessica was on the phone, and I waited by the door until she waved me in.

"So, what's up? Are we working you too hard?"

"It's okay," I said. "I was just wondering. I had these projects that I was hoping to sort of blend in with my studies at Temple."

"What sort of projects?" Jessica asked.

"One of my, um, side focuses is ramps; accessibility."

Jessica offered a confused glance. I had an inkling that her tough demeanor and short hair might be a clue that she was a lesbian, but I didn't dare ask, or let on about myself.

"See, my, uh, roommate is, he uses a wheelchair, and it's always been an idea—"

"Most of the park is flat. Where do you think ramps are needed?"

"Well, I know we can't change all the smaller trails, but what about some of the historic buildings? Just like a ramp to fit over the stairs or—"

"That would require approval from maintenance, and the board. They get very touchy about their properties."

"Okay, but—"

"I'd have to make a budget proposal; could take months. I'm not sure if there'd be funds for something like that."

"Okay, well, it was just an idea."

"I can give you some more hours, if you're up for it."

"Sure," I said, hiding my disappointment. "I just need the last weekend in June off."

"Planning a vacation?"

"Something like that."

"Turkey okay again?"

"Sounds good."

"Bamaytah an' mayoz?"

"Sí!"

Everett and I shared another round of puns and jokes that didn't even require a responding chuckle. We'd established a morning routine of him making lunches with our stock of groceries, and me making coffee, of which I had become dependent on, what with my early work hours. I foraged in the cabinet for a few extra snacks.

Having snagged an internship with one of Philadelphia's council members, he was working as an assistant to a liaison with the Gay and Lesbian Task Force. Although the offices were still a hassle for him to get up to, he had been given a handicap parking space in lieu of a paycheck.

"Any news on the political front?"

"The bill's getting re-introduced next week by Blackwell. He's got eight others lined up to sign on." Everett wrapped our sandwiches in bags.

"Alrighty then!" I replied with a bit of forced enthusiasm, brought on perhaps by the fresh jolt of coffee.

"So soon, you can declare your homo-ness without fear of discrimination."

"I'm sure the flora and fauna will be thrilled."

Everett tossed the paper bag, which I put into my backpack, along with a copy of Thoreau's *Walden* he had given me to read during my lunch breaks.

"Are you making light of all my hard work for equality?"

"No, but you're hobnobbing with city officials while I'm cutting brush and picking up beer cans."

Everett offered a scolding bit of praise. "You're doing God's work!"

"Yeah? Which god?"

He shrugged. "Are you getting next Friday off?"

"Yes."

"Do you still want to go?"

"Yes, as long as we can go to Central Park along with all the gay stuff. It's only a tenth the size of Fairmount Park, but much better designed; Frederick Olmstead's masterpiece!"

"You're amazing."

"Am I? 'Amazing?'" I said, imitating Kenny, our fondly missed summer school kid.

He smiled, admiring me. "Your first time in the greatest city in the world, and all you can think about are more trees."

As we headed out together, eventually in separate directions, I bid my boyfriend a brisk farewell, hoping to keep up my cheerful mood. While attending our first Gay Pride event would be fun, the real reason we were going to New York City filled me with a quiet dread.

Manhattan was only a two-hour train ride away, but from the moment we arrived, I sensed a vast difference from

Philadelphia. New York rumbled, it hummed, it loomed. People didn't politely dodge us; they jostled us.

We'd packed light, since we were only staying two nights. I'd managed to stuff clothes and toiletries in a large duffel bag, and Everett's backpack sagged a bit on the back of his chair, but we managed.

After checking into the hotel, and being snubbed by dozens of taxi cabs, we somehow made it to the address Wesley Sweigard had given us, a brick street in SoHo, which, Everett corrected me, was near How-stun Street, not Hew-stin.

After being buzzed in at a suspiciously funky front door, we entered a cramped elevator, rode up two floors and wandered down a wide bare hallway. We passed an open doorway where a quick glance inside showed a construction crew assembling drywall. Further down the hallway, the man who greeted us at the open door was not the same man from those yearbook photos.

While still tall, he seemed older, thinner, cautious, with an almost grey pallor.

"You made it!"

An awkward hug as Wesley bent down to Everett, then a semblance of a handshake with me, and we were led in to an expansive loft apartment with high windows. Sparsely furnished, the open living room and wood floors echoed our every word. One side of the room opposite the windows shined with metal cabinets and a fridge. On one otherwise blank white wall, a huge poster hung, a Japanese version of a Paul Newman movie. It was all very stylish and cool, more like an idea of a home than a real one.

As we sat and Wesley brought us glasses of water, he told us of the building's history as a sweatshop, like many others on the block, and the growing number of renovations by artists and "the newly successful, like myself." He almost laughed it off as a joke.

We sat, distanced from each other by the furniture, Everett parked beside the long black sofa where I perched. We talked lightly of our studies, our slight travel difficulties, and the weather, and Wesley offered a summary of his few years in New York, his quick rise as a financial investor, anything but why we were really there, until a silence took hold.

"Can I... Reid, do you mind if Everett and I have some time alone?"

One glance toward me, and Everett sighed, asserted himself. "Actually, Wes, anything you tell me gets back to Reid, so you might as well just talk now."

His shoulders slumped a bit, a slow resignation spread across his face.

"You two really are a couple. I wish I had that. Okay, then." He scratched his forehead, looked around the room, at Everett, then at me. "So, I've got it."

"Got what?" Everett asked.

"It. Whatever they're calling it; gay cancer."

"Why didn't you tell me?" Everett asked.

"Because I didn't think you'd come."

"Wes, I would've. We would have."

"Well, you're here."

Another silence, until Everett asked, "So, when did you...?"

Wesley breathed in, then out. "It started with the flu. I couldn't shake it; missed a week at work. Then I got this weird infection in my mouth. Then I had the shits, for like, a month. Then these started showing up." He tugged his shirt up, revealed a few discolored speckles of some sort.

"Are those scars?" I asked.

"Lesions; it's called Kaposi's Sarcoma."

"How did...?"

"The doctors didn't know. But it was pretty easy for me to figure out. I heard about others, and then one of the guys I used to party with just dropped out, quit his job. It had to be from all the sex."

"How much?" Everett asked.

"Enough, I guess. For a while I thought it was the cocaine."

"The what?"

"I had a little habit for a while."

"What's a little?"

Wesley sort of shrugged at Everett, offered a dry huff that stopped short of a chuckle. "Anyway, I made a boatload of money. Funny, it's not helping now. No amount of fancy doctors are working out. My family's already hinting that I should make out my will. Can you believe it? Not like they're getting any."

"I don't know what to say," Everett almost whispered.

"Tell me you forgive me."

Everett looked away, at his knees, over to me. I wanted to take him in my arms, out of that room, away from that city. But we were there, facing his demon, broken and frail as he was.

"I'm here, aren't I?"

Wesley offered a meager smile.

"So, what are you going to do?" Everett asked.

"I already left my job."

"Did they fire you?"

"Not in so many words. My boss... hinted, loudly, that I should take a leave of absence, then he paid me off. And my family's... It's all over. I'm... I just wanted to make amends with you, Mutt, before..."

"Wes, don't..."

"No. I do. I want you to be okay."

"We are."

"Reid, you taking care of him?"

"Trying," I stammered.

"Just so you know. I really don't think I got it until after we... I mean, I never even got fucked until I moved here."

"But you had sex with other guys before Ev–" I blurted.

"I don't think that's relevant," Everett said, attempting to relieve me. It came out as more of a scold.

"Oh, yeah. It's okay. A few. Listen, Reid. I don't want you to freak out or anything."

"I'm trying not to."

"Just to have you here, to share some good memories too, I hope."

"Sure." I blushed.

"Speaking of good memories," Everett said. "Do you have those pictures?"

"Oh my god. You want them back so no one finds them when I croak?"

Neither of us replied.

"Gimme a minute." Wesley walked into another room, his bedroom, I assumed.

Everett gave me a confused look, whispered, "I think it'll be okay if you step out for a bit."

"What? But you said–"

He held up his hand to quiet me.

"Here we are," Wesley returned, tossed a small envelope onto Everett's lap.

"Thanks."

Everett didn't open it, but simply placed it into his backpack.

"I don't know how it all happened," Wesley muttered.

"What happened?" I asked.

"Everything. This city. I mean, I had this image of myself, you know; Connecticut commuter, maybe just a little gay on the side. But after a year of just busting my balls, twelve-hour workdays, a few of the guys at work took me out to a disco, and we ripped off our ties and I got other invites as soon as I took my shirt off. I mean, I got popular really fast."

He shook his head, not in shame, but a cryptic smile of astonishment. "My one roommate got snatched up as a model, spent more time in Europe, and I was, like, snorting at 54 with Grace fucking Jones. And the bathhouses, dude. Unbelievable; just packed with hot men."

Everett and I exchanged a glance. "Really?" he let out a nervous giggle.

Some of this had been filtered down to me; Mom's *People* magazines, Gerard's bragging rants about his weekends in New York. Packed bathhouses hadn't been exactly clarified.

"But guys started getting sick, and I stopped a while ago. I mean, really. A month of bronchitis'll cure the appetite for another orgy."

We all laughed at that, albeit forced.

"So, you guys aren't…?"

"Aren't what?" Everett asked.

"Um, whoring it up?" Wesley offered dryly.

We laughed, and I had to mutely aim my hands to Everett, who replied in a stately tone, "We had a few adventures."

"Dalliances," I offered.

Everett swung a deliberately missed punch.

"Well then, don't worry. If you're not screwing around, it's not contagious other ways, at least not… in the air, or the dishes or anything. If you wanna leave, I'll understand. Everybody else has."

"We're staying, okay?" Everett looked at me, his eyes on the verge of tearing. I noticed the slightest shake of his head, which I thought meant he wanted me to leave. That brief pleading sent a surge of emotion through me; his need for my support made me almost tremble.

"Wes, can I have a word with Reid?"

"Sure. I'm gonna go… do something in my room. I got some other stuff I wanted to show you."

As he left, I could only offer Everett a silent, almost panicked look.

"Can you… leave us for a bit?"

"But you said not to let you–"

His hand pressed against my shoulder. "I'm pretty sure his hypnotic charms are gone. Just for a little while."

"But–"

"It'll be okay. I just want to talk with him."

I nodded.

Wesley returned, shyly, almost, carrying a cardboard box. "All clear?"

"Sure," Everett said.

"Hey, um, anyone hungry?" I asked.

"I don't really have much," Wesley looked toward his kitchen.

"Can we get Chinese food?" I blurted out.

Everett grinned, wiped his face. Wesley's eyes sort of brightened.

"Sure. There's a great place down the block that's pretty good."

"Great," Everett added, through a brief sniffle. "Let me get my wallet," Everett reached into his backpack.

"No, this is on me," Wesley protested as he slowly stood, then handed me some bills, and suggested a few items he knew were good. "Thanks," he said.

But I knew it wasn't about the food.

Outside, a window I found myself staring into displayed a trio of black dresses, shrouds almost, adorning headless suspended mannequins. I couldn't tell if it was a clothing store or an art gallery.

How much time should I give them? What would they discuss? Was I any part of that private talk? Would Wesley beg for one last embrace, or more? What was and wasn't contagious? But what daunted me more was to simply do as Everett asked, to trust him.

After deliberately wandering around the neighborhood, I found the restaurant and waited for the food to arrive in bags.

When I returned, I didn't mention the way they looked, eyes a bit red from what had been some painful heart-to-heart talk. Beside Everett on the sofa were a few books and framed pictures, taken from the box Wesley had brought, then put aside.

We ate quietly. Wesley didn't seem to be eating much, but neither of us said anything about it.

Everett kept it together that day. I listened to several hours of reveries between the two of them about their private school days. It felt odd to hear two guys so young wax nostalgic, but so much had happened to them both.

Perhaps I served as a sort of buffer between them. Maybe I prevented what might have happened, a confrontation, harsh words. But long after we had finished talking, Wesley assured us twice that no, he wasn't up for joining us the next day at the Pride march, but we should go.

"You need to see it, see all the people," he said. "It's not all bad; a few scary drag queens and what have you. But no, you'll be amazed."

As we gathered ourselves and prepared to leave, Wesley's gifts wrapped in my duffle bag, nightfall had darkened the high windows of Wesley's apartment.

He took me aside, offered a handshake that became a brief hug, and whispered softly, but with an almost scolding tone, "You take care of him."

It wasn't until after we approached the busy intersection of 'How-stun,' found a taxi that would actually stop for us and accommodate Everett, until after we were welcomed into the hotel by the staff, and Everett, back in our room, had hoisted himself off his chair and into the bed, out of most of his clothes and into my arms, that he broke down.

Starting with what sounded like a few chuckles, at first I thought he was laughing at some joke Wesley had told. But of course, he wasn't. As I pressed him closer, tighter against me, almost trying to muffle his sobs into me, he really let go, until a wet stain of tears and snot spread across my T-shirt.

"I'm sorry."

"I'm not," he snorted back a mucusy sob. "I mean, yeah, I'm all upset and tired, but... He told me, he told me he was thinking about just…ending it before he's too... I was thinking about when I was first in rehab, and every day I'd get these angry low points, just defying it. 'No, this is not me. I can rise above,' or whatever. And I'd know that wouldn't happen, couldn't happen." He sniffed.

"Take it," I yanked my shirt toward him.

He looked up at me, those near-black marble eyes red around the edges. "But your letters, and those sweet pictures of you in the woods, and your…"

"My what?"

"Your persistence. You never gave up on me. He doesn't have that. I was so afraid of him, but now…"

I wiped his cheek, finally pulled off my soaked shirt, and just held him.

The next morning, we packed for the day, and I carried our small duffel bag hoisted over my shoulder. Everett rolled ahead of me along the crowded streets, until we came upon a loose line of people standing, watching as a stream of marching people, floats, balloons, banners and smiling men, women, even some kids hoisted on parents' shoulders, poured along Fifth Avenue.

We managed to appreciate this shared joy, this buoyant display of openness. Wasn't this what we wanted, what we tried to emulate in our small way? At some point, standing beside Everett, I had taken his hand, finally comfortable enough to do that on the street. Then I just leaned behind him, my arms draped over his shoulders like a sweater.

Some cute guy in shorts and a cut-off T-shirt that showed off his thin waist and belly button called out for us to join him.

I didn't need to ask Everett. His look up to me, those eager dark eyes sparkling in the sunlight, pleaded for a day of desperately needed joy.

"I don't know if we'll get a cab back uptown," I said. "And I want to see Central Park."

"Okay, but I want to try the subway again. Here. Get out my map," he leaned his shoulder around as I unzipped his backpack.

"There's gotta be a station with an elevator downtown that doesn't stink of pee. We could just take the sidewalk. Besides, I want to see it. Christopher Street, homo central."

"Lead on."

And, after a minute of perusing the map, he handed it to me and I stuffed it into his backpack. We joined the slow-moving parade on the street. In between the banners and balloons, the strolling men in shorts, the women with signs who chanted slogans, I felt a growing elation and was able to put aside our concerns for Wesley.

At one point, the parade slowed to a halt as a distant siren echoed a few blocks south. Mustached men casually draped their arms over each others' shoulders, until someone called out a spontaneous, "Kiss In!"

All around us, people embraced, smooched, and I felt a rush of emotion as I leaned down, took in Everett's smiling face as he squinted under the sun, and kissed him, there, in the middle of a New York City street, surrounded by others.

Then, the parade continued to scattered cheers and applause.

"Take my hand," he said.

"But you can't–"

"I'll manage."

With his left hand in mine, he began a sort of cross-stitch push on his wheels, his path veering a bit from side to side. It became a sort of wavering dance, a bit awkward but worth the effort. We continued on our path, and for me, as usual, Everett led the way.

Chapter 31
July 1982

We stayed in Philadelphia that summer, endured the heat, the noise, as if building up our reserves before escaping for our camping trip with Jacob and his girlfriend.

As much as I wanted to distract and cheer Everett, I also hoped for an ultimate outdoorsy spot for just the two of us, with friends nearby.

All of it, the time apart, then together, meeting Nick in Florida, the fight afterwards, the van incident, even meeting Wesley, bonded us more than any of those initial furtive couplings before college.

We shopped for a shower hose, mini tables, a toilet seat and bucket, somebody borrowed a shovel; then groceries were collected at open markets.

When we weren't working, we perused museums like tourists, saw rock bands like Elvis Costello and the Attractions at JFK Stadium with Gerard when he wasn't couch-surfing at the apartments of his friends in New York City. It was as if we dove into having fun, simply to forget discussing Wesley.

But that didn't stop his concern. Free of coursework during classes, Everett continued his obsessive study habits, but with newspapers and magazines. He returned to Giovanni's Room on his own a few times, and bought every gay newspaper they had, then finally ordered a few subscriptions.

He spent hours poring over every article about the constantly changing theories about the 'gay cancer' that kept spreading. One said it was from Africa. Another supposed it was a combination of the sexually transmitted diseases common among "promiscuous" gay men. Another blamed drugs, while another discounted that, citing hemophiliacs in the death toll.

I left him to his research, knowing he would eventually summate his findings, then ask me to read one article or another. I didn't want to think about it, but I listened, all the while growing worried.

While putting away laundry, I had found one excuse or another to look in Everett's clothes drawer, and merely touched the thick small envelope that Wesley had given him. Perhaps it was my sense of respect for his privacy that had kept me from prying.

As if honoring my trust with a surprise, after I'd finished washing the dishes from a light dinner of cold cuts and salad – Mrs. Kukka had stopped by to nibble a bit with us before going out for the evening. I heard Everett in the bathroom. But as I returned to the bedroom, the envelope lay on the bed. I waited until he returned and slipped into a pair of shorts.

"Well, open it," he said.

"Are you sure?"

"I know you want to."

He wheeled over to the bed, hoisted himself up, and I waited for him to settle in. Despite the summer heat, he liked to lay out our quilt in the daytime, the flat green triangles a mosaic at our knees. After unfastening the clasp of the yellow envelope, I sifted out a half dozen Polaroids, similar to the one he had sent me almost three years before.

Most of them were merely cute; others almost blurry or harshly glared flash shots of a shirtless younger version of him. His grin varied but remained a bit coy. In one, his side exposed with the underwear tugged down, his legs, then thicker and firm, showed his familiar fuzzy hair. The last one stunned me, Everett fully naked, his penis thickened, his eyes half-closed, an Adonis in a dorm room, one part a blur, the other defined in harsh flash.

"It's so…"

"Pretty hot, eh?"

"Are these even legal?"

"Well, I was consenting, but underage, so no."

"What are you going to do with them?"

He reached for my shorts, whose contents had grown. "I can tell what you want to do with them."

"Stop! Don't!" I giggled. "Don't stop!" I crouched away from his tickles, nearly crushing one of the photos.

He laid them out on the bed like Tarot cards, perusing them. "You should add yours to the collection."

"But you gave it to me."

"You can have them all."

"Really?"

"For a trade."

"What did you have in mind?"

"Oh, I'll think of a proper occasion."

He continued to gaze at the images as if they were of someone else. And in a way, they were.

"You're a lot hairier now," I said as I crept my hand under his shirt.

"It's funny," he said. "I want to ask you something."

"What?"

"If you met me now, would you still…"

"What?"

"Would you still want to be with me?"

It wasn't an idea I hadn't considered, and perhaps my hesitation hurt him a little bit. If I'd seen Everett rolling along on campus, would I have ever had the nerve to say anything to him without seeming odd? Wouldn't he be surrounded by friends, admirers, another boyfriend, perhaps? But how could 'we' have ever happened?

"I'm just happy I didn't decide to go on that walk in the woods a few minutes later, after you'd…finished."

"My wintry ablutions?" he joked.

"No, seriously, Ev. I don't know how we could have met. You would have gone to school somewhere else. We're so different, but… you know I feel so comfortable with you, most of the time, when you're not driving me nuts."

"You're so easy to confuse sometimes."

"Well, you, you still… I don't know the word."

"Beguile you?"

"Something like that. I don't know." I glanced at the Polaroids before nervously assembling them together in a stack.

I didn't want to think about what could have been, what had and hadn't happened.

He offered a hand in putting the pictures back in their envelope, then placed them on the bedside table. Coaxing me to a comfortable cuddling position, he stroked my chest, toyed with my nose, ears, with his tongue that time, and offered a waxy kiss.

"I would have been such a mess if this had happened and you hadn't been there for me. And I can't stand the idea some other people have about their illness or disability being some kind of 'blessing.' That's crap, I hate it."

I touched him at his cheek, content that he hadn't shaved, that he was with me.

"But it all opened up a new world to me, people I don't think I ever would have noticed, or cared about."

"What would you be doing instead that you aren't already doing?"

"Well, lacrosse, for one thing. I mean, would there ever be wheelchair lacrosse? I dunno. I'm a little busy to… But that was never important. I'd still have an interest in politics. But I was really naïve before. I had this image of myself as some indolent slutty diplomat's assistant, bedding dignitaries' sons in France or Monaco."

"Really?" I chuckled.

"Well, not exactly. But I just took the world for granted. You…" He reached over, offered a caress to my cheek. "You're doing exactly what you want to do, even with me and all this."

"Well, not exactly. I'd probably still think I should hide out in the woods for a career. And now, it's just a little different; you know, tree versus city. But I don't know if I'd ever meet some guy. I'd never meet anyone like you. I wouldn't even have met you if I hadn't met you."

He chuckled, but it seemed he understood.

"Speaking of the woods," he said.

"Yes?"

"Are we all set for camping with Jacob and his girlfriend of the month?"

"Yes. And I believe it's been a few months."

"Okay, then, Suck-my-Hammock it is."

"Susquehannock."

The drive, broken up by our jokes and conversations, and sing-alongs to various songs on the radio, offered a special change of pace, since Everett had deigned to let Jacob drive the van, while his girlfriend Sarah served as navigator. Everett and I nestled together in the back, occasionally poking our heads up to catch a view or funny road sign. But mostly we sat or lay on a pile of sleeping bags, the camping equipment only occasionally wobbling precariously near us.

The road became more winding after we entered the park, and I leaned up toward the front seat to point at a few roads for Sarah to seek out.

Another hundred feet higher and around several more mountains, I pointed Jacob to an almost hidden road. After slowly driving over gravel and dust for a few hundred yards, the trees parted to reveal an expansive view of rolling hills and valleys.

"Wow," Jacob shouted, the first out of the van. He spread his arms wide, taking in the majestic view. We followed, removing equipment as Everett scooted himself to the door's edge, then hoisted himself to his chair after I'd placed it on the ground.

"It's a little rough, but the clearing should be okay."

"I got it." He had to tug a bit harder, but his wheels managed to tread over the dirt.

"Somebody else had a good idea," Sarah said as she set a box of cooking utensils near a small circle of rocks that corralled the ashy remnants of a fire. She tied her long auburn hair into a bun with a hairclip. Despite her small frame, she hauled cartons with ease and determination.

"You seem like you know what you're doing," I smiled.

"Girl Scouts, five years." She held up a few fingers as a saluting oath.

We each set about our chosen duties; Jacob the tents, Sarah the cooking, "fulfilling my gender role stereotype," she joked. Everett decided to focus on filling up an inflatable mattress, using his hands on the foot pump. I chose a less glamorous chore of digging a hole for our communal toilet.

A while later, I returned with another bundle of sticks and kindling, to see an almost homey setting. The two tents bookended the campfire, their openings facing the view.

Uphill, my little contribution was already being enjoyed.

Everett sat like Rodan's "Thinker" atop the plastic toilet placed above the small pit I'd dug. He dared me to take a picture. We'd set up a tarp on one side facing our campground, but Everett enjoyed just sitting there, waiting for something to happen naturally.

"You okay up here?"

"Did we bring any more books?" he asked as he broke the pose. "Damn Chaucer."

A flat clanging noise drew our attention.

Sarah held up an empty pot and a fork, and announced, "Dinner's ready, menfolk!"

"Sinnema…"

"Sinnemahoning?"

"Honig or honing?"

"I forget."

Something about the fresh air made the wine go to our heads. Everett and Sarah sputtered over the name of the river byway village we'd visited on our way up. We'd each bought postcards at the shop and then sent them to each other across the road at the post office.

After a few rounds of jokey Indian-naming, the talk shifted to a more wistful contemplative tone as Sarah asked if any of us knew which Native American tribes had originally roamed the Pennsylvania hills. No one could.

"They probably died off more from the diseases we evil white men brought them," I said.

"Don't look at me," Jacob held up his hands. "My people were busy being slaughtered in Europe."

"It's so strange," Sarah pondered.

"What is?"

"Diseases, plagues, then and now. One of my fellow med students got into this argument over, you know, the gay cancer or whatever it's called, and said that exponentially, it could get so much worse. And then he brought up quarantines and it turned into this nasty argument that–"

"Do we have to talk about this?" I cut in.

"What's the problem?" Sarah said.

"We're here in the mountains, away from all that."

"I'm sorry, I was just trying–"

"We're on vacation. Can't we just…?"

"Vacate?" Everett snipped.

"Yes," I defended.

"Fine," Everett said. "We shall only discuss all things botanical."

"That'd be nice," I replied.

"I'm sorry," Sarah muttered.

"No, I'm sorry. I just–"

"No, it's fine." She shook it off.

Had Everett told them about Wesley? I didn't ask. He wasn't my friend, or whatever Wesley was.

A silence ensued, the crackling of kindling, until Everett struck up a winsome version of one of his Cole Porter favorites.

As we settled into our tents, I waited for Everett to scoot off his chair, then crawl inside.

"Cozy," I said.

"You horny?"

"It wouldn't matter. I'm exhausted."

"I'll bet our compadres are having fun."

Their nighttime intimacies across the campsite were kept to a few quiet giggles.

I felt the long day's effect as well. While it was an ideal situation, Everett and I cuddled in a pair of zipped-together sleeping bags, the air mattress squeaked under our every move. We settled on a sideways position in the darkness.

Running my fingers through his short curls, I smiled.

"You like my summer look?"

"Yes."

"So you did hate the New Wave style."

"I didn't hate it. I just… you're beyond style."

"Easy dodge."

I caressed the beard stubble on his face, with my other arm cushioned under his neck. His hand offered a few exploratory touches under my clothes. We kissed softly, slowly, but somewhere in the middle of it, our moves slowed and we fell asleep.

The next morning, I arose before Everett. Sunlight pressed through the tent, giving his sleeping face a warm orange glow. Despite being incredibly hungry, and needing to pee, I lay next to him, gazing at him for a long moment, and resisted the urge to caress his face. Instead I quietly rose and left the tent.

Stepping downhill from the campsite, I peed, and took in the sweeping panorama. Dawn mist crept through fingery treetops.

Over breakfast, we discussed our day's plans. Jacob craved some rock-climbing, although the map didn't seem to show any potential areas for that.

Jacob asked, "So what led you to this spot, Reid. You said some friend…?"

"I got some pointers from a former coworker's friend. But what struck me was the name of the road we're on."

"Which is?" Sarah asked.

I unfolded the map and handed it to her.

"Dancing Bear Lane?"

Laughs all around, followed by, "And then it's on to Hiney View?"

"Hyner View," I corrected. "It's the most amazing peak, and there's off-road camping nearby, I think."

"How about we just settle here and drive there for the day?" Jacob suggested as he pried at a stuck carabiner.

I shrugged. The camp was set up rather nicely. What I didn't tell him, and what no one else noticed as we turned into the road, was the emergency phone box back up the road only a few yards.

"We could do that. There's also a lake down on the other side, with herons. We could do that tomorrow or the next day."

Jacob seemed preoccupied.

"Let me check something," I said. "Half an hour."

"What's up?" His attention returned to me.

I said quietly, as if conspiring, "A little prepared romantic spontaneity."

I checked the trail map, jogged uphill as long as I could imagine tugging Everett up it, until I found a clearing, with a sort of view, more than a dabble of sky, and raced back down.

"Wagons, ho!"

I tugged. He followed.

"I am so glad you brought this," Everett said. "How utterly convenient."

"I thought so," I said over my shoulder as I pulled the plastic sled. Everett's older sled, a gift from me, lay in a storage bin someplace on the outskirts of Greensburg, awaiting either of his parents to finally divvy up the loot. Instead I'd brought an older one from home.

"My Rosebud," he lamented as I tugged him along the trail in the lost sled's replica.

With a sleeping bag padding him below, Everett lay on the sled, his arms crossed behind his head. There were a few bumps, but since it was impassable in his chair, the sled served well. He let me lead, trusting that our efforts would be worth it.

After we agreed to stay camped at the site, Jacob and Sarah had gone off elsewhere. We each wanted to spend some private couples' time, and I only hoped they wouldn't end up in a poison oak thatch.

I figured a twenty-minute hike up, and perhaps beyond the ridge I'd found, there would be a magnificent view, an inspiration for us both. I had enough supplies in my backpack to last hours, or the night, along with a First Aid kit.

Sunlight spilled in small shafts between the trees, but most of the trail was shady. An occasional rock or root jostled him, but Everett treated it like a sort of bumper car ride.

Finally at our destination, I stopped.

"Wow."

"Wow, indeed."

Before us, a small field of wild grass opened out to sloping hillside and beyond it, an expanse of green hills and valleys. A few distant clouds trailed above, leaving parts of far off foliage in shadow. But mostly, the sun beamed, and multiple shades of greens and browns coated the land.

"Here, scoot up."

Everett pressed himself up as I tugged the sleeping bag from under him, then placed it near the trunk of a small evergreen. Then I hoisted Everett out of the sled.

"Bend at the knees," he scolded as he hugged me.

After unpacking a bag of salted cashews and two cans of beer I'd been hiding, I unlaced my boots, let my toes wiggle, sat beside him. We toasted, smooched, marveled at the view.

It was heaven. It was bliss. We might even make out, if I waited, or I would simply get naked down to my boots before him. Instead, we just peeled off our shirts and sat together, looking at the view, or dozing together as the breeze whispered through nearby trees.

But then he said it.

"Do you think he's going to die?"

I sighed, waited, pulled my thoughts together. "What was it you said? If we live long enough, everyone becomes disabled?"

"Yes?"

"Well, after that, everyone dies."

"You know what I mean."

"I do, and I'm sorry you want to talk about it now, but, yes."

"So, what'll you do with the photos he gave me?"

"Get them framed?" I grinned.

He sighed, shook his head, then thought, "That'll give the cleaning lady a scare. But, you know, they remind me…"

"Yes?"

"Of then, with him, but…"

"What, you want to save them to remember him?"

"No, to remember me."

"Well, I could take better pictures of you."

"No, of me then. I'm standing, Reid, my legs were–"

"Do you want to dwell on that? Fine, like I said, let's frame them and you can look at them every–"

"I'm not gonna feel sorry for myself. I want to… I want to remember, and celebrate what I was, not–"

"It's okay. Whatever you want to do. I… I like them, but we just have to be careful where we leave them. Okay?"

"Maybe a carefully hidden album."

"Whatever. Now can we just enjoy this pretty picture?" I waved before us. The sun was turning half a mountainside from green to gold.

"Okay." He scooted himself closer, we hugged, then settled, until he asked, "So…remember my little proposal of a trade?"

I offered a sly grin. "The camera's in the backpack."

"Better hurry. The light is perfect."

I dug into the backpack and handed him the camera, then walked a few paces away, stood before him.

He snapped a few pictures, then said, "Take your shorts off."

"What?"

"We had a deal."

I shucked them off, adjusted my underpants. The heat of the sun and his admiring glance began to stir my arousal, and my shorts tented out. I bashfully covered my crotch.

"Come on. All the way."

"I'll get naked if you will."

Everett set the camera aside and wriggled himself out of his pants. I thought to walk back to him, but he was naked before

JIM PROVENZANO

I could. He scooted up again, and repositioned his thin legs into a crossed position.

"There."

"But where'll we get these developed?" I asked. "We should have brought a Polaroid."

"I'm sure Gerard can find us some art student who can sneak into a lab." He retrieved the camera. "Now, turn sideways."

As he directed me through a few more poses, I felt myself relax, and my penis stiffened, the breeze and sun grazing my skin.

"God, you're so fuckin' beautiful." He snapped away, then stopped. "Come closer."

I stepped toward him, my erection swaying. He set the camera down, waved me closer, until I hovered over him. He placed a hand on my hip, guiding me lower until his lips met my skin, and the familiar warmth of his mouth, and a sturdy tree trunk to lean on, connected us again.

Chapter 32
August 1982

When I'd started working as a ranger, my enthusiasm overcame the ensuing exhaustion. I saw Fairmount Park as a beautiful ideal made real. My hope to fulfill my aspirations of designing or at the least building ramps for more accessibility were left to the few people with years more seniority. Jessica, my supervisor, had yet to let me know if any such plans would progress. Even so, I'd kept a map of the park, now worn from repeated use, marking problematic paths and rough walkways. Now it just seemed like an endless terrain in constant need of attention.

"Horses, they had; dozens of them."

Ralph was telling me about the old days. A burly fifty-four-year-old from South Philly, he frequently mentioned how long he'd been working at the park, "since I was your age."

It pained me to imagine becoming as old as he was, still picking up brush and garbage with a pair of worn work gloves, as we did while he talked. How was it that bright sunlight in the woods had been so blissful on our camping trip, yet in the city's park it beat down with a heavy weight?

"The Park Guards'd ride down the paths all regal-like, and people respected 'em, know what I'm sayin?"

"I'd love to ride a horse," I said, trying to sound sympathetic. But my comments were ignored.

"They dint have no gangs back then, and even when 'ey started up, people respected the park."

After tossing another bundle onto the pile, I rubbed another scrape on my arm. A cluster of flies had decided to accompany us all day. I swatted them off with a futile gesture.

"Up further, in Cobbs Creek, they'd find bodies, little girls, dead for weeks. Terrible stuff. Then the racial incidents, and fuckin' Rizzo."

Ralph tossed another bundle of dead branches onto the small flatbed on wheels he'd rigged up to the back of one of the motorized carts we drove to tool around the park grounds.

"Fuckin' Mayor Rizzo slashed the budget, and a bunch a other guys and gals got canned. Good people."

One hundred-thirty acres; that was the revised estimate of how much of the park had been each worker's responsibility. According to Ralph, only ten years before, with more employees, that ratio was a third. Despite appeals by my bosses to City Hall, the park's budget had been leveled off for the past several years.

So I should have considered myself lucky, he seemed to hint. The pay was good, I got to spend every day outdoors, and stay in the city. I'd never been annoyed by Ralph's complaints each workday, until he forced my card, the coming out card.

"You know, they even got a little name for the park where they do it, them … gay guys. You hear about that?"

"Why would I have heard about it?"

"I dunno. I just figured you heard."

Ralph had offered a few lewd suggestions about women as a sort of conversational bait, which I never took. But he never came right out and asked. The frustration of the seemingly endless pruning, combined with the heat, sent me over the edge that day, or at least to a point of decision.

"Ralph," I sighed. "I have a boyfriend. And we don't have sex in the park, at least not this one."

"Oh. Sorry." He turned away.

"For what?"

"Whatever. Ain't nothin.'"

He kept quiet after that. I didn't ask him where the cruisy park was. I told myself I didn't care.

As we finished for the day, Ralph's usual cheerful farewell was curt. My train ride home, slower than usual, was made worse by my own sweaty work clothes. At least the other commuters gave me a considerable distance.

My grumpy attitude brightened when I arrived back at the house. Everett, busy in the kitchen, gestured proudly toward a large bowl.

"Primavera pasta!"

"Oh, thank goodness. I thought it was my turn."

"With fusilli!"

I peered into the bowl. "Telephone wire spaghetti."

"Fusilli, silly."

After I took a well-needed shower, we ate. Everett's attempt at conversation became more of a monologue with me grunting and nodding in between mouthfuls of pasta.

"You seem beat," he said.

"I am."

"Why don't you go lay down. I'll catch up."

"But I should do the dishes."

"Ah, ah." He waved me off.

"You're the best boyfriend ever."

Some nights, Everett lovingly massaged my hands, my arms, and my back, as he did that warm night. He sat cross-legged beside me, rubbing his hands with lotion. I lay naked over a towel on the bed.

"How was your day?"

"Full of *Puereria lobata*."

"*Que?*"

"Kudzu."

"A plant, I take it." He kneaded knots out of my shoulders as I winced in pleasurable pain.

"A vine, an evil, treacherous vine," I mumbled into a pillow, then adjusted my head sideways.

"And you conquered it?"

"There's no conquering it; we just cut it back. They grow a foot a day, like some alien species. It's like, taken over half of the South."

"Did you show me any when we went to the park?"

"It's uptown, in this creepy acreage. You know, a few years ago, they used to find abandoned cars under mountains of kudzu."

"Is it native?"

"No, some stupid horticulture expo guy showed it off back in the 1890s or something, and it spread, like a disease. The thing is, it's kind of pretty. It just…it's relentless."

"Do you just cut it?"

"Down to the root, where we can, but the roots go down, like ten feet. One of the guys wanted to get a flamethrower."

"Hold still." He pressed harder, sending tingles through my body.

"What are the vines out back?"

I looked up, peered through the window into the dusk light. Beyond it, in one of the apartments, rock music played and a cluster of voices rose and fell with laughter. If it kept up, as it had on a few weekend nights, we wouldn't get any sleep for hours.

"It's probably just your basic *hedera helix*; English Ivy."

"Which is a more proper plant," he joked, taking on a snooty accent.

"Well, Mrs. Kukka would never plant kudzu. I think she said she planted the ivy because the berries attract birds."

Everett's hands kneaded my lower back, then playfully toyed with my glutes, and between my legs. But before he got too playful, I rolled over. My penis flopped over, then began to rise.

"I see you're feeling better."

"Come here." I reached for him, wrestled him to lie atop me. His face hovered above me as his body pressed against me. I shucked his shorts down, repositioned my erection between his legs, and we commenced a slow, rhythmic humping motion as we kissed. It didn't take long for me to burst, and although our sweat and the lotion made a bit of a mess, I held onto him, holding him, enjoying the heat between us.

With strategically-placed curtains, we could, with the lights off, see a glint of moonlight glimmering over the ivy plants along the fence in the backyard, leaving the window full of silvery green leaves.

Our bed out of range to the top floor apartment beyond, we enjoyed feeling as if we were outdoors, but without the journey. Later that night, after the party across the fence finally died down, a rustling sound disturbed our naked knot on the bed.

Looking up, I stepped to the window, expecting a shadow of someone, but then the ivy quivered, in a path.

I didn't want to ask Ms. Kukka, knowing she would shriek at the sight of them, and probably couldn't even hear them from upstairs, but I knew; rats.

Everett became concerned only after he spotted one of them in the kitchen a few days later. After that, he merely said, at my proposal, "Let's go shopping."

The traps were good enough, but the trail of feed-poison seemed to have worked. What also helped was having a word with the building manager on the other side of the fence, who agreed to cover his trash bins more carefully.

When he didn't, Everett's offhand comment admitting having seen a rat led to Mrs. Kukka making a phone call that led to a few strings being pulled, where afterward, "Some city inspector wagged his finger and took care of that," as Mrs. Kukka said.

I should have felt bad about it, destroying living things. But Everett described my efforts as "heroic."

Our minor pestilence abated, my boyfriend had another reason to be ebullient. The anti-discrimination bill which he'd helped lobby for had passed. There had been celebrations, and parties, including one where we met the mayor.

But after all the celebrations, his work was done. He made a few phone calls about other summer office work, but nothing turned up, particularly when he mentioned accessibility.

For a few days, the heat seemed to drag him down into a languid funk.

So I offered to take him out to see a movie.

"Which one?"

"Your choice."

That time, I again dressed as Brad, and he Dr. Scott. But there wasn't a contest, and most of *Rocky Horror*'s performing cast was out of town. We had fun, but just not as much as the first time, and nobody offered to go to a diner afterward.

The next day, we lay out in the front yard on a blanket. Everett read from a small stack of books and magazines, his face shaded by one of Mrs. Kukka's floppy hats. We had yet to return to school, but he was already diving into the next semester's curriculum.

I lazily grazed my fingers along his back as I lay beside him. Despite all my workdays outdoors, having to wear long pants had kept my legs pale. It felt good to be warmed by the sun. Off near the flowerbed, a pair of wrens hopped by, offered sideways glances, then flew off.

"We should go out to a gay bar."

"Which one?"

"Here. Take your pick." He tossed me a copy of *Au Courant*. I leafed through the pages, which included articles on local entertainers, movie reviews, and a lengthy feature on the recently-renamed AIDS. I'd already read it, and didn't want to dwell on the subject. Any mention of it got Everett talking about Wesley. I instead recited names of bars.

"La Banana Noire."

"If we could go anywhere in the world for a vacation, where would you want to go?"

"No place with rats," I said. "Paris, maybe, since you speak French." I glanced at an ad. "Lickety Split. It's on South Street."

I smiled at Everett, sensing he already had some wild plan up his sleeve. But I didn't try to second-guess him, and instead told him the truth. "The Amazon; the rain forest. Ever hear of buttress roots?"

"No, but I like the sound of that. Although, I do think rain forests have rats. El r-r-r-ratto."

I chuckled. "Or Socotra Island. Ever hear of it?" I remembered one of my nature books that included photos of strangely-branched trees that resembled giant alien sponges.

"It's about two hundred miles off the coast of Yemen. It's got hundreds of different species. There's one called the dragon's blood tree. It's got red sap."

"Wow. You're really into it."

"It's just so unusual; that or Australia. It's got marsupials and all kinds of strange stuff."

"Including some of the Australians." Everett extracted something from his notebook.

"Oh, not another brochure," I leaned up on an elbow. "What is it this time, building wheelchairs out of bamboo in Cambodia?"

"Actually, I was thinking something more pedestrian like …Illinois."

"Okay. Why?"

"I wanna compete in the Olympics for wheelchair jocks."

"And it's in Illinois?"

"Urbana-Champaign. The University of Illinois. I know it's not exotic or anything. There wouldn't be any bleeding dragon trees."

"Ev. Wherever you wanna go, I'll go with you if I can. When is it?"

"Summer nineteen-eighty-four. Different cities have been hosting them for a long time in England, I think since, like the sixties, and they really have their act together with the disability scene."

"Would your team play basketball?"

"I don't know. We don't start up again until November. I'm not sure if we're good enough, or will be, or if the guys can even afford to go. Maybe I'll just do some individual sport; a race or some track and field events. I took an archery class at Pinecrest. It's just the idea of going, you know? Being with a whole herd of other people. It'll be like Up With Cripples!"

I snorted, had to turn away.

"What? Don't laugh!"

"It's just, you're so…Yes." I wiped away a tear from the giggles. "That'd be pretty cool."

"Would you go with me?"

"Sure! I could save up. Illinois can't be as expensive as Paris."

"No, it would be my gift to you."

"Ev, you shouldn't—"

"Hold on. You wouldn't get off so easily, so to speak."

"What do you mean?"

He hesitated, offered a sheepish grin. "I was hoping you could train with me."

"Sure. We did pretty good at the Runfest, and we already go to the gym and the pool."

"Yeah, but this would be more, more focused."

"Well, if it fits around school. Hopefully, we'll have graduated by then, right?"

"*Spera fontes aeterna!*"

"Gesundheit."

As my dream of seeing those exotic Yemenese trees faded, I instead imagined Everett tossing a javelin to a cheering crowd, and considered it a worthy trade.

Those trees could bleed on their own.

As late summer dragged on, the Philadelphia heat made our house stuffy. We didn't have an air conditioner, another home improvement Mrs. Kukka steadfastly refused, and the garbage collectors' strike didn't help. The old-fashioned mini-screens fit into opened windows, but flies got in. We made a sport of swatting them.

But in certain areas, the city stank. Residents were basically allowed to just dump trash on curbs in whatever bags they chose. More than a few times Everett's wheels thumped over scattered debris, including a strewn pile of ketchup packets that splattered under his chair, which he had to later wash off.

The night we decided to go bar-hopping, the Center City streets that Saturday were filled with people eager to be outside in the ghost of a breeze that pushed away some of the odors.

Most of the discos were up a flight of stairs, so we passed on those. "Let's have fun. I'm not in activist mode," Everett said.

We started at Woody's, a bar on Thirteenth Street. I helped Everett up the few steps, and after we endured the expected roomful of stares, I got us beers. The bar's counter and even the tables were set at a level for standing, so we instead found a spot near a wall. A Human League song played loudly, and cigarette smoke curled up around us.

"Why are we here again?" I shouted as I leaned down.

"Anthropological study; gay tribal observance!" Everett replied. "Besides, we might make a few friends."

"Oh, like we did in Fort Lauderdale?"

"Just friends," Everett scowled.

"I don't see anyone looking friendly," I said before taking a large gulp of beer. I hoped that the sooner I finished it, the more quickly our 'experiment' would end. The roomful of men continued chatting among themselves, while other men, mostly older, stood alone, sipping their drinks in a pose of nonchalance.

"Is this what single guys do every weekend?"

"That or the bath houses."

The ads in *Au Courant*, along with porno shops, had intrigued me with their images.

"Are we going there next?" I joked.

Everett shook his head, smirked, and finished his beer. "Let's try that other one, with the numbers."

Expecting cowboys, since its ad depicted a cartoon gunslinger, 247 was instead filled with men in shorts or jeans, sporty T-shirts and a lot of mustaches. After navigating more steps, and the dark entryway where a pair of young guys shoved past us, the cluster of men at the bar didn't stare as much as glare. Whatever jubilation we had felt about being part of the Pride march in June was nowhere to be seen.

As Everett wheeled away from the main area, I got in line at the bar.

"That your friend?" a man standing near me asked. Although shorter than me, his stocky frame and assured stance intimidated me.

"Um, yeah, my boyfriend, actually." It came out almost defensively.

"You guys play around?"

"I'm just getting us beers."

"You know this is a cruise bar."

"Um, okay?"

"Well, don't get all huffy if someone gets friendly."

"Thanks for the tip." I turned away, eager to catch a bartender's eye.

By the time I got back to Everett, a beer in each hand, he was chatting away with another older man who, after a brief introduction, excused himself.

"That guy was telling me about the cruisy park."

"Really?"

"I can't believe you never heard about Judy Garland Park," Everett scolded me, determined to try it out.

So that's what Ralph was talking about.

Did Everett want some ghost of those early days together, arboreal embraces we had shared on our camping trip?

"You're not having fun," he scoffed.

"You're very perceptive."

The music shifted from one unfamiliar disco song to another; Donna Summer, I thought.

A few guys did approach us, or rather Everett, and he endured the predictable questions, and explained about his accident with a politeness, interspersed with a few jokes brought on by the beers.

After they left us, I finished the beer I'd been nursing, set the glass down, and asked, "So, is our little expedition complete?"

"One more stop."

What we found, when we parked near the allegedly cruisy strip of woods along the river, were a few furtive men loitering in various semi-dark paths, who scattered at the sight of Everett's chair.

"Shall we make a go?" Slightly drunk, his naughty grin confused me.

"Here?"

"Why not?"

"You want to have sex here." In the distance, the city's skyline glowed.

He shrugged.

I shook my head. "This," I unzipped, "is about all you get."

Everett made a hokey lunge for my groin as I turned away to pee against a tree trunk. It was not going to happen, despite our blurry desires.

We returned home, me driving slowly. Inspired, or perhaps in spite of the night's events, we attempted a few of the more unusual sex acts described in the *Joy of Gay Sex* book, with underwhelming results.

After our drunken foray in the bathroom, I left him to fumble with his catheter. He wheeled to the bed and promptly konked out.

I was half asleep when a loud siren wailed down the street.

Then I felt a vibration. He spasmed, or his leg did. He stirred, a frantic jolt. Still asleep, he blurted a high-pitched howl, a keening. I grabbed his arm as it flung out, almost hitting me, and held him.

"What?"

"Reid?"

"I'm here, baby. It was a dream."

"No."

"Yes. Tell me."

He jostled, pulled away, wiped his eyes, sat up, groggy, then lay back. "I was alone, riding, wheeling myself across campus, and suddenly, it was empty."

"And?"

"And it was just so empty, and this dog, this hound, English Shepherd or something, was up on its hind legs digging in a trash can, shook itself free and became this woman, this, this banshee. That woman. Remember?"

I nodded.

"She had white hair, like the dog, but these eyes, just pools of emptiness. I was so fuckin' scared to be alone."

"I'm sorry."

"My wheels were frozen, and the entire campus was empty. No people. And I screamed myself awake."

I held him. It scared me, but I put aside any Freudian analysis. He was in my arms.

"Let's go home for a while," I suggested.

"We are home."

"No, I mean my home, and the woods; Greensburg. It's safe. We can go visit your folks."

"Nobody's home."

"Well, then you can stay with me. My dad's birthday's next week. We can throw him a little party. You can debate politics all night."

"What about your park job?"

"Screw it. We're going back to school in two weeks. I'll just quit early."

I would stand to lose a few hundred dollars, but it didn't matter. I had saved up enough money to at least even out my expenses with him for the upcoming semester.

"I thought you liked the park."

"I did, at first. But if I have to pick up one more beer can…" I shook my head. All my labors seemed to amount to nothing. At Allegheny National Forest, trash pick-ups were part of the job, but nothing like that summer's duties. Working at Fairmount Park was almost ruining nature for me.

"Okay."

The next morning, we told Mrs. Kukka our plans, and I called my parents. We cleaned out the fridge, shut everything off, and drove across Pennsylvania.

We arrived in Greensburg just after sunset. Exhausted from the drive, we nevertheless ate some leftovers Mom had prepared, then escaped to my bedroom and slept all night.

The next day, Everett left a phone message for his father. Holly was still working at the summer theatre in upstate New York, and his mother was either in Boston or on Martha's Vineyard.

"Looks like you're stuck with me for a while," he shrugged as he hung up the kitchen wall phone.

"Come 'ere." I leaned down, took his face in my hands, and peppered his face with kisses. Then I got an idea.

"Come with me," I waved him to follow as I opened the garage door. He followed down the wooden ramp Dad and I had made, then watched as I foraged through boxes and Mom's gardening tools, until I found it.

When he saw it, he clapped his hands. "How many of these do you have?"

"One can never have too many sleds."

By the time I saddled him up again and began trudging across the open field, he knew my destination; our tree, the one I'd planted, the gift I'd given him just after his accident.

By then a few inches taller than me, we each gave the still young evergreen's soft bristled branches a few affectionate touches. Nearby trees still loomed over it, but he understood my point. We didn't make out. We didn't need to. But I needed to show him what mattered.

"Do I just mix the baking powder in the flour?"

I had decided I wanted to make Dad a cake for his forty-fifth birthday, more as practice for baking something for Everett, but I didn't let on.

Mom said I should just order one from the supermarket, but I told her I wanted to do it myself. The three of us had conspired to get Dad out of the house by having Everett accompany him to shop for a new lawn mower.

"I ought to figure it out. It's just chemistry."

She guided me through the baking, insisted I use some canned icing she took from a cabinet.

"It's just too much bother. Oh, I should get out my decorating kit."

Mom had tubes and little aluminum caps that squirted out cheese dip and butter cream roses.

"You don't have to do that." I figured I could squiggle out some words with a straw or something. But she dug in a lower cabinet and found them.

As I fumbled with the little metal cones, our conversation shifted when she asked about Everett.

"He's fine."

Everett had said he wanted to cut out a lot of things outside of school, and seemed like he just wanted to finish off the last year as easily as possible.

"How are things?" Mom asked, watching patiently as I mixed ingredients.

"What 'things'?"

"You know, between you two."

"Good."

"Really?"

"Yep."

"Are you being ...careful?"

"What do you mean?"

After an eye roll and a sigh, she said, "You know what I mean."

Although she didn't say it, I knew what she meant. In the living room, for days, a *Newsweek* magazine on the coffee table just happened to be left open to a page with an article about AIDS.

"We're fine, Mom."

My New York trip with Everett had been discussed, but in a heavily edited version, one of many things I couldn't share with her. I felt the growing distance between us.

"Actually, I'm just... You and Dad. You guys dated for a few years, right?"

"He was in college and I was working, yes."

"How did you... Did you have arguments?"

"We had disagreements, but he's always been a bit of a pushover when I get upset, or pretend to."

"So, I dunno. It's just... Everett's a little ...distant." What I wanted to say was, 'Everett's a bit freaked out because his first love, the guy who sort of raped him, is dying.'

"It's tough. He's probably trying to assert his independence. Are you boys still... affectionate?"

"What? You mean sex?"

"No, not just that. Do you feel affectionate with each other? Or is there a distance?"

I hesitated, until she abruptly added, "But speaking of sex."

"Oh, Mom. Don't."

"No, really," she insisted. "I heard about this... thing. It was on Tom Brokaw, these gay men dying of all sorts of–"

"We're not. We're fine, Mom. We don't mess around."

Anymore.

"But is there... Is it spreading? Do you know anyone who has it?"

"We're fine. No. Can we talk about something else?"

"Okay."

I toyed with the batter, wondered why I was supposed to know all about this, as if I was her guide to all things gay.

"So, yeah. People are talking about it, and it's a lot of confusion. But it is contracted through... sex."

"Okay, just so you're being careful."

Careful? In between volleyball coaches, gymnasts and paramedics, yes we were.

"So. Other than that, it's mostly good. He just... I don't know. He seems impatient."

"For what?"

"Everything. To graduate, to make things happen. I'm... he says I'm too protective, and he's really strong, you know? But he acts totally different when we're alone."

"Well, enjoy that, and let him grow. You boys have been together for, well, actually longer than it took for your father and I to get married. I'm just sorry you can't do that, too."

"Really?"

"Well, you never know. And I'm sure he'll love a cake like this one."

"Thanks."

"Oh, and by the way. Your father will probably want to break the news himself, later, but Best Rite's been sold to some company in Minnesota."

"What? So—"

"Well, we're not moving to Minnesota, that's for damn sure. The house is paid for, I have my job, and he's getting a passable severance deal. It's just too bad we spent so much on Hawaii, but it was worth it."

A few of the photos had been framed and put on the mantle in the living room. In them, my parents were sunburned, then tanned and beaming with smiles. It was the first time I'd seen my dad shirtless in years. During our visit, Everett had perused the images and called him 'studly.'

"So, Dad got fired?"

"They prefer other more vague phrases, but yes."

"Wow."

"Yes, 'Wow.'"

"Well, I should help pay for my tuition."

"You don't have to do that."

I scraped the bowl as the last of the batter filled the tin.

"The fees are going up again. I can start working sooner than summer if I ask at the park. Or I'll go to another park. I'll work in a store, anything."

"Reid, please."

"No, Everett's… See, this is something else. I'm pretty far ahead in my studies. I only need to take a few more classes the next few semesters. I could go part-time, and go back to the Parks Department for the spring and summer, and—"

"I thought you didn't want to do that."

"Well, what Dad says. 'That's why they call it work.'"

"We have money for your school. Don't worry about it."

"Okay."

I delicately placed the tin into the oven. "What about the icing?"

"There's a can in the cabinet."

"But—"

"Believe me, they'll say it's delicious," she said. "Just add a little water. I'll tell them you made it."

But then her sardonic edge dropped, and as I was wiping my hands on a dish towel, she wrapped me in her arms in a surprise hug.

As we pulled apart, she wiped her eyes. "That boy is so lucky to have you." She sniffed. "You're so much like your father, so earnest, so…"

"So; icing?"

We laughed, and I felt lucky to have learned a few more of her secrets.

Chapter 33
September 1982

*Everett is part of a men's fashion show, except it's on a plastic
platform in the middle of an outdoor pool, and all of it glimmers in bright
sunlight, including a strange all-plastic chair, with him sitting on it,
showing off his fuzzy legs while wearing only shiny orange shorts and a
pair of sandals. The other models stand near him as the photographer
floats around the platform on a pontoon. The other guys in swimsuits get
closer to him, and I find myself slipping from the edge of the pool into the
water, where he sees me and is then near me, then under me, floating
without breathing, smirking as he aims for my bobbing penis, but I have to
pee and know since I had drunk gallons of pineapple juice, everyone will
see the underwater jets of yellow if I let go I'll…*

His mouth clamped around my erection, I almost knocked
Everett's head off me, until I half-woke, realized it was him,
then thrust my hips up to meet his face. The shock of his
connection, the insistent need to pee and ejaculate, combined
with my anger at his presumption of having begun sex before I
even woke up, inspired an almost violent need.

He choked, withdrew, and gasped as a string of drool
connected from the tip of my erection to his chin.

"Jeez, Ev!"

"What? You don't like it?"

Still a bit disheveled from sleep, his face was as gorgeous as
ever. A glimmer of that abrupt insistence from our first
encounter flashed in my mind. I grabbed the back of his head
and pushed him back onto my dick. Was this what the gay sex
book had called 'S&M?' Did he want it rough? Was this the
kind of sex Wesley Swiegard had forced upon him?

After finally bursting into his mouth, he seemed satisfied, if
not surprised. Yet for me, the tingles were more like the
insistent itch of a bout of poison oak, and I had to pee.

Standing naked at our bedroom door, I peered outside to make sure Mrs. Kukka wasn't downstairs, so I could sneak across the hall to the bathroom.

"I couldn't resist. It was making a damn tent pole under the sheets," he joked.

I turned back. "Just wake me up next time."

"Okay. Sorry," he offered a bashful smile.

"You were like, like a succubine."

"The word is succubus."

"Whatever."

"And actually, that's the female form. You're thinking of an incubus."

He sat up in bed, his hair a mess, his smile almost smug.

"What. Ever."

After returning from the bathroom, where I peed and took a shower, I returned to our room. As Everett ambled around me and into his chair, I got dressed and surveyed what had pretty obviously inspired my strange dream.

Before leaving Pittsburgh, Holly had given Everett a box full of clothes she had tailored to his changed body. His thinner legs and more muscled shoulders and chest had made pants too baggy and shirts too tight.

Once back at our apartment in Philly, Everett had given me a little fashion show, trying on various outfits, but he had yet to put them in the closet or drawers. Along with the clothes, Holly had given us both a stack of men's fashion magazines full of impossibly handsome models, which we had leafed through with amused admiration.

And only days before classes had begun, on one of our first free afternoons, we had taken advantage of the campus pool being nearly empty. A bit of playful aquatic roughhousing included Everett's grabbing for my crotch, which responded accordingly. Everett had laughed, despite the lifeguard's glare, and I had to swim away until my penis had calmed down.

After making breakfast, slowly timing it for Everett's completed bathroom routine, I sat across the kitchen table, looking at him, his damp hair and beaming face almost innocent-looking, as if our abrupt sex had never happened. He chomped on the toast and scrambled eggs I'd prepared, and offered a pleased grunt and a nod.

"Do you ever dream about me?"

"What? Why?" he asked.

"I just…wondered."

He chewed more, swallowed. "Mostly when we're apart."

"Do you still… Are you, you know, walking?"

"I used to. That's funny you ask, because, sometimes we're flying, or we're in the woods. The bad ones are us being separated, like, I can't find you in the woods, and then I'm back in the hospital, tied up in a bed. And then that other freaky one a while back."

There had been a few more nights when he sleep-mumbled, tousling under the covers, until I reached over and held him. I wasn't sure if he remembered those moments. I had grown used to the fuzzy half-sleeping state of feeling his body next to mine, the desire to never let go. Was it our skin touching that connected us even in sleep?

"So!" He pushed his empty plate aside, as if tabling the nocturnal topic. "What say I do the dishes, and then we stop by our respective bookstores and get this semester's overpriced textbooks before the teeming hordes arrive?"

"Sure."

"Okay."

"Mister Incubus."

The profusion of colors in the trees combined with the musty scent of early autumn's decay, and a last burst of warmth in the air, had inspired us to spend a Saturday in Fairmount Park. We had each been apart every weekday since returning to our separate classes. I wanted to show Everett a few of my favorite areas that he had yet to see, where I had helped trim and nurture foliage through the previous summer.

"Now this is beautiful."

"I know, right?"

"Come on. I want to show you something."

My steps increased. I trod a circle around him, then took off, daring him to catch up.

Alongside the Schuylkill River's banks, numerous statues stood in graceful silence. The expansive Ellen Phillips Samuel Memorial Terrace, on the north end, included a large two-man statue of dark brown bronze, which always drew me to admire it whenever I would pass by it on my own.

Called *Welcoming to Freedom*, Maurice Sterne's 1939 sculpture evoked the WPA era, but had been commissioned separately by a local wealthy benefactor.

To the left, a solemn male figure stood looking away toward the river. Clad in a skimpy loincloth of some kind, his muscled frame loomed over the base, his arms upraised in a plaintive gesture of victory or surrender, I wasn't sure which.

The lower male figure to the right was posed sitting down, his arms in a half-crossed pose, one knee raised, the other leg lowered.

Everett had caught up to me, and as I turned back to him, his look of awe let me know he understood.

On trips back and forth from the northern section of the park, I often felt compelled to admire the statues. It wasn't until after the fourth or fifth visit, and my janitorial obsession with removing the small puddles and stray leaves, that I realized what the duo reminded me of, and he saw it.

"It's like us," he realized.

"Sort of, if we were eight feet tall and made of bronze."

"And went to the gym every day."

"Here, I've got a secret."

"What?"

"Get closer. Let me lift you up."

Confused, he gave me a wary glance, but let me hoist him up to the statue's base.

"Oh. My. God." As I had done a few times, he instinctively reached for it.

Nestled inside that bent leg, the seated figure's groin formed a little pool of brackish water. Everett giggled as he gripped it.

"That is the most enormous cock I've ever touched."

"Hey!"

"Well, in non-human form."

"Okay, then."

"Except for Kevin."

I mock-gasped. But he was right. While positioned as flaccid and proportional, the statue's genitals were large and thick. But a tiny pool of rainwater pooled between the legs. Everett wiped his hand on his pants, then clutched his pants. "I think I'm getting a chubby."

"From fondling a statue."

"Whatever works!"

I chuckled, but had to admit they were a handsome pair.

"You brought the camera?"

"You betcha."

"Let's grab the next jogger and pose."

"You read my mind."

"I have a tendency to do that."

And so we added another goofy posed shot to our collection, along with the pictures from our little adventure in Intercourse. Gerard had found one of his design classmates who agreed to develop our more risqué camping photos, which were hidden away along with Everett's Polaroids.

That day, the hapless lady we'd sidetracked into taking the pictures seemed amused as well as we posed at the statue's base. Everett kneeled on the ground, each of us striking imitative poses before the solemn work of art that inspired a few giggles as we moved on.

Continuing on north through the park, we slowed our pace, took in the colorful foliage, until Everett impulsively took off, and I followed and we raced pretty much all the way up to Forbidden Drive and found ourselves at the Valley Green Inn. The historic restaurant appeared to have than the usual amount of visitors.

On the lawn at the riverbank across the road from the inn, rows of white folding chairs sat dormant, facing a white canopy awning where a wedding had taken place.

"Sweet," Everett said. I noticed some autumnal foliage in the decorations that gave the awning an earthy flair.

"Think we can go in?"

"I think it's a private party or something. There's a really cool ramp," I said.

"You've been here before."

"Yeah."

"Well, let's crash a wedding."

We entered the restaurant, but the party guests seemed a bit put off, perhaps more because of our sweatpants. We were put off by the accordion player. We got drinks to go and exited politely.

Sitting outside the inn, a brush of wind fanned over the trees across the river. It felt like a perfect day, me sharing another corner of my refuge, until he spoke.

After a few solid gulps, Everett said, "So, I called Wesley."

"How is he?"

"Not good. He was in the hospital again."

"Oh."

"You don't want to talk about it."

"No, it's okay."

"He said he's fine, but he didn't sound like it."

"Do you want to visit him again?" Please say no.

"He said he didn't want me to. Besides, it's... I don't know."

"What?"

"You wouldn't want to."

"No, I don't. But I would."

"We can't blame him."

"I don't. I just... Even though he's sick, I just don't like him, what he did to you."

"I think it's time you forgave him, because I already did."

I nodded, looked around. Dying leaves are always so beautiful.

The statistical probability of either of us contracting whatever it was that was out there, in the bigger cities, mostly, was explained to me by my father, of all people.

We had established a long-distance bond ever since he had divulged to me his plans to surprise Mom with the trip to Hawaii. He'd been saving for years, along with paying half my tuition. I had thanked him repeatedly, even as the bills continued. He never complained after his job became someone else's, elsewhere. He'd been so stoic, I realized, and more open to me, as we discussed money, and life, and current events.

"You haven't been sick, either of you?"

"No, Dad." Everett had endured a small pressure sore, but it had healed, and we'd both shared a cold a month before. But no, nothing serious had happened.

"Reid, you've had relations with a few…people, and so has Everett, from what you said. But if you remain monogamous, and I think you ought to both get physicals, just get checked out."

It seemed reasonable. Everett was getting his health checked every month at Magee, and with a few medical students observing on occasion, he told me. "This hot Indian nursing student could not keep his eyes off me," Everett bragged.

And so we each got some blood work, reflex tests, and I got a gloved finger up my butt from a not-so-hot campus doctoral student.

And then, one night, after our failed attempt to be turned on under the glare of the porn video, Everett shut it off, rolled himself over to me and my prone body and said, "Look. If we gave it to each other, we already did, but I don't think we did."

"I think we're okay, too."

We kissed, like an old couple. I shut out the lights, and Everett, timed well enough to leave me laughing in the dark, added, "Unless Nick pops into town."

"I think we can make an exception with him. He is a medic."

"A trained professional," he smirked, then mimicked a moment from our shared romp with Nick. That led to a surprisingly heated session of sexual exploration. I just had to stare and marvel at him in the dark after a while, tingling beyond coming, the thrill of watching Everett do so well what he did to me. We weren't gonna let this weird disease stop us.

Chapter 34
October 1982

"We fall but we keep getting' up."

"Over and over and over again …"

It occurred to me after the third time that Everett had pulled this stunt that it was getting kind of old.

If the DJ played the Pretenders song, he'd intentionally spill out of his chair on that line, and plop himself back up on cue, and I'd laugh, because I knew he was going to do it. This time, he managed rather well, considering his legs were wrapped in fins.

Halloween was on Sunday, but all the celebrations were held the night before, including the big gay dance party at Equus that Gerard coaxed us into attending with him.

A hulking football jock, dressed as a hulking football jock, loomed, ready, it seemed, to pound me for laughing at Everett, until I yelled over the blasting music.

"It's okay!!" I nearly spilled my beer on him, shouting into his shoulder. "He does this all the time!" I didn't mind spilling it on myself. To match Everett's merman costume, I was dressed in a bright yellow raincoat as the Gorton's Fisherman, but my fake beard kept falling off, so I put it in a pocket with the pipe I'd found at a thrift store.

"Oh!" The football jock shouted back, still confused.

"He's my boyfriend!"

"Oh." He blinked twice, looked at Everett, then me, then back and forth again. "Oh!"

I saw with that light of understanding in the eyes of the guy, in a gay bar, that silent moment where I could see him constructing the actual possibility that Everett and I had sex, me and that cute guy in a wheelchair, with fins made out of some shiny fabric Gerard had found. Witnessing that realization again, in a stranger's eyes, turned me on more than the idea of actually sleeping with anyone else, even a big husky drunk football jock.

The music shifted jaggedly from disco songs to recent rock favorites. People would pour onto the dance floor or abandon it with a song's first chords. The fact that Everett was dancing with Gerard didn't bother me.

Telling myself that as I sipped my beer, the football jock continued talking to me, and I feigned a fascinated interest in his muddled sympathetic comments, as if being Everett's boyfriend was some sort of sacrifice.

Nodding my head, sneaking glances at Everett on the dance floor, I hoped he would see me with another guy, and that it would draw him back to me. But he wasn't even looking.

Gerard flailed around him in a bulky black and white outfit with huge shiny plastic shoulder pads and a cardboard bow tie. He had colored his hair jet black and wore white make-up, saying he was some artsy singer named Klaus Nomi. People either gave him strange stares or rushed up to him with praiseful screams of recognition.

He could have used a few pointers on how to dance with a wheelchair-using partner. I didn't offer.

And I had a lot of reasons. I finally saw Gerard's interest in Everett to be sincere, thankfully platonic, and apparently, he was a good enough dancer.

To me, it meant he was just like us, trying to find himself through a series of disguises, the latest of which he brought nearly completed that night when he had come over to help sew up Everett's fins, and pretty much his entire costume. After attempting to dab some glitter on Everett's chest, I insisted on taking over, although I did let him give Everett pointers on his turquoise eye make-up.

Gerard had insisted on playing us a few songs by this Klaus Nomi character, which were pretty appropriate for Halloween. Gerard's face was more round than the gaunt singer depicted on the album cover, but he got the make-up down perfectly.

His being so chummy with us that night made me want to warm up to the football player. Something about those black make-up dashes on his cheeks made him sexier than he already was.

Perhaps Everett would open up to another threeway, if we got drunk enough. But with Gerard having left his regular clothes at our apartment, I knew that would be a problem. Perhaps, as I gulped down my beer, I wanted to make a problem.

But my drunken come-ons fell on drunken ears. The football jock swayed, offered a dopey smile, patted me on the shoulder and said, "You're really brave."

"Brave? Why?"

Football jock nodded toward my merman.

Brave? I was scared every day, worried about losing him, losing his interest, being unable to keep up with his ongoing craving for adventures. What was this hulking guy trying to say? I wanted to shout at him, punch him, wake him up, or perhaps lock him in a kiss to make Everett jealous. But he just smiled innocently.

"I'm gonna go dance," I said as I wobbled myself away.

About an hour later, Gerard sidled up next to me as I bought a third round of drinks at the bar. I had switched to a soda, since I realized I would be the designated driver.

"Everett's being adored by his fans," Gerard observed.

I turned back to see a gladiator and his kneeling Cleopatra talking with Everett.

"It's cool. We have our little signals for escape."

"Oh, do you?"

"Yes, we do, Gerard. We do a lot of things together."

"I never took you for the subtle type."

"So, uh, Gerard. We should be heading out soon."

"Sure. That fireman's not coming back."

"When we get back to our place, you're…" I pointed west.

"Leaving?" He huffed. "Yes."

"Sorry. I just want to establish that."

Gerard had slept on the sofa a few weeks before during a well-timed rainstorm. I told myself that his presence wasn't what 'spoiled the mood' in bed with Everett that night. The next morning, Gerard had whipped up a continental breakfast buffet with "whatever I found in the fridge," he tossed off, dismissing Everett's accolades. I tried to ignore having been effetely shown up in the cooking department.

Fortunately, this time, he got my not-subtle message.

"It's okay," Gerard said. "I'll just get a cab or get a ride with some of my *other* friends."

"You don't have to do that."

"It's no bother," he patted me on the shoulder in a patronizing gesture before fiddling inside his cardboard costume to extract a cigarette and lighter.

"You think that's a good idea?"

"What?"

I pointed at his costume. "You're kind of…flammable."

"Oh, now you care about me?" he snapped before sauntering off.

A while later, I had finally coaxed Everett into leaving, despite his popularity.

"But where's Klaus?"

"Who?"

"Gerard, silly."

Everett wheeled beside me, or tried.

"Gerard-een! Where are you?"

I'd rarely seen him push his chair while drunk, and his weaving pattern down a side street induced a few giggles from me, until he ran over my foot. He hadn't even wanted to put a T-shirt and jacket over his chest, whose green glitter he'd sweated off, until I insisted.

"He took off with some of his Transylvanian pals."

"Oh, well." He zoomed ahead of me, until he noticed I had stopped.

"The van's this way."

"Well, alrighty then." Another strong push, and he caught up, then passed me along the sidewalk. Other costumed revelers giggled and hooted down the street. I was about to warn him of a curb he didn't seem to notice, but then his fins got caught in the spokes. He attempted a wheelie to back up from being tangled, and instead crashed backwards onto the sidewalk.

"Jeez, Ev!"

I bent over to help him. He instead pushed up on one arm, then flopped back down, grabbing my arm and pulling me down with him.

"You're drunk."

"You're ubz-observant." He tried to focus on me. "Wherezure mustache, sailor?"

"Lost at sea. Will you get up?"

"It was sexy. Come 'ere. Just lay here with me."

I sat beside him, amused by the green make-up smudge around his eyes.

"Aw, somebody's angry."

"I'm just tired. It's late."

Then he sang, softly, "We are all of us in the gut-tah. But some of us are looking at the stars."

"Very good."

"Did you know?"

"Ev, not now."

"Did. You. Know." He scooted himself, as if for emphasis, making his fins flop.

I sighed. "What?"

"That's actually Oscar Wilde's line. Famous deceased homosexual. Sent to prison."

"Which we'll be, too, if we don't get out of this gutter." I forced his chair up, shoved his fins in place, and pushed his chair from behind.

"Stop that." He swatted behind himself.

Somehow, I managed to pour him into the van and drive us home, where, after stripping him down to his shorts, then disconnecting Mr. Pee Buddy and pouring it out in the toilet and rinsing it out, I returned to the bedroom.

Already half asleep, his eyes closed, he muttered, "You love your little crip, doncha?"

Standing over him, I tried to ignore his remark and pulled the covers up over him. But he yanked them back, exposing his naked body, teasing. He looked up, tried to focus on me. "Come on. Gimme that big dick." He lolled his tongue out in mock hunger.

"You're too drunk."

"What would you do without me?" He sighed, rolled over, his back to me.

In the bathroom, I brushed my teeth, then grabbed a towel, thinking he'd refuse my help in reattaching his catheter. But by the time I returned to the bed, he was asleep. I lay the towel over his waist, and slumped into the bed next to my catch of the day.

Everett's rumpled fins and my raincoat greeted me from the floor the next morning as I tripped over them.

In the kitchen, I noticed a plate of toast and scrambled eggs that seemed to have hardened, wolfed them down as I warily eyed Everett, who sat on the sofa in the living room, his chair nearby.

He was reading a newspaper, actually one in a stack of newspapers. He didn't even greet me a good morning. What had I done, other than flirt with that football player and try to present him as a tribute?

After gulping down half a glass of orange juice, I sat down beside him.

"You're looking studious."

"We're definitely done with fooling around."

"What? Um, good morning?"

"No more messing around, sex-wise."

"Somebody's sobered up. Why are you deciding this now?"

"Read this."

He got the local newspaper along with the campus weekly. Along with his subscriptions to the gay newspapers, Mrs. Kukka had the Sunday *The New York Times* sent weekly. But it was the article in *Philadelphia Gay News* that had a more expansive article.

"And this."

I don't know why I snapped at him that day. Perhaps it was a late case of prescience, along with a mild hangover. Actually, I was relieved to hear him declare our exclusivity, assert his alpha status. The sex with Chuck the volleyball coach and Nick the paramedic had been great. I just felt more advanced with Everett, in tune.

Actually, it was the hangover that made me snap.

I read the article. Some scientists had finally figured out more information about the disease that seemed to be infecting gay men like Wesley.

I worried about him so often. He had fallen from his pull-up bars, slid out on ice patches, and crashed out on the basketball court countless times. But he wouldn't stop. It was as if he thought he could force healing down through his body one bruise at a time.

And then there was his eccentric, if not pleasurable course of study in anal stimulation as a nerve-stimulating and possibly regenerative remedy; my fucking him, slowly, carefully, and, over time, with more than a few thrusts. Knowing he couldn't completely feel it made me wary, move slowly as he quivered from some other touch; my lick inside his armpit or down across his chest. More often it had been merely us lying side by side, jerking each other off like teenagers.

That seemed to be our limited sexual future, since the news articles pretty much confirmed that we could be killing one another through sex.

"I don't even know if we should be having sex at all," he said.

"But we're—"

"We don't know what we are. But we know what I did, with Wesley."

"But that was years ago."

"They don't know what the length of—"

"You're overreacting. This is guys like him, bath houses and orgies."

"We don't know that."

"Well, what do we know?"

"What they know," he almost stabbed the newspaper with a finger, "is that it's about sex, or blood, or sex and blood."

"Okay, so avoid sharp knives."

Everett tossed the newspaper aside. "You're gonna make jokes? Really? Wesley is dying back in New York, and probably a lot of over guys; thousands, maybe."

"I'm sorry. I just–"

"I'm just saying we have to be careful."

"But it's just me and you and Kevin and a few other guys, right?" I asked.

"And Nick, and Chuck–"

"And Gerard?"

Everett almost cringed. "No! Why are you always on Gerard's case?"

I stood, waving my hands around like an idiot. "Well, he's always bragging about his fabulous times in New York. How do you know he hasn't done things like Wesley did to–"

"Reid, you need to–"

"I need to take a shower. I don't want to give you any germs."

I stormed off, cowering in my denial. But even though no blood was spilled, we'd pretty much cut each other.

For a while, we just stopped having sex. Hugging became suspect in its intentions. Our days grew wary, and our nights more chaste.

Everett found more reasons to study on campus, and my own studies and social life started to fill more time on the Temple campus, or for a while, anywhere not with him.

Despite our rift, we knew how to put on a good face, and we dove into activities, made easier when we were in the company of others, and not forced to confront our own problems.

Chapter 35
November 1982

The giant curving metal arches along the ceiling of the Palestra, Penn's sports arena, kept my attention as I tried to ignore the heated discussion to my left. Everett sat by my side, but he spent more time leaning away from me to argue with Jacob about politics, in particular, Israel.

While an appropriate topic, I wished the two of them would just shut up. The Israeli All-Star wheelchair basketball team was trouncing the local Bordentown Elks in a polite exhibition game. Dozens of kids in wheelchairs had been brought in, and Jacob and I sat among them in folding chairs courtside. Nearly all of Everett's own basketball teammates and several people he knew from Magee Rehab greeted him with affection.

Having attended a few games of the Penn varsity basketball team, I'd been overwhelmed with the roaring fans, the noise and mania over every score. Despite his advantage of getting courtside 'seats,' after a few games, I'd declined Everett's further invitations to go with him, and admitted my preference for the less popular sports.

But that night, the arena was quieter, and only a few hundred people watched. The squeaks of wheels on the court, interrupted by whistles and mild cheers, and the quieter atmosphere only made his and Jacob's muttered debate more noticeable. Everett seemed resolute in his position that ran counter to Jacob's understandably pro-Israel sympathies.

"Hey, you two. I'm tryin' to watch the game here," I half-joked.

"Sorry," Everett said. They both quieted down and we watched. Everett eventually became engaged and cheered for baskets, winced at on-court tumbles, and even offered a few explanations of the plays.

"Why do they lean back like that?" Jacob asked.

"They're quads," Everett answered. "Some don't have abdominal muscles. If they don't lean back, they tip over."

Jacob nodded and didn't offer any more comments.

But as soon as we left, they picked up where they left off. The three of us wove through the departing crowds as we headed toward our house. Apparently, Jacob was coming with us, and not to his own dorm. I didn't mind, but the two of them would be joining their fellow debate teammates at a tournament that weekend. Perhaps this was their form of a mental warm-up.

"No, I'm not saying it was worse," Everett said. "But that the eugenics policy of exterminating the disabled preceded the Nazi policy of rounding up Jews."

"And gypsies and homosexuals?" Jacob added.

"Yes! Doctors were already testing the gas chambers. It solidified the later regime's genocide."

"Which you blame on their warped version of Socialism."

"Yes."

"So, a Capitalist regime saved them."

"But Capitalism has its own form of neglect. If a person can't be made useful, it has no purpose to that system. Adam Smith's 'vile maxim.' Social Darwinism, 'weeding out the unfit.'"

After I let out an exhausted sigh, Jacob glanced at me. "Care to chime in, Reid?"

"I suggest we table this discussion and get some hoagies at Wawa."

They laughed, and did stop, thankfully, for a while at least.

"It's just a bunch of us arguing," Everett said as he and I neared the Penn campus that Saturday. "You didn't like it at the basketball game. Why do you want to go?"

"Because you're competing. I only got to see a few of your tournaments, and well, this is the last year, right?"

Everett hadn't understood why, after seeming annoyed by his continued discussions with Jacob, I had actually found a new appreciation for him, a sense of pride when he ripped into his opponent with a cluster of notes he'd assembled that day with his debate partner Donny Yang.

"Besides," I added. "When you get elected to office some day, I want to say that I was there when you got your start in politics."

"Ha!" Everett snorted. "'Ladies and gentlemen, the gay disabled representative from Pennsylvania has the floor!'"

"It could happen."

"We'll see." He pumped his arms, wheeling ahead of me.

Since I had a Chemistry midterm to work on, I brought my books and half-listened as Everett, Donny, Jacob and other students at tables around us in the library whispered as they foraged for quotes to build their case. Everett reeled off a string of publications, even a few specific months, and Donny took off in search of more reference books.

By the time of the debate, held in a small auditorium at Penn, I'd finished my essay draft, notes and even redrew a few charts. It was another of many study skills he'd shared. "If you write it down, if you tell it back to someone else, it goes into your brain." Simple, but I'd too long thought merely reading would be enough.

That grasp of knowledge displayed itself in the first round. The topic that year was whether the U.S. should be barred from military intervention in the Western Hemisphere.

One of Everett's teammates cited the increasing recession and high unemployment figures as an example of a need to, he said, "return our focus on our own country."

While one of his opponents rattled through his references in a style that, Everett had told me, was allowed, he sounded almost unintelligible and rushed.

Everett, however chose one specific example, and from one card, seemed to wing it with the expertise of a political talk show guest. A few abbreviated citations confused me, but overall, he presented a case against weapons proliferation by diverting the argument to solutions; building infrastructures for cultures prone to violence, and finding ways to remove them. "specifically, drug trade, poverty, South American economic strife that not only grows healthy botanical exports in addition to plants grown for drugs or communist regimes."

His opponent countered with examples of failed attempts to convert drug farming to agriculture.

As he went on for a few minutes, I watched as Everett handed his partner a few cards with citations, and Donny nodded. At his response time, Everett quoted an article about charity tourism, and the growth of natural habitats as a diversion to deforestation.

His opponent then fumbled, it seemed, having been put in a position to defend drug cartels via something called Posse Comitatus. It wasn't exactly the case, but Everett had positioned it so.

After a bit of shuffling of whispered voices and notes, the referee made a "call for cards," and the round was summated in some arcane process that eluded me. I was too busy gazing at Everett, and since the room had less than a dozen viewers, eventually, a sly grin tossed my way.

The elation of their victory lent itself to the team discussion over pizza. A six-way argument over where to go resulted in the obvious conclusion; our house. Mrs. Kukka was pleased to have a few more visitors.

Over paper plates and soda, the team sat in various chairs in the front room. Everett had put on one of his cassette mixes that kept the mood light but not raucous; a little pop and jazz. It felt very adult. With several conversations going, I parked myself next to him on the sofa with the front windows behind us.

It wasn't exactly a rowdy event, by any means, but at one point, a toast was raised for the victory, and Donny Yang started a chant of "Speaks! Speaks!" aimed at Everett.

"Could you explain the derivation of this ritual?" I asked in a professorial hush.

"I got the most speaker points. 'Speaks.'"

I nodded. "Cute."

He shrugged his shoulders. "It's safer than lacrosse."

"You want some more pizza?"

"Definitely."

When I returned, Everett, Jacob and a few others had shifted to discussing a lingering local issue, Penn's misappropriation of funds meant for accessibility improvements. The scandal had been in both the university and local papers, a small pile of which Everett had collected; just the pages, in an increasingly stuffed accordion file. Only recently had it been "rectified," according to another article.

"The apartheid protestors are going to force them to divest. I think some sort of action would do the same for this," Everett said.

"It's a legal issue. They pay it back after sucking up to more donors," Jacob added.

"Start the Grace Kelly Memorial ball," another sniped.

"Dude! That is harsh. She only died last month."

The tragic car crash in Monaco that had killed the actress had been extensively covered by the local media, and the student newspaper, given her roots in Philadelphia.

But another lingering issue had not been reported as much. The university had failed to fulfill their already funded requirements to make more buildings accessible, which understandably bothered Everett. He fumed about the lack of resources for disabled possible new students, despite the university's outreach and limited scholarships.

"Yeah, but aren't you different? Aren't you wealthy?" Donny asked.

"Well, I'm not, but my family is."

I didn't add, 'You will be, by a wide margin.'

"What does that have to do with it?" Everett countered.

Donny argued, "You claim to represent a constituency, you say people like you should get disability benefits, yet your family is wealthy. Why should taxpayers support you?"

"I'm a dependent and I don't work. I'm a student."

"But you did work for that summer camp?" Jacob tossed in.

"And we got paid almost nothing."

"And the cabins were far from luxurious," I added.

"And yes, my family has money," Everett admitted. "I'm lucky. My grandfather invested well. If it means I have a car, and better medical care, and am able to travel, so what? If it gets me in the building, great, because there are a lot of people who can't get in the damn building to change that. And my being able to get in, to have the time, not fighting for another welfare check, helps me represent those who have to do that."

Donny and Jacob clapped in approval. But Everett wasn't finished.

"Some problems need to be solved through money, or politics or awareness. But the issue of disability, and how it relates to you, is apparently your primary focus."

Donny blinked at the swiftness of the insult.

"One of the greatest impediments to my qualifications is one of the easiest to solve; architecture."

No one offered a rebuttal, until Jacob called out, "I think we have a winner!"

Everett and I had almost finished cleaning up the kitchen after everyone else had left.

"So, you enjoyed the debate?"

"Which one?"

"Sorry. I got a little worked up," he said.

"You're sexy when you argue."

"You're a bigger nerd than I am."

"Maybe I am."

"Did you know?"

"Did I know what?"

"You inspired one of my most daring points."

"I did?"

"Remember when you were talking about that two-thousand-year-old plant, and how you wanted to go see it?"

"The Mediterranean Cypress."

He gave me an expectant glance, until I remembered; "*Cupe…cupressus sermpervirens.*"

"Good boy. But it's in Iran, which is not the safest place for a couple of Yankee imperialists to visit."

"Right. So?"

"Well, that got me thinking, which is the point of the whole shebang. But we're on the opposing side next time, so it won't be pretty. Unless you can inspire me to defend arms proliferation and the occasional CIA-assisted junta."

It was funny, his ability to argue about anything, but I sensed that he just wanted a night with his friends, so I let it, and him, go.

The next week, Everett considered running for class president, but settled on running for president of the Debate Team. With only himself abstaining, he won overwhelmingly, 5-0.

Chapter 36
December 1982

Beautifully naked, the small fir tree stood in the corner of our living room, with boxes of ornaments set below it on the floor. My parents had once again awaited my return before decorating it.

"What happened to Robot Tree?" I asked.

Mom offered a sassy pose, arms akimbo. "Santa gave it to a needy family by way of the Goodwill."

It was one of several changes I noticed. Mom had also rearranged a few pieces of furniture and added more modern art prints in the living room. Was it a sign of restlessness, their fight against what Mom called the empty nest syndrome? I wasn't sure.

"So you got another cut one?"

"Check the base," Dad said as he hung up his coat.

I knelt before it, taking in the pine scent. The branches seemed moist. Under the holiday skirt, a silver bucket strained to hold a burlap-wrapped bulge of roots and what smelled like damp peat.

"Sweet! This is the best Christmas present ever!"

"Oh, then I can give your other ones to Goodwill, too," Mom joked.

"You can start with any sweaters I'm about to get," I replied, as I admired the little tree. "So, are we gonna plant it in the yard?"

"You're the expert," Dad said.

"Really? Then we can get another one next year and make a whole forest in the back yard."

"Well, we ought to plant a few. Make a great windbreak."

"Fantastic."

Hungry from the drive, I ambled to the kitchen, which pretty much looked the same from Thanksgiving. On the countertop, a large basket sat, full of what looked like...

"Fruit? Yum. Who sent this?"

"Your aunt and uncle."

"Oh." I almost pulled away, but the pears looked nearly perfect. *Pyrus Rosaceae* bounced in my head.

"What are we bringing?" I asked with an obvious tone of dread about a return visit.

"Nothing," Mom replied with barely contained satisfaction. "They have decided to take a holiday vacation to Orlando."

I deadpanned, "This is the best Christmas. Ever."

Until Dad added, "But we're still driving to visit your grandparents."

"And," Mom added, "fortunately, they like fruit." She swatted my hand.

"That's cheating!"

"No, it's being economical."

Despite the pleasant changes at home, I felt an eager anticipation toward visiting Everett in Pittsburgh. His mother had practically crammed his weeks with engagements, meetings with board members of some nonprofit she'd joined; scholarships for "less fortunate" high school graduates, lunches with her new friends. She had even tried to barge in on our New Year's plans. We had decided to skip the opera party in favor of Holly's plans for a gay bar night. That scared their mother off.

We had a bit more champagne than a single toast as the hired limousine pulled up to Pegasus Lounge on Liberty Street.

"Don't be freaked out by the stairs," Holly assured us as she patted my knee. "I took care of everything."

"You had them install an elevator?" I muttered.

Everett, in an attempt to brighten my worries, sang, "He ain't heavy, he's my boyfriend," as he raised his arms in preparation for my shoulder-carrying skills.

The doorman, either charmed or bribed by Holly, let us cut in front of a short line of patrons as the women preceded us down the stairs, holding his chair. Everett hugged me tightly.

"Try to have fun," he whispered.

"You sure it's not too late to join your dad at his old people party?"

While dark, except for flickering disco lights, the nightclub was full of men and women, eager to celebrate. As Everett settled into his chair, we were led to a reserved banquette against a wall. Everett scooted off of his chair, which I set nearby. We chatted up Holly's friends, shouting jovial comments as onstage a series of towering drag queens performed lip-synched songs.

A bottle of champagne arrived, served by a friendly waiter with a paper hat atop his bald head, and we toasted, although midnight was an hour away. I bashfully accepted Holly's invitation to dance, as one of her friends kept Everett company at our table. By the time I returned to the table, I felt better, and offered him a smooch as I scooted next to him.

"Hey! It's almost time," Everett beamed, his face shiny from the heat of the nightclub.

After a few more sips, we'd decided to stay at the table, which afforded us some near privacy as most others took to the main floor to stand ready for the ritual of a cheerful New Year's kiss. Holly's friends were somewhere on the dance floor.

As the buoyant joy to the midnight moment arrived and passed, we kissed again.

"Happy anniversary," he smiled.

Balloons were dropped, confetti strewn, the music grew louder, but we remained seated, until Holly returned.

"So, boys; what are your plans for the new year?" she asked.

"To graduate, hopefully," Everett smiled.

I nodded in agreement.

"But after that?" she pressed.

Everett and I shared a bewildered glance. Back at the house in Philadelphia, a stack of graduate school applications awaited us both. I wasn't sure I wanted to stay in school, or whether I wanted to stay in the city. I wanted Everett to make the first move. The idea of leaving him, being separated again, seemed unthinkable.

Everett offered a giddy, slightly drunk forecast. "We drive off into the sunset!"

Holly smirked, but pressed on. "Has Mother or dear Dad made offers of accommodation?"

Everett assured us that staying with his mother was out of the question. "It's like she's showing off a new pony," he said. "And Dad hasn't exactly jumped in to help me, except to offer that bland studio apartment on the backside of his building, with a lovely view of an alley. Plus, I think he's still a bit skittish about marrying the girlfriend."

"Why?" I asked.

"After our mother, it's understandable," Holly rolled her eyes.

"A lot of reasons, one of them being that she doesn't really like me," Everett admitted. "I kind of creep her out."

"Really?" Holly gasped in mock astonishment. "Because of the chair?"

"She would probably feel the same way about me anyway."

"Why?"

"Well, you know, she pops a kid and there's a will to rewrite."

"What?"

Holly, leaned forward, as if joining me in her conspiracy with Everett. "Reid, my dear boy, let me explain a little bit about a world you'll fortunately never live in. It's called heterosexual privilege. Mom got alimony and Dad never even cheated on her."

Everett added, "And if Miss Alexis Carrington-to-be latches on to him, then if she dumps him, she gets some, too. Just because."

"And we get dumped, too, financially speaking," Holly said.

"You think she's like that?" I asked.

"Oh, we had a little chat a while back," Everett said.

"What did she say?" Holly asked.

"She didn't say anything so much as flash the dollar signs in her eyes while confessing her 'admiration' for my dad."

I tossed in, "Well, what did you expect, 'He's a hot daddy?'"

"What? My dad is not... Okay, but yours is, too."

"He is," Holly giggled.

"This is already weird." I had to change the subject. "Would you like to dance, Mister President?"

"Why, certainly."

"Miss Forrester." I bowed to Holly before helping Everett into his chair. We pushed our way to the edge of the dancing crowd.

That night, the club became our party, our celebration. We danced in that funny awkward way only a couple in and out of a wheelchair can do, until he coaxed me to sit cautiously on his lap, and we nestled, cuddled and celebrated our sort-of anniversary.

We were so happy, because we had no idea what was around the corner.

Chapter 37
January 1983

The news came to us in a strange way, vicariously.

Wesley had left a call for Everett, a strange one, an almost nonsensical combination of Christmas carols. Everett called back, but didn't get an answer. Our Christmas card to him was returned in the mail.

Then a week went by. Everett called again, but it just rang and rang. When someone did pick up, it wasn't Wesley, but his landlord. He was evasive and suspicious, and only offered a number for Wesley's family after some outright begging.

As Everett crooked the phone on one shoulder, he kept nervously folding his legs into different positions. I sat on the edge of the bed in our room, waiting, wanting to support him for what seemed inevitable.

"Three weeks ago?... Yes, from Pinecrest...We were friends... I ... I just...I'm sorry. Yes, I understand. It must have been... no, we saw him last June, and we've talked a few...Excuse me?... Yes, sir."

Despite the lowered volume, I could hear a male voice, tinny through the phone, but growing increasingly terse. Everett's face tensed and he eventually ran out of words.

"I'm sorry about...No, I understand...When you can. Yes, thank you."

As he set the phone down, his gaze remained on it, then the blanket beneath him, his legs, anywhere but toward me. Not knowing what to say, I slid over to the bed and held him.

The fact that we had missed his funeral, and even wondered if we, or just Everett would have, or could have even gone to it –Wesley's family lived in Bradford Woods, a rich suburb of Pittsburgh– added to the lack of closure.

Expecting him to cry, I didn't let go, until he eased back.

"It's okay. I'm... It's not like we didn't expect it. I'm just... a bit stunned."

He didn't cry, not then. We simply lay back in bed, and held each other. I could almost feel him thinking, though, wondering, perhaps the same thoughts as mine. Who could we tell? Who could hear this news and not worry for us or ask more questions? Our parents might panic, and couldn't be told of his close connection. Holly, perhaps. It was then that I realized, perhaps Gerard would be our only true friend who could understand.

After almost dozing off in thought, Everett shifted to roll over, facing me sideways as we lay in the bed.

"Promise me something."

I waited.

"If I get sick…"

"Ev, you're not –"

"Promise me you won't leave."

"Aw, Ev." I clutched him closer, dug my face in his shoulder. It wasn't right to remind him that I was the one who begged to stay with him after his accident, and that if anything happened to him, it would be he who might tear us apart again. "Never. Never ever. You're stuck with me, whether you like it or not."

Despite my assurances, Wesley's death weighed on him like a sledgehammer. He stopped going to classes, stopped going to basketball practice, even stopped eating for a few days, until I practically forced a few sandwiches on him.

He couldn't exactly explain to his parents the depth of his relationship with Wesley. I knew he didn't have that sort of connection to them. And with my last semester underway, I had other creatures to babysit.

Along with a few other near-graduates, I'd been chosen to work on a special hybridization project between the university and the Parks Department to develop and observe the growth of elm saplings. The trees would be grown under observation to make them stronger and hardy enough to grow in the city's smaller parks, to withstand the pollution.

The problem was, we had to visit the Ambler campus, which was about a forty-minute drive north. Taking care of

Everett's obvious depression was too much. I didn't even know if I could leave him overnight for the frequent weekend visits to Ambler.

"I made dinner." I stood in the doorway to our bedroom, which Everett hadn't left all day. The television, an occasional distraction, had become a constant annoyance.

"*Green Acres?*"

"I get allergic smelling hay."

"Funny."

He seemed fascinated by the most banal programs, watching old sitcoms, obviously to avoid facing the duties of his last semester, and me.

"So. Dinner?"

"I'm not hungry."

"Of course you're not." I shook my head, retreated to the kitchen and ate alone.

And yet, hours later, since he wouldn't shut off the TV, I studied in the living room, and heard him eventually roll into the kitchen. A few irritated clunks and crashes of dishware brought me back to see the leftovers spread across a counter.

"I'm fine. Just—"

I stood, waited, then retreated.

And later, in bed, I asked him, "When was the last time you went to your classes?"

"Why are you…? Tuesday."

"Do you want me to go to your lectures, get notes from a classmate or something?"

"No. Jeez, Reid, just… I'll be fine."

"It's not a bother. I'm just doing labs for the rest of the semester."

"No, thank you." He turned away, as if trying to hide himself under the covers.

And he kept at it for another week. This wasn't working.

So I called in the emergency assistance.

"Holly?"

"Reid?"

A casual drive across Pennsylvania usually took about six hours, seven if one stopped for a meal or a break. Holly showed up at the door in five.

"How did you...?"

"I obeyed the speed limit, mostly," she snarled as she unraveled a hat, scarf, and coat.

"Damn."

"Where's the brat?" she growled as she hugged me.

I nodded toward our room.

"Pretty nice digs!" she admired as she preceded through the rooms and to the bedroom door.

"So, I hear someone's having an extended pity party? Should I have brought a gift?"

"Holly!" Everett sat up in the bed, looked to me. "You... You called her. You didn't have to–"

"Apparently he did," Holly said. "Now get out of that bed, get your bony ass in the shower, and we are gonna have a little powwow."

"But..."

Holly snapped her fingers like Mary Poppins and, much to my surprise, Everett obeyed.

As we heard him showering in the bathroom, Holly said, "So, we're just going to talk; old family stuff. Who knows? Maybe you should–"

"I'll, I'm gonna go for a run," I said.

"Okay, then."

"I guess I'm sleeping on that," she said, glancing toward the sofa.

"Yeah. We have blankets."

"You're a sweetie."

"I should... make some food."

Holly shrugged, but I foraged in the fridge. She paced around the living room, then to the side table in the dining room. Among a stack of magazines was Everett's pile of graduate school applications.

"Ooh, UC Berkeley!" she called out, then entered the kitchen. "I had a college friend who moved there. Damn, what was her name?"

"He hasn't even looked at those, so I don't know if–" I couldn't find any bread for sandwiches.

"Well, if you decide to visit, maybe I can look her up."

"You mean if he goes."

"But aren't you–?"

She stopped. Everett finally appeared, dressed, his hair damp yet clean, a sheepish smile on his flushed face.

"Are we eating?" he asked.

I leaned against the counter, unsure of what I was doing.

"Why don't you let me take him off your hands for a bit." Holly then coaxed him out of the house with a lure of coffee and a chat in whatever secret code they had between them. He seemed reluctant but resigned. Holly had driven for five hours, after all.

Left alone, I changed, put on track pants and a T-shirt with the sleeves cut off, chose a hooded sweatshirt, and changed into my running shoes. But then I just felt like not going running.

Mrs. Kukka was off at a faculty retiree dinner. I decided to clean up, even though there wasn't much cleaning to be done, other than some laundry and changing the sheets. Instead I selected a few blankets and spare pillows, placed them on the sofa.

I found myself sitting on the stripped bed, the dryer humming down the hall, and that funny green quilt Everett had bought lying folded on a chair.

That's when it hit me, the calm, silent creeping inevitability of what could happen to us, to him and me, to anyone else like Wesley, or anyone who got too intimate with him. The choking bursts of tears overtook me, then settled after a bit.

Everett had his sister to talk to, about himself, but also about me. Who could I turn to? Gerard, who still rode a jagged balance between his fantastic urban adult life and college, had already mentioned some friend of a friend of his older gay friends who was in some Manhattan hospital with pneumonia. Anything I confessed to him would eventually be shared with Everett in some way, or his new roommates.

My parents were certainly understanding about the situation, but explaining the details would be too much, too exposing. Had we become so intimate to the point of excluding others?

After I finished up cleaning and rearranging the blankets and sheets, the pillows we had shared, I searched in our boxes of souvenirs to find the scrap of paper nestled in with one of my dried palm fronds from Florida, and dialed a phone number.

"Yello."

"Nick?"

"This is Nick."

"Nick, it's Reid. Reid Conniff. We, uh, met in–"

"Reid! Oh my god! You don't have to remind me! How are you, stud? How's Everett?"

"Okay."

"Yeah?"

"Well, actually, no."

"What's wrong?"

After explaining as best I could between another shudder of choked back sobs, he soothed me with his deep voice and that affable accent of his. He listened to my version of Wesley, a truncated variation, and our fears, and I asked for his discretion.

"Look, I'm not gonna lie to you," he said. "I've seen a few guys, cases, emergencies that were way overdue. There ain't that many guys out here in Long Island. It's mostly in the city. But...we had this one guy. His family, he'd come home and they didn't know what to do. He had pneumonia, and they had his room all blocked off and were wearing facemasks and afraid to even touch him. The coroner wouldn't even ... It's lookin' bad, I gotta tell ya." His voice soothed me, despite his news told in quiet outrage.

"But I don't want you to worry. I mean, I'm as healthy as a horse, okay? And as long as you guys are careful–"

"But what does careful mean?" I asked. "Can we even have sex, I mean, just between us?"

"I think you'll be okay."

"You think."

Neither of us spoke. I heard a television in the background, then the sound of him shifting, then silence.

"You still there?"

"Yep," I answered.

"Sorry. Stupid TV."

"It's okay."

"Hey, what if I came out to visit you guys?"

"Oh, I dunno."

"A lil too tempting, huh?"

"Yeah. We're… He's… I'd really like to see you, but…"

"It's okay. Just an idea."

As we exchanged farewells, part of me wanted to erase what had happened between the three of us. The other part wanted him to take us in his big furry arms and hold us.

As I waited for Holly and Everett to return, I sorted through the pile of mail Everett hadn't touched.

He had yet to complete his applications to Yale for PolySci-Public Policy, and to UC Berkeley for a Masters degree in Disability Studies. Temple also had such a program, so I had also begun to fill out an application, but was waiting to see if he even wanted to return there.

For me, working again at Fairmount Park would do for a challenge, but only if he was nearby. I had sent for an application to the Forestry program at Boulder, Colorado, but I wasn't sure if I wanted to stay in academia, or Philadelphia.

We could stay or leave.

But if he stayed in this mood, avoided making decisions, how would that affect our plans? I needed him to be strong, make a choice, otherwise I would have to do it instead.

Chapter 38
February 1983

Birthdays and Christmases had their fumbles on my part. I was never the best shopper. But Valentine's Day had to be perfect.

Of course it wasn't.

Everett had cheered up a bit, and returned to his classes. But despite Holly's visit, an unspoken tension clouded our days. It was as if Wesley's ghost had moved in with us. I imagined him sitting on the sofa, calling out, "Hey, Mutt! Get me a beer."

It got to the point where I couldn't stand it any longer. My consoling was met with indifference. We hadn't had sex in more than a month, which was understandable. But even hugging, holding him in bed, became a sort of cautious grieving gesture. It wasn't about just us any longer, and I didn't know when it would be again.

One night, as I embraced him from behind, he merely tugged down his sweatpants and pushed my hips toward him. My kisses to the back of his neck were met with indifference.

"Ev."

"Mmm?"

"Are you even…?"

"Go ahead," he muttered.

I rolled away. "I want to have sex with you, not on you."

He rolled over, looked at me, then turned away. "I'm just tired."

When Valentine's Day approached, on a Tuesday, I thought a special weekend might help get Everett out of the last of his depression. We both would have the next Monday, Presidents Day, off.

After dinner, where the holiday had yet to be mentioned by either of us, I presented Everett with a card. Inside was a little handmade certificate that read, "This entitles Everett Forrester to a romantic weekend at the Wedgewood Historic Inn in scenic New Hope."

Everett stared at the card, the envelope. "I'm so sorry I forgot."

"We can go this weekend. I made reservations. It's for your birthday, too."

"I can't, sweetie. I did get you something, but I forgot to–"

"Why not? It's even accessible. Well, sort of."

"I'm just not up for it. I'm sorry. We can have sex tonight, if you want. I can get my present, if you can wait a few days."

"That's it? Sex and, oops, I forgot?"

"I'm sorry. I'm just…"

"Yeah, I know; still grieving over the jerk who sort of raped you."

"That's not fair."

"No, but it's accurate, according to you."

"I have to… Listen, I need to go visit a friend at Magee. He's not doing very well."

"Well, I'm glad you're so considerate."

I took our plates and walked off into the kitchen.

He would be gone for hours, but even after returning, a distance kept us quiet, avoiding each other.

That Thursday, I packed some clothes.

"Where are you going?" Everett had been in the living room, catching up on his studies. I had hoped to make a quick and painless exit, but he wheeled into the bedroom.

"I have to work on my saplings for my final project."

"You're going up to Ambler?"

"Well, you don't want go to New Hope, so, I'm gonna work over the weekend."

"Well, maybe it's best that we have some distance."

"No, it's not best, Ev. It's the worst. But I'm not gonna watch you be all depressed about something we can't change."

"There's a lot of things we can't change."

"What do you mean?"

"I can't stand knowing I've robbed you of a normal life."

"Oh, this again." I tossed a sweatshirt into my duffle bag. "Normal? What is normal?"

"You know what I mean."

"Look, we're not sick. We're fine. You need to let him go."

"It's not just that. I tried so many ways to let you–"

"What, let me go? Give me an exit sign? That's not gonna happen."

"Until we know, we can't be normal, and that's on top of all this," he said, gesturing dismissively toward his legs.

"Ev. We've never been normal, not even 'gay' normal. I mean, jeez, the first time we made out, we had sex with a tree, in the middle of winter! That's why I love you."

"I love you, too. That's why I can't–"

"No. Ev? No. I don't want any more excuses. When you are ready to accept that Wesley is gone, and accept being stuck with dopey me, who doesn't know any better, who knows he isn't gonna get sick because of you, and doesn't want anyone else…"

That was where I should have started crying, but I didn't. Wesley's ghost had deadened my tears.

"When you can trust me enough to know, then you come back to me," I said. "And you need to finish those grad school applications."

"Fuck that."

"No, Ev. Do not 'fuck that.' Don't let him fuck up your life any more. Because you're fucking up mine, too."

He sulked. "I thought you liked taking care of me."

"Like?" A fury overtook me. "I do it because I have to, because you're my boyfriend, and I'm yours. Do you know how many times I think about that day, and wish I'd gone to your school and just yanked you off the field and made it never happen?"

"We can't blame anyone for it, Reid. That's…just don't."

I waited. His silence kept me there, standing in the doorway, clinging to his indecision, his doubt, flushed with my own awful admission. And then, as if to offer a truce, he asked, "Do you wanna take the van?"

"No, I'll take the bus. I'll be back on Sunday night."

"But what if I need to contact you?"

"Write me a letter." And then, I added, caustically quoting myself, "We always did good with long distance."

For the next three days, I dug my fingers into the greenhouse piles of dirt with a frenzy. Our instructor, Professor Marsh, was almost shocked by the determination I showed in getting saplings planted, nurtured, sampled. Despite the snowy cold outside, in the warmth of the greenhouse, I sweated.

She had no idea how angry I was, how frustrated, how the low stream of panic running through my veins drove me.

What if this was the real break up with Everett? What if he couldn't find it in himself to let me be his, to settle for the jug-eared nature geek who would not let go?

"Reid?"

"Yes, Ma'am." I'd been jarred out of my worries. Professor Marsh gave me a curious look.

"You seem very intent on your work."

"Oh, sorry, Ma'am. I was just–"

"Can you stop with the Ma'am stuff. You make me feel old."

"Sorry." I stood, wiped my hands of soil.

"Don't be. Anyway, I was going to ask you; didn't you mention having worked at a summer camp?"

"Two years; well, a month for two summers, with disabled kids."

"Yes, that's sweet. So, I was putting together a summer project that… You also worked at Fairmount Park, right?"

"Yep."

"And how was that?"

"Tough, but I learned a lot."

"Well, if you're going to stay in Philly, I might have a job for you, if you're interested."

"Doing what?"

"Teaching kids about nature; planting trees and flowers in the park and on a few day trips up here."

"Oh. That sounds great."

"Okay. Well, the applications will be available in a few weeks. I'll get one to you."

"Thanks."

I didn't bring up the question of whether or not I would stay in the city, because I didn't know. Almost thinking I would have to check with Everett first, I then stopped myself, and wondered if I should. Our growing silences didn't seem to allow such news.

When I returned to the house, he was gone, a note clipped to the fridge; 'B-BALL.'

I didn't know if it meant he had practice or a game I should attend.

He got back late. We spoke little, some perfunctory niceties, but the ice hadn't broken. A few times I walked in on him, headphones on, probably making another mix tape, avoiding me.

The rest of the week became that, him huffing through some task in the other room, or being out early in the morning with a mere nod to go help his friends in need.

By the next weekend, I merely left a note for him; 'Ambler. Back Sunday.'

But I heard back from him sooner than that.

The guest dorm rooms provided for myself and a few other commuting students were sparsely furnished but quiet. I'd slept deeply, having almost forgotten how easy it was to sleep alone.

With a towel and my small bag of toiletries, I was about to leave for the bathroom down the hall when I saw a little green piece of cut-out paper in the shape of a heart that had been slipped under the door. When I opened the door, I found a small package on the floor with one word written on it. LISTEN.

Opening it, I already figured what was inside, a cassette tape. He must have noticed I'd packed my WalkMan and earphones.

Ducking back into the room, I looked out the window to see if I could see his van anywhere nearby. No such luck. How had he, why had he snuck in here and then just left?

I returned to the package.

In between his instructions were songs, music I listened to as I sat on the bus, headed back toward home. His voice told me where to get off, when to stop the tape if the timing wasn't right.

As he had instructed, I got off the bus at the stop. Taped to the stop, right on the map, was another little cluster of hearts.

I walked, as instructed, down Spruce Street, where I found more little hearts, randomly taped or pinned to trees along the sidewalk. At every stop, I plucked them and stuffed them into my pockets. It was my usual route, but each step filled me with hope.

Expecting a room full of little green hearts, I instead saw a trail leading to our bedroom. My best suit, a tie and a white button-down shirt hung on the suit rack, with another heart: PUT ME ON.

Confused to find that he wasn't in the apartment, I changed, again pressed play on my WalkMan. I heard more instructions. 'Take the town car outside.'

And there, outside, was a black sedan.

"Mister Conniff?"

A portly older gentleman in a cap and dress suit opened the door for me. Inside the car, the seat and floor were littered with tiny paper red and green hearts. Okay, the color theme had changed.

'Enjoy the ride,' Everett's voice said on the tape, as Gary Numan's "Cars" piped in. The subsequent music sometimes switched genres, but the songs' themes about love repeated: Pete Townsend's "Let My Love Open the Door," The Spinners, "Working My Way Back to You," Spandau Ballet's "True," and our old favorite, our first song, The Babys' "Every Time I Think of You."

The chauffeur drove downtown, around the Logan Square fountain, and along a street up into Fairmount Park. Still mystified by this journey, I gazed at the passing tree branches, all coated in a fine layer of snow.

The Valley Green Inn at first appeared like Bing Crosby's "White Christmas." Closer inspection showed icicles dripping, slushy grey snow on the road, and the scent of burning wood.

It was mid-afternoon. The driver nodded as I got out.

"Are you…?"

"Staying to take you gentlemen back? Yes, sir."

I didn't know if I should have saluted him.

As I removed my glasses, my eyes adjusted to the darker interior. The rustic restaurant was almost empty of patrons. But there, at a corner table, by the bright light of a window, Everett sat, dressed in a suit and tie, forcing a smile, expectant, nervous, and perhaps relieved.

"What is all this?" I leaned in for a brief hug, and sat across from him. A waiter approached, presented us with a bottle of wine, an expensive one, it seemed.

A few people huddled around tables nearby, sipping hot drinks, but mostly the dining hall was empty, with a few waiters hovering at the edges.

"How did you …?"

"They don't do many wedding parties in the winter."

"Gee, I wonder why."

I rubbed my hands for warmth, then emptied my pockets. His message of love, the paper hearts that littered the trail to him, spilled across the table.

"How long were you waiting here?" I asked.

"About an hour."

"I'm sorry."

"Hey, at least you showed up, finally," he smiled.

"This is… Thank you."

"Before we have dinner, or, lunch, actually, I have something for you."

"There's more?"

He reached into his breast pocket, extracted a small container and offered it to me.

"What's this?"

"Open it and find out."

Inside the small velvet box were two rings. The silvery loops resembled... "Tire treads?"

"I had them made special. I ordered them before–"

He didn't want to say his name, but I knew. Wesley would be with us, perhaps always, just not now.

"I've never had any jewelry."

"I noticed," he said.

"Is the other one for you?"

"If you'll have me." He offered a bashful smile.

"Are we... Are you?"

"Well, we can't get married, so I'm not proposing, exactly."

"But you're–"

"Think of it as a reward for time served, for all the miles you've put in with me."

"Aw, Ev."

"Now, don't get all squidly on me."

"No, I'm going to!"

The clotting feeling in my throat, the little blip of tears on my cheek, softened at the sight of his goofy smirk.

"Well, put it on."

I did, then took out the other ring and took his hand in mine.

"These must have cost a few bucks."

"First thing I'll pay off once the trust fund comes through," he said, proudly holding up his hand.

"And what's next on your list?"

"I reserved us a room at The Four Seasons. They just opened, and they have room service, and a few other amenities, or so Mother said. She already booked a room for my graduation in May."

After an elegantly served meal, and a scenic drive out of the park, his words proved true as we arrived at the hotel.

From the bellhops to the desk clerks, even a few maids in the hallways; no one dared a curious glance.

"So, where are we going to waste your inheritance this summer?" I asked as I stood at the window to admire the view of Logan Circle, its fountain, and the library and museums beyond.

We had agreed to not go anywhere other than our respective homes for Spring Break, what with our previous vacation and encounter with Nick having become so surprisingly eventful.

Everett shrugged, yanked off his tie, unbuttoned his shirt. "I kind of have an idea."

"Rainbow eucalyptus," I blurted.

"What?"

"*Eucalyptus deglupta.* The bark sheds in the most amazing colors. It's found in New Guinea, Tasmania, and even Hawaii."

"That sounds... exotically gay. Actually–"

"We could do Hawaii, but summer's really not the best time to go."

"Actually," Everett repeated, a bit more strongly. "I was thinking in that direction, just not as far."

"What do you mean?"

"Can you look in my bag?"

"What, you got more jewelry?" I joked.

"Not exactly."

I foraged in his duffel bag. Under his extra clothes, I found a large wrapped square-shaped present covered in shiny emerald paper.

"Fancy. Is this it?"

He nodded, a wary look on his face. "It's kind of an early birthday present."

"Oh."

"Well, open it."

Under the green wrapping, I saw more green; a burst of color in a photo of redwood trees.

"'California's State Parks.'" I fanned the pages, each an expansive series of photos showcasing wildflowers, mountains, oceanside cliffs, lighthouses.

"It's great. Thanks." I leaned toward him, offered a kiss, which he accepted, yet somewhat cautiously.

"Wait; inside." He took the book, shook out a letter. "Read it."

Under the letterhead of The University of California Berkeley, I read, 'Dear Mr. Forrester, On behalf of the Graduate Program, we are happy to inform you that...'

"You got in."

He nodded.

"But..."

"I haven't accepted it yet."

"But I–" 'have a job offer here,' I wanted to say. I felt a little dizzy. Was he leaving? Without me?

"Part of why I was moping, it wasn't just Wesley. I... I couldn't decide without asking you. I don't know what I want to do, but I can't... I know maybe you want to stay here, and make a difference, but there's so many opportunities out there. You could go to school, too, or get a job at a park there..."

"I..."

'We can have that here,' a voice inside me said.

"But if you don't, if you... decide to not come with me, just know, you can go off and chase your dreams, but you'll always have someone to come back to."

But I didn't want to need to come back. I couldn't leave him. "Yeah, sure. Fuck it. They can pick up beer cans without me."

And it was as simple as that, I told myself.

"Are you sure?"

I hesitated. "Well, no, I'm not sure. Let me let this sink in."

I found myself fingering the new ring, and what it really meant; not just him thanking me for the miles already shared, but asking me, almost obligating me to put in even more. Leaving my parents would be the hardest part, but Greensburg and Philly? What did it matter, if I could be with him, when I couldn't be without him?

"But how would we–"

"Don't worry about that now. Let's just look at the pretty pictures." He handed me back the book. "Think about it, and we can talk later."

I stood away, began undressing, taking it all in. "How would we get there? Do we ship our stuff?"

"Or drive." He shrugged.

"How about we start with getting a new van first?" I countered. "That thing got two parking tickets last week."

Everett sidled his chair next to the bed, hopped up on it. "How about we start with a few new positions first?"

"How about we start in that shower!" I whistled, pleased as well that a plastic seat had already been provided. "That bathroom's almost bigger than the one at your Dad's."

As our later aquatic amusements commenced, Everett made a ribald joke about my excited state with a comparison to redwoods.

"Think of all those giant California trees," he teased.

"Yeah, but it's got earthquakes, and wildfires…"

"And hippies; oh, my!"

He shut off the shower, and took me in a wet embrace. "So, Scarecrow; to Oz?"

Chapter 39
March 1983

Strapped at opposing sides to four thin wooden poles, the little trees still looked frail, vulnerable.

While our own saplings from Horticulture class remained small and nestled in their planters back at the Ambler campus, we had the honor of planting the previous year's much taller progeny along a wide sidewalk on Temple's main campus.

"But what if there's a cold snap, a late frost?" asked Marco, one of nearly a dozen of my classmates. He held on to one tree, as if afraid to let go, despite the fact that the straps and poles held it securely. The stick-like branches had already sprouted tiny lime green buds.

"It should be fine," assured our professor, a sturdy older man with a handsome beard.

"I guess we'll have to come back in a few years and find out," said Debra, another classmate. Like her, my clothes had become a bit muddy from our shoveling, watering and packing as we planted the trees. Even though I knew I could wash it off, I wore gloves, more to protect my new ring than my hands. I didn't know if I would ever return to see these sprouts grow tall. Other forms of flora were calling.

As the last tree was secured, we all stood back and surveyed our work. Another classmate suggested we celebrate over cheesesteaks and beer. We spent a few hours discussing our future plans after graduation, until I realized what time it was, that I had forgotten to go shopping and was expected to make dinner that night.

My arms full of two bags of groceries from the nearby Thriftway, I almost bumped into a small hatchback parked in the driveway. Then I turned, realizing that I'd passed Everett's van parked down the street.

"Where the hell were you?" he shouted from somewhere in the house the moment the door closed.

"Planting trees," I said as I entered the kitchen. "I told you. I got some groceries, if you hadn't noticed."

I set the bags down on the kitchen counter, befuddled by Everett's anger. He wheeled impatiently toward then away from me.

"You should have called."

"What is wrong?"

"Mrs. Kukka had an accident."

"What?"

"I heard this thumping noise, and I called upstairs and all I heard was this pounding on the floor," he unleashed in a flurry. "So I had to crawl up the stairs and she was lying on the floor holding her arm, and then I had to grab the phone in her room and she's at the hospital and Rosita called her daughter–"

"Why did Rosita call her daughter?"

"No, Mrs. Kukka's daughter."

"Where is she?"

"Driving up from Maryland." Everett fidgeted in his chair, pumping himself up and down.

"Jeez."

"I wish I knew where you were. She broke her arm and maybe her hip and I had to move the van so the ambulance could get in, and one of the EMT guys just wouldn't wait, so I gave him the keys. Did you see where he parked it?"

"Down the street."

"I felt so…dammit, Reid."

"I'm sorry." I leaned down to hug him, but he pushed me away.

"I felt so fucking useless."

"You called 9-1-1."

"Yes!"

"So, you did the right thing."

"Fuck." He wheeled away from me, into the dining room, then shouted something I couldn't hear.

Footsteps descending the stairs drew our attention, then we saw Rosita carrying a small suitcase. "I bring this to the hospital; some of Missus' clothes and things."

"Hi, Rosita."

She had a worried yet determined look.

"The daughter, she be here soon."

"Okay."

After Rosita left, the house was silent. Everett brooded in the living room as I fumbled with dinner. Despite the traumatic events, or perhaps because if them, I was really hungry.

I finally convinced Everett to have some spaghetti and salad, which he wolfed down impatiently before scuttling off outside to sit on the porch. After finishing the dishes, I met him outside. The distant streetlights gave his face a dark glow.

"Is she going to be okay?"

"Hopefully."

I sat, didn't know what to say.

"She couldn't move. It was strange, the way she tried to wave at me with her other arm."

The next day, a different car was parked in the driveway, while the van was still down the street.

I warily entered the house and saw a woman, perhaps in her early thirties, standing in the living room. She turned.

"You must be the tenant."

The woman who must have been Mrs. Kukka's daughter offered a cold appraisal. Her features slightly resembled her mother.

"Yes, one of them."

"The other one's the wheelchair fellow."

"Uh, yes. Everett. I'm Reid." I offered a hand.

"Elsa." She took it, barely holding on for a moment. "I'm sorry. This is… She should have moved in with us years ago. Maybe this wouldn't have happened if she'd only…"

Elsa looked around the house, as if surveying an enormous burden. "I kept begging her to move in with us, but this was our house. My god, it's just full of him."

"Who?"

"My father; their life."

"She told me about the redbud tree she planted."

"Oh!" she gasped, a sigh of resignation. "We all wanted him to be buried like normal, but no, she had to bury his ashes there. So damn sentimental."

"She was very independent."

"Well, I think those days are gone."

"Will she be coming back?"

Another cold stare. "No."

"I'm sorry. I didn't–"

"When she recovers, it'll be either with us or nearby. I don't even know if there's a senior home nearby, or one that we can afford."

"I understand."

"We should have prepared for this. You're not going to like hearing this, but I'm probably going to sell the house."

"When?"

"You're both graduating this semester, yes?"

I nodded.

Elsa corrected herself. "Well, of course, you can stay until then, maybe a month or so afterward."

"You mean...we have to leave?"

"I'm sorry. I just can't manage the property from Maryland, plus I have to decide what to do with her things." She surveyed the room, sizing up its contents. "Even if we don't sell, and rent it, I'll have to hire some movers, and my kids have so many... I suppose Rosita could do some cleaning when we finish. Jesus, my husband's right in the middle of a huge... This just could not have happened at a worse time."

Understandably overwhelmed, she paced across the room, stopped to pick up a small wooden sculpture.

"My father got this in New Guinea. I was twelve. He was always going on another adventure."

Elsa sighed, placed it back on a shelf.

"One thing I learned with Everett."

"Yes?"

"Accidents never happen at the right time."

She sort of crumpled, her shoulders sank and a shudder came over her. She sniffled, held it back.

"She was always so…so pleased with her tenants. Ever since Dad died, we'd be at dinner for the holidays, and she would go on about one grad student or another, his or her accomplishments."

"That's nice."

"But you two." She looked at me, a strange sudden admiration, as if she was seeing me for the first time. "She called you 'the boys.' The last two years, it was, 'The boys are so sweet,' and 'One of the boys won a speech tournament and the other one's cleaning up the park.'"

I smiled.

"I feel like I know you. She really liked you two."

"Likes. She likes us."

"Yes, of course."

That was the moment when I should have grabbed her, hugged her tightly, offered some sort of sympathy. But she stepped further away to survey all the books and primitive knick-knacks.

"There's so much to do."

"If there's anything we can help you with…"

"Oh no. We just… If you could mail the rent checks for now, that would be good. I'll give you the address." She hesitated, overwhelmed.

That night, Elsa stayed upstairs. We overheard her long, almost argumentative phone conversations with her husband, and nervous pacing through the ceiling. She told us her mother only had a few days before she would be transferred to Maryland.

The next morning, Everett waited in the driveway by the van's door as I uprooted a few flowers from the garden.

"You think her daughter will notice?"

"Not sure." I packed the soil into a planter around a few daffodils. "But I know I don't care."

At the side of the house, I washed off my hands under the spurt of the garden hose, sprinkled a bit of water into the planter, then returned to the van and handed the planter to Everett, who nestled it between the folds of a blanket in the back.

As we drove off, he smiled, "You always know the perfect Get Well gift."

I'd only had one morning class on campus, and Everett ducked out of his afternoon senior seminar. The Hospital of the University of Pennsylvania was only a few blocks away, but we didn't want to risk dropping our hastily potted present.

Everett navigated the halls of the building with ease, with me following. As we entered her room, Mrs. Kukka's hoot of surprise roused a sleeping woman in the adjoining bed.

"My boys! Come here!"

She appeared pale and fatigued but in relatively good spirits. I offered a cautious hug, careful of the cast on her right arm. Everett wheeled around the left side of the bed, and they merely clasped hands.

"It's so nice to see you. And what's this?"

"A little bit of home." I set the planter on a nearby table.

"Our daffodils!" She grinned. "So thoughtful."

"How are you?"

"Well, aside from having a few of my brittle bones cracked here and there," she cautiously waved her arm in its sling, "pretty good, thanks to our little hero here." She offered an admiring glance to Everett.

"So, your daughter said she wants to move you to her home?" Everett said.

"Towson," she scowled. "No, it's not bad, a nice town. I visit every year. She's finally won her battle against my independence."

"But they'll take care of you there, right?" Everett asked.

"Oh, I suppose so. You'll have to give me some pointers," she glanced at Everett's chair. "It might be a while before I'm up and about."

The wistful look in her eye, shared with Everett, made me wonder if she would ever fully recuperate.

"And it seems I'll be missing your graduation. You are graduating, aren't you?" She offered a mocking stern glance.

"Yes, Ma'am," Everett nodded.

"Good. Don't let her fussing get in your way. I told her you're paid up through the semester."

"But–"

"Never mind, you," she chided. "You two boys were the best tenants in years, and I want to thank you for a lovely time."

We spent the next few hours together, sharing stories, mostly listening to her stories, all the while ignoring the fact that this might be the last time we would spend together.

The next week was somber, repetitive. Each morning, Everett and I parted ways for classes, studied, yet distracted.

Every time the phone rang, one of us would be startled and race to answer it, expecting a call from Elsa about her mother.

"Hello?"

"I was just reminding you of my fabulous brunch this Sunday."

"Oh. Hi, Gerard." I sighed.

"Could you pretend to be happy to hear from me?"

I reminded him about Mrs. Kukka. We were still waiting for a call from her daughter to let us know how her mother was doing. Gerard sounded genuinely concerned, but determined to get us to make an appearance at his little shindig.

Having not seen Gerard for weeks, I was surprised when Everett politely asked me if we should attend a party, or more of a daytime brunch, at Gerard's new digs in Rittenhouse Square. He'd been living there for months. What made me feel obligated to go was Everett's admission of the number of weeks he'd declined such invitations on our behalf, even before Mrs. Kukka's accident.

After driving across town, we spent a few minutes wandering through Rittenhouse Square before Gerard's brunch. We felt a sort of obligation, yet another anticipated bout of queries from self-described 'queens,' no less. Everett's comic defense system seemed about to go into high gear.

I took my glasses off and he hopped down with me to sit on a dry spot of grass. "They all know your story, so no exploding blimps, okay?"

"If you won't flirt," he teased.

"Deal."

We adjusted ourselves on the ground, our bag of croissants un-smushed.

"Besides," Everett said. "It's mostly older guys."

"What's wrong with that?"

"Nothing. They're all … settled, you know?"

"Are we?"

Everett snorted a chuckle. "Giraffe, we are anything but settled."

"What do you mean?"

"I mean, adventures, my man. After Mrs. Kukka, I just feel… an urgency. Remember that night in the field, in the snow? I've had dreams about that, but you're always too far to whisper to."

"What you said."

"About adventures. We're great together."

"Yeah, we are. Even if we're soon to be kicked out."

"Did you ask about visiting her?"

"I called. Elsa's husband was pretty dismissive. He said she's still in the hospital in Maryland, recovering, or not recovering."

"Oh."

"So, anyway; brunch! The queens await."

"Are we telling them our plans?"

"Do we even know our plans?"

"Yes." I said with a new assurance. "California, here we come!"

"Adventures, wherever."

"Okay." His peck on my cheek sealed it.

"So let's do brunch."

Once back on the sidewalk, Everett wheeled ahead, pointing in tour guide mode. I put my glasses back on, surveying the flora.

"Did you know?" he asked.

"Yes, what should I know?"

"This park was once quite the mating ground for the *Victoriana homosexuala*."

"Was it, now?"

"Yes, and I do believe I saw a flock of pansies over yonder behind that tree."

Despite Gerard's assurance that there wouldn't be any surprises in store, when we arrived, after having trudged up four porch steps, a queenly gasp erupted from a conversation.

The silence was abruptly covered by Gerard's pronounced introductions all around to half a dozen men, mostly older, and one younger slim fellow, the gasper. Since there hadn't been anything done in the way of moving furniture to accommodate Everett, he simply parked himself at one end of a sofa near the room's doorway.

I got Everett a little plate of food, and a drink was brought to him by someone else. I was about to get some for myself, when I was approached.

"I'm so sorry about my little…act," said the gasper, who introduced himself as Russell. A soft hand was offered in a wisp of a handshake. "It's just that we were discussing, you know, all the various diseases and things going around; not exactly appropriate brunch chat, but here we are. Queens always go for the jugular, doncha know, and then you two walked in, or wheeled in. What is the right term?"

"Arrived?"

His laughter reminded me of a macaw.

"So, you two are a couple, yes?"

"Yes."

"So, how does that work?"

"Excuse me?"

"How do you, you know," he said, with an indeterminate flip of his hand.

"Get here? We drove," I deadpanned.

"No," he scowled, rolled his eyes. "How do you...get on?"

"You know... Russell?"

He nodded.

"I'm going to need, like a bagel or something, and definitely a few mimosas, before you go for the jugular." I retreated to the food table. "So, you'll excuse me."

Things turned a bit sour after that, where our togetherness was questioned, in a conversation I more eavesdropped on rather than participated in. I kept to the food table back in the kitchen for as long as possible, until Gerard shooed me out to "mingle."

"So, you're going together?" Michael, one of the hosts asked, as our plans and indecisions had become unfurled, aided by Everett's second drink. Russell seemed to understand enough to keep his distance from me, at least. But Everett always loved an audience. Since the seat next to him had been eagerly filled, I sat at a far end of the room on a dainty chair, occasionally getting poked by a potted fern. The tiny table upon which it sat gave little room for a plate, so I set it on my lap, and the drink on the floor.

"Well, we hope to be together, if that's possible," Everett over-clarified, in an over-enunciated way that he used whenever he got drunk, which seemed to have happened quickly.

Hope. Possible. Not "Definitely," or even "for sure."

"Is there a bathroom here?" I interjected.

"Right down the hall," Gerard said as he pointed.

I stood up too soon, the bagel practically flung itself from my lap and landed cream cheese side down on the rug, knocking over my drink, too.

After cleaning up in the bathroom, I again retreated to the kitchen for a second helping, when one of the hosts approached.

"Reid, is it?"

"Yes, sir."

"Tim, please."

I nodded as he offered a knife for the cream cheese, leaned against the counter. His nearly bald head, and a bit of a paunch, were countered by the boyish sparkle in his blue eyes.

"You know, in my day, things were very different when Michael and I started dating, back in the Cenozoic era."

We both chuckled.

"How long have you been …together?"

"Seventeen years," he said with a combination of pride and bemused exhaustion.

"Wow. That's great."

"And we didn't have these gay groups and bars and parades back then. Well, a few bars, but they were sad places. You kids are pretty lucky."

"Huh. I guess we are."

"Have some more lox." He pushed a plate toward me.

"Thanks." I fumbled with a fork.

"Oh, just use your hands," he scolded.

"So, how do you," I finished assembling my food, but set it aside. "How did you…?"

"Stay together?"

I nodded.

"Persistence, I suppose, and pure dumb luck."

"Huh."

"And a little magic."

"I'm sorry?"

"The magic of being needed by just one person." Tim looked toward the living room, to his partner. Caught by his wistful look, I heard Everett's laughter, then turned with Tim to survey the guests in the room.

Breaking abruptly, he turned back, handed me the plate. "Shall we re-enter the fray?" He smiled, offered a friendly shoulder pat.

"Well, that was a minor disaster," Everett huffed as we finally descended the last of the apartment's porch steps, almost two hours later. Gerard had hugged us goodbye at the door, sensing that this might be our last time together for a while.

"Well, I'm sorry if my social skills amongst royalty are a bit rusty." I almost wanted to give his chair a little shove, but I couldn't think of any lines from that Bette Davis movie.

"You could have been more polite."

"Actually, I had a nice talk with Tim."

Everett stopped pushing his chair, and turned back to glare at me. "I think we're about to have another spousal argument."

"Okay."

"Will there be domestic violence in the form of spanking?"

"No," I muttered.

"Well then, I'm not interested."

"Ev. Are you drunk?"

"Probably."

"No, you said, 'possibly.'"

"I just said 'probably.'"

"No, about us, in there."

"Oh, that. Oh, come on. I was just... Reid."

"No, I'm serious. If we can't stay at the house, what are we gonna do for the summer?"

"I don't know."

"But what if–"

"I said I don't know! Come on. I'll flip a coin, okay? Greensburg, even Pittsburgh, although with the family trifecta nearby, it's not what I'd call an adventure."

"Seriously. Are we staying together?"

"Yes." He nodded himself into agreeing. "As long as you come with me."

As he pushed away, my left hand compulsively grasped the ring on my right finger, and I wondered if it were less than the sort-of wedding ring, and instead more of a consolation prize for a job well done, a job soon to be completed.

'The magic of being needed.'

Barely able to recall the melody, still I dared to call out to him, singing in my off-key tone, "In time the Rockies may crumble, Gibraltar may tumble! They're only made of clay!"

He stopped on the sidewalk, wheeled around, grinned.

I held my arms wide, "Our love is here to stay!"

Someone, unseen in the nearby park, clapped. I bowed to Everett, approached him and squeezed him with an almost insistent hug.

Chapter 40
April 1983

The truck took up the entire driveway. Elsa had called to let us know when the movers would arrive, so I parked Everett's van on a nearby street corner.

We stayed out of the way as a crew of men trundled up and down the stairs. The screech of unrolled packing tape accented the sound of books and other items being dumped into cardboard boxes that descended and left the house in the arms of the movers.

We could have left, perhaps avoided witnessing the disappearance of our landlady's packaged life. We didn't.

A few pieces of furniture, including the rumpled sofa, were left in the living room, out of some sort of blank consideration. The bookshelves were empty and all the trinkets from Mrs. Kukka and her husband's life gone.

By the time the truck departed, we both felt a numbing sort of shock.

"Take me upstairs," Everett said.

I backed myself in front of his chair, felt his arms tighten around my neck, then carefully trod up the stairs, depositing him at the landing. By the time I'd gone down and back up the stairs with his chair, he had already crawled into the central room.

Empty, bare; he surveyed the walls and windows. He didn't even turn back or hop up into his chair.

"And that's it," he said as he sat on the floor, where I joined him.

"It looks smaller empty," he said.

"I know. Strange, huh?"

"I guess our room's next."

"So much for our new home."

Our voices echoed, bouncing back in agreement.

As the semester drew closer to an end, while others around us appeared cheerful and expectant for their liberty, for us, a truncated finality drew closer.

Twirlers, a bugle corps, drummers in silver pants and women with kids in wagons, trucks tugging wobbly crepe paper-festooned floats; all of them paraded around the Penn campus as the annual Spring Fling got underway.

The Park Mall had already begun to fill with hundreds of students seated before a large outdoor stage. I'd politely jostled us as close as I could, and Everett sat in his chair as I knelt by his side. A joint was passed, and we accepted it.

The sun blaring down, and in the middle of it all, I thought Everett was having an allergy attack, when he turned up to me, something or someone on the stage having moved him.

There was a moment, in the middle of it all, with everyone talking and gulping down beers and jostling around, when we realized we were exhausted. It was nearly four o' clock, and we'd had to stick with our spot, a bit too close to the stage for my ears. But wheeling back through the crowd seemed impossible, so I just made sure Everett stayed hydrated and kept his hat on.

Finally, Cyndi Lauper's band came to the stage, and we all sang along. At one point between the bouncy familiar hits, there was a moment where that little elfish red and pink-haired woman in that tattered skirt and about a dozen criss-crossed belts sang a slow song, and she just stopped us, held us all, the entire crowd, and belted out a pealing high note, something about being strong, about breaking down to "cry, cry cry," and I felt Everett's hand clutch mine, hard.

"Are you okay?"

The lawn full of people cheered and hooted around us. He shook his head, a sort of yes. The crowd kept cheering as the band bowed, but I felt I needed to get him out of there, and shoved us through them until we found a place away from the stage and the crowd, off to the side. I crouched before him.

"What is it?"

"It's gonna rain."

I looked up at the sky, a slate of blue, the afternoon sun still beaming down on us. "What?"

"No, I mean, it's going to get worse."

"Oh, Monkey. Stop."

"No, I mean it. I'm sorry." His eyes were red.

"For what?"

"For everything. For everything I did to you, for anything I'm going to do to you."

"Ev, please."

It sort of rolled around in my head for a while until I understood what he meant. Everything was going to change. Graduation was just a few weeks away, and the real world awaited us. Our little bubble of college, as flawed as it had been, had protected us, but was about to pop. I almost saw that immense dark cloud far off in the horizon, moving so slowly that we couldn't yet see it. But we felt it.

"We need to enjoy this, today. I love you," I shouted over the cheers. "We're gonna be okay."

"I hope so," Everett offered a wobbly tentative grin, snorted, wiped his eyes.

In the middle of that herd, I didn't care. In the middle of that noise, I didn't care. I leaned down and kissed him, long and slow, and we heard a strange combination of shrieks, "Whoah!"'s and scattered applause.

It always made me marvel about gleeking. That's when the salivary glands under your tongue simply squirt out a little blast, like skewed windshield wiper fluid.

My tears' ability to spring out of my eyes like that, not merely drip, made me smile.

"He was good, and useful, and he will be missed."

I offered a solemn silent salute as a tow truck driver, having strapped the front end of the van to a hoist, raised the oblong vehicle of our last fours years at an odd angle. It wobbled as if in a few last gasps of existence.

"Farewell, Love Machine," Everett said in a faux-somber tone.

We watched as the tow truck pulled out and dragged our beloved four-wheeled wonder to its final destination, probably a scrap yard.

"You coming in?"

"We need more packing tape."

"The movers didn't leave any?"

"Nope."

"Okay, enjoy your journey."

"It's only three blocks."

"Which you could have driven, if not for our loss." Everett pretended to shed a tear. Perhaps this was his way of really grieving, making fun of the whole process.

When I returned, Everett was in the kitchen, sorting through dry goods.

"You got a package; certified mail. I signed for it."

"Where is it?"

He pointed to the counter top.

Curious, I found a thick manila envelope with an address from a law firm in Bradford Woods. I slid open the envelope and found a small stack of legal papers. I was confused until I saw, among the multiple forms and signatures, the phrase "the estate of Wesley Thompson Sweigard."

Attached with a paper clip was a certified check for twenty thousand dollars.

"Everett!"

The rooms nearly empty, my shout echoed more loudly than I'd expected.

"Did you see this?"

Preoccupied by his kitchen excavation, he muttered, "See what?"

"Your friend Wesley apparently gave me a load of money from the grave."

He finally looked up. "Oh. Well, great."

"What do you mean, 'great'? I can't take it."

"What do you mean, you can't take it?"

"It's…But why me? He was your…"

"Remember when he said he didn't want to give it to his family, that they basically disowned him and were acting like vultures?"

"Sort of."

"Well, maybe he wanted to give some of it to one of his own species instead."

I pondered the utter improbability of it. Then it came to me. "You did this."

"Nope." He tossed a bag of dry pasta into a bag. "I may have mentioned, in one of our phone calls before he died, about your dad losing his job, and how hard you work."

"But you're totally stacked."

"I don't get my trust fund unlocked for a few years. I'm just getting the interest."

"But this is too much."

"Actually, it's not. He told me he was going to give it all away, just to spite his parents. I gave him suggestions on a few charities."

"I have to call this lawyer."

"Let me see that." Everett looked over the papers, then in his officious tone, said, "It's all fair and square."

"I can't..."

"Yes, you can, Reid. He liked you. He was happy for us."

"Twenty thousand dollars worth of happy?"

Everett shrugged.

"So, I'm the rich one now?"

"Which means you're the alpha male, economically speaking, *pro tempore*."

"Damn."

He nodded, rolling away, then back, as if pretending it were some awkward first date. "So, then. Where are we going this summer... sugar daddy?"

I tickled my chin, pondering. "Maui?"

"No M's."

"Not even Madagascar?"

He shrugged.

"Maybe I can buy us a new van."

"I don't think you'll need to do that."

"Why not?"

Everett smiled, the spark in his eyes vowing silence.

The dedication for the portable wooden ramp for the historic yet more often ignored house, set back on a lonely expanse of weedy lawn in Fairmount Park, was sparsely attended.

A few park rangers, one of my professors in landscape architecture, and Everett and I, congratulated each other on the minor accomplishment.

"Finally, one ramp. And all the bureaucracy and inter-departmental paperwork gave fruit," I sighed. A few perfunctory photos were taken.

"It's nice," Everett said. "Now, even crips can be bored to tears by the house tour."

"May I?" I held my hand out, Everett ambled to the base of the ramp, and I helped him up.

Although clean, it still felt a bit musty. The old-time furniture pieces were reproductions, but looked authentic. We played around for a bit, mimicking what we thought was the chatter of the house's long-gone residents.

"Wouldst thou care to frolic on the sofa?"

"'Tis rather creepy inst here. Shall we saunter outside?"

"Oh. Oh, okay."

The few celebrants had dispersed, and we shied off getting a ride back as one of rangers locked the building. A side path led further into the wooded area, and Everett wheeled halfway around.

"One last attempt for floral fun?" Everett smiled.

We wheeled down the street side for several blocks, until a nearly hidden path led his interest.

That afternoon's air thickened with three or four chirping, creaking creatures. We found a small shaded grove away from the main paths. Everett scooted himself down in a sort of cradle between a massive gnarled set of roots. I wiped my glasses to get a marvelous view of the glints of sunlight filtering down between the branches.

"Comfortable?"

"Comfortable enough to get a little naked?" He glanced back and forth, smirking with a jaunty grin.

"Have you...tested it?"

"No, I did not. Although I perused its perimeter, sir." I wasn't sure if I were becoming more comfortable with these tamed woods, but I wondered if I was instead claiming a turf, or if we were bidding it goodbye.

And that's how we recaptured that loamy magical feeling, with a bouquet of communal smooches, some discreet fumbling, and a bit of peat spat off a hand. Spontaneity got a boost from a little exploratory planning.

Chapter 41
May, 1983

Hundreds of cap-and-gowned graduates sat in blocks on the floor of the Civic Center Convention Hall. Seated high up in the bleachers between my parents, that morning, we listened and watched as author Chiam Potok gave an earnest speech, the university's Glee Club sang, and the Provost even noted that one of U. Penn's early commencement ceremonies included no less than George Washington.

But I was only focused on one person. Despite the distance, it was easy to spot Everett; in the front row, one of only two wheelchair-using graduates.

As a student behind him helped him push up the ramp to the stage, a noticeably louder round of applause rose as he was handed his diploma. I felt a swell of pride, fought back a droplet of a tear as my father rubbed my shoulder.

"Oh, there they are," Mom pointed to a much lower row, where Everett's parents sat, while Holly jumped up to cheer her brother.

Anyone who didn't already know him knew of him. They didn't know what he'd been through, or that he was mine, my guy. But right then, it didn't matter.

My own ceremony would take place a week later than Everett's, and in a much more modest setting. But that day, after the ceremonies, our families once again gathered. The polite large dinner, reserved weeks in advance due to the flood of families visiting the city, was endured with all-around joviality, possibly aided by Holly's referee-like presence, but mostly due to talk of my parents' plans for the week's visit.

My mother was never happier, not only to share a bit too much about their visit and upcoming days traveling with Dad, but to trump Diana Forrester, since they were obviously supporting both me and Everett.

"First a city tour, then museums, and after our son's graduation, a weekend in Atlantic City."

Mrs. Forrester seemed to have withheld some disparaging remark, and merely smiled.

"Watch those card sharks," Everett's father warned with a smile.

Holly told us about a recent musical she'd worked on whose scenic designer had borrowed the style of boardwalk sideshows. For a moment, I was silent, listening to different conversations, and I felt a flash of panic. Leaving Philadelphia in days, returning to Greensburg, just to wait for Everett's call; it felt like some kind of impending limbo.

My father and Mr. Forrester talked softly about business. He caught my look, offered a sly wink. Despite Dad having found a job doing the accounts for a small chain of grocery stores, Mom would later confide that, along with the vacation, some corporate managers were met with, thanks to Mr. Forrester, and some form of advancement for my Dad at a new job seemed promising.

"I'm so glad for you both," Mrs. Forrester announced. "I'm so sorry we can't return for Reid's ceremony. I'm only weeks away from my benefit, which I assume Everett has told you about."

"Uh," Everett offered an awkward glance.

"Oh, son. You didn't? Well, I suppose you've been busy, what with graduation and all." She gave him a mildly scolding glance, then announced, "I'm chairing a scholarship fundraiser next month for handicapped high school students."

"Disabled, Mother." Everett corrected.

"Yes. It's at the William Penn, in Pittsburgh, in June. I thought you'd all been sent invitations…"

As Everett's mother continued, I felt relieved that she had once again diverted the conversation back to herself, and not her excuse to miss my graduation ceremony. I didn't tell her she hadn't been invited. Everett's father also had plans, but slipped Everett an envelope that looked promising.

As our meal ended, Dad and Mr. Forrester had a friendly argument over the tab, each of them trying to claim the check. They settled on splitting it.

"Alpha male battle," Everett muttered to me.

Chairs were pushed out, and awkward hugs and handshakes followed.

But then Everett's father interrupted the farewells, as if he'd forgotten something. Mrs. Forrester broke into a grin. It seemed the cat was about to be unleashed from the bag.

"Could you all step outside for a minute?" Mr. Forrester said in a teasing manner.

We all followed, and waited. Something was up. I wasn't sure.

Holly was staying with us for a few days, and asked us to wait, as she had some private discussion with her own parents at the doorway. As we waited in the lounge, my mother inquired about our plans.

"One of our friends is having a few graduates and faculty over," I said. "That's Saturday. After that, we have to pack our stuff. You're taking some in your car after you get back from Atlantic City, right? Ev's dad said he'd–"

"No, I meant your future. With Everett in graduate school, what will you do?" she asked.

"There's a lot up in the air, but I'll probably get a job with the Parks Service. I haven't heard back from them yet. I think we just have to wait until we get there."

Was I supposed to say it yet, that we might be leaving them sooner than they had thought? My mother's anxious look seemed ill-timed, what with all the celebrations.

"We're going to miss you so much," she almost cowered, her face tightening, as if holding back a wave of emotion, until I had to hug her.

Then we saw Mr. Forrester waving us forward, and out the hotel's front door. In the driveway, an attendant approached with a set of keys to a gleaming new small truck, its body a deep orange-yellow.

"Oh, no. It's for him," Mr. Forrester gestured to Everett.

"Fantastic!" Everett shouted.

Although smaller than his recently departed van, it seemed roomy enough, and thick, with wide tires.

"It's a Blazer," Mr. Forrester announced. "Chevy's newest model; got a four-wheel drive."

Everett wheeled around it, inspecting it with curiosity. I sidled up next to him.

"Why didn't you ask for a van?" I whispered.

"I wanted something sporty."

"It's very ... butch... and yellow."

"It's amber," he corrected. "I guess we can put up curtains in the windows, for... overnighters," he muttered with a sly grin and a wink. "Hey, Dad. Did you get the extras?"

His father opened the driver's side door, showed off the extra handles. "And," he tapped above the inside of the door, "a little roll bar, like you asked."

"Cool."

"You want to give it a test drive?" Mr. Forrester offered.

"Duh!" Everett tapped my arm, signaling me to join him.

"Oh, um." Knowing we might not return for a while, all day even, I called out to my parents, "Um, I'll see you guys when–"

"Don't worry!" Dad waved us off. "Just call us at the hotel when you get back."

"Um, Holly?" I nodded for her to hopefully join us.

"Well, alright, if you insist," she rushed up to hop in the back.

Another car approached behind the truck, and our mutual goodbyes became a hurried fluster as the valet gave us an impatient look. Everett tested getting in by reaching up to the roll bar to the seat, then he pulled up his chair, took a wheel off, then hoisted the parts into the back seat, all in about a minute.

"Hop in," he called out.

Before long, Everett, having managed the adjusted handles, toured us around the city. After only a few blocks, we got caught up in a bit of stalled traffic. A few horns blared, and up ahead, I heard the sound of a jackhammer.

Large yellow signs and burly construction workers blocked two parts of an intersection, with pedestrians being guided past a barrier. A man in a hardhat and an orange vest held up a SLOW sign.

"Reid, roll your window down."

Confused, I nevertheless obeyed.

"Excuse me, sir," Everett called out past me. "What's going on?"

The ruddy worker shook his head, almost apologetic. "We're puttin' ramps on the curbs; new city law. I dunno, for handicapped people."

Everett smiled and saluted him. "You're doing God's work, my man."

"Well, he pays, so whatevah."

The jackhammer abruptly cut off Everett's reply. We waited until we'd driven past him before bursting out into a bit of laughter.

"Looks like all that bother might have helped," I said.

"Sowing the seeds," Everett replied.

I fiddled with the stereo as Holly remarked on some of the passing buildings. "I really didn't get a chance to see the sights last time. So, where are you taking us, Ev?"

"Anywhere you want!"

Holly rattled off a list of tourist attractions. But neither of us responded with more than a few grunts. Anywhere we would go, we'd be saying goodbye.

We were each silent for a while, until Holly burst out, "Nancy!"

"What?"

Feigning insult, Everett joked, "We prefer the term pansy."

"Nancy Schuster! My college friend in Berkeley."

"Oh."

"She always sends Christmas cards, with little form letters saying how happy she is, and her successful husband, her beautiful big house, blah blah."

"Your point being?" Everett furled a brow at the rear-view mirror.

"You could stay with her until you find a place of your own."

"I don't know if–"

"Oh, don't worry. She owes me, I wrote three of her term papers."

In between navigating a few turns, Everett looked to me for approval. "Our den mother strikes again."

"So, where are we off to?" Holly asked.

I merely smiled. I longed to say where I wanted to go; home. But I had no idea where that would be.

JIM PROVENZANO

Chapter 42
June, 1983

As Diana Forrester's benefit concluded, guests gradually began to leave the ballroom at the William Penn Hotel. Most of the wheelchair-using kids, grouped in clusters, didn't seem to notice the standing people around the edge of their circles. Everett laughed at someone's joke, out of earshot of me. A photographer took a few last pictures of my boyfriend in his suit and perky bowtie, along with others.

I looked at one of the kids' parents, perhaps shrugging at our apparent superfluous presence. It wasn't the first time I'd been in such a situation, and I knew it wouldn't be the last. I looked up at the banners, the one that featured Everett's smiling face.

The real Everett wheeled toward me, smiling.

"I've got a big surprise," he said. But his smile was a bit cautious.

"I'm getting one of those banners as a parting gift?"

"Wait'll we get back to our room."

"Okay."

My congratulatory hug was interrupted by his proud mother, who swerved in between us. One of the other guests approached Everett, distracting him with a farewell chat.

"Young Mister Conniff."

"Mrs. Forrester." Despite her slightly more affectionate hug, with actual contact this time, I still fought a cringe of fear. After all these years, she still made me nervous.

"I want to thank you for your donation."

"You're most welcome, Ma'am. These kids really deserve it."

"So, it won't be long before you're whisking my son away yet again."

"He's the one leaving, Ma'am. I'm just along for the ride."

"Yes." She offered a hesitant stare, as if waiting for me to melt away.

But I didn't. Instead I blurted out, "You know, I love you."

"What?" Her astonished glare probably continued after I finished hugging her again, tight enough to almost make her squirm. As I pulled away, she remained stunned.

"You gave birth to the most wonderful, amazing guy, and I can never thank you enough."

"Well, I'm... I'm touched."

Before we got misty-eyed, Everett, his glad-handing duties completed, approached. We bid his somewhat bewildered mother goodnight and retreated to our hotel room, where corny as ever, Everett had ordered a bottle of champagne and a bouquet of ...

"Marigolds?"

"Roses are so cliché," Everett grinned.

"Another fancy night. Mister President, sir?"

"Yes?"

"This is living."

Everett sighed in agreement.

"So, what's the big surprise?"

"Remember when I gave you that ring?"

I held up my hand. "Of course."

"And I said how it was thanks for all the miles yet to come?"

"Yes," I replied, slightly confused. "We should get out early tomorrow, since we've got a lot of miles to get back to Greensburg." I had decided to spend a few weeks at the nursery to save up before our move.

And then I saw that look in his eye, that mischievous, daring glint. "What do you say you don't go back right away."

"But I have to start work."

"No, you don't. You're richer than me now."

"Theoretically. Dad convinced me to put most of it in savings."

"What about... another adventure?"

"What kind of adventure?" I asked warily.

"Look, before I get caught up in this rabbit hole of poster boy stuff, let's take a road trip; cross-country. That new truck—"

"The Blazer!" I announced, as if introducing a pro wrestler.

"It's just aching to be broken in. We can travel, see Mrs. Kukka in Baltimore, then pop back here to Pittsburgh, say goodbye to Wesley, then see the country before we land in Berkeley."

"Any other Bs?" Although his plan included visiting a hospital and a cemetery, he kept his tone oddly upbeat.

"Bumfuck; I don't care," he said. "I just… school can wait. Everything can wait."

"Just not our little road trip."

He raised his arms wide.

"Which you've already planned."

"Well, I may have made a few notes on a map or three."

"You're incorrigible."

"That's why you love me."

I leaned in close, offered a kiss, then slowly loosened his bowtie, undid the top button of his shirt.

"We need music." I fiddled with the small radio alarm clock, settling on a jazz station.

"Are you up for it?" he asked.

I returned to him with a sort of cha-cha. "Monkey, I'm up for anything."

"I noticed. Did I tell you how handsome you look in a suit?" he said as I loosened my tie as well.

"You did, Mister Ex-President, but you can say it again."

"Ex-presidents still get called President."

"Yes, Mister President."

"Mister Conniff?"

"Yes, Mister President?"

"You look hot in a suit."

I grabbed my pants suggestively, until he pushed my hand aside to feel for himself.

"I look better out of it. But first…" I took his hand in mine, up and to the side, shifting my hips beside him. "Would you like to dance?"

He spun his chair around in consent. "Mister Conniff, you're a class act," he smiled.

"And that's why you love me."

Chapter 43
July 1983

The sweeping sea and landscape spreads below. Wild yellow poppies shimmer as the breeze grazes the field sloping around us. While not even the northernmost accessible view, our perch on Mount Tamalpais looms over the bay. The land beyond it, behind Angel Island, could be our next home.

Perhaps it's behind another island where he'll go to school, just below the curve of hills, where I start working in a few weeks, if I choose, if we choose.

"So?" Everett smiles at me, his face already slightly sunburned as we sit on a blanket. "Do we just stay in Oz, Scarecrow?"

"Maybe."

It took more than two casual weeks for us to cross the country. We slept in cheap motels or elegant suites, depending on our mood. Canyons, diners, rivers, the enormity of the land, exhausted us toward the end of our trip. And yet only a day after arriving, we're exploring again.

Nancy and her husband told us we can stay in their spare basement room through the summer until fall semester, when Everett's graduate apartment will become available. Basements are different in California. Sometimes they have views, and for us, even a small yard where our hosts' feisty terrier likes to romp.

"We could just have our stuff shipped out," I say.

Everett offers a studious look of agreement, as if it were a novel idea, since he probably already thought of it himself.

I hand him the binoculars and point as he peers over the distant hills and, below them, a jutting clock tower spire. Just uphill from that, somewhere in that speckled hillside, our temporary home lies nestled under oaks, evergreens and the occasional oddly placed palm tree. It's a strange land, one of succulent plants, dry grasses, where almost everyone and everything is an invasive species. And here we are, plotting our own little invasion.

Over on the other side of the expansive view, the city with its own beauty lies beyond the blood-orange bridge. I wonder how much of its pleasures we'll sample, and what we'll have to avoid. It's late in the afternoon, and although we're still under a blast of sun, the brisk sea breeze tugs a blanket of fog, and beyond that, a dark bank of clouds.

As a child, I dreamed of living in the forest, of hiding among the trees to avoid the world of people and all their problems. Instead, I met a boy in the woods, and together we grew and somehow figured out how to become men.

We're still working on that.

ABOUT THE AUTHOR

Jim Provenzano is the author of the Lambda Literary Award-winning *Every Time I Think of You*, the novels *PINS, Monkey Suits, Cyclizen,* the stage adaptation and audiobook edition of *PINS*, as well as numerous published short stories. A journalist, photographer and editor for more than two decades, he lives in San Francisco. www.myrmidude.org
www.facebook.com/JimProvenzanoAuthor
www.jimprovenzano.blogspot.com

If you liked this book, please post online reviews and tell your friends.

Download the book trailer song, Dudley Saunder's performance of The Pretenders' "Message of Love," at www.DudleySaunders.com

CPSIA information can be obtained at www.ICGtesting.com
Printed in the USA
LVOW06s1517120315

430302LV00001B/80/P